A MISTLETOE KISS
IN MANHATTAN

TRACI DOUGLASS

MILLS & BOON

To my wonderful editor, Charlotte,
who always has my back.

CHAPTER ONE

Dashing through the snow...

Emma Trudeau ran from the employee parking lot across the street to the side entrance of Manhattan West General Hospital, unwinding her emerald-green scarf from around her neck. The forecast had been clear earlier in the day, but the weather changed fast in New York City in late November.

She pressed the badge on a lanyard around her neck to the reader beside the door, then pushed inside when the buzzer sounded. A wave of heat and antiseptic scent rushed over her. Hurrying down the well-lit hall toward the front lobby, the soles of her shoes squeaked on the shiny linoleum. For once, Emma wasn't working today in the ER. As charge nurse, she'd picked up more than her fair share of overtime lately for the upcoming holiday season. She rounded the corner at the end of the hall into the spacious lobby area, with its atrium on one side and lots of seating beneath it. A large Christmas tree sat in one corner, adorned with homemade stars from one of the local charities. Kids with disabilities or illnesses that made it hard for them to have happy holidays made them, and people or businesses then chose a wish from the tree to fulfill. Every year, Manhattan West picked one special star to go all out on and this year, Emma was in charge of the project to create the magical wish of one child's dream.

In fact, she was here now—on her day off—to meet with the hospital's chief of staff and the HR director to fill them in on her plans thus far. And she was late.

After passing through security, Emma broke into a near-jog down the long hall toward the other side of the hospital and made it to the small waiting area in front of HR with thirty seconds to spare. She stopped to catch her breath, but before she got the chance an office door opened and the HR director, Jane Ayashi, stuck her head out. "Hi, Emma. Come on in."

Emma tucked her scarf into the pocket of her coat, then smoothed a hand over her long, loose box braids before walking into the office to greet Manhattan West's chief of staff. "Hello, Dr. Franklin."

"Emma," he said. The man was sixty-two if he was a day, but looked at least two decades younger, with a distinct resemblance to Denzel Washington and a deep booming voice like James Earl Jones. "I hope this meeting is worth being late to my granddaughter's Thanksgiving pageant."

"I believe it is, sir. I wanted to let you know my choice of partner on the wish project before the press conference tonight." She took off her coat and draped it over the back of her chair, then sat, her stomach twisting slightly with anxiety. "I think this person will bring a lot to the table."

"Wonderful!" Jane clasped her hands atop her desk. "Are they coming as well?"

Emma's smile faltered. The person she'd chosen wasn't coming to the meeting because Emma hadn't asked them yet. But she would once she got the okay from Jane and Dr. Franklin. She gripped the folder in her lap tighter to hide her shaking fingers. She wasn't nervous, really. Stress was her constant companion working in the fast-paced ER. No, this was more an adrenaline rush. This project was a big deal for her. If she pulled it off well, it could move her to the top of the list for the next big promotion in her department. Meaning more money, more benefits, and hopefully better hours. Now all she had to do was convince the man she wanted working beside her on this project to do it. A difficult task to be sure, considering his reputation around the hospital as the biggest Grinch around. But he had the resources and the clout to grant even the most extravagant wish a kid could ask for, and that's all that was important.

"Uh, no. He won't be here," Emma said, swallowing hard. "In fact, I believe he's upstairs now in surgery."

Dr. Franklin frowned. "Who is it?"

"Dr. Thad Markson."

For a long moment, both Jane and Dr. Franklin just blinked at her, their expressions blank. She began to worry they'd not heard her, but then Dr. Franklin laughed.

"You're joking, right? Dr. Thaddeus Markson? The biggest cardiothoracic surgeon in the city? I'm sorry, Nurse Trudeau, but you better pick someone else. There's no way he's doing this project."

Emma squared her shoulders. "I realize Dr. Markson is a very busy man, but…"

"It's not that," Dr. Franklin chuckled. "Though good luck finding a slot in his surgery schedule. But outside of work, the man's an island. A virtual hermit. Not surprising since he has the charm of an angry polar bear. He'll eat you up and spit you out."

"I think what John is trying to say," Jane said, cutting in, "is that there might be more suitable candidates to work with you on this important project, Emma."

"No. I want Dr. Markson." Emma lifted her chin. "I'm aware of his reputation as being disagreeable toward the staff, but I've done my research and I truly believe he's the best partner for me on this project."

"The Fifth Avenue Grinch? Granting Christmas wishes?" Dr. Franklin managed to get out between guffaws. "He hates the holidays with a passion. I can't imagine his face when you asked him."

Emma had never shied away from a challenge, and she wasn't about to start, not with a possible promotion on the line. She lifted her chin. "He doesn't know yet."

Dr. Franklin sobered fast. "What?"

"I plan to go upstairs after this meeting to talk to him after he's done with his surgery and bring him down to the press conference in the lobby." Emma squared her shoulders. "I just wanted to let you both know first."

"Nurse Trudeau, I've always liked you. You're smart, hardworking, willing to take on anything we ask of you and do it with a smile," Dr. Franklin said, sitting forward, his expression serious. "But please choose someone else for your partner on this. Trust me as someone who's tried to work with him before. Dr. Markson will only make your life a living hell if you get him involved. He's a brilliant surgeon, but he's awful outside the OR. For a project like this one, you need someone with heart and soul, and there are people who'd deny he has either. I only tolerate him because we need his expertise and the privately funded clients he brings into our teaching hospital."

"I hear what you're saying, Dr. Franklin. I do. But I'm used to dealing with difficult people. Most patients in the ER come to see us at the worst moment of their lives." Emma stood firm in her conviction that Dr. Thad Markson was the right man for her project. He just needed a little nudge in the right direction, a dose of sunshine to light his way. And Emma was nothing if not an optimist. "He'll be my partner. Don't worry. Just give me time."

"The wish project must be completed on Christmas Eve," Jane reminded her. "That's only a month away."

"I know. And that's why I want Dr. Markson working with me on this. We need the wealthy donors and connections he can add to this project to make whatever wish our sick child wants granted a reality in such a short time."

Several beats stretched out in silence, until finally, Dr. Franklin shook his head. "You are persistent, aren't you, Nurse Trudeau? I still think it's risky, if not impossible, but maybe he'll say yes just to get you out of his hair."

Now it was Emma's turn to laugh. "Maybe. Just call me Cindy Lou Who."

Jane grinned. "Well, if anyone can do it, it's you, Emma. You worked twice as hard for half the pay as the rest of the nursing student intern friends to earn your first job on the swing shift in the ER. Once you have a goal in mind, Emma, you don't stop until you achieve it."

"Never."

The two women exchanged a glance. Emma was dogged, true. She'd had to be. Raising her younger sister alone since the age of eighteen made her that way. Her strength had come at a price. Profound loss.

Besides, she'd worked far too hard for far too long to get where she was now and no way would one entitled, cranky hermit of a surgeon knock her off her game. "So, does that mean I can head upstairs to wait for Dr. Markson?"

Dr. Franklin and Jane looked at each other, then back to Emma. Dr. Franklin gave a curt nod. "Go. But don't say I didn't warn you. We'll see you at the press conference in half an hour."

Eight hours earlier

Dr. Thaddeus Markson scowled up at the speaker in the elevator where incessant singers went on and on about halls and holly and fa-la-la-la-la—whatever the hell that meant—then jammed the button for his floor again, like that would make the thing move faster.

Christmas was nothing but an excuse to overspend, overindulge and generally overcompensate for all the other days of the year when you were grossly underwhelming. He hated it, more than any other day of the year. Thad would much rather be spectacular in the other 364 calendar boxes and ignore the twenty-fifth and all its overblown pageantry entirely. Which hopefully he'd be able to do just fine because he planned to work all that day, as usual.

Speaking of work, he was here at Manhattan West to perform a delicate surgery only he could do. As the city's top cardiothoracic surgeon, he was used to getting called in when lives were on the line.

Finally, the bell dinged and the doors swished open and Thad stepped out onto the surgical floor.

"What have we got?" he asked Dr. Imrani, the surgeon who'd met him there and now walked with him to the staff locker room. The Iranian man had recently moved to Manhattan from the UK specifically to be part of the innovative cardiovascular team at Manhattan West. "We're sure it's an aortic dissection?" Aortic dissections were rare and involved a tear in the inner layer of the body's main artery, the aorta. Without surgical intervention, the artery could rupture completely, and the patient would bleed to death internally. It was a long, delicate procedure that required steady hands and impeccable skills, both of which Thad possessed in abundance.

"Yes." Dr. Imrani kept pace with Thad as they headed through a set of automatic double doors, and he gave Thad the rundown from the other side of the lockers while Thad changed out of his tailor-made suit and tugged on standard-issue blue cotton scrubs instead. "Patient is a sixty-one-year-old previously healthy male who presented to the emergency department complaining of chest discomfort and shortness of breath."

Once he'd changed, Thad checked the app on his phone that monitored his blood sugar through a sensor Thad wore on his skin and was connected to the insulin pump he wore for long surgeries such as this one, which could last up to eight hours. As a type 1 diabetic, he'd spent years making sure his condition in no way impeded his abilities as a surgeon, and today was no different. He'd eaten right before he'd gotten called in for this procedure, so he should be good to go for a while.

"Any history of blunt force trauma?" Thad asked as he put his phone away, then closed the locker and joined the other doctor to go into a room with a long metal sink against one wall. He stepped on the lever bar below to start the water and washed his hands and forearms with surgical-grade antibacterial soap and hot water. "Car accident?"

"No." The trauma surgeon chuckled. "Believe it or not, the patient was skiing and got hit in the chest by a snowboarder on the side of a mountain." At Thad's blank look, he fidgeted. "'Tis the season and all."

He grunted, scowling as he started soaping up his left hand and lower arm. Another reason to dislike the holiday, apparently. Death by disaster. "What else?"

The trauma surgeon continued. "After the injury, patient got up without incident, developing pain along the left sternum about thirty minutes later, which he said quickly resolved. He then drove the approximate two to three hours home. Patient stated later that afternoon, he complained to his wife of a 'hollow sensation' in his chest that worsened with deep inhalation, and some mild shortness of breath with exertion. He presented this afternoon at the urging of his wife. On initial evaluation, he denied any nausea, vomiting, diaphoresis, back pain or fever, and was comfortable at rest. No neurologic complaints. He did note a contusion of his left lower leg from a fall on ice one week prior. No past medical history, no medications, nonsmoker, exercises regularly, and no family history of cardiac or connective tissue disease." The other doctor scrolled through more notes on his tablet as Thad finished washing. "In triage, blood pressure was one hundred over eighty, pulse seventy, respiratory rate twenty. O-stats one hundred percent on room air, and temp ninety-nine point seven. Heart sounds normal on exam with no murmurs, lungs clear bilaterally, and no tenderness to palpation of the sternum or ribs or external signs of trauma. Abdomen non-tender. A small hematoma noted on the left calf. Neurologic examination grossly normal."

Thad lifted his foot to shut off the water in the sink, then shook off the excess moisture from his hands. "And the EKG?"

"Normal sinus rhythm with minimal nonspecific

T-wave abnormalities. No evidence of pneumothorax, pulmonary contusion, rib fractures or widened mediastinum on chest X-ray."

Thad gave a curt nod. Chest X-rays were not reliable in diagnosing aortic trauma. "And what did the CTA show?"

"Bovine-type aortic arch with both carotid arteries arising from the brachiocephalic artery, and a type-A aortic dissection extending from the aortic root to beyond the bilateral renal arteries." Which basically just meant two arteries shared the same starting point, like two branches off the same trunk, versus two separate trees. Not uncommon really, especially with patients of African descent, as was the current patient. The tear in the artery had occurred right at the point where the kidneys received their blood supply. Not good at all.

He backed out yet another door, arms held up in front of him, into the operating theater. A surgical tech suited him in a sterile gown, gloves and mask before Thad moved to the table where their patient was already under anesthesia and prepped for him to start.

Long procedures like this one took a team to complete, and Thad glanced at the men and women around the table as he took a scalpel from the surgical nurse. Because of the location of the injury, they would first need to perform an open bypass on the patient to ensure that Thad had a bloodless field in which to graft the damaged aorta. The surgical team included not only Thad but a second cardiac surgeon, interventional cardiologists, a thoracic surgeon, and vascular and interventional radiologists. All of them had roles to play as the procedure progressed.

With a curt nod, Thad stepped forward. "Let's get started."

Five hours in, he'd finally sewn a Dacron aortic graft into place on the man's aorta and was currently reattaching the important blood vessels to it as the patient's heart beat against the back of Thad's right hand where it was held in a sling, safely out of the way. The patient had also been placed into hypothermic circulatory arrest, which was a fancy way of saying they'd lowered the man's body temperature to slow the cellular activity and allow them to stop the blood flow temporarily, as needed. The constant low white noise of the heart-lung bypass machine keeping the patient alive helped Thad stay focused and alert as he raced against the clock.

He'd yet to lose a patient and wasn't about to start now.

By the time they finally closed the patient up, the man's heart was beating on its own again and his lungs worked fine. They'd keep him under general anesthesia for another four to six hours, then move him to the ICU for a day or two. If there were no complications, he'd spend seven to ten days at Manhattan West before going home.

Thad scrubbed down again, then returned to the locker room to change. It had been a long night, and a glance at his Omega watch showed it was well into the morning hours now. All he wanted was a hot shower and a long sleep. But what he found, waiting in front of his locker, was a smiling woman wearing a bright green sweater with a reindeer on the front, looking like she'd stepped off the front of a greeting card. For a second, Thad wondered if he'd slipped into some kind of glycemic hallucination without knowing it.

"Dr. Markson," she said, cheerful as one of Santa's elves, setting Thad's teeth on edge. She seemed vaguely familiar to him, but he couldn't place from where and didn't want to bother at that point. It had been a grueling day and he just wanted to go home.

"How did you get in here?" he said, moving past her to his locker. "Only hospital staff are allowed in this area. I could have you arrested for trespassing."

Seemingly undeterred by his churlishness, she continued to smile. "I work here, Dr. Markson. Emma Trudeau." She held out a hand to him, which he promptly ignored. "I'm a nurse in the emergency department here at Manhattan West. We've worked a couple of cases together in the ER."

Well, that explained the familiarity then. Thad turned away to begin pulling out his clothes. "What do you want?"

Most people, when confronted with his brusque manner, either scurried away or simply gave up. It both impressed and irritated him that this petite woman did neither. He did not have the time or patience for this tonight. Normally, Thad would never disrobe in front of a stranger, but given she seemed to have no qualms about invading his personal boundaries, he gave little regard to hers and pulled off his scrub shirt, leaving him bare-chested.

"I…" She stopped when his shirt came off, her bright smile fading a little as her cheeks heated. Then she looked away fast and cleared her throat, her perky tone back in place. "I've been put in charge of the hospital's holiday charity event this year, our Wish Star Program."

"My condolences."

His sarcasm bounced off her like sunlight off an icicle and she continued unfazed. "As part of my pre-planning I was tasked with finding a partner to help me with the event. Someone whose qualities would complement my own and help to make this year's Wish Star Program the best one ever."

Thad paused in the middle of buttoning his dress shirt to stare at her, one brow raised. He didn't like where this was headed one bit. "And that has anything to do with me how?"

"I've chosen you to be my partner." She beamed at him like that was some kind of honor. In other circumstances, Thad might have found her attractive, might have said her smile was nice. Very nice. Now it was one more nuisance he didn't need.

"No." He undid the tie at the waist of his scrub pants. "And unless you'd like a full strip show, I suggest you turn around."

Her wide dark eyes flickered down to his lower half then back up before she swiftly pivoted away, her cheeks pink again. Thad couldn't say the last time he'd met a woman who blushed. Would've been endearing if this whole situation wasn't so annoying. The pump at his lower back beeped a notification, signaling he needed to eat soon. He quickly pulled on his suit pants and tucked in his shirt before zipping up and buckling his Italian leather belt. He did not have time for this nonsense.

"No?" she asked, the word emerging as more of a squeak from where she faced away from him.

"No," Thad repeated as he sat down to put on his shoes. With her turned away, he had a chance to assess her. Slim, with a slight curviness to her hips and behind. Long dark hair, braided neatly, hanging down her back. For a second he wondered if those braids felt as soft as they looked before he shoved that silliness aside. He was exhausted and hungry, that's all. "I have neither the time nor the interest to participate in your little project, Nurse…"

"Trudeau," she said, a tad firmer this time. "Emma Trudeau."

Thad took a deep breath, then tugged on his suit coat and grabbed his phone before closing his locker and tossing his dirty scrubs into a biohazard laundry bin nearby before heading for the exit. She probably wanted money. That seemed to be the most common "quality" people saw in him. "I'll write you a check. How much?"

"Excuse me?" she said, following him.

"If it's over a hundred thousand, it will take longer because I'll have to go through my accountants to liquidate some assets." Thad walked out into the brightly lit hall and toward the elevators, not slowing down for her at all. "If it's under that amount, I'll have someone drop off a check tomorrow. Who should I make it out to? The hospital or the charity?"

"I don't want your money, Dr. Markson," Nurse Trudeau said, waiting with him at the elevators. She was harder to shake than a two-ton snow globe. Her voice held an edge of steel now, her posture stiffer. "I want your help with this project. The planning, the preparing, the execution."

Thad sighed, staring at the metal doors in front of him. "And I've told you what I can do."

"No, you haven't." She stepped a little closer, invading his personal space, a hint of her spicy-sweet scent surrounding him. "Dr. Markson, I realize this might be a foreign concept to a man such as yourself, but sometimes actual physical participation is a good thing."

Thad scowled. "Physical participation?"

"Being present. Being involved. That's what I mean. Getting your hands dirty."

The elevator dinged and Thad hurried onboard, hoping to get away from his new, bothersome shadow, but no such luck. The woman followed him onto the elevator, then shut the doors on them, effectively locking him inside with her. "I need your help. I've already discussed it with the HR director and the chief of staff in a meeting earlier and they agree it would be good for you to participate. You have connections within the city to get this done quickly, and that's what I need. The wish is due on Christmas Eve, so only a month away. That's not long to help a child in need."

Again with Christmas. Why was it haunting him this year? He stared at his reflection in the mirrored wall of the compartment across from him. Connections. She wanted his connections. Of course she did. Thad had learned from a young age that wealth meant power, and power brought out the worst in people. Everyone wanted something from him, even if it was just to disappear off the face of the earth, like his own father had. Well, Thad was through granting favors.

"A check. That's the extent of my offer to you, Nurse Trudeau. Take it or leave it. I have time for nothing else."

They arrived at the lobby and the doors opened. Thad walked out with Nurse Trudeau on his heels and headed toward the side exit, past the atrium. As he passed the Christmas tree, he found himself herded toward a small crowd gathered there, with lights blazing and cameras whirring.

"What the—?" He tried to pull free of Nurse Trudeau's grip on his arm but found her harder to evade than he'd first guessed. "Unhand me!"

She let him go then, her smile back in place as they faced Dr. John Franklin and Jane Ayashi from HR.

"I'd like to file a formal complaint against this woman." He pointed at Nurse Trudeau. "She's been accosting me since I left the OR about some charity thing I want nothing to do with."

"Later," John said, nudging Thad to turn around and face the crowd. A lectern had been set up in front of them. "After the press conference."

"Press conference?" Thad's voice grew louder than the blood pounding in his ears. He felt out of control at that moment and hated it. "I'm not doing any press conference. I've not agreed to anything. My time is too valuable to waste on toy shopping or pizza parties." He glared over at Nurse Trudeau, who now stood shoulder to shoulder with him as they formed a line behind the lectern. "And you can forget about the check now, too."

"Never wanted it in the first place," she shot back, her gaze straight ahead, her smile firm. "Help, Dr. Markson. You're going to help me, and help a sick child, whether you like it or not. It'll be good for you."

"How dare you—" Thad blustered, only to be cut off by Dr. Franklin stepping up to the lectern.

"Thank you all for coming," Dr. Franklin said, his deep voice echoing through the atrium like a herald of angels on high. "Our two Manhattan representatives, Nurse Emma Trudeau and Dr. Thaddeus Markson, are partnering this year to make one lucky child's holiday wish come true on behalf of Manhattan West General Hospital. Nurse Trudeau, if you'd like to select a wish star…"

All eyes turned to the woman beside Thad, and she swallowed hard. Was she suddenly nervous? Good. Thad hoped she was after putting him through all this. He lived like a hermit for a reason and that was to avoid situations exactly like this one. How dare she impose herself like this on him? Who did she think she was?

He watched as she stepped up to the massive tree in

the atrium. The thing had to be at least thirty feet high to reach the top. And the lower third was covered with stars handmade by kids in the Pediatric Intensive Care Unit here at Manhattan West. All colors and sizes and shapes of wrapping paper and glitter-covered cardboard. Thad's chest constricted even more, this time from painful memories of creating a star like this himself when he'd been little. Not that he'd needed charity, but his caregivers had insisted he make one anyway...

In an instant he was back in that cold, lonely hospital room, staring out the window at the snow falling and wishing he was anywhere else but there...

Applause broke out as Nurse Trudeau selected a star, jarring Thad back to the present.

She walked over to Dr. Franklin at the lectern.

"Which child's is it?" one of the reporters asked. "What did they wish for?"

Nurse Trudeau stepped up to the microphone. "This year's Wish Star recipient is Ricky Lynch," she said. "He's nine and he's got a brain tumor." She blinked down at the star in her hands. From where Thad stood he could see the painstakingly neatly printed bold block letters. "He wants a carnival, with free candy and games and a carousel, for all the kids in the Manhattan West Pediatric Intensive Care Unit to ride."

The words slowly penetrated the fog of adrenaline in Thad's brain. *Oh God. A carnival?*

He'd wished for something similar on his star all those years ago. A tiny pinch pricked from the center of Thad's chest, somewhere in the vicinity of his heart.

No. No, no, no.

He refused to allow his past to rule over him again. He'd spent far too long locking it away where it belonged. And certainly not for some woman who'd bamboozled him into this whole situation in the first place.

Not happening.

Cameras clicked and reporters shouted more questions at them, but Thad didn't care about any of it. He only cared about getting out of there and away from all of this horrible mess and even more so away from the woman who was now standing beside him again, smiling and holding his arm like he was a willing participant in all this. Worst of all, it felt nice, her touching him. Oddly comforting. As if he wasn't alone anymore, as he'd been alone so long. And that's when he knew he needed to leave. Now.

With more force than was probably necessary, Thad yanked free and walked away from the crowd, ignoring the calls of his name behind him. All he wanted was to get back to the safety of his town house, get away from these people, get locked away in his study and never come out again. He was Thad Markson, of the New York Marksons, and he did not have time to deal with organizing a charity event or making a kid's wish come true or the most annoyingly attractive woman he'd met in years. Maybe ever.

"Dr. Markson," Nurse Trudeau called after him, but he was already out the door.

Bah humbug indeed.

CHAPTER TWO

THE SUBWAY RIDE from the apartment she shared with
her sister in Richmond Hill, Queens, to the Upper East
Side of Manhattan was a nightmare, as usual, this time
of year. The guy next to Emma had fallen asleep, then
snored and drooled all over her shoulder for nearly the
entire way. Emma had ignored him as best she could,
concentrating on her Kindle instead.

Her phone pinged as soon as she stepped off the train
and onto the platform at the Fifty-Ninth Street station.
Maybe it was Dr. Markson returning her call at last.
She'd been trying to contact him since the night of the
wish star drawing with no luck. Now it had been a week
with no response from him. Thanksgiving had been
and gone, and time was marching on. She'd worked the
holiday, of course, to make up for short staffing in the
ER. She and Karley had celebrated afterward in their
apartment, with turkey subs from down the street and
playing video games together.

But unfortunately, as she scowled down at her phone,
it wasn't a message from Dr. Markson. Just another reminder her automatic payment for her school loans was
due next week.

Great.

With a sigh, she shoved the phone back in her pocket,

tightened her scarf around her neck against the brisk wind and started for Dr. Markson's town house on the corner of Sixty-Third Street and Fifth Avenue, right across from Central Park. Couldn't get an address any posher in New York. The man obviously wanted nothing to do with her or the project, but Emma was undeterred.

If the Grinch wouldn't come to her, she'd go to the Grinch.

As she made her way up Fifth Avenue, Emma smiled behind her scarf at the shops full of Christmas decorations and the stone and vintage facades of the buildings lining the street adorned in red and green lights for the season. Gorgeous. No one did Christmas like her beloved hometown of NYC.

A short time later she stopped and stared up at a four-story building. Red brick on the top two floors, gray stone on the bottom two. Plus, a basement, if the black door to the left of the front stoop was any indication. The place was probably worth more than Emma would make in her entire life. She wondered if it had been passed down in Dr. Markson's family, like many of the places along here. Most of these townhomes had been built back during the Gilded Age of the 1910s by the newly wealthy industrial barons of the time. Emma was something of a history buff, too.

She shook off those errant thoughts. Didn't matter when or how Dr. Markson had gotten his fancy house. All that mattered was him doing his part to make this holiday carnival happen.

Emma took a deep breath, then climbed the granite stoop to the front door before knocking the heavy gilded lion head against the black painted wood door. Soon, an intercom on the wall beside her crackled to life.

"Yes?" said a snooty man's voice. Not Dr. Markson.

Emma would remember his voice anywhere, after hearing him giving one of the residents in the ER hell one day for talking over Dr. Markson in front of a patient. The fact that the information the resident had given was probably incomplete didn't help either, but still.

"I'm here to see Dr. Markson, please?" Emma pulled her scarf away from her face for the camera and cleared her throat. "Thank you."

Several seconds ticked by before the man responded "I'm sorry, but you aren't on the roster. If you have a delivery, the service entrance is in the back alley."

"No delivery. Dr. Markson and I are working on a special project for Manhattan West General. My name is Emma Trudeau and I'm a nurse at the hospital. I must speak with him. It's an emergency."

Okay, maybe the last part was a stretch, but time was ticking.

More time passed. So much so Emma feared he'd stopped answering the intercom entirely. Then, finally, a lock clicked and the door opened to reveal an older man, maybe late seventies, dressed in a gray butler's uniform. Huh. Emma thought those only existed in movies.

The man's chilly stare rivaled the subzero temperatures outside, his expression emotionless. "You may wait in the foyer while I speak with Dr. Markson."

Considering her booted toes were already numb, Emma took the man up on his offer, stepping inside to gape at her surroundings while the older man disappeared up the carved wooden staircase to her right.

From what she could see from where she stood, the gorgeous first floor had once been an old-fashioned parlor, with lots of creamy marble and warm cherrywood trim. Large windows filled the opposite wall across from her and revealed a large garden area in the back of the town house, complete with sculptures and stone benches. While dormant now, Emma bet it was beautiful in the spring.

Emma leaned slightly to peer through the doorway to her right and saw a sitting room bigger than her entire apartment. Light yellow walls, same inlaid marble floors and a huge TV over an elegant carved fireplace that took up practically one entire wall. In front of it were a pair of sprawling cream-colored sofas. If she leaned to her left, she caught a glimpse of what looked like a formal dining room, with a large dining table surrounded by twelve chairs, like something out of Buckingham Palace. Emma tried to imagine the prickly Dr. Markson she knew from the ER living here and had a hard time picturing the stiff, stuffy man ever relaxing anywhere. Then again, the place was pristine, more like a museum than a house, so maybe he only slept and changed in this place.

Emma chuckled and tucked her mittens in her pocket. The rich were a whole different beast. One she hoped to tame to help her with the project, no matter how long it took.

"Sir, there's someone downstairs to see you," his butler said from the door of the third-floor study.

Thad looked up from his computer and scowled. He hated being interrupted during work. "Who is it? No. I don't care. Get rid of them."

Everett, Thad's assistant, valet and now close friend, never changed his stoic expression. Growing up, the older man's stoicism used to annoy Thad, but now he welcomed it.

The butler had been with the Markson family for as

long as Thad could remember. Trained in all aspects of running a household to discreet perfection, Everett's skills were legendary and sought-after in wealthy circles. In his seventies now, the man retained a distinguished full head of white hair, a mustache and a penchant for wearing expensive suits when off duty. He brought a solid presence and capability Thad found soothing. In many ways, the man was more of a father to him than his own had ever been.

And truthfully, he needed Everett. Having the butler around kept Thad from almost complete isolation between his surgical consultations. He wasn't antisocial really; he just had his reasons for valuing his privacy.

A whimper issued near Thad's feet and Thad dropped his hand to pet the black Lab laying there. "What's the matter, Baxter? Huh, boy?"

The dog's wet nose pressed against his palm and Thad smiled. Between his dog and his butler, he had plenty of company. No need to be lonely at all. Never mind the pinch near his heart. It was fine. He was fine. More than enough of everything to last a lifetime.

"I tried to tell her you weren't available, sir. Many times." Annoyance edged Everett's tone. "She said you're working on a project together at the hospital and that it was an emergency. Since the weather is bitterly cold today, I let her wait in the foyer."

Dammit. He'd thought he'd escaped the whole wish mess with that charity event the other night. He'd offered money and it was all he was prepared to give. "Tell her I've left. And to find someone else to help with her project. I'm not available." If she wouldn't take his money, there was nothing more he could offer. Thad had no time to spare with his difficult surgery coming up next month. There were new procedures to study, cutting-edge theories and practices to memorize.

A lifetime of pain and regrets to keep buried.

Thad shook the last thought off. He rarely thought of his childhood these days, how he'd had to scramble for scraps of affection from his father as a child. The grief that had taken over his entire life after the horrible accident that had taken Thad's mother away when he'd been only ten.

He squeezed the pencil in his hand so tightly it broke.

Everett cleared his throat. "Would you like me to throw her out, sir?"

Ah, hell. Thad inhaled deeply, dropping the pencil shards on his desk, then glaring down at the medical journal article he'd been reading on his laptop. He did not have time for this. Any of this. Distractions were rarely a problem for him, not with his usual laser-type focus, but this whole situation had him flustered.

Baxter cocked his head again at Thad, his inky black fur gleaming in the flickering light from the fireplace. He dusted his hands off, his fingers shaking slightly, a sign his blood sugar was dropping. And yes, perhaps he had ignored the alerts from his sensor and pump because he was immersed in studying. He'd eat, later, when it was convenient. His kitchen was well stocked with items to fend off a hypoglycemic storm, if needed. Juices and candy and even special fast-acting glucose gels to dissolve under his tongue. Everett knew where to find them all quickly. He'd become something of a nurse as well over the years, on top of his other duties. Thad wasn't sure what he'd do when the older man retired.

Forcing his mind away from such a melancholy thought, Thad focused on Baxter again, who was licking Thad's hand again. If only the dog wasn't such a big softy, he'd send him down to scare the woman away. Unfortunately, Baxter was more likely to welcome her with a lolling tongue and wagging tail.

Thad tapped a few keys on his laptop and brought up the feeds from the town house's numerous security cameras, scrolling through them until a grainy black-and-white image of a young Black woman dressed in a silly hat and scarf standing in his foyer appeared. She bounced on the balls of her feet, hands in her coat pockets, leaning around to see into the rooms on the first floor. His shoulders sagged. Why couldn't she take the hint? He wasn't going to meet with her. Not today. Not ever. "Let her wait. Eventually, she'll get tired or bored, and leave."

His butler nodded, but the older man's gaze held a hint of doubt. "As you wish, sir."

Good. Done. Thad never second-guessed himself. A quality that made him a great surgeon. He returned to reading his article. Once that was done, he logged into a special website to watch the video of the surgery being performed, committing each step of the delicate operation to his memory. Closed his eyes and imagined himself working on the patient, going step-by-step to repair the damage to their cardiovascular system. He'd studied this particular procedure for close to a year now, making minor tweaks as needed to meet his patient's specific situation, going through each step over and over, in preparation.

Next month, he would finally perform it to save a woman's life.

Doing the procedure itself and having a successful outcome were accolades enough for him. He wasn't charging the patient or her family at all for his services. They didn't have much, so Thad had also arranged to pay for the hospital and any other expenses associated with the surgery—including the patient's travel from Central America—through the private foundation he'd set up via his attorneys years ago. Everything totally anonymous. A way to give back without the world knowing his business. Another way to rinse away the stain of his family's sins. He couldn't save the world, but he could give his patients a new, healthier future.

Time passed in a blur as Thad absorbed the detailed images playing on his screen, until finally, he sat back, neck stiff and spine cracking. "All done, Baxter."

The Lab yawned.

"Now, let's go eat, huh?" Thad stood from behind his desk and stretched.

They walked downstairs from his office on the third-floor to the second-floor kitchen, Thad's balance a bit wobbly. The pump at his waist, tucked into his pants, again beeped ominously. Damn. He just needed a quick hit of sugar to stabilize things. It would be fine. Yes, as a doctor, he should know better than to let things get out of hand like this, but he'd been working. And his work was everything to him. He stepped into the massive chef's kitchen, Baxter whimpering and nudging his leg, and opened the fridge for a bottle of apple juice, glancing at the flat-screen monitor on the wall and freezing.

Son of a...

The digital clock above his Viking range showed nearly two hours had passed since he'd told Everett to let the woman wait, figuring she'd leave eventually. But no. There she was. Still standing in his foyer, stubbornly facing his camera now. Even with the grainy footage, her loveliness made his heart skip a beat. Dark eyes surrounded by lush lashes. Full lips slightly parted as if waiting for a kiss. Still bouncing on the balls of her feet, too, like her body could barely contain all the energy inside it. An unwanted tingle of awareness warmed Thad's belly, spreading quickly outward before he quashed it.

No. This was not happening. He refused to be attracted to this woman.

Frustration coursed through him. Why couldn't the world let him be? Outside the windows, snow fell heavier and the wind howled. A storm was coming, in more ways than one.

Pissed, he set his bottle of juice aside, unopened. She wanted to see him? Fine. Thad would make sure she never forgot the experience. His hands were trembling so bad now he gripped the edge of the counter to keep his balance.

Everett stood in the doorway leading to the stairs. "Sir, do you need—"

"Show her up," Thad growled, aware that at least some of his anger was due to his lowering blood sugar, but beyond caring at this point.

"Sir, I—a..." Everett started toward him, his expression concerned.

"No!" Thad shouted, then lowered his voice, the trembling worse. "Get her up here now. I want this over with, once and for all."

The butler stared at him a moment, then hurried down the stairs. "Yes, sir."

Baxter nudged Thad's leg with his nose, whimpering louder, and everything went sideways.

"Follow me," Everett said, turning toward those stairs again, moving faster now. "Hurry."

The urgency in the older man's voice surprised her, but Emma wasn't about to lose her chance to see Dr. Markson. Not after she'd waited forever and a day here.

She shook out her stiff legs and followed the butler, scared to touch anything for fear she'd leave a mark on the gleaming wood. They'd made it halfway up a second flight of stairs when a shattering of glass split the air.

"Hurry, ma'am," the butler said again, showing admirable agility for his age.

Emma's pulse stumbled as they raced up the rest of the stairs. "What's going on?"

They entered an enormous kitchen, which should have been a showpiece, too, but instead was in complete disarray. Cabinet doors open and food scattered everywhere across the countertops. In the open doors of a huge, professional-sized double-sided refrigerator, Dr. Markson stood with his back to them, rummaging inside, a shattered crystal tumbler and a cowering dog at his feet. He didn't seem to notice them or the mess.

Everett immediately ran to a drawer and pulled out a pack of glucose gels. "He's a type 1 diabetic, ma'am. He doesn't always take care of himself as he should."

"Right." Emma moved into action. Carefully kicking the broken glass out of the way with her boot, before placing a hand on Dr. Markson's back and noticing the bulge of an insulin pump at his waist. "Why don't you have a seat, Dr. Markson, and Everett will help you feel better."

He spun around, blue eyes wild and glassy and face gaunt. Classic signs of hypoglycemia. Neglecting himself was one thing, but letting your blood sugar drop to dangerously low levels could be life-threatening.

"Don't touch me. Leave me alone!" Dr. Markson growled, turning back to the counter to scatter more food around. A banana flew past her head, then a jar of jam, which broke into a sticky mess on the gray marble floor behind her.

The dog gave a startled yelp and Emma reached down to give the poor thing a pat, noticing the collar embroidered with Service Dog in white. "It's okay, sweetie. We're here now and we'll take care of him."

"Don't need care," Dr. Markson hissed, pushing Emma out of the way hard with his hip, causing her to stumble back a little and barely miss stepping on the dog's paw. "Don't need anyone."

"We could use those glucose gels over here," she called to the butler. "And juice. Something to get in his system fast."

Everett handed her the package of gels, then grabbed the apple juice Thad had pulled from the fridge earlier. "Ready when you are, ma'am."

"Okay. Good." Emma switched into ER nurse mode then, her tone brisk and efficient. "Help me get him to one of those stools at the island and sit him down."

While Everett steered Dr. Markson away from the fridge, Emma got the juice bottle open while keeping the dog back with her foot. The butler got her patient onto the stool, and Emma crouched in front of Dr. Markson, smiling. "Hello, there. Remember me? Emma Trudeau, a nurse from the hospital. Can you take a sip of this juice for me, please?"

She held the bottle to his lips, but he batted it away. "No! I don't want your drink. I don't want you here! Leave me alone!" Emma's heart sank a bit at his cruel tone, but she held her ground. Aggression was a common side effect of low blood sugar. This wasn't him. Not really. He needed some sugar in his system. Easier said than done, though, given that Dr. Markson had more muscle on him than she'd previously noticed. Still, she persisted. "Come on. Please. Just a little drink."

His eyes were more unfocused, as if the world around

him made no sense. Screw it. Time for the gels. Emma normally used them as a last resort in the ER, since they were pure sugar and could easily send a patient in the opposite problem if not carefully monitored, but desperate times called for desperate measures. She ripped the top of a sachet and prepared to squeeze the contents into Thad's mouth. "Hold his head for me."

The older man did as she asked, his face tight with worry, and Emma squeezed the gel into his mouth. She'd guessed on the dosage based on his size, but they'd deal with the consequences afterward. She held his mouth closed until he swallowed.

Slowly, Thad began to quiet. Five minutes passed and she was able to get him to drink some juice, too. Part of her itched to check his sensor to see his levels, but she didn't want to disturb him again until he was stable.

"Will he be all right, ma'am?" Everett asked, a bit of his color returning. "He hasn't been this bad in a long time."

Emma straightened and leaned her hip against the edge of the giant granite-topped island. "He should be all right. We'll need to wait and see."

CHAPTER THREE

AN ANGEL FLOATED before him. An angel with long black braids and bright dark eyes. She also had a pink hat on her head with a ball on top that flopped around whenever she moved. Weird. His dreams didn't normally look like this.

The angel patted his hand and talked quietly to him, her voice calm and soothing. The voice he'd wished for as a child on those long nights after his mother had died and his father had grown cold and distant. The voice of reason and truth and kindness. He smiled.

"Sir?" Another voice interrupted his fantasy, dissolving the cloudy, comfortable heaven in his head. Thad moved and winced, his back aching. And cold. He was so cold. A shudder ran through him as he straightened, doing his best to shake off the fuzziness surrounding him. "Are you feeling better?"

Everett. Yep, he recognized that voice. What he didn't recognize was the edge of fear in the butler's voice. Thad could be a bit brusque and broody sometimes, but Everett had never been scared of him. Probably because the man had seen Thad in diapers. Hard to fear a man you'd seen in his undies.

A cold nose nudged the strip of bare leg between the top of Thad's sock and the hem of his pants. Baxter. He absently reached down to pat the Lab's head to reassure him. Good old Baxter. His father had never let Thad have pets in the town house, so the first thing he'd done after his father died five years ago had been to rescue Baxter. The dog had returned the favor many times over.

Thad's mystery angel still hovered around the periphery of his vision, though, speaking again. "Hi, Dr. Markson. Glad you're back with us." She didn't wait for his answer. Just as well, with his thick, dry mouth. He licked his lips and tasted apple. Huh. He didn't remember drinking juice.

He sat there until his brain functioned again and tiny puzzle pieces fell into place—working upstairs; pushing himself too hard for too long; the trip to the kitchen for food.

His angel touched his arm and all Thad's senses sparked to life. Normally, he didn't like people touching him. So invasive. Left him feeling unsettled and vulnerable. Thad hated being vulnerable.

Frowning, he shrugged off her touch and blinked hard to clear his vision. Turned to look at her, his movements slow and awkward. "Who are you?"

The woman smiled, her teeth white and even against her darker skin, and held out her hand. "Emma Trudeau. We've met before. I'm a nurse in the ER at Manhattan West and your new partner for the hospital's holiday wish project."

Thad shifted his attention to his butler, who stood near the fridge now with Baxter, a broom in one hand. "Everett, what's happening here?"

His words sounded funny to his own ears. Slurred as if he'd been drinking, but Thad never touched alcohol. Dulled the senses and affected the reflexes. As he took in the chaotic mess in his kitchen, Thad's scowl deepened. He did stand then, his wobbly knees accepting his weight thankfully, though he still held on to the island just in case. "Will someone please explain what the hell happened in here?"

The last thing Thad remembered was getting into the fridge. He ran a shaky hand down the front of his black cashmere turtleneck, before giving Emma Trudeau some serious side-eye. She'd helped him…apparently, and he wasn't sure how he felt about that. Thad didn't like surprises. Or changes.

Tonight, he'd had both.

His stomach plummeted as the realization of what had happened struck him hard. Oh God. He hadn't let things slip that badly with his blood sugar since way back in his teens, after he'd first been diagnosed with type 1 diabetes at twelve. At the time he'd first found out about his disease, his life had been in turmoil anyway. His beloved mother had died unexpectedly two years prior, and his father had not handled it well. He'd thrown himself into work, leaving young Thad to deal with his grief on his own. Then, after Thad had gotten sick and been hospitalized because of his blood sugar and received his final diagnosis, Thad's father had basically shunned him. Said he was deficient, weak, useless, because of his illness. Part of Thad's drive to not just succeed but excel came from the deep hurt of his father's rejection back then. His father had died five years ago, but those wounds lived on, festering inside where Thad had buried them because it was easier that way. He was fine. It was fine.

Or he had been, until now.

Dammit. Why hadn't he taken two seconds to check his blood sugar earlier like he'd intended? He certainly knew the drill by now, the symptoms to look out for that meant he was headed for trouble. He even kept snacks all around the town house just for such emergencies.

Shame heated his cheeks as his father's voice echoed through his head from the past.

Deficient, weak. Useless.

"Dr. Markson?" the nurse asked again. She tapped his arm to get his attention. Her smile had been replaced by a serious expression now. "Where is your glucose monitor? We should check your levels now after what just happened."

He knew that. Of course he did. But having her tell him, like he was a child, only made him angry. Rather than answer her, Thad walked to the sink instead, broken glass crunching under his shoes. He scowled down at them. "Who broke this?"

Thad hated disorder. That was another reason he preferred to live alone. No one around to make a mess.

Everett rushed over with a broom and dustpan from the closet nearby to begin sweeping up the shards. "I wasn't here to see it happen, but we believe you did, sir."

"We?" Thad's exasperation reached a breaking point. What the hell was happening in his own house? And since when did Everett join forces with anyone against him? They'd known each other for decades. Then a nurse shows up and suddenly they're a team? No. He didn't like that at all.

The older man threw the broken glass in the trash then turned back to Thad. "Yes, sir. I brought Ms. Trudeau up here as you'd asked and when we arrived, we found you going through the cupboards and refrigerator. We weren't quite sure what you were doing."

The final missing piece of the puzzle fell into place for Thad with a heavy thud in his head, his humiliation complete. "I did this."

It wasn't a question.

Emma stepped in beside him. "Is there somewhere we can talk, Dr. Markson?"

"No, Ms. Trudeau," Thad gritted out, his inner discombobulation and embarrassment at having lost control like that erupting into anger. "There isn't. We have nothing to talk about. I will not be participating in any project with you, and I want you to leave my home right now. I want you to leave me alone, period. Understand?"

Usually when Thad lost his temper, people jumped. Not Emma Trudeau, though. Nope. In fact, she didn't look surprised or fazed at all. The woman stood her ground, crossing her arms like she had no intention of going anywhere. "What I understand, Dr. Markson," she said, "is that we're both busy people and I for one don't have time to deal with this nonsense. We—" she gestured between them "—have an important project to complete in order to make a very sick child's holiday wish come true. In addition to that, I have way too much riding on getting this thing done that I won't allow you or anyone else to stand in my way. Do you understand?"

He blinked at her, too stunned to respond. No one talked back to him like that. Ever.

"Now," she said, leaning forward slightly, enough for him to catch a whiff of her rose-and-cinnamon scent. "We are going to talk. Here or somewhere else in this palace, that's up to you. But it's happening."

When had the kitchen gotten so hot? Emma took off her coat, hat and scarf and handed them over to Everett, who waited to take them, seemingly as anxious to escape the tension in the room as the black Lab took up residence at Dr. Markson's side once more, lying down on the tile floor. Good service dog and not uncommon for people who had chronic conditions like Dr. Markson's. Her face burned hotter than the sun and Emma desperately wanted to fan herself but doubted it would help. Not with Dr. Markson watching her from such close quarters. Something about the man seemed to set all her senses abuzz. Even with the icy glare he currently directed her way.

Working with him, even temporarily, would be a baptism by fire, no doubt. But Emma had never been one to run from a challenge and she refused to start now. The clock above his fancy stove said it was nearly eight o'clock, meaning she'd been waiting to see this man for hours. Hours she could've spent at home with her sister, Karley, relaxing. Maybe catching up on the latest episodes of the new rom-com that had dropped earlier in the week on streaming. Emma had precious little free time to begin with and it seemed Dr. Markson would be eating into what small amount she had left. At least for the next three weeks or so.

She gestured toward the pump at his waist, then the sensor on his arm, hidden beneath the sleeve of his soft-looking black turtleneck sweater. "Looks like you've got the latest equipment, so I'm guessing your blood sugar is monitored through an app on your phone?" He gave a curt nod. "Good. Where is it?"

He didn't answer at first, just watched her closely, as if sizing her up. She did the same to him, receiving the full effect of Dr. Thad Markson. Those piercing icy blue eyes and chiseled jaw. The perfectly swept-back dark hair. A hint of stubble beneath the skin of his jaw. His sculpted lips were currently compressed into a thin white line, but she imagined them relaxed, full and soft and…

Whoops. Girl, stop. Now is not the time and he is definitely not the man for you to fantasize about.

Not that she had time for that anyway. Romance was way at the bottom of her to-do list. Especially with a man who practically had a flashing neon sign above his head warning Do Not Touch.

Emma took a deep breath and placed a hand on her hip, waiting for his answer, hoping her inappropriate thoughts did not show on her face.

Finally, Dr. Markson pointed toward a corner of the counter. "On the charger over there."

She turned, mentally shaking off the unwanted fuzzy warmth this man had fizzing inside her like champagne.

You're here to talk about the project. That's it. Get the phone and get on with it.

After getting his phone, she brought it back over to the island so he could unlock it and pull up the app. Dr. Markson cursed under his breath, crimson dotting his high cheekbones, as he scrolled through the screen of information. It was obvious he was embarrassed. She almost felt sorry for the man. Almost.

Their arms accidentally brushed as she sat down on the stool beside his. Zings of awareness raced through her nerve endings while Emma didn't miss how he flinched away from the brief touch.

He shook his head, scowling. "I haven't had an episode that bad in years. I use the latest, best automated insulin delivery system available. Cutting-edge technology. This never should've happened."

"When was the last time you ate?" she asked, clasping her hands in her lap to avoid any accidental brushes against each other again. Dr. Markson clearly didn't like to be touched. Not by her, anyway, if the way he'd pulled back like she'd burned him before was any indication. "Even the best pumps can fail if the patient doesn't follow the proper guidelines."

"I know," he snapped, without glancing at her. "I've been dealing with my condition since I was twelve." He tapped the phone screen a couple of times, then exhaled slowly. "Returning to normal."

"Good."

He set the phone aside and they sat there, silence gathering around them faster than the steady snow blanketing the city outside. Eventually, Dr. Markson hung his head. "I don't want to do your project, Nurse Trudeau. I don't have the time. I'm preparing for a very delicate surgery next month and need to focus all my energy and attention on that."

"It won't take much of your time, actually," she countered, ready for this argument. "I'm prepared to do the bulk of the work. Your connections within the city are what I'm most interested in. To get things going and keep things moving at a steady pace until Christmas Eve. I'll handle the rest."

He did look at her now, all narrowed gaze and pursed lips. Yep. Very kissable indeed. Not that she'd noticed. Nope. Not looking at them at all. "And what makes you think I have connections?"

She almost blurted out the fact that he was rich, but that was rude. Instead, Emma chose her words more carefully. "Your family name is well known in New York. It holds clout with the wealthy and powerful. You have access to people and places I could never approach on behalf of the charity project. Don't you want little Ricky Lynch to get his wish?"

"First of all." He straightened, his color returning. "Do not try to guilt me into participating in your little project, Nurse Trudeau."

"Emma."

Dr. Markson blinked at her, then gave a dismissive wave. "Fine. Whatever. Emma. My point is things have happened in my life you can't even imagine. I understand what Ricky Lynch is going through better than most. Don't ever assume you know me or understand what makes me tick because I can assure you that you don't." He inhaled deep. "And as far as those connections you mentioned, most of them were my father's and I will never, ever use anything that man made. If you'd done your research properly on me in the first place, you'd know why. And you never would've asked me to participate." Slowly, he slid off his stool, as if testing his legs to see if they'd support him. "Now, if you'll excuse me, Everett will show you out."

He was halfway across the kitchen when Emma said, "I know that your father cheated a lot of people out of their money and their homes with his dodgy real estate deals. I know that if he hadn't died five years ago he probably would've been in prison for securities fraud. And you're right. I can't know exactly what it was like growing up with a parent like him. But I did do my research, Dr. Markson. Because I also know you immediately took all the assets your father had left, once he was gone, and set up a foundation to pay restitution to those harmed by your father's actions. I know that you continue that foundation today, even though those affected by your father have long since been compensated and now the foundation funds outreach and all sorts of social welfare programs throughout New York City to better the lives of others. And I know you kept this town house to save it from being torn down and have filed paperwork to have it added to the historic preservation list."

She stood, too, crossing her arms. "Believe me, Dr. Markson. I did my homework, and I understood the assignment. You might be able to intimidate other people at Manhattan West, but I've dealt with far tougher in far worse situations and you won't intimidate me. I've worked too hard for too long to not complete this project. One, because Ricky Lynch deserves whatever joy he wants for whatever time he has left. And two, because if I get this done—and I will—I have a great shot at a promotion in the ER that will give me more money and a better house and allow me more time to spend with my sister outside of work. So I will camp on your front porch if I must, but we will grant this wish, and you will help me. Do you understand?"

Dr. Markson stood there so long, so still, his back to her, that Emma started to worry maybe he would pass out again. Then, finally, he scrubbed a hand over his face, a bit of the tension in his broad shoulders relaxing as he murmured something to her over his shoulder she didn't catch.

"I'm sorry?" Emma said, stepping closer, in case she needed to catch him before he hit the ground. He was quite a bit bigger than her, but she'd been trained to move large patients without hurting herself, so...

"Thad," he repeated, louder this time. "If we're going to work on this thing together, you should call me Thad. At least here in the town house. Dr. Markson is too formal."

Emma smiled slowly as she did an inner fist pump. Yes. At last she'd made progress here.

Before she could get too excited, though, he turned to face her again. "I need to eat something." He leaned past her and shouted. "Everett?"

She shook her head. "I can get it for you. I'm already here. What do you want?"

"It's his job," Thad said, frowning and making his way back to his stool at the island, still shakier than Emma would've liked. "Everett likes taking care of me."

"The poor man is probably tired after the ordeal you just put him through." She snorted and got him settled at the island before walking back over to the fridge to peek inside. "How old is your butler, anyway?"

"Seventy-two." He pointed toward the food still strewn across the counters. "I'll just have some toast with peanut butter."

Emma nodded, then raised a brow at him.

"Please," Thad added after a moment.

"Better." Grinning, Emma grabbed the whole-grain bread and jar of peanut butter and carried them over to the toaster sticking out of the carnage. She stuck two slices in, then rested her hips back against the edge of the counter to wait. "You should check your app again. Make sure your numbers are still stable."

Thad scrunched his nose. "Are you always this bossy as a nurse?"

Emma laughed. "Always."

For a second something changed. The tension between them disappeared and he smiled in return, the glory of it shining down on her like the star of Bethlehem. She doubted Thad smiled much, so it was a rare gift indeed. Shame, too, because it was a very nice smile.

Ding!

The toast popped up, breaking her out of her reverie. She pulled it out and spread it with peanut butter before setting two plates on the island, one for him and one for her. At his surprised look, she shrugged.

"What? You made me wait so long I missed dinner. I think you owe me a piece of toast. Want something to drink with it, Thad?"

"Cup of tea," he said, almost absently, staring down at his plate like it might blow up any second. "Bags are in the cupboard to the right of the stove. Kettle is on the stove."

She started boiling the water, then searched for cups. He was probably right that calling in the butler would've been easier, but she felt sorry for the older man. Besides, making him food felt like getting to know Thad better. Which she needed to do for the project, not because it felt nice, being here with him and let into his world, however briefly and reluctantly.

His icy gaze still tracked her movements from across the room, sending small shivers of awareness up her spine. He ate a bite of his toast.

In the reflection on the glass door of the microwave over the stove, she caught sight of Thad behind her, running his free hand through his hair, mussing it, and her breath caught. Not just because it was sexy, which it totally was. But also because it made him seem a little less perfect, a little more vulnerable. *Like the rest of us.* Her chest burned with yearning to make him smile again, to see him let his walls down and just be happy for a while. Given all he'd accomplished by the age of thirty-six, he worked hard. Perhaps too hard. Of all people, though, she understood the drive to achieve, and the fear of disappointing those who depended on you. Maybe she and Thad Markson weren't so very different after all?

The kettle whistled, startling Emma. She splashed some milk into the bottom of each cup, then poured the boiling water over the tea bags and carried both cups to the island before taking a seat beside Thad again. Using first names was nice. Friendly. "Maybe now would be a good time to discuss the basics of the project?"

Slowly he lifted the mug to his mouth and took a sip. "Later, please."

Sighing, Emma swallowed a bite of toast. "Okay, but we're already behind on prep because of the Thanksgiving holiday and we can't afford to lose much more time."

Thad looked like he wanted to argue with her, but instead reached down to give his dog a bite of peanut butter toast. "Hey, Baxter," he said, scratching the dog behind the ears. "Good boy."

And there it was. The smile again. This time, Emma had to stop herself from staring and covered it quickly by gulping her tea.

When he straightened again, Thad gave Emma some serious side-eye. "I do believe you'll be nothing but trouble, Emma."

"Trouble's my middle name." She winked up at him, then froze, realizing what she'd done. Flirting wasn't part of the plan, no matter how endearing the man had suddenly become. Baxter the dog came to her rescue then, too, gruffling and wagging his tail, paws prancing on the tile floor in hopes of more treats.

"You've had enough, boy," Thad said, chuckling, the dark timbre of his voice soothing the dog and causing him to lie back down on the floor at Thad's feet. Unfortunately, his tone had a similar effect on Emma, making her heart flip and her entire body sigh with pleasure. If she wasn't careful, she'd end up in a puddle of goo at Thad's feet, just like Baxter. Man, his voice should be bottled and sold like expensive perfume. Intoxicating, sensual, made to whisper naughty things in the deep of the night, then to be followed up with some equally naughty actions.

Stop it!

Alarm bells went off in Emma's head. She had no idea what was wrong with her. She wasn't a woman who swooned over men. Especially ones who were so obviously off-limits. Yet here she was, studying Thad from beneath her lashes as he frowned down into his teacup. From the dark jeans encasing his long legs to the black turtleneck she'd bet her life was made of the finest cashmere and which emphasized the breadth of his shoulders to perfection. Yep. Dr. Thad Markson was a complete stud. Even if most people didn't notice it beneath his churlish demeanor. Even sitting there slumped over his kitchen island, the man exuded a certain power and prowess Emma found intoxicating. She'd always had a thing for competent men, and Thad was the most competent cardiothoracic surgeon in the city. Didn't get more attractive than that for her.

She glanced up at his face again and her throat constricted as her eyes locked with his.

Busted.

"Right." Fresh heat prickled her cheeks and she turned away slightly on her stool to grab her phone from her pocket and pull up the information sheets on Ricky Lynch and his wish she'd received from the charity. She slid her phone over toward Thad so he could see the picture there. "I'll forward these documents to you as well, but this is Ricky Lynch, our wish recipient. He had a brain tumor."

Thad swallowed hard, staring down at the photo of the little boy smiling on her phone screen, his head bald from the chemo. One of his front teeth was missing. He looked too thin, and his skin had a bluish cast. But

his eyes still sparkled with life and excitement and reflected back a cheerful happiness remarkable for a kid
who'd been through so much in his young life. Beside
the boy in his hospital bed was a black Lab with a service dog vest on. Kind of reminded Emma of Baxter.

"What kind of tumor?" Thad asked, his voice gruffer
than before.

"Grade four glioblastoma."

Thad winced. "Poor kid."

"Yeah. He was diagnosed at eight. He's nine now.
Been in and out of the hospital for the past year. His
wish is to have a winter carnival and invite all the kids
in the Manhattan West PICU to attend, along with their
families."

Thad shifted to look at her phone screen, causing
the dog to stir, raising his head to make sure his master
didn't disappear on him again. "So, how do we start? I
don't know the first thing about carnivals. We'll need
a big venue. Those will be hard to come by around the
holidays, especially on short notice."

"I'm working on that. It will probably need to be
indoors as well since we'll have children with various
health conditions there. And ADA accessible too, obviously."

"What about a trip to Disney World?" Thad asked.
"We could book him and his family in down there for
a week of luxury and fun. Solves all our problems."

She took a deep breath. "I thought that, too, but with
his current condition, traveling is impossible. Plus,
Ricky wants to share his carnival with his friends in the
PICU, so we need to stay here. So I spent this morning
calling all the businesses on the list the charity gave me
for donations, but with our time constraints, it's going
to be hard to get it all together in time."

"Hmm." He frowned. "Sounds like we need a miracle."

Emma sipped her tea, regarding him thoughtfully over the rim. "I don't believe in miracles, Thad. I grew up poor and it taught me to believe in the power of people and their choices. Now, you say you don't know anything about carnivals, but you do have resources. And where there's money, there's a way. I have a list of vendors who are willing to come and can get the booths and rides here before Christmas Eve, barring any bad weather. Maybe your foundation can help coordinate that if you contact them. I'll take care of the organization and invitations and ask for donations from the hospital staff, too. But honestly, you're the only person I know who could pull something like this off. That's why I chose you." From Thad's horrified expression he was ready to bolt again, but she reassured him. "I just want you to see this isn't about waiting for a miracle. It's about working together to put on a winter carnival for Ricky, and all the other sick kids in our PICU. To buy them a few hours of happiness and distraction before they go back to reality, and in some cases, before they are no longer with us. Then you can disappear back into this mansion and your privileged life and never have to hear from me again. All I ask is that you help me now."

She took a deep breath before adding, "This carnival can give something to these kids, something priceless. A memory. A good memory. Something they can pick out, dust off and remember with a smile when things aren't going well. Don't you think they deserve that?" She paused and looked him. "Don't you have memories like that, Thad?"

Emma had a few moments like that to remember: twinkling lights, festive rides, people laughing and having fun. But Thad didn't look like he had any pleasant answers to her question. In fact, when he looked at her at last, his gaze was cold enough to give her frostbite. "No, Emma. I don't."

For a moment she thought about pushing him more but knew it wouldn't get her any further with him. Best to leave things as they were and take the progress she'd made so far tonight. It was getting late, too, and she didn't like leaving Karley alone at night. She stood and smoothed a hand down the front of her beige sweater and jeans. Everett, ever the good butler, was right there with her coat, scarf and hat. "Okay. Well, I think we've made a good start," she said as she tugged on her hat. Not really accurate, but at least she'd sat down with him and talked. That was something. "We, uh, should probably set up our next meeting to plan our next steps. I'm working in the ER tomorrow but can take a break in the afternoon. Say around three. Will that work?"

He took a deep breath, scowling into his tea again. "Fine. But make it three fifteen. I'll find you."

"It's a date," Emma said, then bit her lip when she realized how that sounded. "I mean, not a *date* date, but…"

Stop talking now.

She turned to follow the butler downstairs, but Thad's words stopped her. "If we do this, I want my name kept out of it. Use the foundation's name instead. I'll have my people there do some research on possible venues for us and give you an update tomorrow at our meeting."

It wasn't exactly rousing support, but she'd take it.

"Great." She stood on the threshold of the kitchen biting back a grin of triumph. "I'll see you tomorrow afternoon."

Things were about to get interesting.

CHAPTER FOUR

"Trauma one, probable UTI," Emma said to one of the residents standing nearby as she stepped out into the hall and closed the curtain behind her. "White blood cell count is twelve thousand, with neutrophils slightly elevated. There's a trace of blood and plus four bacteria in the urine. The patient reports tenderness in the abdomen and in the mid-low back."

The resident nodded, then glanced down the hall toward the nurses' station. "There's, uh, someone here to see you, Nurse Trudeau."

"Who?" Emma frowned. They were slammed today. Nothing major yet, but lots of flu cases and colds. She handed her tablet containing the patient's chart to the resident, then headed toward the nurses' station, checking her smartwatch along the way. Only two thirty, so too early for Thad.

Yet when she rounded the corner, there he stood, scowling at their assignment board like it was his worst enemy.

Emma sighed. After yesterday, her thinking about him had shifted. Oh, the man was still intimidating, no doubt. At least the rest of the department seemed to think so, seeing how they all gave him a wide berth. But witnessing his vulnerable side in the kitchen the previous night had made a difference for her. She could no longer think of him as just a means to an end to get the charity carnival done. Nope. Growing up, her parents had always warned Emma her soft heart would get her in trouble one day, but it had become one of her greatest assets in her work. Allowing her to understand and empathize with others in a way that built their trust in her and got them to tell her their problems. Of course, she'd learned to put limits on it, too, put up walls to protect herself from those who wanted too much, who drained her energy until there was nothing left. And yes, maybe she'd grown too good at keeping others out over the years, which explained why she was still single at twenty-eight. But Emma was happy with her life and grateful for what she had. Even if what she had at the moment was her partner on the carnival project glaring at her with those icicle-blue eyes.

Despite her wishes, her chest squeezed with unwanted attraction. The man was hot, maybe more so because of his air of cool untouchability. Was it weird to lust after a Grinch? Maybe. Probably.

Get it together, girl.

She shook off the silly thoughts and forced a polite smile. "You're early, Dr. Markson."

"What?" He didn't look away from the board.

"Our meeting isn't until three fifteen, Dr. Markson," Emma said, used to his brusqueness now.

His nose twitched slightly, and he blinked at her, then shook his head. "I'm not here for that. I was called down for a consult on a suspected case of acute decompensated heart failure?"

"Oh." Emma said, focusing on her work and not how handsome he looked in his lab coat. "Okay. Yes, that would be Ms. Lovelace in trauma bay four."

"Right." He started that way, then stopped and said over his shoulder, "I'll need assistance, Nurse Trudeau."

Emma quickly filled in one of the other nurses to help the resident with the UTI, then followed Dr. Markson. Used to Thad's "bedside manner," Emma hurried to enter the patient's room before him and stood by Ms. Lovelace's side to act as a friendly buffer from what she expected to be Thad's more formal exam questions.

Sure enough, Thad started bombarding the older woman the moment he stepped into the room. "You have difficulty breathing and swollen feet. Show me."

Emma cringed on behalf of his less-than-charming social skills and smiled down at the patient. "He's extremely talented as a surgeon."

"He'd better be," the older woman said, shooting Dr. Markson a dubious stare. The woman was a frequent flier in the ER with her dicey insurance situation. Normally thin, tonight Ms. Lovelace looked downright gaunt. From her pinched expression and messy, gray-streaked hair, Emma wondered if she'd been neglecting herself. The woman had no one to care for her; she was in her eighties and not married, nor did she have any children.

While Thad poked and prodded the woman's ankles, Emma tried to discover more about her home situation. "Do you have groceries delivered, Ms. Lovelace? Should I call Meals on Wheels for you?"

"Child, I have all the food I need." The older woman waved Emma off, her attention laser-focused on Dr. Markson. "What kind of doctor are you again?"

Emma bit back a smile. "He's a heart surgeon."

"Cardiothoracic surgeon," Thad corrected from the end of the bed.

After giving him a look, Emma continued. "He's a

specialist who's here to evaluate your heart. Based on your symptoms tonight it sounds like you're having problems again?"

"Lord, yes," Ms. Lovelace huffed. "And I'm so tired all the time."

Thad gave a curt nod. "Fatigue is normal. Three plus pitting edema bilaterally." He next moved to the patient's chest, using his stethoscope to listen to her breathing.

"Damn, son!" Ms. Lovelace scowled up at him. "Warn a lady about your cold hands, why don't ya?"

This time Emma coughed to cover her laugh. Leave it to the elderly to tell it like it was.

"What about water, Ms. Lovelace?" Emma asked, walking to the keyboard in the corner to pull up the patient's file and enter the vitals Thad gave her. "Last time you were in, I believe the resident had ordered you to drink at least sixty-four ounces a day."

"Well, I'm not." The older woman sighed. "I mean, I do drink when I'm thirsty, but then I have to go to the bathroom more and it's hard for me to get around. Plus, I'm not sleeping well at night, so sometimes I fall asleep during the day and miss meals. Which is just as well because the charity group that used to bring me food every month is low on donations, so they can only come every other month now. Sometimes I catch my neighbor when he goes to work but his hours are odd and I don't always get him."

Emma typed all that in, along with the other findings Thad called out to her like they'd been a team forever.

"And when did the breathing issues worsen?" Thad asked, straightening at last.

"Two nights ago," Ms. Lovelace said. "At first, I

thought it was bronchitis messing with my lungs again, but this morning I couldn't catch my breath."

Thad walked out of the room without another word, leaving Emma to make apologies before chasing after him.

As she hurried down the hall, Emma didn't miss the looks both she and Thad received from the staff, including Emma's best friend, another nurse named Danielle. Emma had told Dani about the project and her plans to recruit Dr. Markson. Now though, she was regretting letting her bestie in on the secret, based on Dani's too-inquisitive stare.

"What are your orders, Dr. Markson?" Emma asked once they'd stopped at the nurses' station again.

"The immediate goal is to reestablish adequate perfusion and oxygen delivery to the patient's organs," he said, as if just now noticing that Emma was there. Laser focus. It's what made him such a brilliant surgeon, and such a pain in the butt to wrangle. "Prop the patient's head up, give her oxygen, morphine if she's in pain, IV Lasix and enalapril, along with some nitrates and digoxin for the slight arrhythmia I detected on exam. If that doesn't work, we'll look at more drastic interventions."

"Drastic measures?" Emma only knew the patient through the ER, but still she cared.

"Yes." He washed his hands in the sink nearby while Emma typed the orders into the computer. "If it turns out her kidneys are failing, then we'll need to handle that issue as well."

Emma swallowed hard. Kidney failure would mean dialysis, which would mean regular trips to a clinic and more burden on poor Ms. Lovelace. She was so caught up in her thoughts, she didn't even realize he'd come up behind her until he spoke, his warm breath near her ear making her shiver.

"I don't expect it's that bad though," he said, his voice low and deep, intimate, for her ears only. "Also, thank you for assisting me in there, Emma."

"You're welcome," she squeaked out past her constricted vocal cords, turning slightly to look at him over her shoulder. He was close, so close that if there hadn't been people around and she'd been braver, she could've risen on tiptoe and kissed him. He smiled then, teeth even and white, lips soft and sinfully sexy, and…

Oh, boy.

Emma turned back around fast, cheeks hot and mouth dry. "I'll keep you updated on the patient's progress."

"Perfect." Thad walked away, seemingly oblivious to the fact he'd just rocked Emma's world. "See you at three fifteen, Nurse Trudeau."

But unfortunately, fate had other ideas, because the busy ER got busier and Emma and Thad were thrown together again on a case, this time an overweight man with a sharp tightness in his chest. When she'd offered to have one of the residents take the case instead, Thad had brushed her off.

"I'm the only one in my department, and I like to stay busy," he said, like that covered it. As far as Emma knew, Thad normally avoided her department like an Ebola outbreak, but suddenly he was around today. A lot. With her. She didn't want to think too hard about why that was occurring because honestly, they were short-staffed and could use all the help they could get today. She and Thad worked on the obese patient, doing an EKG, which showed left ventricular hypertrophy and a possible blockage. They stabilized the man while awaiting the results of his cardiac enzyme tests.

"I've read your chest X-ray, Mr. Trotter," Thad said to the patient about twenty minutes later. "And your heart is enlarged. Part of that is due to your high blood pressure and congestive heart failure, but you still shouldn't have the chest pain. One of the heart enzymes in your blood, called troponin, is elevated, suggesting your heart muscle isn't getting enough oxygen. So—" he turned then to Emma "—let's get the patient moved up to the cardiac-care unit for closer observation. And schedule a cardiac catheterization in the morning. That way, if there are any blockages, I can repair them immediately."

Emma prepared the transfer information while Thad answered questions from the man's wife. By then it was nearly time for Emma's break and their meeting. She finished up with Mr. Trotter and his wife before clocking out and going downstairs to the basement cafeteria with Thad to discuss the carnival plans in private.

She settled at a table in the corner to wait for Thad while he got his drink and pulled out her phone to take notes on their project updates. When he finally sat down, though, he had a whole tray of food.

He put a napkin on her lap, then looked up at her. "What? It's time for me to eat and I didn't want to be rude by doing it in front of you. So I got enough for two. Wasn't sure what you liked. Vegetarian? Gluten free? Pescatarian? Vegan? There's a bit of everything."

"Oh. Um." She shook her head. "I'm not on any special diet, but thanks. I guess."

"You're welcome." His voice once again stroked against her skin like velvet and Emma battled another shudder of awareness from rippling through her. They were here to discuss their progress on the carnival, not for her to drool all over him. She sat back and refocused on her notes rather than her inappropriate attraction to Thad.

"Here." He passed her an unopened bag of pita chips before digging into his chicken Caesar salad. "Eat those."

"I'm not really hungry," she said, setting the bag aside.

"What time did your shift start today?" he asked between bites of food.

"Seven this morning. Why?"

"And when did you last eat?"

Emma had to think about that for a second. "Dinner last night. But I had a whole burger and fries, so I'm still full."

He snorted, then shook his head. "You need to take the same level of care with yourself as you do for others."

"I…" Emma frowned. She took care of herself. She ate well, or tried to, between her busy work schedule and Karley's school activities. And she certainly got enough exercise running around the ER all day. Defensive, she tried again to get their meeting back on track. "We're here to talk about the project."

"Do you always do that?"

"What?"

"Deflect away from yourself?" Thad wiped his mouth on his napkin, then narrowed his gaze. "You don't like being in the spotlight."

"I have no problem—"

"It wasn't a question," he said, cutting her off. "You prefer to let others shine. I see it very clearly."

"Do you?" Heat prickling her face, she compressed

her lips. The fact that his words had hit far too close to home only unsettled her more. Part of her wanted to tell him where to go and how to get off, but the other part of her felt far too exposed and raw. She didn't like being the center of attention, it was true. But that was a good thing, right? Her sister didn't agree. Karley was always on at Emma to stand up for herself, to toot her own horn, as Karley called it. Maybe if she did, Emma still wouldn't be waiting for a promotion that was long overdue by any standards. But she felt more comfortable in the background. Not that she would let Thad Markson know it, though. She raised her chin and waggled her phone between her fingers. "I've only got twenty minutes left on my break and we have a lot to do. And if we're going to talk about people's life choices, why are you being so nice to me all of a sudden, bringing me lunch? Yesterday you wanted nothing to do with me."

Thad gave a slight shrug, then ate another bite of salad. "I don't like to eat alone."

"But you live alone."

"Everett is there."

"Does your butler eat with you?" Emma found that hard to believe.

"Sometimes," Thad said, surprising her. She couldn't imagine the staid older man breaking protocol like that. "And there's Baxter, too..."

And damn. Now he'd gone and made her feel sorry for him again. She resisted the urge to rub the sore spot on her chest over her heart as she pictured Thad eating alone at the granite island in his massive kitchen. Apparently, that old adage was right. Money wasn't everything. Distracted, she reached for her bag of chips and accidentally brushed her hand against Thad's free one on the table. Her nerve endings zinged, but this time

Thad didn't pull away fast as he had before. Their eyes met and she saw the same shocked awareness she felt in his gaze.

Oh boy.

Emma opened the chips and popped one in her mouth, looking away fast. And yeah. Fine. She was kind of hungry.

"How old are you?" Thad blurted out, his expression unreadable.

"Uh." She frowned. "First of all, that's rude. And second, twenty-eight. How old are you?"

"Thirty-six." He pushed away his now-empty salad plate before starting on a bowl of yogurt with blueberries. "Have you always lived in New York?"

"Yes." Emma exhaled slowly and ate another chip, losing hope for their planning session. "You?"

"Same." He stared into his yogurt. "What made you want to be a nurse?"

"I didn't have time for medical school." She devoured a few more chips and at his curious look, continued. "My parents were killed in a car accident when I turned eighteen. I had a full scholarship for a pre-med program, but with my little sister to raise there was no time. And I had to bring in income to keep a roof over our heads. So I put aside my dreams of being a doctor and went to community college at night instead, so I could hold down a full-time job to support us. Took me longer than I wanted to graduate, but I got there. Got a job here at Manhattan West after graduation and worked my way up."

Everyone reacted differently to her story. Some pitied her. Some applauded her gumption. Rarely, though, did Emma feel like anyone really saw her. Not her looks or skin color or tragic past, but her.

But when Thad looked at her, she felt seen. Right down to her core. So much so she had to fight not to squirm. It was uncomfortable and unsettling and more than a little unbelievable. Because of course it would be the one man she could never imagine herself with in a million years who finally got her.

Silence stretched taut between them until he finally changed the subject. "Tell me what you've done so far on your plans."

While she told him about the vendor calls she'd made that morning, Thad wrestled with his rioting emotions. He wasn't sure what he'd expected Emma's life and past to be like, but he hadn't been prepared for her truth. Even with his own mother dying when he was just ten from cancer and living with his cold, distant father afterward, Thad knew his life had been privileged.

But hearing her speak about losing her dream of becoming a doctor because of such horrible circumstances and the choices she'd been forced to make to survive, well… Thad swallowed hard. It was heartbreaking. Still, she managed to remain upbeat, optimistic, happy despite the scars grief inevitably left inside you. She'd persevered, finding new opportunities to move forward when others closed on her. She'd turned her troubles into triumphs and damn if Thad didn't admire Emma for it.

And now she'd turned that same dogged determination to helping a sad, sick little boy get his dream come true. He remembered the image of little Ricky Lynch from the project brief, clutching the neck of his service dog. A dog who looked remarkably like Baxter. And that dog wasn't the only thing he and Ricky had in common, either. Thad had spent more than enough time in hospitals as a kid. Scared and lonely and sick as they'd worked to regulate his diabetes. Sometimes, if he closed his eyes, he could still hear the beep of monitors and smell the disinfectant.

"Thad?" Emma asked, jarring him back to the present.

He started, blinking at her, the sound of his name on her lips still ringing in his ears—sweet and soft and a tad sultry. Deep inside him, something tightly coiled unfurled. "Yes?"

She looked concerned. "Everything okay?"

Thad resorted to his usual brusque business mode again, same as he always did when he felt too raw. "Fine. I think we need to consider the venue carefully, given we're dealing with extremely ill children here. Can't have them traipsing about outside in the snow and freezing temperatures. I need to do more research to find a suitable location."

He kept his eyes locked on his yogurt bowl the whole time to avoid gazing at Emma like some smitten schoolboy. It was ridiculous. He was never besotted. He was a Markson, for God's sake.

"Agreed," she said, tapping her phone screen. "I thought about that, too. But it will need to be a pretty big venue for all the rides and booths and things. Plus have good ventilation and access to bathrooms. Not easy to find this close to Christmas."

After considering that a moment, Thad said, "I've got my foundation on it. They should get back to me soon with a report." At her expectant look, his pulse tripped. He'd grown up seeing his father throw his financial weight around and the consequences of that with his shady real estate deals had not been good. People had lost their homes, their life savings, because of his father. Thad was hesitant to do anything even remotely similar to his father's, using money and influence to push things through he wanted, but this was for a good cause and Emma had him fired up. "And I'll make some calls too. See if I can move them along any faster." He finished his yogurt, then stacked his things back on the tray. "I'll try and coordinate the mechanics of the rides as well, since you already started on the vendor list. What should we get? Ferris wheel, Scrambler, fun house? Maybe a bouncy house or fun slide?"

"A Ferris wheel might be hard to fit indoors." Emma practically beamed at him now and Thad found himself enchanted. "Maybe something smaller. Like a carousel?"

"Is that your favorite ride?" He wasn't sure why he'd asked, but it seemed important he know.

"It is." Her bright smile faltered before she looked away. "I remember riding one with my parents as a kid. Everyone was so happy and carefree."

He studied her wistful expression, her smooth skin and lovely dark eyes and those lips, so soft and kissable and…

Whoops. No.

Thad shoved those thoughts from his head and forced himself to get up and throw his trash away instead before they headed back to work. At the elevators, Emma yawned and stretched, her blue scrub top riding up slightly to reveal a sliver of bare skin at her waist. Thad looked away fast, throat tight.

"I think we got a good start," he said, his voice gruff to his own ears.

"We did." The elevator dinged and Emma stepped on board, holding the door for him. "I'll text you with our next meeting time?"

"Yes. Good." He cleared his throat, clasping his hands behind his back and staring straight ahead. "And thank you for helping me last night in my kitchen." Uncomfortable heat climbed his neck from beneath the starched collar of his dress shirt. "I look forward to your text."

The elevator dinged and the doors opened on the first floor. Emma got off, then turned to look at him. "You're welcome, about the kitchen thing last night. And thanks for the chips."

Neither moved. Thad held the doors until they beeped.

"So—" Emma stared.

"Maybe—" Thad said at the same time.

Both laughed. Then Thad said, "You go first."

"I was thinking we should meet Ricky in person. Tell him what we're planning and see if he has any more ideas we should incorporate. Maybe one day next week?" Her cheeks flushed a pink and she stared down at her toes. "If you're available."

"Yes." He cleared his throat. "I'm free on Wednesday around lunchtime."

"Good. Me, too." Thad felt her answering grin like the sun breaking through a cloudy day. "Next Wednesday it is."

CHAPTER FIVE

As soon as they arrived on the sixth floor of Manhattan West the following week, it was like being in another world. Like being home, in a weird way. Children's wards were one of the few places, beside the OR, where Thad felt entirely relaxed, entirely himself. Here the temperature was different, the mood was different. Even the lighting was different. Everything felt softer, warmer, kinder. Even if it was all just an illusion.

Several huge Christmas trees dotted the floor. One near the elevators at the entrance. Another at the end of the main corridor. And yet another still filled a corner of the kids' playroom, its colorful decorations creating a rainbow effect. Beneath each tree awaited a bevy of wrapped gifts for their small patients, brought by family and friends and staff. Paintings made by the kids in the ward decorated the walls with Santa and reindeer and snowmen in all shapes and sizes. And even the kids in isolation because of infection risk had fiber-optic trees outside their windows in the hallway, the ever-changing lights reflecting joyfully back inside their rooms. The staff in the PICU bent over backward to make each child feel special at this time of year.

They always had.

Chest tight, Thad stepped up to the desk at the

nurses' station and cleared his throat. "I'm Dr. Markson and this is Nurse Emma Trudeau. We're here to see Ricky Lynch."

The middle-aged Latina woman behind the desk whose name tag read Perla smiled wide. "He's been waiting for you two to arrive." She looked from Thad to Emma. "You work down in the ER, right? I think you helped me a month or so ago when I had to bring my mom in."

"I do." Emma smiled back. "And I remember you now. How's your mother doing?"

"Much better, thanks. We finally got her blood pressure regulated, which was a big deal. She's also on a special diet and moving more, so she's doing really good." Perla finished typing something on her computer, then stood. "Right. Let's go see Ricky. Follow me."

The atmosphere here was the opposite to what Thad was used to in the high-pressure, competitive world of specialist surgery. Staff in the PICU never held any airs or graces. Never jockeyed for position or shouted orders at one another. In fact, at one time, Thad had considered going into pediatric surgery instead of his chosen field. But that was not good enough for his father, who had always insisted Thad be the best, do the best, have the best, or else he was worthless. Being back in such a gentle, soothing, supportive environment now felt like an opposite universe from what Thad had become familiar with growing up with his horrible father. Still, a part of him deep inside remembered this place, and a tiny sprout of warmth broke through the hardened soil of his soul. Perhaps his heart wasn't completely dead after all.

Perla pointed toward the end of the main corridor.

"Ricky's in room three. His parents are working today but left word for you to go on in and speak with their son. Oh, and McCoy's in there too."

"McCoy?" Thad frowned.

"His emotional support dog," Perla said, her expression a bit sad. "Helps him deal with things."

"Right. Thank you." Thad started down the hall. The floor had been updated since his last stay there as a child, but he still remembered the layout. Emma followed behind him, oddly quiet.

Thad slowly opened the door to the room in case Ricky had fallen asleep so as not to disturb him. Chemotherapy and radiation tended to zap all of a person's energy. But when he peeked inside, the young boy was wide-awake, talking to the large Lab on his bed. The sprout of emotion in his heart grew larger, choking the air from his lungs. Baxter meant so much to Thad now, the unconditional love and support of an animal. Back when he'd been Ricky's age and stuck in here, with no one to visit him except Everett, Thad would've given anything to have a friend like McCoy by his side.

Both Ricky and the dog looked over as Thad and Emma entered, the dog whimpering slightly because they were strangers. Ricky looked the same as he had in the photo from the project brief. Bald from the chemo, skin so pale it was almost translucent and blue. But a smile so wide and earnest it made Thad's newly resuscitated heart ache.

"Hello, Ricky," Thad said, his voice a tad gruffer than normal. "We're here to talk about your wish."

Ricky's blue eyes sparkled with excitement. "Yay!"

"My name's Dr. Markson, but you can call me Thad." He stood beside him. "And this is Nurse Trudeau."

"Emma," she said. "May I pet your dog?"

"Sure, Emma," Ricky said, grinning at the Lab. "McCoy loves attention."

They both greeted the dog, then pulled up chairs to the boy's bedside. "Now, about the carnival you wished for," Thad started.

"I want cake," Ricky said, tossing away the covers and throwing his legs over the side of his bed.

"Cake?" Thad frowned. "We didn't bring any cake."

"No, silly." Ricky shook his head. "There's cake in the TV room. Come on, McCoy."

The dog jumped down, trailing along beside the boy, nudging Ricky's hand with his wet nose to let him know he was there, much as Baxter did to Thad. The boy stopped at the door and gestured to them. "You want cake, too? I'm sure there's enough."

Emma shrugged, then glanced at Thad. "Cake sounds good to me."

They went back down the corridor to a room with several round tables in it and a large flat-screen TV on the wall showing cartoons. On another table against the wall the staff had set out plates of cookies and bottles of drinks and a large sheet cake in the shape of a rocket. Emma got Ricky and McCoy settled, then joined Thad near the refreshments.

"Wow," she said, scanning the assortment of stuff. "This is quite a spread. I wonder if it was someone's birthday or something."

"I doubt it." Thad shrugged. "They usually keep some kind of food around at all times in this ward. Some of the kids can't eat at usual mealtimes because of their treatments. Most of the time it's healthy snacks like veggies or granola or fruit. But considering the state some of these children are in health-wise, they can be lenient, too, and give them sweets as well to keep them happy." He picked up a plate and filled it with fresh veg-gies and hummus while Emma grabbed some cake for herself and Ricky. "If the patient is midway through chemo and can't face regular food the staff will give them anything they want to get some calories in them. I remember when I was in here one time, a nurse made a mad dash at midnight just to find a kid the kind of candy bar he craved."

The minute he said the words, Thad froze. He hadn't meant to share so much with Emma. Gaze trained on his plate, he added a few whole-grain crackers to his as-sortment of healthy snacks, hoping perhaps she hadn't heard him.

No such luck.

"Do you spend a lot of time up here now?" Emma asked, her intense gaze burning a hole through the side of his head. "Or was this when you were a child?"

Thad grabbed a bottled water. "It was a long time ago."

Emma looked like she wanted to ask more, but Thad stopped her. "Please not now. We're here for Ricky. He's having a good day and I don't want to spoil that by fo-cusing on me and my past."

Before she could respond, he rejoined the boy at the table. Emma followed and soon they were discussing everything about the carnival.

Ricky seemed very chatty, asking lots of questions while slipping McCoy bites of his vanilla cake with strawberry frosting. "What about pony rides?"

"No pony rides. Too many health concerns and reg-ulations," Thad said. He felt for the kid, but there were limits. "Not to mention the cleanup and waste—"

"We're thinking games instead, Ricky," Emma intervened, giving Thad a look. "All free with prizes, even if you didn't win."

"Oh, I love prizes!" Ricky clapped and wriggled in his seat a little. "What kind of prizes?"

While Emma and the boy discussed the toy options, Thad ate his veggies and marveled at how good she was with people. His mom had been great with people, too. But Thad had never learned that skill. First because of his isolated childhood after his mother's death, and later because he valued his privacy far more than the risks of social interaction. Of course, he knew people complained about his bedside manner, but once his patients recovered from things others had said were impossible to cure, they forgot about his terseness soon enough. And yes, maybe he did feel lonely sometimes, even with Everett and Baxter there for company. Everyone got lonely. It was fine. All fine.

Normal part of life. Had nothing to do with the sudden appearance of Emma Trudeau in his life or the odd sparks of emotion bursting forth like fireworks inside him whenever she was around. It would pass. It always did.

After about an hour, Ricky yawned and sagged in his chair, pushing his empty plate away. "I think I need a nap now."

They quickly cleaned up their table, then walked the boy back to his room, making sure he was warm and comfortable in his bed with the dog by his side before Thad and Emma made their way back out to the elevators in the lobby. But instead of leaving right away, she led him over to some chairs behind the large Christmas tree. Thad figured she wanted to go over what they'd learned from Ricky about the carnival, but instead she patted the seat beside her and looked up at him.

"Tell me about being in this place as a child."

Thad frowned, his guard up. "Why? It has no bearing on what we're doing here."

"It could," Emma argued. "You have personal insight into what these children go through in here. We could use that to make our carnival even more fun for them."

"I don't see how," he groused, reluctantly sitting beside her. This. This was exactly why he didn't talk to people, open up to them. Because they wanted more. Always more. Poking and prodding and making him feel raw and vulnerable and like he was right back in the dark corners he used to hide in as a child to avoid the wrath of his father and later the intrusiveness of the press and anger of the people his father had cheated. He'd repaid them all, every last cent, and still they continued to hound his foundation. No. Letting people in only meant they could hurt you. His father had taught him that lesson well.

But from the determined expression Emma wore, she wasn't letting this go until he told her something. Thad sighed and squeezed the bridge of his nose between his thumb and forefinger. "Fine. What do you want to know exactly?"

"Were you here because of your diabetes?"

"Yes." He hoped that one-word answer would suffice. It did not. She continued to stare at him until he continued. "Why are we doing this, Emma? I really don't think it will help with the project at all and I'm not comfortable talking about myself."

"Because of your family."

"Because of a lot of things."

They sat there in silence for a while, staring at the massive tree in front of them. Finally, Emma huffed out a breath. "I thought talking about ourselves might make working on the project go more smoothly, that's all." She shrugged. "How about we try a different topic. One not quite so personal? Tell me why you don't like Christmas."

Thad hid a wince, barely. In truth, that question was even more personal than the first one she'd asked. He tried to deflect instead. "I never said I don't like Christmas."

"Seriously?" she snorted, raising one brow. "You know they call you the Fifth Avenue Grinch, right?"

He gave her a side glance. "How childish." *How true.*

Thad's chest squeezed tight with old pain. As a skinny kid who'd had to check his blood sugar often, he'd been bullied a lot and had the inner scars to prove it. But considering what else he'd been called in his life, especially by his own father, Thad figured a Grinch wasn't so bad.

She sighed and looked over at him again. "But it's not true. You're…"

"I'm what?" He gave her a deadpan stare.

"Complicated."

He pressed his lips together to stifle a smile. Complicated. He could live with that.

They watched the tree some more, the lights twinkling and ornaments sparkling. It wasn't often that Thad spent time doing nothing, but it was rather…nice. He was on call, but otherwise there wasn't anything pressing he needed to get to, other than home.

"So," Emma tried again. "What is it about the holidays that bothers you so much?"

"Besides the commercialism?" Thad took a deep breath. "Why do you care so much?"

"Because I—"

He shook his head. "Forget I asked."

She was always so ready to talk, so ready to open herself to anyone who asked, that it made Thad frightened for her. Hadn't anyone told her of the dangers of letting people in, letting them close? It brought out a strange protectiveness in him, wanting to keep her safe from anyone who'd harm her. Weird that. The only other people he felt that way toward were Everett and his dog Baxter. And his late mother. But she was looking at him again, watching him, and those darned fireworks were bursting in his stomach, urging him to tell her something, to make her happy, so he blurted out, "Something bad happened to me a long time ago around Christmas, so that's why I hate the holiday."

"Oh, Thad." Emma reached over and took his hand, shocking the hell out of him. "I'm so sorry. Christmas can be rough for so many people. If there's anything I can do—"

"Unless you can bring back my dead mother, there isn't." He tried to tug his hand free from her, embarrassed and raw from saying way more than he'd intended. He never talked about his mother's death anymore. Thad had buried it so deep he rarely thought about it. He'd thought he'd put it all well and truly behind him, but apparently not. What was it about this woman that unearthed all these painful things inside him and brought them rushing to the surface? Emma didn't say anything more, just sat there, holding Thad's hand while he battled the roiling emotions inside him for control. Fierce grief, fresh as the day he'd lost his mother, clawed his throat, making it burn. He blinked at the tree, forcing the words out before they choked him. "I was ten when she died of cancer. It all happened so quick. Six months from diagnosis to death. There was no time to process, no time to prepare."

There. He'd answered her question; now they could get up and get out of here.

Except his heart pounded against his rib cage like it wanted to escape. His temples throbbed and his gut knotted. Thad stared at the tree again as he returned to the awful day of her passing. Christmas. A time when the whole world rejoiced. But not the Markson residence. In his mind, Thad still heard the ringing phone, the sound of his father's voice as they'd told him his wife was gone, the smell of coffee and raw anguish curdling the air. "She was only thirty-eight. Too young."

"Oh, Thad." Emma's voice caught on a sob and she squeezed his hand, her skin warm against his chilled fingers. "I'm so sorry. I didn't realize or I never would've asked."

Without thinking, he found himself turning his hand over to entwine their fingers, the need to comfort her, too, suddenly overwhelming. "I associate the holiday with her death. All the decorations, all the people so happy, only reminds me of what I lost. My mother, the center of my universe." His face twisted slightly. "My father went downhill after that, too."

Part of him screamed for him to stop talking, stop spilling all his secrets to this woman he barely knew, but Thad couldn't seem to stop himself. There was something about Emma that made him want to open up, want to be vulnerable. It both terrified and tempted him to do more, be more, with her.

Another small eternity of silent seconds passed before she scooted slightly in her seat to face him, reaching up slowly to smooth the hair at his temple. "Thank you for telling me that, Thad. I know it wasn't easy for you and I appreciate your trust."

Trust? Thad looked at her then, as if seeing her for

the first time, this woman who'd crashed into his life out of nowhere and somehow, suddenly made it…better. For the first time it dawned on him, that yes, he did trust her. As much as he trusted anyone these days. But there was still so much about her that was a mystery. He'd been vulnerable, now it was her turn. "What about you?"

"What about me? I love Christmas. Obviously," she smiled and sat back, her hand falling away from his face. Thad missed the touch immediately.

"No, I mean what was it like raising your younger sibling?" Now that Thad had started asking about her past, he couldn't seem to stop. "Do you resent having to give up your dreams for her?"

"What? No. Of course I don't resent Karley." Emma frowned. "She's my sister and I love her. We're the only family each of us has left. We have to stick together. The accident that killed our parents wasn't her fault. She was only seven at the time."

He nodded. "Still, it must've been hard for you. Thinking about what might have been."

She crossed her arms and scowled at the tree. "Not really. Honestly, I don't think like that."

"How can you not?"

"Because it's a luxury we couldn't afford. At eighteen, I had to step up to the plate and be the adult. I couldn't sit around wallowing and feeling sorry for myself." She shook her head. "Don't get me wrong. I still grieved. Hell, sometimes I still cry for my parents because I miss them, especially this time of year. But I had to keep moving forward for Karley's sake. To take care of her and to set a good example."

"Eleven years is a big age gap between kids," he said, doing the calculations in his head, way more interested in Emma's life than he'd let himself be in another person's in a long time. "Did your parents plan it that way?"

"Not really." She smiled and glanced over at him. "They tried for a while to have another kid, but it just didn't work out. Then, one day, when they'd stopped trying…there came Karley."

"Huh."

"Yeah. Funny how things work out sometimes, isn't it?" she asked, smiling at him again.

That tug of connection Thad felt for her tugged tighter. "How do you do it?"

Emma gave him a puzzled look. "Do what?"

"How do you remain so positive when you've lost so much in your life?"

She took a moment, then shrugged. "I mean everyone loses something in life eventually, right? It's how we choose how to deal with it that matters. I guess I choose to be happy."

Thad couldn't look away from her, his chest buzzing with warmth and compassion for this brave, beautiful woman who'd stepped in when no one else could. First for her sister, then with him. They were close now, so close her warmth breath fanned his face. He heard a catch when she inhaled and saw her pink lips part, and his long-dead heart jumped with excitement, swelling bigger in his constricted chest until he thought he might die from the sheer anticipation. He closed his eyes, whether to sear this memory into his brain or because it felt like too much, too soon, he wasn't sure. Whispered her name like a prayer, "Emma."

Then suddenly they kissed. He wasn't sure who leaned into whom, but Thad couldn't get enough. He cupped her cheeks, her skin silky and hot beneath his fingertips. Emma stilled at first, then clutched his shirt, right over his heart, in her fist, keeping him right where he was. Time slowed and the world narrowed to only them, only now, only this kiss.

Ding!

The elevator doors nearby *whooshed* open, reminding him of where they were, who they were. Thad pulled back, resting his forehead against Emma's, their rapid breaths still mingling between parted lips.

What the hell am I doing?

Unfortunately, Thad had no answer to that question because he had no clue. Disoriented and unsettled, his skin felt too tight for his body. But he couldn't let her go. Not yet.

Neither moved nor spoke for a long while, hidden behind the tree. Until, at last, Thad sat back, inhaling some much-needed oxygen. Words stuck in his throat, which was probably good because he feared anything he said right then would sound ridiculous. Kissing Emma made no sense. Neither did telling her about his past. But he didn't regret it. Not yet anyway. He stared down at his hands in his lap and managed to croak out, "Thank you for setting this up today."

"Of course," she murmured, looking anywhere but at him, seemingly as flustered as him. "Ricky's a great kid. I'm glad we can make his wish come true."

You could make my wish come true.

And if that wasn't a sign to get the hell out of there, Thad didn't know what was.

He stood fast and raked a hand through his hair. "We should…uh…" *Stop stammering, idiot!* His father's cold voice resonated through Thad's head. "We should go."

Emma nodded and stood, following him to the elevators. "Yeah. I guess we should."

Thad spent the rest of the ride down to the first floor

berating himself. All his good intentions, all the barriers he'd spent years building around his life, his heart. All thrown out the window over one kiss. Was it worth it? His newly awakened heart said yes. But his mind, ever wary, wasn't so sure at all.

Restless after she left Manhattan West, Emma wasn't ready to go home yet, even though she had the day off. She needed some time and some space to think about everything that had happened in the PICU, especially the kiss with Thad. It was warmer today and sunny, so she got on a train for Brooklyn and decided to stop by the cemetery to see her parents.

She got off at the Ninth Avenue station and stopped at a street vendor to buy two small pretty poinsettia wreaths, then headed across the street into Green-Wood. The place was peaceful, as always, a tiny oasis in the chaos that was Brooklyn. A layer of freshly fallen snow covered the ground and many of the historical markers there. Her parents had loved this place when Emma was little and had brought her there often for walks in the summer, pointing out graves from the Revolutionary War onward. Some were huge and ornate, others small and quiet. But all marked lives that had been important to someone. They had outdoor concerts here in the spring and summer, too, and there was even a public art exhibit here, where people could write their innermost secrets and put the note through a slot in the special headstone to help them release whatever was troubling them.

Emma followed the trails through the huge 478-acre park, passing the frozen pond and gorgeous sculptures, until she reached the little ridge where her parents rested side by side. She placed the wreaths on their headstone and cleared the snow from atop the granite marker, then took a seat on the little bench nearby. She'd come here at least once a month—sometimes with her sister, sometimes separately—since they'd died, just to talk to them and clear her head and heart. Today was no different.

Sounds of the winter birds and the distant clop of horses' hooves from the carriages that ran through the cemetery lulled her into a more meditative state. She smiled softly at her parents' graves and said quietly, "Hello. It's me. Back again."

Some people might think it was silly, talking to dead loved ones, but Emma found it comforting. Like they were still there, looking out for her even though she couldn't see them.

"Things are going well," she said, nudging the snow with the toe of her boot. "Karley's applying for colleges. Fingers crossed she gets into Howard this fall."

Hushed voices nearby had her glancing up to see a small group of people walking by on a tour. She waited until they'd passed, then turned to her parents again. "Work's been busy," she said. "I'm working on a special project. Granting a Christmas wish for a sick child." She huffed out a laugh, the sound frosting on the air. "I have a partner. His name is Thad. He's…different." Emma thought about that for a second. "Surprising. Maybe that's a better word."

Yep. Thad had surprised her all right. And it wasn't just the kiss earlier, either. Though that had been something. Sitting here, her lips still tingled. She raised a mittened hand to them, remembering the feel of his mouth on hers, the warmth of his nearness, the soft flick of his tongue against hers.

Heat prickled her cheeks despite the cold temperatures.

Other things about Thad surprised her, too. She'd

always had this vision of how wealthy people lived, formed mainly through what she'd seen on TV and in social media. That they had entourages and people around to do their bidding. But Thad had money, lots of it if the town house was anything to go by, and yet he lived quietly and alone. Other than the dog and Everett.

But the most surprising thing about Thad was how vulnerable he was just below his tough surface. Not only because of his illness, but also all the things he'd been through. He kept most people at bay and the fact he'd let her in felt, well, special. It pulled at her heartstrings, which both terrified and thrilled her. For a woman who'd done it all on her own for so long, could she afford to let him in now?

"Do I want to?" she asked aloud.

She realized she did. She liked Thad Markson. He was bright and interesting and sometimes stubborn to a fault, but then wasn't everyone. He could be an ass, but he could also be immensely kind and caring, too. He saved lives. He needed saving himself.

Emma. If she closed her eyes, she could still him whispering her name, so much hope and hesitation there. She felt the same emotions coursing through her, too, about him.

A gentle wind rustled through the bare tree branches above her, and one lonely leaf fell, bright red, into her lap, like a sign from above. She chuckled and picked it up, holding it out toward her parents' headstone. "Is this supposed to be a sign?"

"Tweet, tweet," a bright red cardinal chirped from atop a cross on the graves next door.

Red had been her mom's favorite color, too.

And while Emma wasn't a member of any particular religion she considered herself quite spiritual and took a hint when one was given. "Okay. Fine. I do like him. Probably more than I should. Not that I'll go crazy over him because that's not me. But I might give him a chance. See what happens."

"Tweet, tweet!" the cardinal said before flying away, as if his mission was done here.

Emma smiled and snuggled down in her coat, standing to straighten the wreaths once more before stepping back. "Well, I should go. It's cold out here and I need to get home to Karley. I'll come back around the holidays. Love you both and miss you."

She blew them kisses, then headed on toward the exit, underneath the massive Gothic archway, leaving the haven of Green-Wood and walking toward home. She didn't have many more answers than when she'd started, but she felt more settled, as if she had guardian angels on her shoulders, watching out for her.

Thad was a puzzle, wrapped in an enigma. Each layer she peeled back revealed another. But the longer she spent with him, the more she wanted to know him. And if they kissed again? Well, she wasn't the type to make out with virtual strangers, but there was something between them—warm and precious and unexpectedly real—and she wasn't ready to close the door on that special gift just yet.

CHAPTER SIX

SATURDAY AFTERNOON, Thad stood at the window in the study behind his desk and stared out at south Central Park. In the distance he could see Wollman Rink, and dots of red and blue skating around on it. Then there was Heckscher Playground, the ball diamonds covered in tarps and snow now. And the octagonal building housing the historic carousel from the earlier 1900s. Back when he'd been younger, Thad had spent many a long hour up here, watching all the other children play while he was stuck inside studying because his doctors had deemed him too ill to go out.

His mind returned to little Ricky Lynch in the PICU. How small and fragile and vulnerable he'd looked. Thad's chest felt oddly hollow and cold. He remembered all too well having those feelings himself when he'd been in the hospital for the umpteenth time, and he never wanted to feel that vulnerable again.

He forced himself to focus on something else. The plans for the carnival, the things he needed to do for that. What he needed to talk to Emma about when she arrived here in a few minutes.

Emma.

With his past and his trust issues, Thad didn't do long-term relationships. He had needs, like everyone else. And those needs for intimacy were taken care of through short, carefully arranged affairs where both parties knew the rules and no deep emotions were involved. Afterward, they parted ways, both satisfied physically and with no ties or bad feelings emotionally. Not exactly fairy tale stuff, but it worked for him.

Or it had, until Emma arrived.

It was still hard to wrap his brain around their kiss. If it wasn't for the fact that his fingers still tingled with awareness from where he'd tangled them in her hair, or how when he licked his lips he swore he still tasted her there, he'd have denied it ever happened.

Most unsettling, though, had been the way she'd looked at him afterward. Like she'd seen him for the first time. Really seen him. And understood him. It was scary, being revealed like that, and Thad just didn't know what to do about it.

Part of him felt like maybe it was more about his return to the PICU and the emotions that always ran high when sick children were involved. He hadn't been there in years, doing his best to sequester the painful past away. But having Emma there with him today seemed to have widened fractures in the already-crumbling stone encasing his heart. Trouble was, he wasn't sure how to close the newly developed crack in his otherwise impenetrable armor.

With a sigh, he abandoned the window and walked over to sit in front of the crackling fire in the fireplace instead. Thad pulled up the app on his phone to check his blood sugar again, thinking perhaps his strange maudlin mood might have something to do with that. Ever since the episode in his kitchen, his blood sugar had fluctuated a lot and the exhaustion drove him nuts. He had things to do. Procedures to perfect. He couldn't sleep all day. For a man who'd always been up early and awake until the wee hours at night, it was unacceptable. In the past, once he'd gotten his insulin and eating schedule back on track things regulated quickly, but so far his diabetes was kicking his butt. Maybe he was getting old. Thirty-six was hardly ancient, but perhaps his underlying health condition was taking its toll.

In his mind his father's voice reverberated from beyond the grave.

Nothing but a sickly waste of space. Weakling. Good for nothing.

Thad scrubbed a hand over his face and shoved those hurtful memories aside. Ever. The awful man had died of a heart attack in South America five years ago, running away from his crimes to the end. He'd managed to avoid arrest, but hopefully had been punished just the same. Never putting down roots, always looking over his shoulder. Regardless, the man was no longer allowed to take up precious real estate in Thad's mind, though when he was tired or stressed, it was easier said than done.

In the corner of the study sat several large boxes marked Christmas Decorations on the sides in his mother's handwriting. His heart twisted again. He'd asked Everett to bring them down from the attic, thinking perhaps they could use something in there for the carnival, but it seemed rather silly now.

"Sir," his butler said from the doorway, as if conjured from Thad's thoughts. "Ms. Trudeau is here to see you."

"Thanks," Thad said, sighing. She'd texted him earlier that she had the day off and suggested they meet about the carnival plans. "Send her in."

Emma entered a few moments later, her braids loose once more as she walked across the huge Persian rug to sit in the chair opposite Thad's. Today she wore a pair of figure-hugging jeans that drew his gaze like a magnet to the sway of her hips. He looked back at the fire, forcing his attention from her pink lips and the memory of how soft and sweet they'd felt beneath his.

God, what's wrong with me?

"So," she said, clasping her hands atop the folder in her lap and breaking him out of his inappropriate erotic thoughts. "After meeting with Ricky on Wednesday, I think we need to take into account his wishes for the carnival."

Thad shifted in his seat slightly. "We are not having pony rides. The poop alone would be too much to deal with."

"No. Not ponies. I agree." She chuckled and shook her head. "Don't want to go there. But we need to nail down a location soon, so I can let the vendors know the space they'll have to work with. Also, seeing how fragile Ricky is only confirms for me that we need to keep it indoors and smaller, so these sick kids won't have issues getting around. Has your foundation had any luck securing a place?"

"Not yet. They contacted several places, but so far nothing's a done deal," he said, glad for a topic that didn't involve anything related to kissing. He told her about several spots around the city the Markson Foundation was looking at for the carnival and Emma took notes accordingly. Then awkward silence fell as he ran out of things to say.

She nodded and closed her folder, then tucked some braids behind her ear. Thad's fingertips itched, remembering how soft they'd felt against his skin. He had the crazy urge to slide his hands through them again, draw her near and kiss her until they were both breathless. Instead, he clenched his fists at his sides on the leather seat.

"How've you been feeling?" she asked at last, fiddling with the small sparkling stud earring in her earlobe. "After what happened in your kitchen the other night. Are you back on your schedule again? I'd hate to see you have another attack like that again."

He imagined running his tongue along that sensitive spot where her neck met her ear, feeling her shiver beneath him, moaning his name and…

Oh God. Stop thinking about that.

His throat constricted, making speech difficult. "I'm fine," Thad managed to squeak out, several octaves higher than usual. Restless and shaken by his emotional response to a woman he'd known such a short time, he pushed to his feet and paced the room. Not to mention the fact that he hated being fawned over. "Stop worrying about me."

"I'm a nurse. It's my job to worry about patients," she said, crossing her arms and forcing her breasts higher beneath her bright red turtleneck like she was presenting them to him as a gift.

Don't. Do not look at them.

Except now that was all Thad could seem to focus on. "Not that you're my patient," she went on quickly. "That would be weird. But I still feel responsible because I was there when it happened, and I care about you…" Her voice trailed off. "Because of the project, I mean."

I care about you…

There were times in Thad's past when he would've given up everything to hear those words from someone other than Everett. But part of the reason why he'd built such strong barriers around himself was so he didn't need them. Now, with Emma right here, offering him his innermost secret wish, Thad found himself completely flummoxed.

He turned away fast and stalked back to the window, away from temptation and yearning and the deep, aching, embarrassing need blossoming inside him, his face burning like the sun. He'd survived this long through sheer fractiousness and he couldn't turn his back on that now, not with Emma threatening all his long-held beliefs about himself and the world and everything he thought he had to be. It was too much, too soon and way too terrifying.

Thad turned back to face her; his tone harsh from desperation. "We're here to talk about the carnival, so let's stick to that, please."

Her dark eyes flashed fire for a second and Thad thought she'd argue with him about his abrupt change in topic. She moved closer and his pulse stumbled. If she touched him again now, all would be lost. He'd crumple like wet paper in her hands and tear apart just as easily. But she didn't touch him. Just stood a feet away, looking at him like she saw right through his BS and knew he was being a coward instead of facing up to what was happening between them. "Fine. Let's work."

After an hour and a half of planning and coordination, they took a break so Thad could check his blood sugar and give himself a small shot of insulin. Once he'd put everything away, he looked up at her from behind his desk while Emma studied the books on his shelves. It was an interesting assortment of everything from nonfiction to mysteries and thrillers to the odd women's fiction and romance story.

"You must read a lot, huh?" she asked him, eager to steer clear of the tension from before. This could be an interest they shared. "I love books. My mom used to read to me a lot as a kid and it stuck. When I was a teenager and we started reading the same stuff, we used to talk about them after, like our own little book club." Emma stopped, clearing her throat from the lump of sadness there. "Well, until she died, anyway."

God, this man made her so nervous. Why? Thad shouldn't make her heart race or her blood pound in her veins. And yes, they'd kissed back at the hospital, but that had been a mistake. A horrible, inexplicable mistake, completely not what she wanted at all.

Right?

Her uncertainty was even more unsettling. Because maybe, just maybe, if she was honest with herself, she kind of had wanted to kiss Thad Markson. Maybe still wanted to kiss him now, despite him sending off clear don't-touch-me vibes. There was something so endearing, so intoxicatingly broken in him that called to the healer in her. The fact that he'd let her into his inner world that day in the PICU showed her he wasn't beyond redemption, no matter what he might try to portray to the others.

No. Emma knew in her heart the real Thad was still in there somewhere, the sad, sick, scared little boy he'd been before the death of his mother and his monster of a father had gotten to him. She wanted to help him find his way back to that boy again, if he'd let her.

But from the way Thad was avoiding the whole subject now, though, it was obviously not the time. He wasn't comfortable at present and neither was she. Best to focus on the project for now and get on with their planning. They could revisit the kiss and where they wanted things to go later, if they wanted. Time to change the subject. She looked over at the boxes in the corner and grinned. "Are you getting ready to decorate?"

"Huh?" Thad looked up from his laptop and frowned before tracking her gaze to the corner. "Oh, that." He gave a dismissive wave. "I had Everett bring those down from the attic earlier thinking we might be able to use them at the carnival, but it was a bad idea. He'll take them back up shortly."

"Why? Have you looked in them? Maybe there is something we could use." She got up and went over to peek inside the boxes. There was everything here—a tree, ornaments, garlands, wreaths, everything to make a home festive. Probably not the best choices for their carnival, he was right there, but why not use them anyway here? "I bet this place would look lovely all done up for the holidays. How about if we take a break and put up this stuff here in your office? I'll help. We could get this all unpacked and up in no time."

"Oh, I don't—" Thad started, but Emma already had part of the artificial tree out and on its stand where she started fluffing out the lower branches.

"Come on. It'll be fun," she said, grinning over at him behind the desk. And for the first time since their kiss, if felt like her nerves disappeared. "I promise."

For a moment Thad stared at her, then finally shook his head and joined her, grumbling under his breath about silly traditions and ridiculous extravagance as they got the rest of the tree up. It was bigger than she expected—at least eight feet tall—and moving into the spot he wanted in the corner was awkward, too, forcing them both to work together to avoid being buried under a mass of prickly fake pine.

Finally, with one last shove, Thad straightened, his high cheekbones flushed from the effort. "There. Satisfied?"

The tree stood to one side of the fireplace, a bit crooked, but they'd fix that in time.

"Not yet. But I will be." She winked at him, then began opening more boxes from the stack, pulling out swags of red, green and gold garlands. "We can use these on the tree and whatever's left over we can drape across the fireplace mantel. It will look beautiful."

Thad scowled as he pulled out handfuls of lights and gold stars and glittering berries from yet another box. "This is my private office, not the North Pole. I don't want anything to be garish or silly."

"Why not? It's Christmas. Everything is garish and loud and overblown this time of year. That's the joy of it." Thad gave her a look, then started throwing the lights on the tree haphazardly, with big wads of tangles everywhere. "No, no. That's not right." She pulled them off, then handed him the cord. "You need to plug them in first to make sure they work. Haven't you ever decorated a tree before?"

He hesitated for a second. "Not since my mother was alive."

Damn. Her heart squeezed. She should have connected those dots better. But now that she'd stepped in it, she needed to clean up her mess. Emma cleared her throat and tried again. "Well, then. I think it's time we started a new tradition ourselves, huh?"

Thad shrugged, then walked over to plug in the lights. They flickered at first, then glowed a warm gold color, twinkling off the silver star and berry ornaments piled on the floor beside them.

"Wow. These are beautiful. Leave them on while we decorate." Emma strung the lights around the tree. "Did both of your parents work?"

"Only my father. Too much." He fed her more lights,

pointing out empty spots as she worked. "My mother was on the board of several charities in the city, but mainly she stayed home, with me. At least until she got sick."

His voice trailed off and Emma looked down at him from where she'd climbed the ladder to reach the top of the tree. "That must've been so hard for you, losing her support."

"It was," he said, moving in behind her at the bottom of the ladder to steady it, essentially caging her in while continuing to feed more string lights to her and making sure she didn't fall. If Emma didn't know better, she'd think they'd landed in one of those cheesy TV holiday movies where she falls and ends up his arms, sharing a first kiss under the mistletoe.

Or another kiss. Because she and Thad had already kissed behind a Christmas tree.

And it had been nice. More than nice. Sweet and warm and seductive and…

"Here." He handed her the rest of the lights in the bundle. "I'll grab another from the box."

Emma turned back toward the tree, feeling a bit shaky. This was no movie and Thad Markson was not her romantic hero, even if he did have that whole broody, gorgeous grump thing going for him.

Do not go there. Emma repeated to herself, like maybe it would stick. *This is for Ricky. Not you. Don't screw up your chance at a promotion over a man. People leave. People die. Be responsible.*

The ladder wobbled a bit as Thad climbed up behind her and his weight settled on the wood. "These are multicolored." He held out another string of lights to her, his body so close to hers now she could feel the heat of him through her clothes and smell his woodsy, clean aftershave. "Not ideal since they don't match the others, but they're all that's left in the box."

"Uh…" Emma made the mistake of looking back at him over her shoulder and, oh, boy. His face was right there, near enough to kiss him again, if she wanted. And man, did she want. Except no. They weren't doing that again. Not now. Maybe not ever. To distract herself from the need now churning through her system, Emma grabbed the lights from him and weaved them in with the others, inching closer to the top of the tree. Each time she moved up a rung, Thad did the same behind her, increasing the sizzling tension between them that apparently only she could feel because Thad continued scowling at the lights like they held all of his attention.

Once they finally got the entire tree lit, Thad stepped down off the ladder, followed by Emma. She stepped back to admire their handiwork and accidentally brushed against his chest with her shoulder.

"Sorry." She moved away, doing her best to concentrate on the task at hand and not the hunky surgeon beside her as she picked up another box full of gorgeous red and gold glass ornaments. The mesmerizing iridescent sheen on them showed their quality and cost. Probably handmade. Way out of her price range to be sure, but they reminded her of the old hand-me-down ornaments her parents had used every year. Same magical feel, way less expensive. The lower cost never affected their beauty. "These are amazing. I've never seen decorations like this before."

"My mother bought them from a Bavarian market one year," he said, holding one up in front of him so the lights from the tree cast rainbow shards around the room. "They were her pride and joy."

The sudden tenderness in his voice had Emma blinking hard against the unexpected sting of tears. The last thing she wanted to do today was start crying in front of Thad, so instead, she gestured toward the tree. "Since all this was your mother's, I think you should have the honor of placing the first ornament."

"Oh, I…" Thad frowned, as if only then realizing she was still there. "Let's do it together."

She took a deep breath, her heart pinching again. "But it's obvious this meant so much to your mother and…"

He continued watching her, waiting.

"Fine. It's making me sad, okay?" She threw up her hands, exasperated. "You're not the only one with fond memories of your long-lost parents. All this reminds me of when my mom and dad used to decorate the tree with me and Karley. The holidays are hard for everyone. Doesn't mean we still shouldn't celebrate them."

Saying it out loud seemed to open the floodgates of her past, causing a tidal wave of memories to rush back to her, just as vivid and real as the day they'd happened. The scent of the pine incense her dad used to light. The jolly sounds of Christmas carols on the radio. The sweetness of the cookies and eggnog they set out for Santa. Bittersweet now, all of it. Emma had tried hard to re-create those memories for Karley after their parents were gone, but it never felt quite the same.

Thad, thankfully, seemed to realize she needed some space, because he stopped questioning her and began decorating the tree alone. She held the box and handed him the ornaments while he hung them. Like clockwork they went, making a good team—same as they'd done in the ER—until the last box was empty. They stood shoulder to shoulder across the room then, admiring their work. Magical.

Soon though, the mood in the room changed. Thad's arm bumped Emma's, sending fresh waves of awareness through her nerve endings.

"My father wasn't around very much after my mother died. Which was good, since he hated me."

Stunned, Emma glanced up at him, noticing for the first time the row of tiny freckles covering the bridge of his nose. "I'm sure that's not true. No parent hates their own child."

"He did." Thad stared straight ahead at the tree, his voice low and devoid of emotion. "He never missed an opportunity to tell me what a disappointment I was to him. How my disease made me weak and defective. How he wished I'd never been born. It's those words that spur me on today. The burning desire to prove to him that he was wrong. In so many ways."

Something clicked for her then. That's why he acted the way he did, keeping everyone away. Not because he was truly a Grinch, but because of what had happened to him growing up. "You aren't, you know," she said, watching his throat work as he swallowed hard. "Defective or weak. You aren't a disappointment at all, Thad. You have nothing to prove to anyone."

"Hmm." He continued staring at the tree. "Perhaps. But you don't forget those scars. Not ever."

A red and gold glow bathed the room now, lending a new warmth and intimacy to the space. Emma felt like the final walls between them had crashed down and for the first time she saw the real Thad. The one she'd suspected lurked beneath his grouchy exterior the whole time.

"I remember being in the PICU after my mom died," Thad continued, his voice monotone as more painful memories surfaced. Emma didn't interrupt, knowing he needed to get this out to help him heal. "He told them to keep me. That he didn't want me around until I was normal again." A tiny muscle near his jaw worked. "I knew, even then, that it had to be the grief talking. He was upset about my mother dying. I loved him. He was my father. I didn't want to think the worst. But even after they got my blood sugar stabilized and I came home, nothing changed. Well, except my father. All he cared about from that point forward was his work. He became obsessed with money. Making it, spending it. His wealth consumed him. And when he was threatened with the loss of that wealth, he took whatever means necessary to keep it—even if it meant hurting and cheating other people to do it. If he hadn't died from a heart attack when he did, I fully believe he would've been investigated by the SEC and found guilty. As it was, he died and left me with a mess and a scandal to clean up. I did both. And I've never taken a cent of his dirty money. All of it went to his victims and to the foundation to help other people and do good in the world. Even this town house is owned by the foundation. When I die, they have instructions to donate it to the city to be used as a museum or school or whatever else they need. His was a legacy of pain. I refuse to continue it onward. The pain stops with me."

"Oh, Thad," she whispered again, not knowing what else to say, her own heart breaking for him. Without thinking, she entwined her fingers with his and he let her. "You've been through so much and deserved none of it. But what you're doing now, it's so good. You'll make a difference to so many people."

He still wasn't looking at her, but she saw the sheen in his eyes. "The only person who was ever there for me after my mom died was Everett. He sat with me, helped me with my homework, played with me. He's more of a father to me than my own ever was."

She'd sensed there was more of a relationship between the two men than employer and employee from the first night she'd come here, but now it made so much sense. "I'm glad he was there for you, Thad. Every child needs someone to care for them. I've tried to step in and be that for Karley, too." Emma sighed. "Not sure I've done enough, though. Weird, but it's easier taking care of other people as a nurse than it is those closest to you sometimes."

Thad finally looked at her. "I haven't met your sister, Emma, but I bet you've done a wonderful job. You're one of the kindest people I've ever met."

"Thank you. I appreciate you saying that."

He put his arm around her shoulders—a bit stiffly, as if he wasn't used to showing affection—and drew her into his side. Emma didn't move at first, stunned, then slowly shifted to face him. Most people feared Thad, but not Emma. Never again. Not after tonight.

The flames in the fireplace crackled and shadows played in the glow from the tree, making the moment seem moody, mysterious and infinitely romantic. She licked her lips and he tracked the tiny movement with his gaze. Her breath caught as he dipped his head, thinking he was going to kiss her again. But then his cheek brushed hers as he buried his face in her hair and inhaled deep.

"I'm glad you're here, Emma," Thad said, his voice deep and rough.

"Me, too." The words didn't come out as firm as Emma wanted because just then Thad's lips trailed around her ear, moving slowly across her cheekbone and down to her mouth. This time was different from their sweet kiss in the PICU lobby. Now it felt hot and needy, enough to rock her world like a shaken-up snow globe. Thad held her tight to him, as if afraid she'd disappear. After what he'd been through as a kid, maybe he was. Emma wanted to heal his wounds, make his holidays warm and bright and happy for once. She slid her hand from his chest, the soft hair at the nape of his neck tickling her fingertips, urging her to sink into him even more…

It took her a moment then to process the cold rush of air between them. He returned to the window, alone. Her lips tingled and her head felt stuffy with emotions. She hugged her arms around herself against a shudder. "Thad, I…"

"I think you should go," he said, still staring outside, his breath fogging the glass. "Have Everett get your things and call you a taxi home. I'll pay for it."

"But…" she whispered, still feeling a bit dazed.

Thad stalked toward the office door then, his words a rush as he passed her. "My foundation is setting up a holiday fundraiser for the end of next week for all of the charities we support, including the wish project. I'd like you to accompany me to the event."

She blinked at him, still trying to process his abrupt change in mood, let alone his words. "I, uh…"

"I'll text you the exact date and time," he said to her, stopping on the threshold of the doorway to glance back at her. "It will be formal, so I'll have one of the local stores send something to your apartment for you to wear to the event. Just give Everett your sizes and he'll arrange everything else. Good night, Emma."

He walked out, leaving her to stare after him, wondering when exactly she'd become Cinderella in their crazy Christmas fairy tale.

CHAPTER SEVEN

"WOW!" KARLEY SAID when Emma came out of her bedroom the following Friday evening, dressed in the figure-hugging, scarlet, off-the-shoulder, below-the-knee cocktail dress one of the fancy designer boutiques on Fifth Avenue had sent over earlier, per Thad's promised orders. And it wasn't just the dress, either. There'd been shoes and jewelry and even a small beaded handbag to go with it.

Part of her wondered exactly what kind of game he was playing—and if she was bold enough to go along with it. They hadn't really spoken much since the kiss at his place, other than quick texts and calls about the carnival, so she had no clue where any of this was going. She'd thought about canceling, but no. Tonight was important for the carnival, so she needed to be there.

And another part of her told her to just enjoy the ride. She worked hard. She deserved some fun. And really, it was all just fun, right? This thing between them couldn't actually go anywhere long-term. Their lives were too different. They wanted different things. She loved her independence too much.

Emma did a little spin on her red high heels and grinned at her reflection in the mirror. Okay. Fine. She did feel like she'd been visited by a fairy godmother this afternoon, instead of just the normal delivery guy. And damn if she didn't like it. Probably more than she should.

After a final adjustment to her dress, she stepped out into the living room and cleared her throat to get her sister's attention. "So, you like it? You don't think I look silly all fancied up this way?"

"*Silly* is the last word I'd use to describe you, sis." Karley looked up from where she sat on the sofa, watching TV and typing on her phone, her expression suitably impressed. "Wow! You look like you're ready for the red carpet or something."

"Thanks." Emma blushed and smoothed a hand over the silky fabric of her gown. She'd never worn a garment so expensive in her life and she rarely had a chance to dress up these days, so tonight was special. And important. In more ways than one. She knew it was important to convince the donors to give money at the fundraiser and she needed to look the part of a wealthy, successful project coordinator in order to do that. But part of her also secretly hoped Thad liked how she looked, too.

They'd only texted each other since the night in his office when they'd put up the decorations and then… Lord help her, Emma's whole body still tingled at the thought of their steamy second kiss.

It had been good. *Really* good.

Then things had cooled off fast between them.

At first, she'd been hurt. But then she'd remembered what he'd told her about himself and his past, and she understood why he was hesitant. She wasn't ready to jump into anything either, to be truthful. She'd dated before, off and on, and been with other men. Nothing serious, though. Emma was too focused on her career and building a life for herself and her sister to go all gaga over some man. Then along came Thad Markson, and for some odd reason, he'd ticked her boxes. Gotten around her barriers and laid her vulnerabilities bare. At first glance he wasn't the type she usually went for—funny, kind, outgoing. But his brokenness called to the healer in her. The very brusqueness and broodiness that drove others away drew her like a moth to a flame. Maybe because she'd suffered great loss early in life, too. Maybe because she knew what it was like to forge ahead alone, making up for what you lacked. And maybe it was just the fact that deep down she knew he hurt and she wanted to let him know he wasn't alone…

"Ready to wheel and deal for your charity event?" Karley asked, breaking into her thoughts.

"I think so." Emma shook off the pensiveness that had settled over her as she'd thought about her complicated relationship with Thad and walked over to sit on the opposite end of the sofa to wait for the driver to arrive. "I'm not really a big schmoozer, but if it means being able to grant Ricky's wish, I'll try." She checked her watch. "Are you set for dinner? Okay here by yourself for a couple hours?"

"I'm fine, sis." Karley managed not to roll her eyes at Emma, though it was implied in her tone. "Stop worrying about me, Em. I'll be eighteen in a few months, the same age you were when Mom and Dad died. Practically an adult. By this time next year, I'll be away at college and doing my own thing."

"Don't remind me."

"So." Her sister shifted slightly on the cushion to face Emma, tucking one leg beneath her. "You like this guy, huh?"

"What? No." Emma did her best to hide her smile

and failed miserably. "We're just partners on this project, that's all."

"Uh-huh. Sure." Karley sounded completely unconvinced. "Well, whatever it is, I'm happy for you. Haven't seen you glow this much in a long time."

"I'm not glowing!" Emma looked up sharply, her cheeks prickling with shock. "Am I?"

"Oh, yeah. Definitely glow happening there." Karley gestured toward Emma and grinned. "You deserve it, sis. Go for it."

Before Emma could say anything else, a knock sounded on their apartment door. Damn. Her driver. She took a deep breath and stood, still not sure how she felt about her attraction to Thad being so obvious to everyone. "I need to go," she said, pulling her coat from the closet and slipping it on. "I'll be back by eleven."

"Don't hurry on my account," Karley said as Emma grabbed her tiny evening bag and opened the door. "Have fun!"

"I'll try." She started out into the hallway with the driver, then said over her shoulder. "Be good!"

"Be better!" Karley shouted back. It was kind of their ritual.

She followed the driver downstairs and thanked him for holding the back door of the black limo open for her. Emma climbed inside and looked over to see Thad across from her, looking like he'd stepped right out of a high-fashion modeling shoot in his tailored tux and crisp white shirt. Then the driver closed the door, and the overhead light went out, leaving them in sudden darkness.

"Good evening, Emma," he said from the shadows. "You look lovely. I knew that color would suit you well."

"You picked this out yourself?" she asked as the limo

pulled away from the curb and merged into traffic. "I thought you had surgeries booked all week."

"I did." He turned to look out the window beside him at the passing Christmas lights. "But I gave the personal shopper strict instructions on what I wanted and your sizes. It looks like she did an excellent job."

"Thank you for all this," Emma said, clutching her tiny bag like a shield in her lap. "It's very generous of you."

"It's necessary to make a good impression on the people we'll meet tonight." They stopped at a light, and he looked over at her again, those icy eyes of his skimming over her like a physical touch. A shudder of awareness went through her before she could stop it. Emma hugged her coat tighter around herself. "Not that you aren't beautiful the way you usually are. It's just I find presenting a certain image acts as additional armor."

I know. Emma bit back those words and swallowed them down. Thad exuded a low-key disdain to keep others at bay. It worked a lot of the time, too. Except with her, because she saw through it. *Armor* was a good word to describe Thad's attitude. Push others away before they did the same to you. The fact that Emma was here tonight felt even more special, taken in that light.

"Well, I appreciate you thinking of me."

"I always think of you these days, Emma."

Oh boy. Her chest tightened at his quiet words; she was thankful he couldn't see her face because it had to be as red as her dress now. He couldn't mean… Unless he did. Had he been thinking about their kisses as much as Emma had? Imagining what might have happened if they hadn't stopped there? If he'd led her up to his bedroom and locked the door and…

Inside she flailed with want, struggling to keep her breath calm.

As they rode through blue-collar Queens, Thad glanced at the passing scenery. "So, this is your neighborhood?"

"Yes." Emma smiled, grateful for the mundane topic. "Long way from your Fifth Avenue town house, but we like it."

"We?"

"My sister and I."

"Right," he said, frowning at her. "Karley. How old is she again?"

"Seventeen, going on thirty." Emma's grinned with pride. "She's great. Straight-A student. Working toward a full scholarship to Howard University after she graduates."

"That's impressive." Thad shifted a bit in his seat, light filtering in through the window illuminated the front of his tux jacket, reminding her again of his broad shoulders and tight torso. "What does she want to study in college?"

"Premed," Emma said. "God help her."

Thad chuckled. "It's challenging, no lie. But worth it if it's the right fit for you."

"I think it is, for her." She met his gaze. "But no matter what she wanted to do, I'd support her."

"I'm sure you would."

The ride to the small event center was quiet after that, Emma's stomach filling with nervous butterflies. Not so much because of the fundraiser, but because of the man across from her. She kept reminding herself that this was not a date. Though, wow. It really did feel like one.

Once they arrived, the driver held the door for Thad,

then he came around himself to help Emma out. He took her hand and kept hold of it, his grip firm and warm. Comforting. After making their way inside and checking their coats at the booth near the entrance, they walked into a banquet room decorated like a winter wonderland. White linen tablecloths, huge bouquets of white roses and lilies and paperwhites adorning the center of each table. From the sparkling champagne flutes and real silverware to the dangling lights and iridescent streamers, the entire place screamed wealth. There was even a small string quartet in one corner playing live Christmas music. Emma hesitated on the threshold, taking it all in. Despite her wishes, it really did feel like a fairy tale.

"Everything okay?" Thad asked near her ear, his expression concerned. "You look a bit flushed."

Any warmth now was because of the tickle of his breath on her cheek, the brush of his body against hers as they walked, the reassuring squeeze of his fingers. She had it bad for him, and that wasn't good.

Stop. Enjoy tonight for what it is.

She took a deep breath, then smiled. "I'm good. There are so many people here."

"Yes." Thad winked. "But you're the only one here with me."

Those words surrounded her like a fuzzy blanket as they entered the room and Thad introduced her to person after person, enough to make her head swim after a while. So many of the city's powerful and elite. Given what he'd told her about his family and his father's scandals, Emma knew what a big deal it was for Thad to be here tonight, and she wanted to support him in any way she could, so she stayed by his side. He put on a good show of being above it all, but still. It seemed everyone wanted to greet him, talk to him, be around him. Everyone carefully avoiding the subject of Thad's father, she noticed, which Emma was grateful for. Thad even managed to get several of the guests to commit to sizable donations to their charity project.

They got a short break during dinner, where they were partially hidden from the others at their table by the large centerpiece and out of the immediate spotlight. She glanced over at Thad then and noticed the tightness at the corners of his mouth and eyes he couldn't hide, showing the toll being here had taken on him. Emma placed her hand over his chilled one on the table and squeezed. He was picking at their delicious chicken and roasted veggies. From the artful arrangement of the food on the plate, she was sure it was gourmet expensive, but she'd have been just as happy with a burger and fries.

"Here," she said, picking up a nearby basket of fancy whole-grain artisan rolls. "Eat one of these. You should, to keep your sugar balanced. And have some water. You look stressed."

"I'm fine." He shook his head and exhaled slowly. "I'm just looking forward to leaving."

"I understand." She squeezed his hand again. "And thank you."

"For what?"

"For being here tonight. Hopefully, we'll raise all the funds to make Ricky's wish come true."

"We will. I'll make sure of it."

After the delicious dinner the quartet played several holiday-themed ballads, and couples moved around the dance floor set up in one corner. Emma watched them sway to the music while Thad chatted up yet another donor. She lost herself in the beauty of the music until Thad held out his hand.

"Care to dance?"

"Oh." She blinked at him a moment, her heart tripping over itself. "I don't think…"

Not a date. Not a date. Not a date.

"I do," he said, taking her hand and leading her toward the dance floor. And damn if she didn't feel like a princess being led by her Prince Charming. Or Grinch Charming in this case. Though it was getting harder and harder to associate Thad with that green cartoon figure.

Thad took her in his arms just as the band started playing a rendition of the waltz from *Anastasia*. Even with her high heels, she had to look up at him.

"Have I mentioned how beautiful you look tonight?" he asked, his gaze skimming over her. "Because you do, Emma. You really do. Scrubs don't do you justice."

"Yes, you have. And thank you, Thad." They continued around the floor, him deftly steering them around the other couples around them. Emma was impressed. "You're a good dancer."

"My mother gave me lessons when I was young. It's like riding a bike." Thad glanced down at her and almost smiled before admitting, "One of those things you don't really forget."

Eventually the music changed to her bittersweet favorite, "Have Yourself a Merry Little Christmas." With a contented sigh, she laid her cheek against Thad's chest, soaking in the magic of the evening.

They swayed together, bodies brushing, his heat melting her like a marshmallow in hot cocoa.

"You always smell so good," he said, nuzzling the top of her head. "Like cinnamon and roses."

She grinned, murmuring against his tux lapel, "You smell good, too."

From the corner of her eye, she spotted several of the

people they'd talked with earlier watching them with curiosity. Emma straightened.

Thad frowned down at her. "What?"

"We should be careful," she said, glancing around. "Everyone will think we're a couple."

He stilled, scowling. "I don't do couples, Emma."

Despite knowing this wasn't a date or anything serious, her stomach still sank with disappointment. "I didn't say we were one. Just that people might think that."

It was silly to be hurt by his words. Emma knew that. She had no right getting upset over something that was never meant to be in the first place, regardless of the fairy-tale setting. Still, her heart ached and her temples throbbed. Fine. Maybe she'd let herself believe there was the possibility of something between her and Thad after they'd kissed. Anybody would, right? But she wasn't a fool. She didn't belong in his world of glittering banquets and fancy houses and expensive clothes. She was just a normal woman with a normal life. If Thad wasn't interested in that, in her, she wouldn't try to convince him otherwise. He could take her or leave her. She didn't need to change for a man. She had plenty going on in her life without him. She was more than fine with who she was.

Emma stepped out of his arms and crossed her own. "We should probably go. It's getting late."

He studied her, clearly confused. "I'm not sure what's happening here."

"Neither am I. And that's the problem." She walked back toward their table, eyes prickling. She refused to cry. Emma never cried. Not since the day of her parents' funeral. Thad followed behind her, his heat at her back a constant reminder of what she couldn't have, shouldn't have, but wanted desperately anyway.

They said their goodbyes and thanked the people who had donated to Ricky's cause, then went to get their coats. Thad helped Emma into hers, then kept his hands on her shoulders, taking a deep breath. "You're right."

Now she was confused, frowning up at him over her shoulder. "About what?"

"Us. This. Whatever it is." He gave a vague wave between them before walking her out to their limo parked at the curb once more. Thad held the door for her, then climbed inside to sit across from her again. "We came here tonight to fundraise, but..." He huffed out a breath, then stared out the window next to him as they drove through the New York night. "I don't know. Something's changed."

"How?" Emma asked, feeling like if they didn't get it out now, they never would.

Thad shook his head, still staring out the window beside him at the crowds gathered at Rockefeller Center's ice rink. "I can't stop thinking about you, Emma. About that kiss in my study."

The butterflies inside her swarmed and her throat constricted, making words difficult. But she managed to whisper the truth burning a hole inside her. "Me neither."

He moved then, sitting beside her, the length of his body pressed against hers, the sound of his breath as ragged as her pulse. "I want you, Emma. I haven't stopped wanting you since the night in my office. Seeing you now, looking so beautiful and holding you as we danced. I know we shouldn't, because I meant what I said about relationships. I'm not good at them and I don't do them."

The pain in his voice overshadowed any sting in his words. He was broken inside. Broken and beautiful and so beyond anything she'd ever experienced before, she was completely hooked. Emma didn't need a cheesy holiday film ending, she realized. She just needed Thad. More than she'd needed anyone in a long, long time.

She cupped his cheek, forcing him to meet her gaze. "What do you want?"

"Emma," he whispered against her forehead, his jaw flexing beneath her palm. Thad pulled back to meet her gaze, icy eyes flashing fire, possessive and primal and potent.

She slipped her other hand around his neck, toying with the soft hair at his nape, twirling the silky dark strands around her finger. "I don't know what's happening here or how any of this will turn out, but I do know that I want to find out. With you."

For the hundredth time that week, Thad wondered what in the hell he was doing as Emma texted her sister to let her know she might be late and to not wait up and he let the driver know to head to his town house instead of Queens.

But it was so difficult to think rationally, to keep his cool, to push his emotions aside when Emma was this close to him. She was stunningly beautiful, soft and warm and giving. And she wanted him.

Throat tight, he focused on keeping some semblance of sanity in the back of that car despite the desperation to have her clawing inside him. This was no way to be together the first time—frantic and fumbling in the back seat where anyone could see them. No. If this was going to happen with Emma, he wanted it to be perfect.

So he needed to keep his mind off the sweet scent of

her washing over him in the tight confines of the limo. Speaking of tight, his pants were becoming increasingly uncomfortable as they constrained a certain part of his anatomy responding directly to the press of Emma's thigh against the side of his. Not helpful. What also wasn't helpful was how each time he closed his eyes, he pictured Emma gazing up at him as they'd danced, looking at him like she saw only the good, the right, the admirable in him. Worse, it made him yearn to be that man for her. Like it was that easy.

And maybe he would be with her by his side.

But no. There'd be no sides, no support, because this would only be a one-night affair. That was all it could ever be.

Right?

Right. Because Emma deserved better than him. If she stayed by his side, Thad feared his father had been right. That he was truly worthless and weak and he'd drain all the good right out of whatever this was between them. Not on purpose; things happened. They always did with him. She'd told him people called him a Grinch at the hospital, and they were probably right. He lived alone—except for Everett and Baxter—he rarely let anyone close to him for a reason. He'd become used to the self-imposed isolation.

At least until Emma had arrived.

Now Thad wasn't so sure. About anything.

"Done," Emma said, slipping her phone back into her impossibly tiny purse, then kissing his cheek. "Karley's alerted and has secured herself in the apartment for the night."

Thad then took a deep breath, wondering if the adrenaline racing through his veins like Santa's reindeer was a sign of excitement or caution. Ten minutes later they pulled up to the curb on Fifth Avenue and the driver opened Thad's door for him, jarring him from his thoughts. "We've arrived, sir."

"Thank you." Thad climbed out and adjusted his top-coat, his heart slamming against his rib cage so hard he feared it might burst out onto the sidewalk. He was no virgin. He'd been with plenty of women in his time, but this thing with Emma felt different. Perhaps because he'd told her things about himself, his deepest, darkest secrets, and instead of running away or breaking his confidence, she'd accepted him. His chest squeezed tight with what that might mean, for him and for the future.

Thad walked around to open Emma's door and help her out of the vehicle. The same crackling chemistry between them flared hotter, and suddenly there was no more time to debate his actions. He needed Emma upstairs, in his bed. Now. They hurried inside, Thad bypassing Everett with a muttered word about his butler taking the rest of the night off, and Thad took her to his private suite on the top floor.

"Oh my!" Emma gaped at his luxurious surroundings as he shut and locked the door behind them. This room was his sanctuary, the place in the town house he spent the most time, other than his office on the third floor. He'd had it redecorated a few years earlier, with lots of darker colors and soothing fabrics. Everett had lit a fire, as usual, and turned down the white satin sheets on Thad's huge king-size poster bed. "This place is like a dream world." Her grin turned wicked, and his taut body tightened even more. "A fantasy."

Thad removed his coat and draped it over the back of a chair, then took Emma's as well and did the same with it. "I don't bring many people up here."

"I feel honored," she said, her tone teasing.

Thad wasn't a man who was teased often, but from Emma he loved it. Loved her wonderful, giving nature. In fact, the more time Thad spent with her, the more he craved. She was like a drug, and he was addicted, for better or worse.

Emma believed in the goodness of humanity. She gave of herself without asking for anything in return. The cruelty of Thad's father had taught him differently. But for a few shining moments, Emma made him feel better, less alone. Made him believe again. Even as she made him forget everything else but her.

And that's how he knew he should stay away. Because if he wasn't careful, he'd start believing those things as well and his armor would be gone. He couldn't allow that to happen. He feared it was already too late.

"Come here." He pulled her into his arms and kissed her, hoping to stem the tide of helplessness flooding his system. Control. He needed control here, even as the sweetness of her lips threatened to rob him of it. She gasped and he swept his tongue inside, tasting her as he slid his hands down her body, touching, caressing, claiming.

Instead of pulling away, though, Emma met him kiss for kiss, tangle for tangle, pressing against him, holding him tighter, as if she wanted to remember everything about him, too. She shoved his tux jacket off his shoulders, leaving it in a pile on the floor. Undid his bow tie and tossed it aside.

When they finally pulled back for breath, Thad whispered, "I want you so much."

She slid her leg up the outside of his thigh in answer, taking that red dress with it.

"God, Emma," Thad groaned. All that smooth flesh

exposed for him made him crazy to touch it. He nuzzled her throat, nibbling down to the base of her neck. The heat of her scorched his lips, bringing the simmering need within him to a full boil. His steady surgeon's fingers fumbled for the zipper at the back of her dress, drawing it open as she growled low and buried her face in his throat, loving how responsive Emma was to his touch.

"Hurry." She wriggled against him as his hand slipped inside her dress to stroke her exposed back. "Please…"

"You like that?" He smiled against the side of her neck, then licked the raging pulse at the base of her throat. Emma shivered, her head thrown back, eyes closed in wild abandon. "Tell me what you want."

"You. I want you."

That's all Thad needed to hear. The red dress slid off Emma, pooling around her feet, and for a second, he just took in the sight of her in only her lingerie and heels. The image would be seared into his mind forever. He pulled her back into his arms to rain kisses on her shoulders. "You're perfect, Emma. The closest thing I'll ever find to heaven."

God, he couldn't remember ever wanting anyone else this much.

She took his hand and led him to the bed. "Lie down."

Thad did, swallowing hard when she climbed atop him to straddle him. Emma made quick work of his shirt, running her hands over his torso as if to memorize every inch of him. Then she kissed the middle of his chest, right over his thundering heart, and Thad melted like a snowman in a furnace.

He thought of facts, figures, medical journals. Anything to blunt his need, anything to make this last longer, because he wanted this to go all night. Wanted to kiss every inch of her.

But where Emma was concerned, he only had the time setting—now!

Ending her sweet torture, he rolled her beneath him and took charge, pinning her hands beside her head, enveloped in her legs around his waist, the heat between her thighs rocking against his hardness.

"I need you, Thad," she urged. "Please."

"I need you, too, Emma." More than he'd ever imagined possible. Rolling slightly to his side, Thad quickly removed Emma's bra and panties and his own pants and boxer briefs, leaving them both naked, hot and panting. His lips went to her breast, teasing her nipple with his tongue, while her hand slid down to close around his length, making him shudder and groan. So good. He kissed lower, making love to her with his lips and tongue until she arched and cried out her first release.

It was all too much. It would never be enough.

When Thad could take no more, he rolled away to grab a condom from his nightstand drawer and put it on before stretching out atop her once more. He rested his weight on his forearms on either side of her head, his gaze locked on her sated one, his tip poised at her wet entrance. "Ready."

"So ready," she said, then pulled his mouth to hers for another kiss.

Thad sank into her in one long thrust, savoring the tight heat of her body around his. Then he held still, allowing her to adjust to him until she grew restless and demanded more.

"You feel…" she said, gasping as he began a slow, steady rhythm that had them both careering toward ecstasy all too soon. Her hands were on his back, stroking his skin in slow, rough caresses before she dug her nails into his butt, meeting him thrust for thrust. Thad felt like every nerve ending in his body was on fire, demanding release of a powerful, stormy, wild hunger that stole his breath.

Emma cried out again, riding the waves of her second climax and pushing Thad past the point of no return. Soon, he let go as well, throbbing with his own pleasure.

Eventually, they floated back down to earth, limp and tangled together in his big bed, his head on her chest, her fingers in his hair. Reluctantly, Thad got up to use the restroom, then returned to pull a limp, sated Emma into his side. She sighed and cuddled closer.

"That was…" She kissed the pulse point at the base of his throat. "Wow."

"Hmm." He closed his eyes, his head blissfully clear and blank for a while. "Agreed. When do you need to get home?"

"Soon," she whispered, kissing him again. "But not yet."

"Good." Thad smiled as he drifted to sleep. Eventually Everett would call her a cab and she'd go back to her life and he to his, but for now, Emma was here with him, and he wanted to enjoy it for as long as it lasted.

CHAPTER EIGHT

THE SOUND OF cold reality woke Thad early the next morning.

His cell phone.

With a groan he rolled over and stretched an arm out to grab his phone from the nightstand, painfully aware of the patch of cold mattress beside him where Emma had been earlier. He peeked open an eye and saw a hastily scrawled sticky note stuck on her pillow saying, "Thanks for last night. Call you later," followed by a string of *x*'s and *o*'s. His heart gave a little pinch and his lips twitched into a smile.

So sweet, my Emma.

Thad bolted up in bed, now fully awake, and not just because he was on call that day. Damn. When the hell had he begun having…*feelings*…for Emma? Beyond desire, beyond attraction. Beyond anything he'd felt for anyone in a long, long time and far more dangerous than he'd ever intended. Lo—

Buzz. Buzz. Buzz.

His phone kept him from finishing that last word, thank goodness. Because Thad Markson was not a man who fell head over heels. Oh no. He was far too precise and orderly and career-focused for that. And not even someone as kind and lovely and sexy and perfect as Emma Trudeau would change him.

Maybe she already has...

Dammit. His orderly universe had been rocked and for once in his life, he wanted to ignore the call, but couldn't. Duty called. Literally.

Scowling, he hit the answer button on the phone and tossed the covers aside, padding across the room to the attached master bath as he spoke. "Dr. Markson." The woman from the after-hours service gave him the run-down on the case as he raked his fingers through his disheveled hair and stared at his reflection in the mirror. "I'll be there in half an hour. Have them prep an OR and take the patient up."

He ended the call and hopped in the shower, then quickly shaved and dressed. The patient was one he'd seen in the ER the week before—an elderly woman named Lovelace. She'd returned to Manhattan West last night complaining of chest pain and sudden shortness of breath. They'd been running tests on her since, thinking it might be related to her heart failure, but Thad disagreed. Given the woman's history, he suspected a pulmonary embolism, which could be life-threatening if not handled quickly and properly. He exited his bedroom and called for Everett as he descended the stairs toward the kitchen. "I need to go in to the hospital. Emergency case. Can you have the driver meet me out front, please?"

"Certainly, sir," Everett said, already waiting for him with hot coffee, oatmeal with fresh berries, and an early edition of the financial newspaper on a tray for Thad. The older man set it all on the island's granite counter-top, then turned to walk out of the kitchen.

That's when Thad noticed the slightly grayish pallor to his butler's complexion. Given it was predawn, it could be the early hour, but Thad was still concerned. His closest confidant wasn't a spring chicken anymore. "Everything all right, Everett? You look unwell today."

"Fine, sir. Fine," the older man said, waving off Thad's worry. "Bit of insomnia, that's all. I'll alert the driver of your impending departure."

Thad stared at the empty doorway a moment longer before turning his attention to his breakfast. His insulin pump and sensor were both waterproof, meaning he could wear them in the shower, which was great. But the hot water did cause his body to absorb his insulin more quickly, so it was important for him to keep his blood sugar regulated now. Plus, if he had to take the Lovelace patient into surgery, which he suspected he would, he may not have a chance to eat again for a while.

He quickly paged through the stock reports, but his focus was elsewhere. Mainly on Emma and the blissful night they'd spent together. It had been amazing, being with her like that. Their chemistry was off the charts, and they'd been so in sync, like two pieces of the same puzzle, almost knowing what the other needed before they said anything.

Baxter came up and nudged Thad's leg with his nose, tail wagging and tongue lolling. Thad smiled down at him and bent to scratch the dog behind his ears. "Hey, boy. Good morning to you, too."

"The car is ready for you, sir," Everett said, reappearing the doorway.

"Thank you." Thad finished the rest of his food and coffee fast, then stood. "I should be home for dinner tonight. Usual time."

"Very good, sir," Everett said, then turned away to cough.

"Are you sure you're all right?" Thad stopped next to the butler and put a hand on the older man's shoulder. "Do I need to examine you? Maybe you're coming down with something?"

"No, sir. Really," Everett said, holding up his hand. "It's just a cold. Nothing to worry about."

Thad watched his old friend closely for a moment, then nodded. "Call me if you change your mind."

"Yes, sir." The butler helped Thad into his coat, then held the door for him as he exited, waving from the top of the stoop. "Good day, sir."

Even early in the morning the Manhattan traffic was busy. Once he was in the back of the car, racing toward the hospital, his focus usually turned to the case ahead, the work he needed to do. But today, Emma overwhelmed his thoughts. Unexpected and unsettling. Part of him wished they'd woken up together, maybe stayed in bed a while and talked, enjoyed each other's company. But the other part of him knew that was both impractical and impossible. Impractical because he had to work. So did she. If he remembered correctly, she'd mentioned having a shift today in the ER. Impossible because regardless of the strange feelings he had toward her and the odd way he kept imagining what a future between them might look like, there was no way it could ever happen.

Sleeping together was nice. Way more than nice, actually. Amazing. But that's all it could ever be. What he'd told Emma about him not doing relationships still stood, even after their wonderful night together. And soon enough, Emma would realize what Thad had known all along. She deserved more than him. Deserved better than a grouchy recluse with serious boundary issues. She was sunshine and he was darkness. She saw the positive in everything, the good. She trusted people. He kept everyone at bay and trusted no one.

They were too different for it to ever work between them long-term.

Even if Emma had made him want to forget reality for a little while.

"I'll be waiting right here for you, Ms. Lovelace, when you get out. Promise," Emma said, holding the elderly woman's hand as they walked down the hall toward the OR. "And I'll check with social services, too, to see what we can do about help for you while you recover. Don't worry about a thing. Just get better."

"I'm here. Let's get the patient prepped," a familiar deep voice said, causing a shiver of awareness down Emma's spine. She looked up to see Thad join the group of people flanking the gurney. His hair was a bit mussed, and his scrub top was on slightly crooked, but he still looked gorgeous to her. Their eyes caught from across the gurney and despite the situation, she couldn't help smiling at him.

Something flickered through his icy eyes—warm and comforting—before those too-familiar walls slammed back into place and his usual brusque demeanor returned. She should have been used to it by now, but after the intimacy they'd shared the previous night, her stomach still sank a little.

She returned to focus on the patient instead, who was gripping her hand like a lifeline. "Don't worry, Ms. Lovelace. There is no surgeon more capable in this city than Dr. Markson to handle your case. He's the best."

They hit the double doors into the OR then and Emma halted while the rest of them went through. Thad glanced up at her once more, their eyes locking briefly again before the doors closed and she was left alone in the now-silent hall.

Rather than wait for the elevator, she took the stairs, figuring the exercise would do her good and help keep her alert. To say she hadn't gotten much sleep last night would be an understatement, but she wouldn't have changed it at all. Dating and sex for her had been luxuries ever since she'd taken her sister in ten years ago. Between her busy schedule at work and handling a teenager, there wasn't much time for Emma to focus on herself and her needs. Usually, it didn't bother her. Flings and quickies here and there. No strings, no attachments. No real disruptions to the life she'd built for herself and Karley.

But then along came Thad. A man who many feared or loathed, but Emma found to be a squishy marshmallow beneath his arctic snowman exterior. Sure, he could be difficult and prickly and sometimes downright wrong, but couldn't everyone? She was an optimist, yes, but Emma wasn't naive. She knew trying to do any sort of normal "dating" with Thad would be hard with the weird obstacles they face—location, time, social circles—but still. The connection they had was strong, and rare, and Emma wasn't ready to consign it to the quickie pile just yet. They needed to talk about things once they had a moment in their busy days. Yep.

But that moment was a long time coming unfortunately. Because while Emma had been upstairs with Ms. Lovelace, apparently there'd been a gas leak in a building nearby and now the ER was running nonstop with all the new patients flooding in from that. Emma kicked into high gear, efficiently triaging patients into those who needed admits versus those who could be treated and released. The fact that they were chronically short-staffed didn't help either.

By the time they got the trauma rooms cleared and she had a chance to take a breather, it was afternoon. Emma clocked out and headed to the employee break room in the back of the ER to grab a bottled water. Then she checked with the OR to discover Ms. Lovelace was out of surgery and recovering well in the ICU, though still heavily sedated. She wouldn't wake up until the morning, so Emma didn't plan to go up and see her until then.

Back aching, she slumped into a chair in the otherwise empty break room and took a sip of her water. Her lack of sleep the night before was catching up with her now. She checked her smartwatch. Five more minutes of rest before she needed to go back. She closed her eyes just for a second, only to be awakened by that low, familiar voice again.

"You look tired," Thad said from the break room entrance, one shoulder leaned against the doorframe.

Emma opened on eye to peer at him. "So do you."

Which wasn't exactly true. Where she felt harried and probably looked a mess, Thad was back to his crisp, perfect, chilly self again. His hair combed and his pristine white lab coat in place over fresh blue scrubs. How a man could look that good after making love all night, then spending the morning in surgery, she had no clue. The only signs at all of his fatigue were the slight shadows beneath his eyes, but most people wouldn't notice because most people avoided making eye contact with him for fear he'd go Grinch on them. Not Emma, though. Not anymore.

"You should go home," he said, pushing away from

the doorframe to walk over to her table. "You can't get sick now. We've got too much to do for the carnival."

She yawned, then smiled. "I'm on until five. And I'm not going to get sick. Don't worry. I wouldn't leave you in a lurch. Sit down and share the last—" she checked her watch again "—two minutes of my break with me."

He sighed, then sank into the chair across from her. "Emma, about last night…"

Oh boy. Those words were never good. She straightened and clenched her water bottle tighter than necessary. "Thad, now really isn't a good time. Maybe we can meet up later, where we'd have more privacy?"

A small muscle ticked near his tense jaw as he gave a curt nod. "I just… I've been thinking a lot about us."

"Me, too." Honestly, she hadn't really stopped thinking about them. Maybe they could try to make this last if they were both willing.

His dark brows drew together. "I don't know what we're doing, Emma. None of this makes logical sense."

"I see." She shouldn't be disappointed, because it wasn't like he hadn't told her up front he didn't do relationships, but yet she was. This time had felt different for her. She thought it might be the same for Thad, too. Still, she tried to play down the growing sting of hurt inside her. "It doesn't have to make sense. We're two consenting adults who had a good time last night. That's all. I like you, Thad. I thought you liked me, too."

"I do like you, Emma." He looked at her then, his gaze panicked. "More than I should. More than I intended. And that's a problem for me because I don't do that sort of thing. I told you that." Thad licked his lips, his posture rigid. "I don't want you to get hurt, Emma. Do you understand?"

Emma watched him for a moment, frowning. "I'm a big girl, Thad. I can take care of myself. You won't—"

"But I will," he said, cutting her off, his tone taking on a desperate edge now. "I will hurt you, Emma. Eventually. Because I can't be what you need. I'm no good. I'm distant and aloof. I hate going to parties and being social. I prefer my quiet office and my dog to most people. That isn't the kind of life you want, is it? Isolated. Alone. People hurrying away when they see you coming. Because that's what it would be like with me, and you deserve better."

"Thad, come on." Emma tried to reach over and take his hand, but he pulled away. She sat back and crossed her arms. "Look, I know you had a hard time with your father. I know you've got demons you're dealing with from the way he treated you. But we all have things we deal with. People can change if they want to. And I know that's not who you are inside. I've seen the real you, Thad, and you're wonderful."

"No, I'm not." He stood, his voice vehement now. "I'm not wonderful. You see what you want to see. You only see the good in others, Emma. But the truth is, the only good thing about me is my surgical abilities. Without those, I'm nothing. Therefore, my work always has and always will come first. It's the most important thing for me and there's no room for anything else. I'm not good for anything else."

Wow. Stunned, Emma just blinked at him. His father's lies had left scars even deeper than she'd realized. She cursed the dead man and how he'd made his son think so little of himself and what he had to give the world. Thad was amazing, both in and out of the operating room, but if he didn't believe it himself, there was no way she could convince him otherwise.

Her smartwatch beeped, meaning her break was over. She took a deep breath and stood, pushing her chair in. "I have to go. We should talk about this more later. I'll text you when I'm done working and maybe we can meet up later."

"No." He crossed his arms, staring at the floor instead of her. "I don't think there's anything more to discuss about us. We should stick to the carnival plans from now on."

She closed her eyes and counted to ten before opening them again, surprised hurt scorching through her usually sunny outlook. Thad wasn't the only one who'd taken a chance last night. Up until now, Emma had steered clear of romantic entanglements, far too busy with work and focusing on her sister and getting promoted than love. And while she liked Thad—more than liked him, if she was honest—she was just as scared and uncertain of how quickly things had intensified between them. Sleeping with a man was one thing. Opening her heart and her past to him, as she had with Thad, was another. But if he couldn't see that or didn't value it, she refused to beg. "Fine. If that's what you want. Perhaps we should avoid face-to-face meetings then. Stick with texts and phone calls from here on out. We should be able to get the carnival finished that way."

"Yes. It is what I want, and I think your idea is a good one." He let out a slow breath, looked relieved. "I'm glad you understand."

"Actually, I don't." She shook her head. "But if you don't trust me enough to work through this, then there's no point."

"Em—"

"Stop," she interrupted, holding up her hand. "I need to work now. But let me end by saying I like you, Thad.

A lot. And I thought last night was amazing. I'd like to explore that more with you. But you obviously don't so, fine, end of story."

He opened his mouth, as if to argue, then hung his head. "You can do better than me."

She nodded, projecting confidence even though she was crumbling inside. "You're right. I can."

She left the break room, and damn if those weren't some of the hardest steps she'd ever had to take. Because that connection between her and Thad still burned bright, urging her to go back and hug him, tell him that he was good, that there was hope, even though she knew there wasn't. He'd made his decision and there was no point arguing. Change happened fast and the best you could do was ride it out and try to keep your head above water. Emma knew that better than most. She'd lived it for the past ten years and survived. She should've known better than to veer out of the happy lane she was in.

Well, no more. If Thad was satisfied playing the Grinch of Fifth Avenue, then let him. She had more than enough to keep her busy. She had the carnival to plan for Ricky. She had Ms. Lovelace upstairs who needed her. She had Karley at home. She had a promotion to win here in the ER.

But what she didn't have was Thad Markson. And right then, he was the only thing that mattered.

CHAPTER NINE

"Sis, what's up?" Karley asked, leaning her hip against the edge of the kitchen counter in their apartment. "You've been quiet for days and that's not like you. Didn't even try to cheer up cranky Mr. Lewis next door when he brought over the mail that got misdelivered."

Emma sighed and looked up at her younger sister, standing there with her arms crossed waiting for an answer. With the holiday rush, it had been a busy time for both sisters and today was the first day in a week they'd both been home together. Emma had hoped a quiet Sunday would help settle her before the last big push to get the carnival done. They had less than a week now until Christmas Eve.

"I'm fine," Emma said, trying not to let her inner sadness show. Seemed like an eternity ago now that she'd been with Thad, like a fairy-tale dream she'd wakened from too early. Or maybe too late. Either way, she was still reeling from their whiplash breakup and wasn't sure what to do about it. Part of her felt silly even calling it a breakup, considering they hadn't ever really been together—not in the relationship sense, anyway. But she missed him. Even with his prickly nature and lack of social skills and overall allergy to anything remotely bright and cheerful. Or maybe because of it.

Go figure.

The man couldn't be more different from her and yet they shared the same deep connection. A connection that still tugged at her heart each time her phone buzzed, hoping maybe it was Thad.

He'd stuck to their agreement, only contacting her by text or call, mainly the former. And damn if she hadn't caught herself glancing around the ER during her shifts this past week, trying to catch a glimpse of him. It was silly. It was infuriating. It was ridiculously confusing.

She was the happy one, the sunny person who made everyone else's day brighter. Like the Cindy Lou Who of Manhattan West. And she'd allowed her light to be snuffed, at least temporarily, by the Grinch of Fifth Avenue.

How in the world had that happened?

She didn't know.

All Emma did know for sure was she'd spent the last few nights since her fight with Thad tossing and turning, despite being bone-deep weary. Her usually pleasant dreams were haunted by memories of them together, his kisses, his taut, muscled body pressed against her, moving inside her, driving her to the heights of pleasure.

"Hello?" Karley stood beside the table now, waving a hand in front of Emma's face. "Earth to sis. Is this about your partner? The cute doctor who took you to that dance?" Karley crossed her arms, gaze narrowed on Emma, waiting for an answer. When one didn't come, her eyes widened. "Oh my God, sis! It is, isn't it?"

"What? No." Flushed and flustered, Emma shuffled the papers in front of her on the table, avoiding Karley's too-perceptive stare. "Of course not. We're just working on the carnival together. That's all."

"This conversation is inappropriate and I'm not

having it with you." Emma did her best to refocus on
her vendor lists, but it was no use. Her mind was too
cluttered now with anxious adrenaline, and the words
blurred before her eyes. "Don't you have homework or
something to do?"

"Already done." Karley grinned and leaned forward,
resting her forearms on the table, clearly not going anywhere. Perfect. Not. "So, you like this guy, huh? I can
tell by the way you're acting."

"I'm not acting any way at all," Emma snapped, the
heat in her face rivaling the surface of the sun. "And
how I feel about Dr. Markson isn't important." *Not anymore.*

Her sister frowned now and sat back. "Why? Did
he hurt you? Want me to go over there and smack him
for you?"

"No!" Emma didn't look at Karley then. "He didn't
hurt me. We just had a misunderstanding, that's all."
Her chest squeezed tighter, and she swallowed hard before staring down at her papers again. Good Lord. She
blinked hard against unexpected tears. She would not
cry about this. Nope. Especially not in front of Karley.
"I'm just under a lot of pressure right now to make sure
this wish project turns out well, so I have a better shot
at that promotion at work. After Christmas, I'll be back
to normal. Promise."

Karley gave her a flat look. "You work harder than
anyone I know, Em. You always put everyone else first,
do whatever you can to make everyone feel better. But
if this guy doesn't appreciate it, then he doesn't deserve
you. End of story."

"Dr. Markson appreciates me," Emma said, rising to
his defense though she didn't know why.

"Sure." Karley shook her head. "Whatever."

"He does. He's actually a really good man."

Her sister responded by raising a skeptical brow at her. "If he's so good, then why are you sitting here miserable now instead of being at his fancy Park Avenue town house with him?"

"Fifth Avenue," Emma corrected before she caught herself. "And you shouldn't judge someone just by where they live. Just because his family had money doesn't mean there aren't problems to go along with it."

"Maybe." Karley shrugged. "Is it nice there?"

"At the town house? Yes, very nice."

"Does he have servants?"

"A butler. Older man named Everett." It was Emma's turn to scowl now. "Why?"

"So it's just him and his butler living alone in that great big house?" her sister asked.

"Yes. Oh, and Thad has a service dog named Baxter."

"Service dog?" Karley perked up a little at that. "Why would he need one of those? Is he sick?"

Oops. It wasn't her business to talk about Thad's illness. Realizing she'd said too much already, Emma stood and picked up her paperwork for the vendors. "I think I'm going to take a nap."

Her sister protested as Emma brushed past her. "Hey, sis. Don't get offended. I'm just trying to figure out why he's got you so torn and twisted."

"I'm not…" Emma's voice trailed off. She was tired. Exhausted, really. She sank onto the couch in their living room and buried her face in her hands, her voice sounding raw to her own ears as she said, "Please, just forget it. Okay?"

Karley joined her in the living room and put her arm around Emma's shoulders, pulling her into a much-needed hug. "Hey, it's okay, sis."

"No, it's not," Emma said, her words catching on a sob. God. This was not how it was supposed to work. Emma was the older one, the strong one, the one who should be comforting Karley, not the other way around. Yet she couldn't seem to stop her tears. "Everything's a mess."

Despite her wishes, the whole sad tale of what had transpired between her and Thad over the past few weeks came tumbling out—well, except for the sleeping together part. Some things needed to stay private, even between sisters. Still, Karley was smart enough to connect the dots. Seventeen going on thirty indeed.

"Wow," her sister said, sitting back a short while later and pushing Emma's braids away from her face. "Yep. Sounds like a mess all right."

Emma laughed through her tears, swiping the back of her hand across her damp cheeks. "Thanks for agreeing with me." She sniffled, then shrugged. "It probably would've been easier to move on if we didn't still have to stay in contact because of the carnival, but little Ricky's depending on us and I won't let him down, so…"

"There's the Em I know." Karley smiled and got up, returning a minute later with a box of tissues from the bathroom. She handed them to Emma, then pulled one out to dab the tears from her sister's cheeks. "The optimist with a spine of steel. Honestly, I'm not an expert on men."

"That's good to know."

Karley gave her a look. "Seriously, though. It sounds to me like you need to take charge of the situation if you want to fix things with him. And you need to do it face-to-face. Go to his town house and talk to him."

"Oh, I don't know." She blew her nose, then scowled

down at the tissue as she twisted it in her hands in her lap. "We agreed not to see each other again and he's so reclusive, I'm not sure how I'd even get in."

"Hmm." Karley sat back, her expression thoughtful as she stared at the coffee table. "What about those papers you're working on?"

"The vendors?" She blinked at the stack of papers she'd been working on earlier. "He hasn't given me the specifications for the site yet and it's getting down to the wire."

"That's good." Her sister nodded and grinned. "Go over and fib a little. Say you'd been trying to call him all day but couldn't get through. Tell him one of the vendors is pressing you for the specifications. Then when you get inside, sit him down and have a talk about things."

Before Emma could respond, Karley's phone buzzed.

"Need to take this. My bestie's having a man crisis, too." Karley leaned over and kissed Emma's cheek, then stood. "Good luck, sis. Can't wait to hear how it turns out."

Emma watched her sister walk away, then leaned back into the cushions and stared at the ceiling. She hated to break the agreement with Thad about sticking to phone communication only, but how else were they supposed to mend fences between them? And needing to know specifics about the venue was important. With only a week left until Christmas Eve, they did need to get confirmation from his foundation on the location for the carnival. So far, Thad had brushed her off when she'd asked, but as a partner on the project, she had a right to know. Still, she didn't feel right just showing up at his town house again, nor did she want to wait all day like he'd made her do before. She pulled out her phone and stared down at the screen, her stomach lurching. Should she text first? That would be easier. But no. He could ignore a text and it could come across wrong. Best to call and get it over with. She pulled up his number and waited as it rang once, twice…

"What?" Thad's deep, growly voice rolled down the line and over her like velvet and sin.

For a moment, Emma couldn't say a word. Then she blurted out, "It's Emma."

A pause. Thad exhaled slowly, sounding about as worn out as she felt. "What do you need?"

You. I need you.

Emma gripped her phone tight, her heart slamming against her rib cage and her throat dry. "I need to speak with you about the vendors. We need specifications for the vendors so they will be able to set up properly," she said, praying she hid her nervousness well. "We only have a week left."

"I know how long we have left, Emma." His tone turned sharp. "Now is not a good time."

"Are you at the hospital?" she asked. Dammit. She really hadn't thought this through as well as she should have. If he was in the middle of an important case, she didn't want to interrupt him. "Sorry."

"What? No. I'm home. But I…" She heard the sounds of leather creaking and pictured him getting up from behind his desk in the study, pacing back and forth in front of the tree they'd decorated together. He cursed under his breath. "Fine. Yes. What time can you be here?"

"Half an hour?"

"Okay. I'll call my foundation and get as much information as I can from them. Have you eaten yet?"

The question took Emma by surprise. "Uh, no."

"Good. Everett serves dinner at six. Will that work?"

"Sure."

"See you then, Emma."

He clicked off and she sat there staring at the wall in her living room, stunned. It had worked. She and Thad were going to talk. About the carnival, but it was better than nothing. Pulse racing, she straightened and walked over to knock on Karley's bedroom door. Her sister was still on the phone but stopped as Emma stuck her head inside. "Can you do takeout for dinner?"

Karley nodded and gave her a thumbs-up. "Go get him, sis."

Around five forty-five Thad finished up the phone call with his foundation. They'd pulled a lot of strings to find a venue to meet their needs, but in the end, they'd managed to secure an amazing place. In fact, if everything came together as planned, they'd be able to invite not only the children from the PICU at Manhattan West, as Ricky wanted, but also all the other hospitals' PICUs in the city. Thad was nothing if not an overachiever and besides, it soothed an old wound inside him that had festered too long. Granting little Ricky's wish was like throwing the party Thad had always wanted as a child himself and never received.

Now that he'd solved one problem, he faced another. Emma.

Inviting her to dinner had probably been a mistake. He should have stuck to his guns and insisted they handle the carnival issues over the phone as they'd agreed. But man, the thought of seeing her again after time apart made his battered heart sing.

Which made no sense. For once since this whole debacle started with her, he'd thought rationally and acted from logic, not emotion, when he'd said they should work apart from now on. Then all it had taken was one phone call from her to crumble his resolve. How would he ever survive if he pushed her away again? How would he ever survive if he didn't?

Thad was still stewing over that dilemma when Everett knocked on his office door to announce, "Ms. Trudeau is downstairs, sir."

"Thank you," Thad said. "I'll be right down."

The butler left and Thad watched his old friend go, still concerned about the man's condition. Everett still had a slight limp and his coloring had not improved much. Thad had tried to get the older man to let him examine him again last night, but Everett had waved him off once more, stating he had an appointment with his own physician the next day and that it was nothing. In fact, Everett had insisted he felt better, even if he didn't look it.

Anxiety buzzed through his system even as he tried to tamp it down. Not just over Everett's condition but also the fact that Emma was there, in his home, once more. Not for a social call or date, but for business. He needed to remember that and keep his emotions out of it. Never mind that each time he closed his eyes, Thad remembered the feel of her beside him, beneath him, around him. Could still smell her spicy-sweet scent and taste her lips. He needed to forget those things. She wasn't meant for a man like him. Love wasn't meant for a man like him.

Resigned, he headed downstairs to find her already seated in the large formal dining room where Everett would serve dinner tonight. Normally, Thad ate in the kitchen where it was smaller and homier. But considering what had happened in there with Emma on the first night she'd been here, Thad didn't want reminders of the past to muddle things any more than they already were.

"Hello, Emma." Thad stopped on the threshold to meet her gaze down the length of the long mahogany table. She wore a silly red sweater tonight with Santa on the front and looked more beautiful than ever. Yearning constricted his throat and he swallowed hard against it, battling his rioting emotions. From the moment Emma Trudeau had entered his life, all of his ideas about himself and the world had exploded into a million pieces. She didn't think he was broken or a monster. She'd asked him for nothing except his help and his kindness. She had scars and had suffered hurt, but she used her pain to bring light to others, not hide away. She made him question his decisions, and for a man whose patients lived and died by those decisions, it was terrifying as hell.

"Thad?"

Her voice startled him back into motion. He headed for the chair across from hers. "Yes?"

"Are you okay?"

She watched him warily, like he might have another hypoglycemic episode. Dammit. He'd been in the same room with Emma for less than five minutes and already his plans for a quick professional meeting were derailing.

"I'm fine, thank you." He gave a curt nod to Everett, hoping to keep the rest of the evening on track. "We're ready for dinner."

The older man disappeared through a doorway into the kitchen, Baxter sticking to the butler's side like glue. Odd that, since he rarely left Thad's side when he was home, but Thad didn't have the brain space to worry about it now. They sat in awkward silence as Thad studied Emma from beneath his lashes. There were faint shadows under her eyes, suggesting she'd had sleepless nights, too. Before he could ask her, however, thankfully Everett returned with their meals, grilled salmon and quinoa, Baxter trotting beside him.

"So," she said, after thanking the butler, then placing her napkin atop her lap. "Did you speak with your foundation?"

"I did," he said, taking a sip of his water. "They've secured an excellent venue. One I hope you'll be as happy with as I am."

"Oh." She blinked at him, looking surprised. "Good. Where is it?"

"They actually originally had two that met our specifications. Large, good ventilation, heated." He ate a bit of salmon, watching her. "I settled on the second one. Madison Square Garden."

She froze with her fork halfway to her mouth, eyes wide. "*The* Madison Square Garden?"

"Yes."

"How… What…" Emma shook her head, setting her fork down carefully, then wiping her mouth before continuing. "Do we have the donations to cover that expense? I'm sure it's not cheap."

"Far from it." Thad smiled, satisfied that she seemed suitably impressed with his work. "And yes, we have the funds to cover the rental." *With my help.* "It took some finagling by my foundation, too, to get the Christmas Eve date we wanted for the arena. They wanted to use it for some sporting event, but I pulled some strings and now it's ours." He cleared his throat. "With the capacity, our vendors should have no problems setting up the booths and rides in there. And we could also invite more people."

"Who?"

"I'm thinking children and their families from other PICUs in the city."

"Uh, wow. Okay." She took another bite of her food and chewed slowly, as if considering all that he'd said. Then she looked behind her at Everett. "This food is excellent."

"Thank you, ma'am," the older man said, bowing a bit awkwardly.

Emma laughed, then shook her head. "You can call me Emma, Everett."

"As you wish, ma—" the butler stopped himself. "Emma."

Thad regarded their exchange with astonishment. In all the years Everett had been with him, he'd never asked the man to call him Thad. He felt bad about that now. Scowling, Thad shifted his attention back to Emma. "May I ask you a question?"

She ate a roasted carrot and Thad tried not to remember how soft her lips were. "Sure. If I can ask you one in return."

"Fine. How exactly do you remain so happy all the time?" He waved his fork around at the room in general. "Stay so friendly and open and joyful, with the state of the world?"

Emma didn't respond at first, her expression serious. "First of all, I'm not always happy, Thad. Some days are harder than others." He managed not to wince at the thinly veiled reference to their conversation in the break room the previous week. "But then I remind myself that I can't fix every problem in the world. All I can do is get up each day and improve my little corner of it. The rest is up to the universe."

"The universe?"

"Or God, or whatever you believe in that's bigger than you. Divine intelligence."

He shook his head, the idea of leaving anything up to chance only spiking his anxiety more. "I don't know what to do with your concept."

"I know." She gave him a small smile, her eyes kind. "But I always remember what my mother told me when I was little. Sometimes it's braver to surrender what you can't control."

Part of Thad recognized she was trying to get a point across to him. But another part, the part conditioned by his dead father to believe his worth came from the results he produced, balked.

Emma chuckled. "I think that's the first time I've seen you speechless."

He shook his head and finished the last bite of his food. "Your answer just surprised me, that's all."

"Hmm." She sat back for Everett to take her empty plate, then waited until the butler took Thad's as well and disappeared into the kitchen again before saying, "Now it's time for my question."

His heart skipped a beat and Thad gulped more water. "All right."

"I want to know the real reason you pushed me away."

Tell her. Tell her the truth. Let her see you for who you really are. Let her in. Open up.

It was the hardest thing he'd ever done, harder than losing his mother, harder than suffering his father's emotional abuse, harder than all those long nights in the hospital as a scared little boy alone. But he wanted this, needed this, needed her in his life, more than he needed his next breath.

"I—" he started, only to be cut off by a loud crash

from the kitchen followed by the dog's frantic barks. Thad scowled, his attention snapping to the door behind Emma. "What the hell? Everett?"

No answer.

Anxiety soaring through the roof now, Thad was up out of his chair and pushing into the kitchen in a flash. "Everett, is everything—"

No. Everything was not all right. The details of the scene before him registered all at once, flooding his mind with information. Everett on the floor, unmoving and deathly pale. Baxter by his side, nudging the older man with his nose and crying plaintively. The heat of Emma as she ran into the kitchen behind him, then stopped short.

"Help me, Emma. Now!" Thad's medical training overrode his shock and he dropped to his knees on the tile, not caring about the shards from the broken dishes cutting into his knees.

"Call 911. We need an ambulance here now!" he yelled to Emma as he turned over his butler, noting the bluish tint to his lips and his greenish-gray complexion. He checked the older man's pulse and breathing and detected neither. Not good. Not good at all. "Then get down here and help me start CPR until they arrive."

His blood froze.

Please don't die on me. You're the closest thing I have to a father. Stay with me.

Thad ripped open the front of Everett's black butler jacket, then his shirt to reveal the man's bare chest. Then he placed his hands over Everett's sternum and began compressions, counting in his head. He thought back over the last week or so. The unusual limp in Everett's walk, his unhealthy pallor. Given the man's age and the fact that he was overweight, chances were high he had elevated blood pressure and heart disease. A stroke was highly possible. Thad cursed himself for not insisting on taking his butler to the doctor earlier.

"EMS is on the way," Emma said, kneeling on Everett's other side and tipping the man's head back to clear his airways, and began giving him lifesaving breaths. "Had he been feeling unwell lately?"

"Yes. This is my fault," he growled, checking for a pulse again and this time finding one—thready and weak. "He's been limping for the past few days. And he didn't look good. But I let him brush me aside instead of taking him to the doctor. If he dies…"

No. That last thought was too horrible to bear. He couldn't let Everett die. Wouldn't let him die.

Sirens grew louder outside and Emma rushed to the door to let the EMTs in, a hand on Baxter's collar to keep him out of the fray. As the paramedics worked to get Everett stabilized and onto a gurney, Thad gave them his assessment. If it was a stroke, which he suspected it was, time was of the essence. "Take him to Manhattan West. I'll call one of my colleagues and have them meet us there."

Emma accompanied them to the door. "I'll follow you."

"No."

Dammit. He hadn't meant to say that as harshly as he had. But he was stressed and sick with worry and berating himself for being so self-absorbed that he'd allowed this situation to get to the point it had. Thad turned to see Emma's stricken expression. "I have to go." He glanced out the door to the ambulance at the curb where the EMTs were loading Everett into the back. "I'll check in with you later and give you an update."

Then he was running down the sidewalk, barely

stopping to tug on his coat before climbing into the back
of the rig and hurtling toward the hospital, the life of the
man who'd taught him what it meant to be a real man,
one who loved and cared for others more than themselves and their own comfort in life, in dire jeopardy.

CHAPTER TEN

EMMA GLANCED OUT the window of Thad's office upstairs, watching the lightly falling snow glittering the air over Central Park in the distance, her phone in hand. Karley was on the other end of the line, sounding about as stunned as Emma felt.

"He what?" her sister asked.

"Rented out Madison Square Garden arena for our carnival." Even saying it sounded unbelievable. Or maybe that was just her shock from seeing poor Everett lifeless on the kitchen floor. She was a medical professional, yes, but when disaster struck close to home, no one was immune.

"Isn't that wildly expensive?"

"Probably." Emma shook her head, still trying to wrap her brain around what had happened that night. "But the reason I called was to let you know I won't be home tonight. I'm heading to the hospital to be there for Thad and Everett."

"So you guys made up then?"

"No. Not exactly." She rubbed her throbbing temple. "But Everett is all Thad has in this world and if he doesn't make it, Thad will need all the support he can get. Even if it's from me."

"Emma," Karley said. "I appreciate you want to help, but if he doesn't want you there…"

"I've got a shift in the morning anyway," she said, swiveling back to stare at the tree across the room, still glowing cheerfully as if Thad's world hadn't avalanched down around him tonight. "So once I check on him, I'll just start early. I'm sure they can use the help in the ER. You be okay by yourself?"

"I'm fine," her sister said. "Just don't do too much, okay? I know you want to help, but don't force it. Give him time to accept it."

"I will." Emma could picture her sister's dubious stare in her head. "I promise. Make sure the doors are locked before you go to bed."

"I'm not seven anymore, sis. I got this."

"I know." She started to end the call, then added. "I love you."

"Love you, too," Karley said. "And call me with an update when you know something. I don't know the old man, but still. That's no way for a person to go."

"Will do."

Emma ended the call, then sank down into Thad's chair behind the desk. Baxter walked over and nudged her hand with his wet nose for a pet. Poor thing was probably still as traumatized as the rest of them. She smiled down at the dog, scratching behind his ears. "I know. You were such a good boy, Baxter. Alerting us to trouble."

The dog snuffled and whined, then lay down with his head on Emma's foot.

She sat there for a while, thinking of all the things they could do with the new venue. Thad had mentioned inviting all the kids and parents from the other PICUs in New York, and that was a great idea. They'd have to make provisions, based on each child's illness, and perhaps group them accordingly. Maybe stagger the times of entry to the carnival to accommodate everyone without crowding people too close together. There was still a lot of work to do, but Emma could handle it. Thad had done more than enough getting the venue.

And wow, what a venue it was.

Determined not to let his hard work and sacrifice go to waste, and knowing he'd have more than enough to deal with over the next few days regardless of Everett's outcome, she sat forward and started jotting down lists of things to do on a pad of paper sitting atop Thad's desk. Okay. With the new area to cover, they would need more spotlights set up so people could see properly. They'd planned to hold the carnival for four hours, but if they were inviting more people and staggering the entries, they'd need more time. She would need to ask Thad for a contact person at the arena the next time she talked with him, so she could get schematics for the event. Hard to believe in less than a week, they'd transform Madison Square Garden arena into a winter wonderland and make little Ricky's dreams come true.

Hard to believe I've fallen for the Grinch...

The thought caught Emma off guard, but not because of her feelings for Thad. Tonight, when her heart had broken for him at his anguished pleas for Everett to stay with him as they performed CPR on the man together, Emma knew her caring for Thad went deeper than platonic. How deep exactly? She wasn't sure yet. But the emotions were there for her—warm and wonder-filled and full of future possibilities just the same. Time would tell if those emotions went anywhere or if Thad felt the same toward her.

The one thing Emma was certain of, though, having worked with Thad these past few weeks, was that he wasn't the man everyone thought he was. He wasn't a Grinch. People at the hospital seemed genuinely surprised to learn from Emma how helpful he'd been on the project, and she secretly hoped this could lead to a new beginning for Thad at Manhattan West, if he wanted it. A fresh start, free from the burdens and fears heaped on him by his horrible, abusive father. Thad deserved to be welcomed and praised for what he was now—a successful, highly skilled surgeon and a generous philanthropist—not for the antisocial ways he'd shielded himself from his painful past.

And Emma intended to help with that transformation of his image, whether Thad wanted to continue seeing her after the project was over or not. In the same way he'd used his personal resources to secure the perfect venue for their carnival. Not because of any hope of reward, but because it was the right thing to do.

If that didn't prove he wasn't truly a Grinch, Emma didn't know what did.

She returned to the kitchen to make sure Baxter had enough food and water to last him until someone could return to the town house the next morning, then took him out back into the gardens to potty before grabbing her coat from the closet off the foyer Everett had hung it in. Everett. She prayed once more the man would be all right and make a full recovery. He was the closest person in Thad's life. The only person in Thad's life that Emma knew of. Well, besides her now. And she wasn't going anywhere. Not without a fight.

Emma locked up the town house, then used the fresh air and exercise to hone her focus. She was about a block away from his place when her phone rang. Thad's number flashed on her caller ID. Heart in her throat, she answered. "What's happening?"

"They're still running tests, but they think it was a stroke," Thad said, a bit breathless. She imagined him pacing the halls of the hospital, his hair a mess from running his fingers through it and his cheeks flushed from adrenaline and stress. She wished she could be there now to hug him and show support. To tell him everything would be okay, even if it wouldn't. "My colleague Dr. Kinkaid is handling the case. He's the best in the business, besides me, so I trust him."

I trust him.

The words were bittersweet for Emma. She was glad Thad had found a good doctor to treat Everett, but she hoped someday Thad might trust her, too. It felt like the holy grail with him, being vulnerable and trusting. They weren't there yet, but maybe someday.

"I'm glad Everett's in capable hands." She meant it. The old butler had always been kind to her, and he'd helped tremendously during Thad's initial hypoglycemic attack. And despite their rather formal arrangement, the fact that Everett had stayed by Thad's side all these years had shown a loyalty and caring you had to admire. She couldn't imagine what Thad must be going through right now. "How are you doing?"

"I'm fine," he said, far too quickly.

"Thad. I don't believe that." Emma kept her tone low and calm, but firm. "Stop trying to be strong here. I was there when we did CPR on him, I could see the fear on your face. Everett is your friend, your confidant, your closest companion. You said as much yourself. This had to be traumatic for you."

The squeak of his shoes on the floor that had echoed through the phone line since the start of their conversation stopped, letting her know he stood still now. "It's my fault. I saw signs he hadn't been up to par the past few days and I let him dismiss them with me. I'm a doctor and his employer. I should have insisted he go in for treatment."

"What? No. None of this is your fault." Emma had seen it more than enough times in the ER. People blaming themselves because of "if onlys." If only they'd done this or that. If only they'd responded soon or made a different decision. Hindsight was always twenty-twenty. But she feared Thad would try to suppress all of his rediscovered emotions over this and retreat back into the safety of his cold, lonely, emotionless cave again. "Everett was a grown man, and while he worked for you, you were not the boss of him personally, no matter what you might think. He needs you now, Thad. Be there for him, the way he's been there for you from the start."

Thad didn't respond at first and Emma feared she'd gone too far. Then he sighed. "I need to get back to his exam room. They'll be taking him up to surgery soon."

"I'm on my way into the ER now," she said. "Figured I'd start my shift early since I'm already up. I'll try to find you later and see how things are going. If you need me for any reason before then, you know where to find me."

"Thanks, Emma," he said, his voice rough and strained. "For everything."

The call ended then, leaving Emma at the top of the steps leading down into the subway terminal, blinking tears away hard. It was still hours until dawn, but she prayed for light anyway.

Everett's surgery turned out to be long and hard, including an emergency craniotomy to relieve pressure on his brain from the subarachnoid hemorrhage and the neurosurgeon clipping the vessels that had ruptured. The next several hours in recovery would be crucial to determine how successful the procedure had been and whether Everett would ever regain consciousness.

Thad had spent the two hours his old friend was in the OR wearing a hole in the carpet of the waiting area, stewing over everything that had happened the past few weeks with Emma, and with Everett for his entire life. All the tumultuous feelings of guilt and shame and hope and yearning left him weary to his bones. But Emma had been right. Everett had been there for him all these years. He couldn't leave the older man now. Wouldn't leave him.

Please, Everett. Stay with me.

He sat in the private ICU room he'd secured for Everett, by the man's bedside. Monitors beeped around him and from somewhere down the hall, through the open doorway, he heard far-off hushed conversation at the nurses' station. Thad closed his eyes for a moment and pictured Emma, downstairs in the ER, helping patients feel better. Knowing she was there, at Manhattan West, made him feel better, too. Outside the windows across from him, the first rays of sunlight pierced the horizon with streaks of pink and gold and purple. A new day had arrived.

Time ticked by and Thad's eyes grew heavy. He didn't sleep, but he did reminisce. About all the times Everett had helped him when he'd been younger. Teaching him how to take care of his blood sugar. Tutoring him on his homework. Comforting him after the endless fights with his father.

Those memories soon morphed into his more recent times with Emma. The first night he'd seen her in his kitchen, mistaking her for an angel. The fundraiser, breathtaking in her red gown. Decorating the tree in his office. Visiting young Ricky in the PICU. Their first kiss behind the Christmas tree in the lobby. The second kiss in his office. Making plans for the project. Making love in his bed.

Emma had seared herself in his life, into his heart, without him realizing it and now he wasn't sure how he'd ever let her go. They only had a few days left until the carnival and then she'd be gone, and his life would return to the same sad, dreary, lonely existence it had been before.

His eyes opened and he sat up straighter.

Did he want that? No. He didn't. But how to change that? Circumstances were still the same as they had been. Thad had opened up a lot more during his time with Emma, but he was still a busy surgeon with a demanding schedule and a penchant for solitude. He couldn't ask Emma to change for him. She loved people. Loved being out in the world experiencing new things and new ideas. He preferred the safety of his office and ordered searches on his computer. And there was her sister to consider, too. She still had a family, a life, separate from his. How would that work? Would they, could they, blend the two? If Everett survived, he'd need help and care at the town house to recover. Thad was happy to provide that for him or hire someone to do that, but it would require even more of his precious free time, leaving even less to spend with Emma after this project.

Most of all, though, he feared she'd had enough of him. Enough of his isolation and grumpiness. Enough of his wariness and pushing new things away. Deep down, he knew that it wasn't her who needed to change here. It was him. But was he capable of it? Even for Emma?

Everyone loses something in life eventually... It's how we choose to deal with it that matters... I choose to be happy.

Her words looped in his head, urging him to try. Was it that simple, though?

Thad wasn't sure. The only thing he was sure of at the moment was that Emma was everything he never knew he needed. Fate had brought them together through some Christmas miracle and now that he'd found her, he never wanted to let her go. Could he change himself enough to keep her, though? To make her happy, as she'd made him? To allow her to see him, really see him, with no filters, no barriers, no fear, and to do the same for her?

It would be the most difficult thing he'd ever done in his life, including his delicate surgeries, but he wanted to try. For Emma. For himself. For the future they might have together.

If she'd still have him.

"Thad?" Her quiet voice carried from the doorway as if conjured by his thoughts.

He straightened in his seat and gave her a tentative smile, gesturing to the chair beside his, his pulse pounding in his head. "Come in, Emma."

"How is he doing?" she asked, looking at Everett in the hospital bed, tubes and wires attached to him, the rhythmic whoosh and hiss of the ventilator keeping him breathing and alive. "The surgery went well, I hope."

"As well as can be expected," Thad said, grateful for her warmth beside him as Emma settled into her chair. She was wearing scrubs again and her braids were tied back at the nape of her neck. She looked tired and overworked and so beautiful it made his chest ache. He forced his attention back to Everett. "We got him here quickly after the stroke, which is crucial, and they began anticoagulation therapy fast. That, plus the surgery should minimize the damage from the bleeding on his brain, hopefully. We won't know the extent of his injuries, though, until he wakes up."

If he wakes up...

Thad swallowed hard and stared at the monitors for fear he'd break down completely. This was like losing his mother all over again. Except this time, he knew what was happening and there was no Everett to comfort him because his old friend was the one who was sick.

Then Emma took his hand, entwining his cold fingers with her warm ones and squeezing gently. "I'm sure this is very scary and painful for you, Thad. But please know I'm here for you. Whatever you need. Just let me know."

Normally, he took such things as flippancy. Stuff people said to make themselves feel better when they didn't know what else to do. It had happened after his mother had died, and even now, his colleague had mentioned the same today when he'd filled Thad in after the surgery. Thad knew better than to take them at their word. But now...

Let her see you... No filters, no barriers, no fear...

His earlier realization came to bite him in the butt. He wanted to let her in, wanted to rely on her, wanted to accept her support, her caring. The fear part, though, was strong.

Do it anyway.

Those words were in Everett's voice in his head. Nudging him toward the truth.

And the truth was, these two people had become his family. Small and odd, maybe, but still. Everett and

Emma were the two people he'd let closest to him in the world. And family wasn't by blood, necessarily, it was who you trusted. Who was there for you no matter how difficult the situation, or how terribly you screwed up. People who had your back and you had theirs.

People like Everett and Emma.

"I want you to be here," he blurted out before he could stop himself. "I... I want your help and your friendship and whatever else you want to give me, Emma. And I want to give that back to you, too, tenfold, a thousandfold. Anytime, anywhere. Anything I can do, just name it. I just... I don't want this to be over."

Emma just looked at him for a long moment, and he cringed inside. Man, he was so bad at this stuff. Probably because he had no framework to base it on. And the man who'd always advised him on matters of emotion and the heart couldn't currently tell him how to handle this.

Finally, though, she laughed. It was the last thing Thad had expected and the thing he'd needed most right then. The awful tension and gloom in the air shattered like icicles, raining down prismatic rainbows of hope through the quiet ICU room. Even Everett's color and vitals improved and for the first time in forever, Thad felt a rush of something very akin to optimism.

It filled him to bursting, like his heart had grown three sizes bigger in a matter of seconds, filling him with happiness and joy and peace regardless of the circumstances. Not unpleasant, per se. But definitely different from his usual reserve.

"Oh, Thad." Emma cupped his cheeks, then leaned in to kiss him right there in the ICU and he didn't even care. "I'll stay as long as you want me. Promise."

He kissed her again then, just because he wanted to

and it felt so good, then they sat side by side in Everett's room, holding hands and leaning their heads together.

"Does he have anyone we should notify?" Emma asked after a short while. "I can call them after I get back downstairs from my break."

"No. Not that I know of," Thad whispered. "He told me once he was married, back when I was still a baby, long before my mother died."

"What happened to his wife?" she asked, her tone sounding a bit sad.

"Cancer. She died at thirty, he said. Way too young." Thad nestled closer to her warmth, more grateful than he could say to have her there beside him. More hopeful than he'd ever been that his future might be different from the vast empty desert he'd pictured for himself. "I don't think he ever tried to find anyone else after that." Thad shrugged, remembering what Everett had told him during that conversation. "He said when it's right, it's right."

Emma raised her head then to look at Thad, leaning in to kiss him softly. "Everett's a wise man."

"Yes," Thad agreed. "He really is."

Eventually, Emma had to leave the peace of the ICU and return downstairs to the controlled chaos of the ER. Good thing, too, because the first patient she walked into an exam room to see was her friend. "Ms. Lovelace? What are you doing back here?"

"My Christmas tree topper was crooked," the older woman said, shaking her head. "That nice young man from the community center came and put it up for me last week after I got home from my surgery. The star wasn't right. And since I live by myself, I had to fix it."

"Oh, dear." Emma gave the elderly woman a look.

"Why didn't you call me? Or Karley? We're just down the block."

"Because you're busy, dear." Ms. Lovelace looked at her like it was obvious. "And New York blocks are long. Anyway, I got out my stepladder and climbed up. Almost had it, too, except the tree tipped."

"And you fell." Emma sighed, looking over the chart on her tablet. "You could've injured yourself badly."

"I'm fine." The older woman waved her off. "Only reason I'm here is the fellow who drops off my meals found me and panicked. Apparently, I passed out for a bit."

A bit? Emma read through the story the community center worker had given the EMTs who'd brought Ms. Lovelace in. According to the notes, the older woman had been unconscious for an undetermined amount of time. Not good. Rather than argue with her, though, Emma just nodded, then headed for the door. "All right. Let me find a doctor to examine you. I'll be right back."

By the time she'd corralled a busy resident, then called down both a neurologist and an orthopedic surgeon for consults and ordered all the tests and images both doctors wanted, more than a couple hours had passed. According to the clock on the wall, it was closer to noon now than morning, and Emma was ready for another break to see Thad again and check on Everett. What had happened upstairs earlier had been... amazing. Astounding. Absolutely better than she'd ever imagined things going.

But she was still concerned about pushing him too far, too soon. With the situation with Everett still in the balance, Thad was running on fumes both emotionally and energywise. And sometimes decisions you made and things you said when under duress, you regretted later. She never wanted him to regret anything they'd done or said together, so she'd be patient and wait. Emma was good at waiting.

She finished typing up her notes on Ms. Lovelace's case, then clocked out and headed for the elevators. But when the doors opened, Thad nearly ran her down in his haste to exit.

"Hey," she said, grabbing him by the arm, her stomach plummeting at his harried expression. "What's going on? Is it Everett?"

"Yes," he said, his words falling out in a tumble. "He's awake."

"Oh, Thad!" She threw her arms around him and hugged him tight. Not caring that they were in eyesight of the ER and her nosy coworkers might see. She didn't care what they thought. All she cared about was Thad at that moment. "That's wonderful."

"Yes, it is," he said, holding her tighter for a moment before pulling back. "The neurosurgeon is examining him now, so I thought I'd come tell you."

"I was just on my way up," she said, moving slightly to the side as the other elevator dinged and a couple of techs wheeled off a patient. "Oh, Ms. Lovelace," Emma said. "You remember Dr. Markson?"

"Of course," the older woman said to him. "Back again, just in time for the holidays."

"What happened?" Thad asked, glancing between Emma and the patient. "Not your heart again."

"Nope. Fell off a stepladder," Ms. Lovelace said. At Thad's raised brow she added, "I'm fine. Sore and a bit stiff today. My head hurts, too, but I think I'm okay."

"How about we let the doctors be the judge of that, eh?" Emma shook her head, then chuckled.

"I'm in my eighties, child," the patient scolded

Emma, though there was no sting in it. "I know my own body."

"Hmm." Thad looked her over quickly, then asked, "What day is it?"

"December nineteenth. I know that because I've got gifts being delivered five days from now on Christmas Eve. Had to pay an arm and a leg for them to get there that fast, too, but what are you going to do?"

Thad glanced over at Emma, biting back a smile. Seemed he really was a different man than before. The old Thad would never have smiled in front of a patient. "Very good on the date. You should really be more careful, though, Ms. Lovelace. You're still healing from the surgery I did for you, and at your age one fall could spell disaster. No more ladders."

"I know, I know." She waved him off, too. "But I'm old, Doc. Not dead. I can still do things."

"I'm sure you can. You're tough, Ms. Lovelace. I know that firsthand, but you're not invincible." He winked down at the older woman. "Next time perhaps wait until this Daniel from the community center comes by again, then ask him to help you."

Ms. Lovelace harrumphed. "He only comes three days per week, and I don't have the patience."

"Patience is hard, it's true." Thad leaned a hip on the edge of the patient's bed, catching Emma's gaze once more. "But sometimes, the things we wait longest for are the best ones."

Yes, they are.

Emma cheeks heated and she looked away fast, but not before Ms. Lovelace's shrewd gaze caught her. The older woman glanced between her and Thad, a knowing look in her eyes. "Ah. Right. Yep. Waiting definitely has its benefits. I see your point, Doc, and I promise I'll think about it."

The techs rolled the patient back toward the ER and she and Thad stepped into a private consult room nearby for a moment. Once inside with the door closed behind them, Thad pulled her into his arms again to kiss her, then hold her close. They just stood there, holding each other for a long while. Finally, he pulled away and they sat down at the tiny table for two in there, Emma's heart still spinning from all the new possibilities between her and Thad.

He pulled his chair around in front of her, then sat down, putting them face-to-face. "You look tired."

"Gee, thanks."

"I'm exhausted, too. But you're still beautiful, Emma." His icy blue eyes were now lit with earnest fire. "The most beautiful woman I've ever seen."

Still, she tried to play it off, not used to such blatant compliments. "Stop flattering me."

"Not flattery. Truth." He took her hands in his. "I should probably wait to talk about all this with you, but it feels too important."

"What does?"

"What I'm feeling. What I realized sitting upstairs watching over the man I love like a father and praying he'd survive."

The sincerity in his tone sent ripples of tenderness through her. "You said Everett had woken up. That's a good thing, right? I mean, recovery might take a while but—"

"No, no. I know." He frowned. "I'm very relieved about that, believe me. But there's more. I realized sitting next to his bedside that he's my family, Emma, not my employee. That even though Everett and I are not related by blood, the bond we share is stronger than that. He's been there for me when no one else was."

"Oh." Emma blinked, taking that in, a sharp, unwanted pinch in the center of her chest. She was happy for Thad. She was. Happy that he'd realized that he did have a support system, people who cared for him and would support him, no matter what. That was so important. She had that with Karley, too. But there was still that part of her wishing she and Thad shared those feelings about each other. That it wasn't one-sided on her part. When he'd brought her in here and hugged her, she'd thought maybe he'd confess to wanting that same connection with her, too. Beyond the great sex and the great partnership they had on the project. Still, she didn't want to let her disappointment show. This was a big day for Thad, and he deserved the joy at his discovery. "That's wonderful."

He tilted his head and narrowed his gaze. "But?"

"But nothing," she added with faux cheerfulness. "I'm so glad you found family with Everett. You'll both need to rely on that for the next couple of months as he recovers."

"True." He stroked his thumbs over the inside of her wrists and Emma stifled a shiver. "I was hoping you might help, too."

Right. She was a nurse. She should've expected this. "I'm happy to assist in whatever he needs, Thad. But I might also be busier, too, if I get the promotion I want." Honestly, she hadn't really thought about the new job at all the past few weeks. She'd been so wrapped up with the carnival and with Thad, she'd lost sight of her original goals for taking on the project in the first place. At first, she hadn't cared so much, thinking she was building something more important than a promotion with him. But now, perhaps her decision to put him before her goals had been a mistake. Especially if he was only including her in his future as nursemaid to Everett.

Hollow and hurt, she checked her watch, then stood. "I, uh, I should probably get back to work."

"Emma," Thad said, holding on tight to her hands and shaking his head fiercely. "Please, don't go. I know I'm not handling this right at all. Saying all the wrong things at the wrong time instead of what I really feel. But all of this is new to me. No excuse, but it's the truth."

Suffering emotional whiplash and her lack of sleep and stress catching up with her, Emma's patience snapped its tether. She slumped back down in her chair, exasperated. "Oh, Thad. Just say it already. You know me. I won't judge you or berate you or whatever else you fear might happen. After all we've been through here, can't you trust me now?"

"I'm trying," he said, scowling down at their joined hands. "But I'm so used to protecting myself, to not being vulnerable. Trust is hard. But I realize I've been living on autopilot. Not really living at all. And life is so short. What happened with Everett drove that home for me. I've been so wrapped up in my past and my pain and my career that I missed so much." He looked up at her then and cupped her cheek. "So wrapped up that I almost missed the best thing that ever happened to me."

Emma struggled to understand what he was saying, her pulse racing harder than Santa's reindeer. "I care about you, too, Thad. I hope I've shown that over the past few weeks. I told you I wanted to continue seeing you after the project was over, but you shut me down." Despite her wishes, tears ran down her cheeks and she wiped them away with his thumb. "I can't do this alone,

Thad. Relationships needs trust. And they need two people who are committed to making them work. I'm there, but only if you're fully there with me. Otherwise, I can't." She sat back, needing to get this out before she couldn't. "You think you're the only one who's scared here? I've lost people in my life, too, Thad. You know that. And while I've coped differently with it than you have, I really don't want to lose anyone else I care about, including you. But I will, if you're not ready to do this thing with me. Because it's going to take both of us putting one hundred percent into making it work. All day, every day. Rain or shine. Are you willing to do that, Thad? If not, please respect me enough to tell me."

He took a deep breath, hesitating, then nodded. "Yes, Emma. I'm ready. I'm terrified, but I'm willing to do whatever it takes to make this work because if feels too precious not to." He leaned his forehead against hers. "I have that same wobbly, shaking feeling I did that first night in my kitchen." At her worried look, he laughed. "I'm not hypoglycemic now though, I promise. One of the nurses upstairs brought me a meal and made sure I ate it all. My blood sugar is fine." He inhaled deep through his nose and his gaze turned serious. "This time it's all because of you, Emma. In the short time I've known you, you've taken everything I thought I knew, everything I thought I was, and turned it on its head. With you, all bets are off. My filters are gone. I feel things, say and do things before my logical brain can react. I lose control around you, and I like it." He kissed her gently. "I want to keep feeling this with you for as long as you'll have me. It's far too soon to tell where this will end up, but for now, I want you to know, Emma Trudeau, that I care about you very much, and I'd like to date you."

She bit her lip, then burst into happy tears. "You silly, silly man. I care about you, too. And yes. I will date you."

"Good. That's settled then." Thad kissed and hugged her, and her tension dissipated under the flood of relief in her body. He'd taken a chance with her, and she couldn't have asked for more. In fact, she didn't want to ask for more. Not yet, anyway. Because sometimes the very best things came from the most unexpected places.

CHAPTER ELEVEN

ON CHRISTMAS EVE, just after sunset, Emma and Thad walked into the arena of Madison Square Garden and entered a dazzling, enchanted winter wonderland. The carnival vendors and ride owners had worked with the arena staff to pull off an incredible feat of both engineering and magic. From the Ferris wheel and the carousel they'd set up inside the space, to the snow falling gently around them from the artificial snow makers perched in the rafters, it was amazing. Most spectacular was the fact that it was all accessible to every one of the children, regardless of their situation.

"We did it," Emma whispered to Thad as they stood near the edge of the festivities, watching as the families of the PICU patients from around the city made their way around the carnival.

"Yes, we did." He kissed her sweetly, his hand atop hers on his forearm. Thad still couldn't quite believe that he'd finally, after all these years, done something to prove he was worth something outside of his surgical skills. They'd made little Ricky's wish come true, because of all the hard work and effort of the woman beside him. The same woman he now got to call his girlfriend. There'd been so many lonely nights where he'd stood at the window in his office, watching life pass him by, fearing he'd never be a part of it. Not knowing how to be a part of it. But Emma had shown him the way. She'd given him a path to return to life. And that was a gift he could never repay.

"Look over there," she said, pointing at two giant snowmen near the carousel, greeting the riders as they waited for their turn. "Did you hire them?"

"I did." He grinned. "Well, actually my foundation did, since I've been busy with surgeries all week. But I gave them carte blanche to get the very best the city had to offer."

"Nice." They began walking the circuit around the carnival, nodding to families as they passed. Near the center of the enormous arena floor, a small ice rink had been set up as well for the kids to enjoy. Enough snow had fallen now, too, that people were making snowballs and snow angels. Thad had worried it would be a mess to clean up afterward, but the staff had assured him it was not a problem.

As they neared the carousel area, tinkling Christmas tunes drifted their way and they stopped in front of it to watch and listen. It was a beautiful piece of early twentieth-century art, with the carved wooden horses painted in bright, vivid colors, with polished gilded poles. Interspersed with the ponies were winter carriages and sleds large enough for wheelchairs.

"It's so beautiful," Emma gasped, clapping her hands. "We should ride it later."

Thad wrapped his arms around her waist and pulled her back into him, resting his chin atop her head. "We should. Do you think the carnival turned out well?"

She turned to gaze at him. "I think it turned out perfect. Thank you for helping me."

His pulse skyrocketed at the words, and he swallowed hard. "No, Emma. Thank you. This was all you from start to finish. I just got the venue."

Even with all his epiphanies and moves forward in his private life, coming here tonight had been a bit of a struggle, he wasn't going to lie. Socializing with so many people was a lot for him, but he refused to let Ricky and his parents down and he'd summoned his courage. Because with Emma by his side, he could do anything.

Eventually, they continued on around the arena floor, stopping at vendor booths to buy hot chocolates or check out the items they had for sale. Emma even won a stuffed dog at one of the games. Thad did his best to soak up all the sights and sounds of childhood heaven he'd been denied as a kid. The scents of cotton candy, hot dogs, popcorn and fried doughnuts. The colorful game booths showing off huge silly toys for prizes. Music blasting through the speakers, and his eyes dazzling with the blinking array of rides and ornaments and tinsel for the season. Delight and satisfaction swelled inside him.

We did this. Together.

His only regret was that Everett wasn't here to enjoy it with them. But he was doing better, awake and alert and even speaking again, though with a slight slur. The doctors expected him to make a full recovery in time, with help and lots of rehab. Thad intended to be by the man's side for all of it.

"Oh, look who's over there." Emma pointed. "Dr. Franklin and Jane Ayashi from HR. And they're with Ricky Lynch and his family. We should go say hello."

She tugged on his hand but for a moment Thad couldn't move, couldn't breathe, as a long-forgotten memory rushed back. His mother had brought him to a carnival like this as a small boy, before everything had gone sideways in his life. They'd had such fun, just him and his mother, and if he listened closely, he swore he heard the lilt of his mother's laughter on the air, like a sign he was on the right path now. For himself and for the future. Thad closed his eyes and said a silent thanks to his mother, or fate, or whoever had brought Emma into his life. She'd given him back his heart. His soul. She meant everything to him.

"Well, well," Dr. Franklin said as they approached. "You both pulled it off. Congratulations."

"Thank you," Emma said, squeezing Thad's hand. "We make a pretty good team. Just like I thought."

"Hmm." Dr. Franklin nodded at Thad. "I never knew you had it in you, Dr. Markson."

"That makes two of us," Thad joked, and they all laughed.

"It really is amazing." Jane Ayashi beamed, looking around at it all. "Can't imagine what it took for the two of you to pull this off so quickly."

"Elbow grease," Emma said, winking at Thad. "And a whole lot of trust."

"Exactly." Thad kissed Emma's mittened knuckles, ignoring the looks of their two colleagues.

"Dr. Markson, how is your friend in the ICU?" Dr. Franklin asked. "I heard it was thanks to your and Nurse Trudeau's quick reactions that he's still alive."

"Yes." Thad straightened, taking a deep breath. "Everett's awake and alert and from the last report I got earlier from his neurosurgeon, he should make a full recovery. I plan to move him out of Manhattan West as soon as he's ready and set up a private rehab unit in my town house for him."

Before anyone could ask more questions, a small, excited voice broke into their conversation.

"Dr. Markson!" Ricky Lynch yelled, running up with his parents. For someone so sick, Thad was astounded at the kid's energy. Then again, it was a magical night, and this carnival was proof miracles could happen, if you just believed enough. Ricky hugged Thad first, then Emma, his pale cheeks flushed with excitement. "Thank you, thank you for my wish. It's more than I ever imagined."

"You're welcome, Ricky." Thad patted the boy's back, then straightened to shake his parents' hands. "And it's good to finally meet you, Mr. and Mrs. Lynch."

"Same," Ricky's dad said, shaking Thad's hand, then putting his arm back around his wife's shoulders. "Our son was just enrolled in a new clinical trial for his specific type of brain cancer. The results have been incredible and we're feeling hopeful. Several kids with the same type of tumor as our son have gone into full remission, so we're cautiously optimistic."

"The best kind of optimism to have." Thad smiled. He was still attempting to go full optimist like Emma, but some days were easier than others. "I've read the findings of the study you're talking about, and I think it's great you got Ricky a spot in the trials. He will hopefully do very well."

The clinical trial was the result of more than thirty years of research and used a viral immunotherapy injected directly into the patient's tumor, causing their own immune system to attack and destroy the cancer itself, without the use of harmful chemotherapy drugs. So far, they had a 90 percent response rate in pediatric patients with the same form of brain tumor as Ricky had, and the overall survival rate of the children in the study had more than doubled.

"And how do you feel about the trial, Ricky?" Emma asked, crouching to put herself at eye level while still holding Thad's hand.

"I'm just glad my parents aren't so worried anymore." Ricky glanced up at his mom and dad, who were smiling and looked happy. "I try to tell them that I'll be okay no matter what, but then they cry, so…" He shrugged, his knit hat crooked on his bald head. "Anyway, I don't want to talk about that stuff. Tonight's all about fun!" He hugged Emma around the neck, then pointed at a nearby booth. "Can we get some cotton candy, please? And then I want to go on the Ferris wheel with all my friends from the PICU. This is the best night of my life!"

He ran off to play with his friends and Emma straightened, sliding her arm around Thad's waist and hugging him tight. "We're both really thrilled for you and Ricky with the new trial. He's a strong kid with a great attitude. That will take him far in life."

"Thanks," Ricky's mom said. "We hope so. And thank you both again for all of this. It's such a blessing to us and to all the other families of sick children here tonight. It helps take them away from their problems for a little while. And that's such an important thing. You really have given us all the merriest of holidays."

They spent the rest of the evening walking around the carnival they'd created greeting guests. shaking hands and treating each family like they were the most important people on the planet. Emma still had to pinch herself every so often to make sure all of this, and Thad, were real. There'd been such a transformation in her life in such a short time. Her life before him hadn't been bad at all. She'd had her work and her sister and plans for the future. But now she could see how much better it all was with Thad in their lives. It had nothing to do with his money and everything to do with the amazing person he was inside.

And speaking of amazing…

People continued to approach them as one group of families left and another arrived. Grateful families continued to thank them personally and Thad pushed further and further beyond his boundaries and his Grinch-like past to blossom before her eyes, chatting and playing with the kids, even picking some of the smaller ones up—with their parents' permission—to give them a friendly cuddle. He spent time discussing each child's condition with their parents and even offering information about medical studies he'd seen or giving them names of experts to contact about this or that. All trace of his previous coldness and awkwardness seemed to have vanished. Even with his colleagues he was more open and friendly. And when Emma's sister Karley showed up with a couple of her school friends, Thad greeted them with the same enthusiasm he had the other kids, talking and even cracking a couple of jokes. Emma was impressed. And more than a little smitten with her newfound ho-ho-holiday hunk. As Thad walked Karley's friend over to one of the game vendors, Karley sidled up to her sister.

"I like him," her sister said. "And I can tell you do."

"I do," Emma agreed, any denials about her feelings for Thad way behind her. She wasn't quite ready to say the L-word yet, but things here definitely headed that way. "I really, really do."

"Good. I'm glad."

"You are?"

"Yes. I didn't want you to be alone when I go off to Howard next fall. Now you won't be."

"You sound awfully sure about yourself." Emma nudged her sister with her shoulder as they stood side by side watching Thad. "It's not like we're committed or anything."

Karley scoffed. "Girl. I see how he looks at you. And that man adores you. He's not going anywhere."

"You think?" Heat prickled Emma's cheeks despite the snow still falling around them.

"I know. Maybe you should take him to Green-Wood. Meet the parents, after the holidays." Karley winked, then pulled away from her sister. "I'll go rescue him from my friends and send him back. Have fun tonight."

"You, too!" Emma called, feeling so blessed to have such a wonderful sister. She took a seat at a nearby table to wait for Thad's return. She should take Thad to the cemetery. It was a special place to her, and she wanted to share it with him. In fact, she'd ask him about it later, after they got home. They could write their secrets and add them to the collection. Hers? Well, she'd met her Prince Charming, disguised as a Grinch, and won him for her very own. Not such a secret, maybe, but still the one that made her heart sing this Christmas.

Woof!

"What the—" Emma barely had time to turn around before a familiar black Lab ran up out of nowhere to put his paws on her jeans-covered knees, his tongue lolling out of the side of his mouth. She laughed and scratched the dog behind the ears. "Hello there, Baxter. How'd you get here?"

"I had someone from the foundation staff stop by the town house to bring him," Thad said, strolling up to her table. "He could use the exercise and since I'll miss his nightly walk, I figured this would be as good a place as any for him to run around. Plus, the kids seem to love him."

"Of course they do," Emma said, snuffling his adorable doggy face. Usually it was verboten to distract a service dog from his work, but Baxter was off-duty tonight and it was Christmas Eve. He deserved a little fun, too. "Who's a good boy, huh? I think you are. Yes, I do. Aren't you, Baxter?"

"Having a good time?" Thad asked, straddling the bench on the other side of the table.

"The best time." She grinned over at him. "We should grab a couple extra hot dogs from the vendor over there for a treat for Baxter. If that's okay with you?"

She glanced over at Thad then, only to find him watching her. She wanted to ask him what he was thinking, but then Ricky Lynch and his parents walked by their table again. They were on their way from the carousel to the Ferris wheel, and she'd never seen the boy look happier. As they passed, Baxter pulled at his leash until Thad nodded and Emma let the dog go and run up to the boy, licking and nudging Ricky, who laughed and laughed until Thad finally collected the dog and brought him back to their table.

The rest of the night passed in a blur for Emma, caught up in more people wanting to thank her and Thad, or pet Baxter. It seemed like she'd talked to more people that night than she had in all her years in the ER. And not one person commented on Thad's old reputation as a Grinch. Nope. It seemed that had disappeared as quickly as footprints in the falling snow.

And when it was all over and only Thad and Emma

were left in the arena as the vendors tore down their booths and carnival rides, Thad held out his hand. "Emma, would you ride the carousel with me?"

Heart swelling with joy, she gave him a dazzling smile. "Yes, of course."

He escorted her to the now-empty pavilion and claimed one of the carriages, large enough for both of them and Baxter. They rode around and around, holding hands and laughing, same as the kids had done earlier, as the dog barked happily.

When their magical ride ended, he leaned in to kiss her, whispering, "I'm so glad I found you, Emma Trudeau. I can't imagine my life without you now."

She blinked hard against her tears of happiness. "Me, too, Thad. Me, too."

They kissed, sweet and deep, before he pulled back slightly to say against her lips, "Should I buy this for the gardens in back of the town house?"

Emma laughed with delight. "Nah. Let's wait until Everett's better, then we can all celebrate together."

"Deal." Thad grinned, then kissed her again.

EPILOGUE

Early Christmas Day, one year later

AT THE SOUND of Emma's voice echoing up from the foyer downstairs, Thad turned from where he was working in his study. It was only 6:00 a.m. Emma never got up that early on her days off. Dammit, he wasn't done with what he was working on yet.

Still, he finished pulling on his Santa suit with Everett's help, then looked at himself in the mirror.

"Wish me luck," he said to his old friend. The man was improving every day and could now walk and talk and even carry out most of his butler duties the same as before. But Thad made it a point not to overwork the man anymore. Everett was no longer an employee. He was a treasured member of Thad's found family and was treated as such.

The older man shook his head as he met Thad's gaze in the mirror. "None needed. Go get her."

Nerves on high alert, Thad went downstairs, waiting until he got to the first floor before uttering a somewhat subdued, "Ho, ho, ho!"

He felt ridiculous, but if it made his Emma smile, it was worth it.

"You know my sister's still sleeping, right?" She eyed

him up and down from where she sat in the living room, her arms crossed over her red plaid flannel pj's and her baby bump showing ever so slightly beneath. "And what are you wearing?"

"I'm Santa," Thad said, adjusting the velvet bag over his shoulder. "And I'm doing my job. Delivering gifts. And yes, I know Karley's still asleep." She'd moved into the town house along with Emma. The sisters were a package deal, he'd learned. Now Karley stayed here whenever she wasn't at Howard University pursuing her premed degree.

Thad walked past Emma into the living room on the first floor to deposit his presents. Lots and lots of presents. Packages of various shapes and sizes, all brightly wrapped and now overflowing beneath the tree. It had cost him a small fortune to hire personal shoppers to scour the stores of New York to find everything on the list Emma had given him last month, but if you were willing to spend enough, a person could do most anything. And he was counting on her sister staying asleep for a good long while yet.

"Why would you do that?" She stood in the doorway, staring at him and looking befuddled. "You don't even like Christmas."

"Maybe I've changed my mind." He scanned the gifts, then frowned as "White Christmas" played on the town house's sound system for the millionth time. Okay. Perhaps he'd become overzealous when he'd turned on the Christmas tunes. And with the gifts. And the decorations. But hey. He had a lot of time to make up for. Thad straightened then, set his empty bag aside and shrugged. "Women aren't the only ones allowed to change their minds. Apparently I just needed to be reminded of the real meaning of the holiday."

"Oh, you needed that all right," she scoffed, eyeing him suspiciously. "You changed your mind about Christmas, huh? Why?"

"You."

"Me?" This time she laughed with a great deal of irony. "I changed your mind about Christmas?"

"You changed my mind about everything, Emma. About life. My life. And the life I want with you."

"Aw. That's sweet." She crossed the room to stand next to him, staring at the tree. "But why now?"

"Because now I'm sure I'm ready to move on to the future. With you. And our little one."

She placed a hand over her stomach and smiled. "That is a pretty good reason."

He put his arm around her and drew her into his side. "Someone once told me Christmas Day was the most magical day of the year. A day when miracles can happen." He kissed her temple, then tucked her head beneath his chin. That Christmas magic had surely shone down on him last year. Brought him the gift of a new lease on life, a woman he loved, and a new, found family of his own. A future he never could have imagined before, too. "I love you, Emma. And I plan to spend the rest of my life proving to you how much. You and our baby. Every single day."

He'd been so miserable before she'd arrived in his life. A fool. He'd pushed everyone away out of fear. Fear of feeling again. Fear of loving and losing. Fear of feeling, because with feeling came the risk of pain.

But you had to overcome those fears, had to risk that pain, had to risk rejection, because the alternative wasn't acceptable. He took her hand and pulled a small blue box from the pocket of his Santa suit. This one didn't go beneath the tree, because if all went well, it would end up on her finger.

He got down on one knee and Emma put a trembling hand to her mouth. "What are you doing?"

"I've loved you from the first moment I saw you here in my kitchen, looking like an angel, Emma. And I want you by my side for as long as you'll have me. Please give me the chance to be the man you deserve." He swallowed hard and opened the box to reveal the sparkling diamond-and-platinum engagement ring. "Will you marry me?"

Tears trickled from her lovely eyes as she nodded. "Yes, Thad. I will marry you. I love you, too."

He slid the ring onto her finger, then stood to take her into his arms and kiss her soundly.

Emma didn't think she'd ever seen so many presents in her life.

Sitting on the floor, she picked up a box, shook it prior to carefully unwrapping it to reveal a beautiful aqua-colored baby blanket. He'd bought gifts for their baby. And now she was crying all over again. Running her fingers over the soft fuzzy material. "This is so beautiful."

"I'm glad you like it." He handed her another box. They repeated the process until she was surrounded with baby items. Some pink. Some blue. Some a mixture of pastels. They didn't know what they were having, wanting to be surprised for the first one.

Karley and Everett were in the dining room, playing a spirited game of Scrabble, and Baxter was happily enjoying his new toys in the corner. Their little family was happy and content.

"Wow. You've been busy." Emma bit her lip, taking it all in. "When did you have time to shop?"

"I had help, but don't hold that against me." He glanced at the two in the dining room, then gave a crooked grin. "Even Santa utilizes elves."

"Uh-huh," she said, knowing her sister and Everett had probably shopped for most of this, given her fiancé's busy work schedule these days. He was still as in demand as ever, though he'd cut back considerably on his hours, preferring to spend more time at home when he could. Still, it was sweet he'd thought of her and the baby and she loved all the gifts she'd gotten, even if she did feel bigger and more awkward each passing day. "Thank you, sweetie. I love everything."

Emma met his gaze and her breath caught at the intensity there, the vulnerability in his icy blue eyes. No protective walls. No barriers. Those were gone now, leaving only the man she loved with all her heart.

The music changed to "Have Yourself a Merry Little Christmas." Their song, the one they'd danced to last year at the fundraiser for the first time. Then it had been bittersweet for her. Now it was all goodness and light. Because this year, they would have a merry little Christmas. Together.

Thad held her close as they swayed slowly, his gaze reflecting back to her the same emotions she felt inside—love, gratitude, affection, desire. "I didn't think I'd ever feel this way about another person, Emma. Sometimes I wondered if I could love someone at all. But I do love you, my darling. More than I could ever say. Always and forever. And I can't wait to meet our baby."

"I love you, too." She wrapped her arms around him and kissed him, pulling back to laugh when their baby kicked hard between them. "I'd say our child shares our sentiments."

"Agreed." Thad grinned. "Merry Christmas, wife-to-be."

"Merry Christmas, husband-to-be," she said, cuddling into him again as the music switched to "It's the Most Wonderful Time of the Year." Corny, absolutely. But as Andy Williams warbled away in the background, Emma also knew it was true. This holiday was wonderful. The best ever for her. Knowing no matter what the future held, she and Thad and their family would face it together, for the rest of their lives.

* * * * *

THE PRINCE'S
ONE-NIGHT BABY

JULIETTE HYLAND

MILLS & BOON

For my sister…because she said I had to!

CHAPTER ONE

Dr. Kostas Drakos slid into his first-class seat and immediately put on his headphones. The first leg of his journey from Washington State to his home island of Palaío was almost six hours, and he had no desire to spend any of it talking to a stranger. He had almost twenty-four hours' worth of flights before he got home. Twenty-four hours before Dr. Kostas Drakos reverted from obstetrician to prince. A day before the man he'd become over the last twelve years was thrust back into the royal spotlight full-time.

He pulled up his phone and reread the email from his brother. Ioannis had asked him to return following the retirement of the capital's primary obstetrician. Another might have been able to refuse, but Ioannis wasn't really asking. It was a brother's question couched to hide the summons from the king.

When Ioannis had taken the throne last year, Kostas had returned to the island only long enough to fulfill his sanctioned duties. His brother's son already three, Kostas was currently second in line to the throne. Ioannis's delightful wife, Queen Eleni, was pregnant, and he suspected he'd fall several more spots given the love between Eleni and Ioannis on display for the entire country to see whenever they were ever together.

And that was fine with Kostas.

However, his distance from the crown did not mean he didn't have obligations, as Ioannis's request had gently reminded him. Rolling his shoulders, Kostas tried to get comfortable, though he doubted it was possible, no matter how nice the first-class area was. He was returning to Palaío…returning to the palace…and to the press.

That he'd never sit on the throne hadn't stopped the island's press outlets from speculating about his princess prospects. They'd run headlines for his entire trip about the Prodigal Prince and whether he was finally home to choose a bride. Only his brother's coronation had briefly kicked his name from the front page.

His brother was Palaío's golden child, put on an elevated pedestal at birth. Kostas…well, Kostas was less respected.

Eleni had offered to introduce him to one of her friends so he wouldn't have to attend the coronation alone. She'd told Kostas that the woman was kind and understood that he wasn't staying. No need to worry about a long-term connection.

It had been thoughtful, but there were no short connections with a royal. Royal life had destroyed his mother, and it had burned the one girl he'd gotten attached to as a teenager. Both had left the island following the press's sensational lies.

As the prince, the one born into the family, the press often speculated but kept their cruelest words couched in flowery language. To the best of his knowledge, the one time his teenage love, Maria, had come home, the reporters had met her at the airport. A simple visit to her parents a decade after their connection had resulted in questions about their supposed teenage pregnancy and loss. It was a salacious rumor, made up by a jealous acquaintance, that the media had devoured. He'd been raised to expect his life to belong to the public, but Maria had simply made the mistake of thinking a young prince was cute.

And it had nearly ruined her life.

Kostas had no intention of putting another person in the same position.

When he was on Palaío, he was Prince Kostas. The rebel son, who'd really just wanted to be a regular teen, but they'd thrust microphones in his face and he'd said terse things about his father, about wanting to leave the island, about hating being royal. It had made headlines on the usually quiet island, which meant that his life wasn't truly his. He'd never inherit the throne but he'd always be royal, and that also meant that if he fell in love, the woman would stand beside him in the gilded cage.

He'd serve the clinic for a while, find a new obstetrician, and then head back to Seattle. A year, no more, on the island was all he needed.

A hand touched his shoulder and Kostas jumped, his headphones sliding. He looked up to find a dark-haired beauty staring at him. Her hazel eyes captured his as she held his gaze.

"Can I help you?" The woman was stunning, but she seemed out of place. Her patched-up backpack, her jeans and oversized sweatshirt were not the designer styles he typically saw in first class. *Have I been recognized?*

British royalty fascinated Americans, but they rarely recognized royals from other countries. Still, occasionally someone would know him, and a few women had foolishly hoped the connection might lead to a fantasy ending.

But real royal life wasn't the stuff of television movies. Happily-ever-afters were for other people.

"Um…" She looked at her ticket then up at the seat numbers and back at him, color tinging her cheeks as she bit her lip. "I think you might be in my seat."

"What?" Kostas reached into his back pocket as he saw the flight attendant start toward him.

"I'm 2F, or at least I think I am." She bit her lip, her eyes darting to the flight attendant.

He could see concern floating through her. *Great, a nervous flier.* Hopefully, she'd be all right for their long flight. He didn't really want to deal with the questions and concerns that sometimes came from individuals who rarely took to the skies. It was selfish, he knew it, but Kostas was trying to prep himself for stepping off the plane in Palaío.

"Is there a problem?" The attendant smiled at Kostas as she looked at the woman standing in the aisle, not trying to hide the judgment in her eyes. She saw what Kostas did: a woman out of place.

And they were both assessing her.

Kostas mentally kicked himself. He wasn't in Palaío yet. There was really no reason for his suspicions.

"I…" She looked down at her ticket and then back at the numbers above.

Kostas looked at his ticket and wanted to kick himself even harder. He was in her seat. "No. There isn't a problem. I wasn't paying attention. I'm in 2D not 2F."

He started to stand when the woman held up her hand. "You can stay there. It's okay. Unless you want to move?"

"Can I see your ticket, ma'am?" The flight attendant took a quick look and nodded. "You a standby?"

"Yep," the woman responded, her tone overly bubbly, the kind he heard some of his nurses use when they were trying to put their patients at ease. "Weather canceled my flight, and they told me I could head to New York tomorrow or try to get on tonight as a standby—" She cut her words off and slid into the seat as the attendant wandered off to continue getting ready for takeoff.

Kostas nodded and slid his headphones back on.

"Should have worn something besides the old sweatshirt and comfy jeans, Calla. Maybe then you'd look like you belonged in first class."

The whispered words weren't meant for him. He was sure Calla had assumed he had music or something playing in his headphones. But Kostas had caused the incident that had made her so uncomfortable.

Pulling his headphones off, he turned. First-class seats had more room than business or coach, but he was still uncomfortably close to the woman next to him. She had her eyes closed, and a few tears ran under her glasses and down her cheek, over the freckles dotting her nose.

"I'm sorry." Kostas kept his voice quiet. She was upset, and he knew that when he was upset, the last thing he wanted was an audience. "I am going home. My family's expectations…well, I am a little tense about returning to prying eyes. I took that annoyance out on you. Which is more than a little unfair. There is nothing wrong with how you look."

She wiped her hand across her cheek and offered him a smile. "You're headed home and I'm leaving mine." She sucked in a deep breath. "Which is the reason for the tears. Not the flight attendant or you thinking I didn't belong in first class. Tonight is hardly the first time someone has judged me."

There was a story there, but not one that two perfect strangers shared.

"But thank you for apologizing." She offered him a smile then turned her head toward the flight attendant as she started giving the mandatory safety instructions.

His seatmate clearly wasn't expecting any further conversation, which wasn't surprising given his initial rudeness and headphones. He typically hated flying with a chatty seat neighbor, but he wanted to know more about the woman beside him.

Maybe it was her statement about being judged; he understood that better than most. It was a driving need he couldn't explain. "I'm Kostas. Will you be away from home for long?"

Her hazel eyes studied him and she looked like she was weighing her answer. A skill he'd developed while living in the royal household, though he wondered where she might have learned it and if it was part of the judgment she'd experienced.

"Calla Lewis," she sighed, shrugging as she pulled her legs into her lap.

He was a little jealous that she could adjust her frame in the uncomfortable seat. At six feet five inches, even the legroom in first class was a tight fit.

"I took rotation assignment for a year. I'm a replacement for a woman on maternity leave." Calla pursed her lips, "Anyways...hopefully, I'll be back after that. But life—" She blew out a breath and pushed a strand of hair that had escaped her messy bun out of her eye. "Life has a way of changing any carefully made plans. At least, in my experience."

"Mine too." He laughed.

Calla let out a soft chuckle. "The best laid plans are no match for life's chaos." The plane started forward and she leaned a little closer. "Would you mind if I looked out the window? I've never left Seattle."

"Of course." Kostas wished they could switch seats now. Wished he'd not taken the easy answer of staying in place during their awkward exchange. But they couldn't switch while the plane was taking off.

She leaned across him and energy seemed to race across his skin as her light scent invaded his nose. He took a deep breath, trying to control the unusual response. He didn't react...especially to strangers.

"No way to do this without invading your personal space." Calla smiled as she glanced at him yet he could see the unshed tears in her eyes.

She was a stranger, but he'd left home before. Fled was a more accurate term. He remembered the mixture of excitement, dread and homesickness that had accompanied that first flight. "What's your favorite thing about Seattle?"

"The rain." She put her hand over her mouth as the lights of the city became smaller. Then the entire landscape disappeared below the clouds.

Calla leaned back in her seat, though she kept her body shifted toward him. "I love the rain. I know people come from elsewhere who complain that it feels like it's always raining—which it's not."

"But it happens enough to feel like it's always." Kostas grinned.

"Statistically, we get less rain than much of the US. It just happens on more days than most places."

He laughed and leaned a little closer. Discussing rain shouldn't be invigorating, but he enjoyed seeing the hint of fire in Calla's eyes. "That sounds like something only someone born in Seattle would brag about. There is moss growing on the buildings."

Calla opened her mouth but instead of defending her home city, she clicked her tongue and pointed to him. "I supposed you're headed some place sunny and warm."

"Sunnier and warmer than Seattle. But that is a low bar to climb over." He winked, answering the question, but not directly. He loved the island of Palaío, but he didn't want to talk about home. Didn't want to think of the responsibilities waiting for him.

"Is New York your final destination?"

If Calla noticed him shifting the topic away from himself, she didn't acknowledge it. Instead, she shook her head and yawned. "No. Though part of me wishes it was. It's the first stop in my four layovers. From New York to London and then on to progressively tinier airports."

"New York to Paris for me. Then on to one tiny airport and a ship."

"Adventure!" Calla smiled, but he could see the worry in her eyes as she looked toward the window. Seattle was far behind them; with the speed of the airplane, they were likely two-thirds across the state by now.

The airplane shook and Calla grabbed his hand. Her cheeks colored as she immediately pulled back. "Oh, my. Sorry. I… I have clearly never been on a plane."

His fingers ached to take her hand back. To touch her. It was such a dangerous thought. He didn't know Calla, and their paths were only passing on this one flight, but part of him felt like he should want to know her. Should want to hold her hand. It was an uncomfortable sensation, but one he didn't want to push away.

"I don't mind." He put his hand on the shared armrest and winked. "It's here in case you need it. But I hope the plane doesn't experience any real turbulence."

"Have you ever experienced that?" She twitched her nose before hitting her palm against her head. "Chalk that up as questions a nervous flier shouldn't ask their seatmate. Especially since there is no chance we will be on the same flight once we hit our destination."

She pursed her lips as she shifted in the chair. "Though even if we were on the same plane, we wouldn't be seatmates since I am very much flying coach the rest of the way. But this is nice!"

It was nice. He knew she meant the extra legroom and quick service. But he'd flown around the world since he was a small boy, and Kostas had never had such a fun experience. She let out another yawn and he knew their banter was ending.

That was the problem with red-eye flights. This one was supposed to land in New York at four in the morning. His plane left for Paris at six and he'd never see the woman next to him again.

A touch of sadness ran through him as she covered her mouth for her third yawn in less than five minutes. He reached up and flipped off the small reading lights above them. "You should get some rest. You'll be exhausted with all the travel, but sleeping now will help with the transition. Trust me."

"Well, you seem to be a travel expert...or as close to one as I can ask now. Thanks for making me feel better, Kostas. The last year..." She paused as she looked at the window before letting her eyes wander to his in the darkened cabin. "It's been rough. Anyways... thanks, again."

"Anytime." It was a phrase so many people threw away. A conversation rejoinder that really meant nothing. But for the first time in forever, Kostas wished it truly meant that she could reach out to him anytime. That they had a connection.

Clearly, his nerves were more frayed at the thought of returning home than he wanted to admit. But at least Calla had given him a few minutes of relief.

Midwife Calla Lewis was tired, but she didn't think she could sleep. The exhaustion floating through her body refused to take over her brain's wanderings. She was really on the first leg of her twenty-four-hour-plus journey to the small island off the coast of Greece.

When she'd first talked to the recruiter for her international travel nursing program, Calla hadn't really expected it to lead anywhere. It was just one of the many options she'd explored to pay off her debt as fast as possible. But then the recruiter had let her know there was an opportunity on the small island nation of Palaío; one of their midwives was on her twelve-month maternity leave. It was a posting that came with a furnished apartment and an excellent salary to compete with the international shortage of nurses.

She'd been warned that the clinic was going through some changes. The main doctor was retiring after serving nearly sixty years, according to the recruiter, and there were only two other midwives plus a traveling OBGYN.

The island community was small, but the women deserved the safest option when they were delivering. And the king of Palaío was determined to recruit the best for his subjects with the understanding that the nurse she would be replacing planned to return from maternity leave. It was a year rotation with the opportunity to stay on, if the clinic needed it. But one year was all she needed. One year to get back on her feet.

Calla still couldn't wrap her mind around the fact that the king of Palaío was taking such a close interest in the clinic. He'd not been able to attend the interview panel that had met with her and the agency representative, yet had sent along his apologies. It was a little overwhelming.

But overwhelming didn't really matter. She owed Liam almost forty thousand dollars.

Liam.

In another world, today she was supposed to be honeymooning in Jamaica. She pinched her eyes, as if she closed them tighter the memories would float away. Her thumb wandered to the missing ring on her left finger.

It had been gone for almost a year. At first, she couldn't believe that after five years together, after planning a life, after supporting each other…after she'd done everything he'd asked of her to impress his impossible parents, he'd still chosen his family money over her. Then demanded she repay the "loan" he'd given her for her masters in midwifery program. *Loan…*

She hadn't asked him to pay off her student loan. He'd done it because his parents had already thought she wasn't good enough for their son. It had taken her three months after her broken engagement to realize that Liam had never thought she was good enough for him, either.

That stung. Not that her ex was a jerk, but that she'd let him control her. Done her best to fit the mold he'd wanted. Dyed her hair when he'd said he preferred blond, dressed the way he and his parents preferred. The only thing she hadn't done was give up her career.

And that had been the deal breaker. That was fine,

but asking for repayment on what he'd called a gift was the reason she was on this plane. The reason she was traveling thousands of miles away from the only place she'd known.

The salary included room and board. With any luck and some thriftiness, she'd repay him and have her life back on track by the end of the contract.

The plane shuddered again and Calla almost reached for Kostas's hand. She wanted to, so badly. He'd offered, and she'd thought the offer was genuine, but then, it had taken her over five years to realize who Liam was. She wasn't sure she could trust her gut anymore.

Luckily, the plane stopped its tremors after a few seconds. It was just the normal bumps that, supposedly, accompanied air travel. With any luck, by the time she landed in Palaío, she'd feel like a true travel veteran. But she doubted it.

She yawned again and shifted in her seat. Her shoulder connected with Kostas's and her body heated at the simple touch. That was the thing she missed the most about being in a relationship. The little touches.

Hand-holding, hugs after a rough day, bumping another's hip at a joke, falling asleep on someone's shoulder. It had been a year since she'd shared those simple pleasures. A year of loneliness.

Still, she'd take lonely to the control she'd let Liam exercise over her. Every single day for the rest of her life, if necessary. Calla liked who she was, and she wasn't changing for someone again.

She yawned for what felt like the hundredth time since she'd stepped onto the plane, but her brain finally drifted away. She sighed as her body slowly lost its fight against exhaustion.

* * *

It didn't feel like she'd been asleep for long when the pillow under her shifted and her lopsided glasses dug into her cheek. It took a moment to realize that she didn't have a pillow and for mortification to creep up her spine as Kostas moved beside her.

Dear God. She'd fallen asleep on his shoulder. The man was gorgeous. Tall, with dark, curly hair and a five-o'clock shadow. He wore slacks and a loose shirt that screamed designer goods. A model compared to her sloppy travel gear. And she'd fallen asleep on him!

"I'm sorry to wake you. They've put out a request for a doctor." Kostas's voice was warm as he hit the button to call the flight attendant.

"No. I'm sorry. I didn't—" She stopped as the flight attendant stepped up beside them.

"Are you a medical professional?"

"I'm an obstetrician."

The response sent the final fog of sleepiness from Calla's brain as she registered the conversation.

"Oh, thank God. We've got a passenger in coach who thinks she's in labor."

Calla unbuckled her seat belt as she stated, "I'm a nurse practitioner and midwife."

The flight attendant visibly relaxed. Having any doctor onboard was a gift, but having the exact right combination of needed medical professionals was a miracle.

Kostas nodded. "You're perfect, aren't you?"

Perfect. Calla tried not to flinch at the term. Perfection was what Liam had demanded, and she'd always fallen short.

"Not really. Want me to get washed up first while you check on the patient or do you want to wash up first?" An airplane was not the best place to sanitize one's hands, and if she couldn't deliver a baby in a hospital, there were at least a dozen other locations she'd pick before an airplane thousands of miles above the earth. But you worked with what you had.

"I'll check the patient first. Hopefully, it's strong Braxton-Hicks."

Calla nodded to acknowledge she'd heard Kostas as she made her way to the bathroom. She hoped it was false contractions, but if it wasn't, they needed to be prepared.

The attendant followed her and Calla turned to ask, "Once we've washed our hands, do you have non-latex gloves in case we need to check the mother?" Less than one percent of the general population had a latex allergy, but she'd prefer not to take any additional risks.

"Yes. I'll grab them."

Calla washed up as quickly as she could professionally manage in the tiny compartment. She quickly gloved and went to find Kostas and their patient.

Stepping into coach was like stepping into a different world. The whole back of the plane was awake, and she could see a few phones out. No doubt this would be on people's social media platforms as soon as they landed. *If not before.*

She made her way to the woman sitting close to the front and noticed the small pool of liquid under the seat. *Amniotic fluid?*

Calla looked from it to Kostas and saw him nod.

"Becky, meet midwife Calla."

Then he turned to the flight attendant. "Why don't we move to first class? More room…" He nodded to the number of phones being held up. "And more privacy."

"Of course."

Kostas smiled at Becky. "Calla is going to go with

you to first class and check you while I get cleaned up."
Kostas's tone was soft but commanding. "Calla, this
is Becky. She is thirty-three weeks pregnant with her
second daughter. Contractions are steady at six minutes apart."

So this was the real deal in the air! When she'd
thought of this next step as an adventure, she hadn't
meant for it to kick off with such a bang.

"My OB cleared me to travel." Becky's bottom lip
trembled as Kostas guided her to first class and then
helped settle her onto a blanket on the floor.

"I'm sure he did. You did nothing wrong, Becky.
Nothing."

Calla wasn't sure Becky registered Kostas's words,
but they were absolutely the right ones. She had done
nothing wrong and preterm labor was not a punishment.
It was just something that happened.

The good news was that at thirty-three weeks,
Becky's daughter had an excellent chance of being able
to tell this story to all her friends as a teenager.

"It's lovely to meet you, Becky. Let's get you checked,
so we know how far along you are." Calla kept her tone
level, trying to calm the scared mom despite the most
unlikely situation.

She watched the flight attendants hold up blankets
to give the women some privacy, though the other four
first-class passengers were kind enough to look en-
grossed in their phones.

Calla smiled as she checked Becky, but she couldn't
stop the shift of her face as she felt the cord in the vagi-
nal canal. *Prolapse.*

"What?" Becky's face was white as she stared at
Calla. "And don't say it's nothing. I can tell it's not."

"You're right." Calla kept her voice steady as she

gently pushed the cord up to give the baby some relief. "The umbilical cord is prolapsed, which means…"

"I know what it means. I remember from birthing class. We're on a plane. Oh, my God."

"First, I know this is hard and scary. But I need you to take a deep breath. With me." Calla breathed in and out then did it again as Becky followed her.

"Now, I am going to remove my hand. I want you to get on all fours, then put your head down on the ground."

"Puppy pose."

Calla raised an eyebrow but didn't ask as Becky moved into position.

"I'm a yoga instructor. I…" She let out a soft sob. "What now?"

"Now, I keep the cord lifted until we get you to the hospital." Calla repositioned herself and found the cord immediately.

Before she could alert the flight attendants to the situation, Kostas peeked over the blankets. He saw the position Becky was in and Calla watched as his shoulders tensed before he calmly looked at the attendants.

"We need to be on the ground. As soon as possible, with an ambulance waiting to take us to a facility capable of performing a cesarean. Alert the pilot now. This is a medical emergency."

Becky let out a sob and Kostas bent to her level. "I'm sorry, Becky. But we will get you the best possible help as soon as possible. Until then, if you feel the need to push, I need you to do your best to avoid it. Understand?"

"Yes."

Kostas turned his attention to Calla. "They are going to perform an emergency landing. It will be a quick descent and air regulations require passengers in their seats."

"We can't do that." Calla shifted her legs to brace them against the chairs on either side of her. She could feel the baby move against her hand. The little girl was still okay. If she moved or Becky sat in a chair, the cord compression could kill the child.

"I know. But they are going to ask." Kostas looked at her and she saw the same determination she felt ripping through her. Becky and her daughter were their patients now. And they'd do their utmost to make sure she got the best outcome possible.

Directing her attention to Becky, Calla asked, "Are you willing to risk staying here on the floor? I have my feet braced against the seats to keep us from sliding."

Becky reached out and grabbed the legs of the chairs beside her. "Anything for my daughter."

Calla nodded and looked at Kostas. "You need to sit and buckle in. If something happens, one of us needs to take care of Becky and her daughter."

He opened his mouth like he planned to say something, but no words escaped as he shut it and looked at the empty seat. The one where she'd fallen asleep on his shoulder…the one that was actually his. He buckled in just as the announcement started.

"Ladies and gentlemen. As many of you are aware, we have a medical emergency on board. We will land in Dayton, Ohio, in ten minutes. Flight crew, prepare for landing."

The attendants holding the blankets handed them to the passengers opposite Kostas. The man continued to hold his end up as the flight attendants began giving orders.

The plane shifted and Calla braced herself. This was going to be the longest ten minutes of her career.

"Calla." Kostas's tone was steady as she met his dark gaze. "You've got this."

She nodded, not trusting her voice to not wobble as the plane started its descent. She hoped he understood how much she appreciated the faith she heard in his voice.

They barely knew each other. Theirs was a passing connection now forever bound by a medical emergency. When the plane landed, she was going to the hospital with Becky. He was headed on to Paris.

Even if he wanted to treat Becky, he'd said he practiced in Washington, so he didn't have permission to treat patients at whatever hospital they were headed to. It hurt to know that the handsome stranger who'd let her sleep on his shoulder, who'd offered a genuine connection—the first one she'd had since before Liam's falsehoods—would disappear. It had been a balm to her soul she hadn't known she'd needed.

As soon as the plane's wheels hit the ground, she let out a soft cheer. The worst part was nearly over.

Kostas unbuckled and got down to Becky's level. "How are you doing?"

"Still…here." She let out a rough breath as another contraction took her.

He looked up at Calla and raised a brow. "And you?"

Calla offered what she hoped was a reassuring smile. "Still here."

Kostas stood and looked out the window. "I can see the ambulance."

The main door to the cabin opened and he bent for what Calla knew was the last time. She looked at him, desperate to remember his handsome features so she could recall them when she told the story in the future of the sweet and handsome physician who'd assisted her with the most trying delivery of her career. His dark eyes sparkled and there were a few freckles along his nose. It would have to be enough.

"Good luck, Becky."

"Thank you."

"It was nice to meet you, Kostas." Calla hoped the few words contained all the emotions she was feeling.

"It was nice to meet you, too, Calla. Good luck on your assignment."

"Good luck at home. I hope it isn't as stressful as you fear." She offered him a smile as the EMTs stepped up behind him.

Kostas nodded as he turned to tell the medics what was going on. Then he faded into the background of the plane's chaos.

She was sad to see him go. There were other things to focus on, but a part of her felt bereft at the idea that she'd never see him again.

CHAPTER TWO

CALLA TRIED TO cover the yawn as she looked in on Becky and her daughter. While the race to the hospital in Dayton had felt like it had taken forever, from the time the plane landed to when the doctors at Miami Valley Hospital had brought Becky's little one into the world, it had been less than forty minutes. An impressive feat.

And now that the adrenaline was wearing off, Calla was dead on her feet and suddenly very aware that all her belongings, including her purse, with a way to pay for her to get back to the airport were…

Well, they were somewhere. Calla did not know where. That was a problem for after she said goodbye to Becky.

Her daughter was stable and breathing without extra oxygen. She was a little bigger than the average thirty-three-week infant. A great sign.

Becky and her newborn would be here in the hospital for a few days at least, but their prognosis was excellent.

She knocked on the door and entered when she heard the soft call from the other side.

"Calla." Becky's eyes held that tired but blissful look that all new moms shared after delivery. "I can't thank you enough. Without you…"

Becky's eyes filled with tears and Calla moved to her side. The combination of the last several hours of stress, giving birth, and the hormones that elevated then dropped following birth were enough to unseat anyone. "Everything is fine. And I am so glad that Kostas and I were there."

Kostas...

The name on her lips made her breath stop. She'd known the man for less than four hours and spoken to him for less than twenty minutes. His dark brown eyes, with flecks of gold around the edges, shouldn't be so easy to recall.

It should be a passing connection. *It was a passing connection.*

"I will always be thankful that you were there. And…" She offered a watery smile. "My daughter, Caroline Calla, will know about the nurse who saved her."

There was no way to express the emotions pouring through Calla. It was such a sweet tribute. She squeezed Becky's hand. "Thank you." The words were soft, but she hoped Becky knew how much the honor meant.

"My husband is on his way." Becky looked at her phone. "He started calling for flights the second we landed."

It was great that Becky's husband was en route. "How did he know?" Calla hadn't meant for the question to slip out. Maybe a medic had asked while she'd focused on making sure the umbilical cord didn't compress.

"Kostas." Becky let out a soft chuckle. "No idea how, but he called Mitch, and I'm too tired to worry about the how."

Calla took that as her cue. "You should get some rest. Congratulations on your little girl. I wish you a lifetime of happiness and love." She headed for the door before Becky could argue. She needed her rest.

How did Kostas reach him? The thought niggled in the back of her brain. Airlines were known for their rigid rules and privacy concerns. However he'd done it, it was sweet.

His dark eyes flashed in her memory, *again*, as she moved down the hallway and Calla mentally shook herself. She needed to find a way to the airport and hoped all her things hadn't flown on to London without her. Even her cell phone was in her backpack, which she'd also left behind on the plane.

Pushing open the waiting room doors, her feet stopped in their path. Kostas sat in one of the most uncomfortable-looking chairs she'd ever seen. "What?" The word echoed in the room as he smiled at her and stood.

It was then that she noticed her luggage at his feet. Her lip trembled as she saw the old secondhand suitcases her parents had purchased at a thrift store almost twenty years ago. Ugly but functional was the best description, and she'd never been happier to see the faded green bags in her life.

Kostas handed her the backpack she'd left on the plane. "Figured life would be easier if you had these things."

"Thank you," she whispered as she looked at her things. "But your flight home?"

He shrugged. "There will be other flights. I let my family know about the delay. My brother is disappointed, but that is nothing new."

"Kostas." She laid her hand over his, reflexive.

He squeezed her hand as he added, "I fly out tomorrow morning. Paris to Italy to…" He hesitated for a moment before finishing. "To home."

The hesitation struck her. She was an only child, and her family had loved her unconditionally. If her parents were still alive, they'd celebrate her return home, no matter the circumstances. She hated that not everyone had had the same experience.

Growing up, her parents were the ones everyone wanted. The ones cheering at her soccer games, never missing a band concert, and clearly infatuated with each other. Losing them to cancer within a year of each other had nearly destroyed her.

But she knew she'd been lucky. To have seen their love, to know it was possible. So many of her friends went home to a house that lacked love…or worse.

Liam's parents had controlled every aspect of their son's life. The sports he'd participated in, the schools he'd attended, even his degree in engineering had been mandated by his father.

And the woman he'd married last weekend had been their choice too.

He'd had a chance to leave that life. Their life together would have been less privileged than he'd known, but she'd believed love could overcome that. Except he hadn't loved her…not really. And she would never settle for less again.

She didn't know Kostas's story, but a man who sat for hours in a hospital waiting room with a practical stranger's luggage was someone she wanted to know. He called to her in a way no one had before.

And he was attractive…actually, he was hot with multiple T's. The man looked like he belonged on billboards; his curly hair dipped over his ears and his shadowed beard gave him a rugged look that would make anyone's mouth water. His dark eyes seemed to see straight to her soul.

Kostas's looks were enough to make her want to dream of kissing him. His thoughtfulness, his compassionate spirit, made her want to follow through with the action. Shame they were basically two ships passing in the night.

He squeezed her hand. He leaned close and, for a moment, she thought about what might happen if she lifted her lips and grazed his cheeks.

Kostas held her gaze, the energy between them crackling, then he dropped her hand and reached into his pocket. "You need to call this number to reschedule your flights. I rented a car, so if you can get out today, I can get you to the airport."

"And if I can't get out until tomorrow?" Calla looked at him and saw the corners of his lips tilt up. It was as forward as she'd ever been. But she wanted to spend the day with him, wanted a memory to keep her warm during the lonely nights to come in Palaío.

"Then we'll have to grab something to eat and see what we can do to keep ourselves occupied until we head out." His mouth broke into a full smile then, and her body heated at the desire pooling in his eyes.

A day with the man before her was the perfect way to start her adventure.

Kostas grinned as he watched Calla step to the side and call the number he'd given her.

Unbeknownst to her, he'd spoken with the airline and made sure they'd upgraded her to first class for her entire trip. The customer service rep had refused to give him her itinerary, which he understood, but had accepted his credit card number and put it in Calla's file, agreeing to just call it an upgrade for the service she'd provided Becky.

Calla had earned the pampering and extra space on her long trip. If the luggage and worn backpack at his side were any indicators, she rarely got pampered. And she'd more than earned it. He also knew that there were generally open seats in first class on overseas flights in the current economy. That meant it was possible he'd take her to the airport as soon as she hung up the phone.

His brother's secretary had taken the news of his delay with more grace than he figured Ioannis would. Significantly more than his father would have. But his delay couldn't be helped.

Mostly...

Kostas could have stayed on the fight with the other passengers. If he had, he'd be on his way to Paris now. But he wouldn't trade the look on Calla's face when she'd seen him in the waiting room for anything.

He wanted more time with the nurse who'd fallen asleep on his shoulder, risked her safety during landing, and hadn't even asked the flight attendants to grab her backpack as the EMTs had loaded her and Becky into the ambulance. The woman had touched a part of him that had been dormant for so long.

Kostas kept to himself. The few women he'd dated in Seattle always complained that he held them at arm's length. Complaints he understood. But how to explain that it was for their own good?

That the life of a royal bride was far from the fairy-tale ending. That your life was never truly your own. A gilded cage was still a cage.

Living in the States had given him more freedom than he'd had in Palaío, but it hadn't changed who he was. Dr. Kostas Drakos was the title he'd earned, the one he loved. But it didn't replace the title of prince of Palaío. Didn't strip away the responsibilities he was returning to.

It was easier to remain single. Besides, no woman had made him want to challenge that thought.

Calla… His heart rate picked up as she put her phone back in her pocket. Calla intrigued him. He'd wanted to see her again. Wanted to spend more than the few hours they'd had on the red-eye together—hours that had been cut painfully short.

This wasn't a forever love story. But for a few hours, he could pretend that the woman who touched his heart, who seemed to understand his hesitation to return home, might be someone special. Then they'd get on separate flights and he'd go back to being Prince Kostas once more.

"So I can't get out until tomorrow morning, either."

"Are we on the same flight to New York?" Kostas couldn't keep the grin from his face. If she wasn't sitting next to him on the plane, he could ask someone to switch seats with them. A few extra hours.

The frown appearing on her lips twisted his stomach.

"I'm not going through New York now. The quickest way to get me to my final destination is through Charlotte. I'll be a day late. I let my contact know and they understand, but…"

"But nothing." Kostas reached for her hand and squeezed it. "You need to get where you're going." Her stomach growled and he quirked a brow. "Sounds like we need to find sustenance."

"Not hospital food." She bit her lip as he laughed.

"Of course not! I don't know what we might find in Dayton, but I figure we can find something better than the hospital cafeteria."

He grabbed her ancient luggage as she put her back-pack on. "What sounds good?"

"Anything!" Her grin sent a wave of happiness through him. "I am not picky…particularly when I am hungry."

The small diner boasting the best burgers in town hummed with conversation as Calla dipped a fry in ketchup. "So, Kostas…where did you work in Seattle? I was at Regional Midwives. Mostly home births, but I was in and out of Seattle General a few times. Never saw you."

The word *did* in her sentence sent a chill down his spine. Kostas didn't like to think of his time in Seattle as over. He'd promised Ioannis he'd run the clinic in Palaío for a while and recruit a few more staff. Ioannis believed he was staying, but that wasn't Kostas's plan. Still, he couldn't ask his administrator to keep him on staff while he was gone. So he'd turned in his resigna-tion. Hating the decision, even though he'd known it was the right one.

"I had admitting privileges at Seattle General, but saw most of my patients at Grace Hospital."

"Ah." Calla dipped another fry, and he watched as she ate what was more ketchup than fry before putting more of the condiment on her plate.

She saw his gaze and laughed. "My parents always said I could just eat straight ketchup, but I don't."

He chuckled and shrugged. He'd never gotten much into the tomato-based condiment, but if it made her happy, Kostas didn't care. "I prefer mustard."

"On fries?"

He nodded, enjoying the look of horror cross her face.

She playfully shuddered as she held up another red-covered fry. "Bite your tongue!"

He laughed and held up both hands. "It's good. Promise."

"I am going to take your word for it…and ignore it." She winked and her knee pressed against his. It had happened a few times in the tight booth, and she'd moved it away each time. This time, she left it.

The small connection sent heat pouring through him as her hazel gaze held him. Then she yawned, and he couldn't keep the yawn from his lips, either.

"You're exhausted." Calla smiled as she dipped her final fry.

"You yawned first." Kostas tapped her leg with his, enjoying the pink rising in her cheeks. She was lovely.

Calla waved to the waitress and asked for the check. When Kostas made for his wallet, she held up her hand. "You brought my luggage, sat and waited for me, and somehow convinced the airline to upgrade me for the rest of my trip. I got this."

He started to argue then held his tongue. Her eyes blazed with seriousness. She wanted to pay. He could force the issue, by why take away something that was important to her? So he reached for her free hand as she put the money on the table and told the waitress that she didn't need change.

Calla looked at his hand in hers and the pink invaded her cheeks again as he ran a thumb along her palm. The easiness between them was something he'd never experienced. Maybe because there was no agenda between them. They each understood that whatever this was, it had an expiration date.

The clock would strike tomorrow morning. His heart clenched as he thought of that. He didn't want to think of the eventual goodbye. But she was also exhausted, and he was nearly dead on his feet.

It was barely three o'clock local time, but now that they had full bellies, they were each fighting the fatigue. A fight they were destined to lose.

"I have a hotel room." Her eyes popped open as he raced on. "It's the penthouse suite, so it has two full bedrooms." He wanted her, craved knowing what her lips felt like, how she tasted, but he'd never force his advances.

Calla looked at their fingers entwined, as if they'd known each other for days or weeks rather than hours.

"And if I didn't want to stay in the extra room?"

Before he could answer, she let out another yawn. As much as he wanted to follow the thread she was also clearly interested in, they were both too tired to really enjoy it. "You're free to sleep wherever you want. But I think we both need a hot shower and a few hours' rest. Then we can see where the rest of the time goes. Fair?"

"Fair," Calla agreed as she bit back another yawn.

As the hot water streamed over her, Calla tried to gather her thoughts. She was in the penthouse of a luxury hotel, in a bathroom that was bigger than her Seattle apartment. It was a little unnerving.

She felt like a fish out of water, except she was enjoying the experience. Far too much, maybe. Calla had never gone to bed with a man she barely knew. Never even considered it. But something about Kostas called to her.

In fiction, this would be the soul-mate moment, the fate of mates destined for each other. Instant connections happened, but they were mostly rooted in lust. And she certainly lusted after the man.

Her nipples were hard as she pulled the towel around herself. Kostas was showering in the other bathroom. *A hotel room with two full-sized bathrooms.* Even when she was with Liam, they'd never stayed in a place like this.

Yet Kostas didn't seem concerned with helping her, didn't seem to mind the very apparent differences in their bank accounts. He seemed to just like being around her. That was intoxicating. She dropped a long shirt over herself and stepped into the room.

Kostas was already lying on the bed. He set his tablet down. He was shirtless, but had on a pair of comfortable-looking blue jeans. Her mouth watered at the sight of his chiseled chest. Man, he was gorgeous.

Part of her wished she'd stepped out in some lacy nightgown. A ridiculous thought given their short acquaintance—and the fact that she didn't have any fancy nightgowns.

Nerves cascaded around her body as she stepped to the bed. Kostas smiled and she nearly melted. But he didn't rush her, clearly realizing that part of her was still uncertain.

"Calla…"

Her name on his lips made her decision. She wanted to lie next to him. Wanted him. She slid into his arms, enjoying the feel of his warm skin against hers. Before he could say anything else, Calla pressed her lips to his.

Kostas's grip tightened as she opened her mouth. His tongue darted across hers and she sighed. This felt right. It was a fantasy; she knew that. But a fantasy that felt so perfect.

She deepened the kiss, willing the yawn she felt building in the back of her throat away. She had a lifetime to rest; she had less than fifteen hours with Kostas, and she wanted to make them last.

"You're tired." Kostas broke the kiss, his fingers tracing along her side as if he couldn't keep from touching her.

"So are you." She dropped a kiss at his lips. "I don't care." It was the truth. She didn't want to miss whatever chemistry was driving them. Calla could sleep on the plane tomorrow, but something in her screamed that if she missed this opportunity, if she missed being with him, she'd regret it for the rest of her life.

Calla kissed him again then pulled back. "But if you need sleep…"

He pursed his lips as he stared at her. "I need you." The words sounded primal as they escaped his lips, his eyes dilated with passion.

His hands slipped up the shirt she was wearing and found her nipples. He ran his thumbs across them as he kissed her again. Each touch sent flickers of flames along her skin as he explored her.

Kostas let out a guttural noise as her lips trailed his neck and she smiled against him, loving his reaction. He lifted the shirt over her head and leaned back, studying her.

Maybe she should feel self-conscious. But the shame or nervousness she thought she'd feel if she ever fell into bed with a man she'd just met failed to appear. Her body longed for his touch, craved it. That was a gift she refused to push away.

"You are so lovely." His deep voice covered her as his hand slid to the top of her thigh. "So very lovely."

"You already said that." She let out a sigh as his mouth trailed along her stomach.

"It bears repeating." His lips caressed her nipples, suckling each one with a gentleness that consumed her.

"Kostas…"

His fingers dragged across her inner thigh, so close to where she wanted him. *Needed him.*

She felt him smile against her chest as he stroked her nipple with his tongue before drifting down her body. His motions were slow, achingly slow. And she loved each touch.

He reached her belly button and then moved back to her nipples, lingering as she sucked in a deep breath. Kostas's fingers feathered her body; sketches that varied from the lightest brush to a touch that felt like he was barely holding back from claiming her.

His tongue traced her as he finally meandered down her body again. His fingers teasing as he trailed so close to her sex. "Kostas…"

"I enjoy the sound of my name on your lips, Calla." His thumb pressed against her bud and she let out a cry, arching her back as her body exploded. "It may be the most perfect sound. Look at me, sweetheart."

She opened her eyes, quivering as his fingers pressed into her. He smiled as he touched her, grinning as he watched her enjoy the scorching pleasure he was bringing her. It was thrilling.

His thumb pressed against her as his fingers stroked her. "Calla."

Her name dripping from his lips as he pleasured her sent her over the edge again.

"Kostas…" She was breathless. She should feel sated after the two breathtaking orgasms, but she wanted more. Needed more.

"I need you."

He dropped his lips to hers, but she grabbed either side of his face, halting his attentions. "I want you… all of you. Now."

Only after getting her demand out did she join their

mouths, loving the taste of him as she reached between them and undid the button of his jeans. Unzipping him, she slid her hand in, finding what she craved most.

"Calla." He whispered her name as he stripped his jeans off. He pulled a condom from the back pocket, and she reached for it.

Holding his smoky gaze, she opened it, sheathing him. Then she straddled him, watching his lips part as she eased her way slowly down his length.

His hands gripped her hips, but he didn't rush her.

He spent forever driving her closer and closer to the edge before finally giving her what she needed. She planned to repay the favor in the most delicious way possible.

Kostas's eyes held hers as she gently rocked their bodies, refusing to yield to her body's demand to move faster. She wanted to savor every moment.

His fingers drifted to her nipples again, swirling them in perfect symphony with her movements. They melded together, and everything else seemed to disappear. Kostas sat up and she wrapped her legs around him as he kissed her.

The sensations were almost too much. She let out a groan and finally gave in to the heady needs claiming them both. When she came for a final time, it was with Kostas's name on her lips.

Calla's soft snores echoed in the dark room as Kostas pulled her into his arms. Their alarms would go off in less than an hour. And in less than four, they'd be on different planes, their paths forever moving in different directions. And he hated the thought.

It wasn't fair to want more from her. Particularly when he knew he couldn't bring her to Palaío. On the island, the man he was, the man he wanted to be, transformed into a prince. And this time he was determined to kill the "rebel son" label he'd earned as an angry teen. Now he'd be the man the kingdom needed, a skilled doctor, but cold, distant, always ensuring he followed protocols.

He'd fled after what had happened with Maria. After his father had refused to refute the ugly and untrue rumors. He was a grown adult now, and he would not let lies stand. But for the next year or so, he doubted there be much news for the press to latch onto. He had a role to play, expectations to fulfill. And he'd be perfect.

Perfect!

That didn't mean he didn't want to beg Calla to visit him. To want to show her the crystal-clear water as it lapped onto the beaches. Needed to show her all the places special to him.

It was beyond selfish. If she landed in Palaío and the press saw the connection between them, they'd make her life a living hell. She'd grow to resent him, just as Maria had.

It stung when Maria had fled, but he'd understood.

He barely knew Calla, but he suspected seeing disappointment grow in her eyes would be just as bad. *Maybe worse.*

This day, this one twenty-four-hour period, would have to sate his desires for the rest of time. He let his fingers trail along her delicate body, enjoying the little sighs escaping her lips. She was so beautiful.

He dropped his lips to the base of her neck, right where her shoulder and neck met. The place where, when he'd trailed his lips along it last night, she'd cried out his name.

Kostas lightly stroked her hip. Her skin was so soft

under his fingers. He wanted to memorize how she felt, how she tasted, how perfectly she fit with him. He let his hand travel to her breasts, running a finger along her nipple, smiling as he felt it harden.

She rolled over in his hold, her eyes meeting his in the room's dim lights. Her lips traced his chin as her hand moved south. "Can I help you, Kostas?"

He didn't bother to mince words, didn't want to hide the need he felt. "I want you, Calla. So badly."

She ginned as she kissed him. "The feeling is very mutual."

He gripped her and rolled with her, losing himself in the sensations that were simply Calla.

CHAPTER THREE

CALLA WALKED ALONG the beach in Palaío, holding herself tightly as she watched the sun rise along the edge of the ocean. She'd been on the island nation for less than seventy-two hours, and most of those she'd spent sleeping.

And dreaming of Kostas.

Their parting at the airport had been the stuff of movies. The tragic ones that people sat on their couches clutching tissues, waiting for the inevitable relief that tears brought. And she'd replayed it repeatedly in her head.

He'd stayed with her until she'd boarded her flight to London. His hand clasping hers. For a moment, she'd pretended he was coming with her. It was only when she sank into her plush first-class seat alone that she'd let the emotion of their last kiss at the gate float through her.

She'd spent most of the trip trying to keep her weepiness in check. It was ridiculous to cry over a one-night stand. A beautiful one-night stand. A memory she'd cherish forever, though one might think she'd left her soul mate in Dayton. It was ridiculous, but part of her had wanted to run back down the ramp, jump into his arms and tell him she wanted to see if the connection between them was more than lust.

But she had a job in Palaío. The income would let her cut the final ties to her past. Getting on the flight to Palaío had been the right move.

Calla blew out a breath as the waves crashed close to her feet. She'd done the right thing. That didn't mean that she didn't wish another option had been available.

She started at the Palaío Women's Clinic today. She was still kicking the last of her jet lag, but Calla didn't care. Once she was at the clinic, the work would take prime focus in her mind. She loved working as a midwife. It consumed her.

Then she could let the memory of Kostas, the thoughts of his kisses and touches, slip to the back of her memory. Calla heard her scoff echo in the early morning light and hugged herself even tighter.

At the very least, the memory couldn't occupy all her thoughts while she was working.

She picked up a shell, fingering the ridges as she let out a breath. Squeezing the shell tightly, she brought Kostas's face into her memory. Calla let her mind trace his high cheekbones, the five-o'clock shadow he wore so perfectly, and the dark eyes that saw her so clearly.

"Goodbye, Kostas." She raised the shell above her head, getting ready to throw it. A silly ritual she'd schemed up when she'd tossed and turned in her bed last night. But her hand refused to let go.

Pathetic, Calla. Pathetic.

She wrapped her hand around the shell. In a few days, she could complete the ritual. But for now, she turned to head back to the apartment the clinic had secured for her. It was lovely, larger than her place in Seattle, and furnished with furniture nicer than she'd ever had. Palaío was great, and if she hadn't met Kostas, her heart would be happier than she'd ever been.

But she had met him.

Another soul walked the beach, and her breath caught in her throat. He walked like Kostas, carried himself in the same, almost regal, way he had. Her throat closed as she watched the man, her heart urging her to run toward him.

Luckily, she still had some of her senses. The odds of it being Kostas were so minuscule she refused to even calculate them. If she ran to the stranger, she'd be disappointed when it wasn't the man she craved.

And he'd likely be terrified of a stranger racing at him in the early morning. She looked at the man in the distance once more then purposefully started back for her apartment without looking back.

Kostas let the wet sand sink between his toes as he stared at the departing woman further up the beach. For a minute, he'd wondered if it was Calla. In the distance, with the morning's shadows, it had been too easy to pretend it might be her. He pushed a hand through his much shorter hair and turned to look out at the ocean.

He was in Palaío. Had been for almost three days, and the casing of Prince Kostas, second in line to the throne, had wrapped around him as soon as he'd stepped into the palace. He'd cut his hair after multiple comments from his brother's advisers.

Kostas wished he'd stood up to them. Explained that having the loose curls falling around his ears looked no less professional than the close cut worn by his brother. But he hadn't wanted to argue.

If the advisers thought it best that he have short hair…well, he could grow it out again as soon as he left. He'd wear the mask of Prince Kostas, the reformed rebel. That was all.

Besides, all he'd wanted to do since landing was to think of the woman he'd kissed goodbye at the airport. Nothing seemed to matter much. He was mourning a relationship that had never been.

But could have been.

He shook his head as he stepped into the ocean, letting the waves wrap around his ankles. It was silly to keep replaying their last kiss. Silly to wish he'd asked for her email or phone number. They were on different paths, but he'd spent most of the last few days looking for her. Thinking he might see her in the street or on the beach.

His mind was intent on conjuring her. He heard a noise behind him and turned to see a photographer with a long lens above the dune. He turned back to the waves as the truth of his position weighed on him.

Even if Calla was in Palaío, which he knew she wasn't, it wouldn't matter. Here, he wasn't her Kostas. Wasn't the man who'd cradled her in sleep. On this island, he was Prince Kostas.

He shook his head. Today was a new day, and he needed to focus on his role at the clinic. It was his first day…and the new midwife's first day, too. When he'd heard that, he'd nearly screamed for Natalia to tell him the name, his mind wrapping around the possibility that he and Calla might have taken very different routes to the same place.

His personal assistant had nearly jumped away from his outburst. Then she'd apologized profusely for not knowing the information. She'd promised to get it, but Kostas had waved her off, expressing regret for his outburst. Besides, he'd find out everything about the midwife when he arrived.

His watch beeped and he closed his eyes as he faced

the rising sun. Today started his countdown. Maybe when he left, he'd see if he could locate Calla.

How?

That question had hovered around him for days. He knew her name was Calla Lewis. But he knew nothing else. He hadn't memorized the address on her baggage tags—a mistake he'd castigated himself for most of his trip to Paris.

He knew how she kissed, how her skin felt against his, but there was no way to trace her from those notes.

"Goodbye, Calla." The whispered words carried across the sand and he turned. He needed to focus on his actual mission. Do what the island needed…and then get off it. For good this time.

"I hope those photographers aren't planning on camping outside the clinic every day," Alexa muttered as she leaned against the desk in the small office where she and Calla were waiting for the new OBGYN to arrive.

"Why are they here?" Calla looked over the charting tablet the nurse practitioner had handed her when she'd walked in.

Alexa had smiled when Calla had arrived almost an hour before her shift. Calla had claimed it was because she'd wanted to organize herself, to get to know the clinic and procedures before their patients arrived. But she'd been going a little stir crazy in her apartment. Looking over the patient records, figuring out her schedule was calming.

And it lets me think of something other than Kostas.

There'd been a photographer sitting in a car when she'd first arrived, and more had appeared in the last hour. In Seattle, she'd occasionally seen journalists and photographers at the hospital, but never near the maternity wing, and usually only after a terrible accident.

"Waiting for our new OB." Alexa let out a sigh as she looked out the window. "A few of them camped out back there, too. Guess they want to make sure they covered all potential entrances."

"Did he work as a movie star at some point?" Calla chuckled as she looked up. The nurse's stare cut the sound out of her throat. "Seriously, he was in the movies?"

"No." Alexa looked at her and crossed her arms. "Did they really not tell you that you'd be working with King Ioannis's little brother? Prince Kostas?"

"Kostas?" Her throat went dry as she processed the name. No way her Kostas was a prince. He would have said something…right?

Uncertainty pooled through her. Would he have told her? Their physical connection had been deep, electric, magical, but they'd not actually spoken of where they were going.

She'd called this an adventure and he'd only said he was going home. *And that he wasn't looking forward to his family's expectations…*

No. That didn't mean anything. Far too many people had family expectations that were overburdening.

She and Kostas hadn't shared too much, but that was a protective measure, one to guard their hearts as the heat between them burned but didn't allow for any future. At least, that was how Calla viewed it and had assumed it was the same for him.

But what if was something else?

It had taken Liam almost a year before he'd told her how much wealth his family had. He'd claimed other girlfriends had used him for his family's money.

She chewed on her lower lip. Surely, her Kostas, the man she'd spent the most passionate day of her life with, wasn't a prince. It was just a name.

"If he looks half as good as he did at his brother's coronation, then he could be in the movies. But Palaío's Prodigal Prince chose medicine." The tinge of annoyance at the words *Prodigal Prince* sounded almost maternal. As if Alexa understood the desire but couldn't quite countenance the choice the royal had made.

"Where was he working before?"

"Some city in the US. Starts with sea…" Alexa tapped her finger against her chin. "Sea—"

"Seattle." Calla set the tablet down as she leaned against the desk.

"That's it!" Alexa stated.

Kostas. Her mouth was dry. Kostas *was* here. Her heart hammered as she tried to figure out what this meant. *Does it mean anything?*

They'd had one blissful night together. But they'd given in to passion because they'd never expected to see one another again—or at least that was why she'd followed her needs.

Her cheeks heated as the memory of his fingers on her skin lit up her mind.

"I said leave. This is a medical clinic, and the patients don't need cameras in their faces. They need support for their babies!"

His voice carried across the clinic and Alexa left the office. Calla couldn't seem to get her feet to move. She'd dreamed of reuniting with him since she'd kissed him goodbye in Dayton. But she'd never expected to fulfill the fantasy.

Certainly not in Palaío or after discovering he was a prince. This was the stuff of TV movies, not real life.

"Prince Kostas. It's so nice to see you." Alexa's tone was cordial, deferential, as it drifted to the office.

How was she supposed to address royalty? Particularly royalty she'd clung to? Naked.

"Dr. Drakos or Kostas will be fine, Alexa. And please don't bow. I'm second in line to the throne and soon to be third when my sister-in-law delivers. I don't want our patients uncomfortable. In this clinic, I am Dr. Kostas Drakos, nothing more."

He cleared his throat and added, "When does the new nurse midwife arrive?"

"She's already here. Calla?"

She could hear Alexa turn; no doubt surprised she hadn't followed her to greet the doctor. *The Prince.*

Calla grabbed the tablet chart and raced around the desk. "Here. Sorry, I just…" Her eyes met Kostas's and her heart cried out to go to him. He looked tired. He'd taken several planes to get here, just as she had. But the exhaustion clinging to him looked like it went deeper. The curls he'd worn so well were gone; the short hair looked regal.

But it didn't suit him.

Kostas stared at her, clearly as surprised by her appearance as she was by his. The air in the room felt thick as she dragged it in. What was she supposed to do?

Alexa cleared her throat and Kostas broke the connection with her.

"I just realized that Calla worked in Seattle, too. Did you two work together?"

"No." His voice was tight as he shook his head. "We've never worked together. It's a huge city. There are several major hospitals in Seattle. It's a big place. It's nice to meet you, Calla."

She blinked as she registered his words. They didn't

have to acknowledge the exact nature of their acquaintance, but to just dismiss her, to act like she was a complete stranger… The warmth in his eyes that she'd fallen for was gone.

The prince stood here now. In Seattle, or Dayton, she was good enough for a night. But here, in his home, she was a stranger.

Liam hadn't considered her good enough, either.

Liam had been wrong, but Kostas was actual royalty. Her throat tightened, but she refused to let him see how much his words cut. She pushed the pain radiating through her down. She'd deal with it tonight…alone.

If he wanted to act like they didn't know each other, fine. She could follow that script. "It's nice to meet you, too, Prince Kostas."

"I prefer Kostas." He looked at her, his features softening for just a moment.

She knew that. Had heard him correct Alexa. But she was using his title for herself. A reminder to Calla Lewis that she'd spent the past few days yearning for a man who considered her beneath him. A man who wouldn't even acknowledge that they'd known each other.

Hell, they could have even shared the story of helping Becky when she'd gone into labor thirty-thousand feet above the earth. There were so many ways he could have handled it besides this one. Ways to acknowledge her.

But if he didn't want to. Well, fine!

"I look forward to working with you, Dr. Drakos." Calla kept her tone even, not trusting herself to say any more.

He opened his mouth but shut it quickly. Whatever he'd planned to say evaporating as she nodded. "I need to see to a few things in the office, before my first patient arrives."

He walked past her without another glance. Alexa followed, chattering about the day's schedule, the patients and island gossip.

Kostas met Calla's gaze briefly before he closed the office door, but he didn't smile, didn't show any reaction to her presence at all.

Calla raised her chin and closed her eyes. She'd mourned her relationship with Liam. Nursed the heartache for months before realizing it was her she was missing. The woman she'd been before she'd tried to fit into his mold.

As soon as she'd reclaimed her true self, Calla's heart had stitched itself back together. She'd sworn that she'd never change herself for another again. Never let someone have that much control over her.

Her escapade with Kostas was a fun memory. But she would not chase a man who didn't want her. Wouldn't acknowledge a prince who greeted a lover with no kindness.

She was in Palaío for a reason that had nothing to do with Prince Kostas Drakos. And she wasn't leaving, so she hoped His Royal Highness didn't expect her to wilt under his controlled gaze.

Kostas wanted to tell Alexa that he didn't care about island gossip. That he didn't know the woman she was gossiping about and didn't care that she'd married her best friend's nephew. Or that she was pregnant. When she arrived at his clinic, he'd treat her just like any other patient.

This was one of the many aspects of the life on Palaío that he hadn't missed. The country was home to a little over one hundred thousand people. Each of the island's towns, even the capital where they were, operated as small towns. Everyone still knew everyone's business, particularly the scandals. *Or perceived scandals.*

The city of Seattle had over seven times the island's population, and twenty times the capital city's population. There, it was easy to get lost in the daily hustle. Easy to only see his patients in the office. If he occasionally passed them at the grocery store or Starbucks, he'd wave, say a few pleasantries and then move on.

For the first time in his life, Kostas had been nearly invisible. Able to be just the man he wanted, without the trappings of a title. That Kostas could have taken Calla on a date without worrying about photos and rumors and… He inhaled and discarded the thoughts. He wasn't that Kostas—no matter how much he wished for it.

"Do you mind giving me a few minutes to look over the records here alone?" Kostas saw Alexa glance at her watch as he cut off her story in midsentence then look up at him.

She nodded and headed for the door. "It's nice to have you home, Your Highness."

Before he could comment on her use of the honorific, the nurse disappeared. Calla walked by the open office door, but she didn't stop or look at him. Not that he could blame her.

His body had ignited the moment he'd seen her. Only Alexa's presence had stilled his movements. When she'd asked if they knew each other, he'd seen the hint of excitement glowing in Alexa's eyes. She'd wanted to hear the word *yes.* Wanted to deconstruct its meaning, pass it along to her friends that not only had Prince Kostas returned to Palaío, but he knew the nurse from Seattle, too.

The rumor mill would spin out of control. So he'd lied. And he'd seen the hurt in Calla's eyes. Seen her swallow so many words. Then she'd called him "Prince Kostas," and he was almost certain she'd done it intentionally.

He just wasn't sure why.

Rolling his neck, he wrapped the need crawling through him and forced it into the mental compartment he'd carefully constructed following the disasters with his mother and Maria. The photographers had followed him from the airport to the palace to the office. Hopefully, in a few days, they'd get so bored by his activities that they'd disappear.

But if word leaked that he was interested in Calla... That he'd spent the night with her... The gathering outside would look like nothing compared to the frenzy they'd experience. He couldn't do that to her.

Wouldn't.

Better to cause her hurt now than to subject her to weeks and months under the microscope. Even if part of him wanted her to join him, wanted to see if she might not mind the invasion to her life. That was the selfish inner voice that he'd learned to ignore years ago—though it surprised him how much he wanted to give in to the urge now.

"Yes, I am glowing! Look at my bump. You'd think I was having twins. Which maybe I am!"

Kostas pulled on his face as his sister-in-law's voice carried into the office. He knew Eleni didn't have an appointment this morning. So what was she doing here?

Checking on him. He sighed as he stepped into the waiting area.

Her eyes met his as she cradled her bump. "Twins." Eleni let out a chuckle. "That story ought to keep them busy for at least a few days." She looked lovely and, at eight months pregnant, she did not look like she was carrying twins.

"You don't have an appointment, Eleni." Kostas raised an eyebrow as he leaned against the door to the office. He'd looked over his list of patients last night, and Eleni was not on it.

Though the queen had a habit of doing as she liked, much to the chagrin of her security detail, she kept a much looser schedule than Kostas or Ioannis. Besides formal functions, her daily schedule was more general ideas than actual appointments. Particularly now. She'd started her maternity leave when she'd entered her third trimester and only had a handful of royal appointments.

"Not with you!" She grinned as she turned and waved. "I assume you're the new midwife?"

"I am. Calla Lewis, Your Majesty. Right on time for your appointment."

"Oh, pish! Call me Eleni, please. There is no need to be formal. I've heard so much about you from Ioannis. He was thrilled when you accepted the position. He thought you and Kostas would work well together."

Color crept up Calla's neck as she cleared her throat. "I suppose we'll find our way. If you'll follow me..."

Eleni looked to Kostas, her dark eyes laying into him before she followed Calla. There was little that got past his sister-in-law. She'd undoubtedly seen Calla blush, but being around royals often made people uncomfortable. Hopefully, Eleni would accept that answer if she pressed him on it later.

It was a minor problem for later, but Kostas followed behind them. He wanted—needed—to be near Calla.

"Do you need something, Doctor?" Calla raised her

chin, challenging him at the door. "I promise you, I am more than capable of taking care of your sister-in-law."

She was right, of course. There was no need for him to follow them. Calla was perfectly capable of doing Eleni's check. At thirty-three weeks along, he knew his sister-in-law had been coming in regularly. And doing so before the other patients arrived granted her at least a little privacy.

Assuming the photographers outside left.

"I like her!" Eleni winked at Kostas. "Everyone here treats you like a prince, or a little brother. No one just stands up to you."

"You always have." Kostas crossed his arms and let his eyes wander to Calla for an instant before redirecting his attention to his sister-in-law.

"I'm different. I'm family." Eleni slid onto the table and waved to the heart monitor sitting on the counter. "I don't care if he stays, but I would like to hear my baby's heartbeat."

Calla grabbed the wand and turned all her attention to Eleni, ignoring Kostas completely. "Are you having a boy or a girl?"

"We haven't found out." Eleni grinned as the heartbeat rang out in the room. "We found out with our first, as is tradition on Palaío, though I was pregnant before we got married, which was a new tradition for Palaío!"

Eleni let out a giggle as she looked at Calla. "Those photographers followed me for months, guessing that I'd conceived before the wedding, though we've never officially confirmed it."

"It's none of their business." Calla nodded as she grabbed the gel. "This will be cold." She looked at Kostas. "We should get warmers for the gel. It isn't cold for long, but warm gel is better." Then she turned her attention back to Eleni, ignoring him completely. "So you and Ioannis are going for surprise on the sex for this little one. How fun."

He noticed Calla didn't have any issue using his brother's first name. That shouldn't hurt. He bit his lip as he looked at Calla, wishing they were someplace else. Anywhere else.

Eleni sighed as the wand found the heartbeat. "We are. I put my foot down and demanded we do something different. Traditions are nice, but change can be good too."

His sister-in-law didn't look at him, but Kostas knew the message was intended for him. She had never cared about traditions. Raised in a neighboring kingdom by a royal mother and commoner father, Eleni was the breath of fresh air the monarchy needed.

She and Ioannis had fallen for each other hard and quickly. Their love was evident to anyone paying the smallest bit of attention. Still, the press had had a field day with her. Insinuating that she wasn't royal enough for the king of Palaío, wasn't queen material, wasn't virginal—which wasn't a requirement, or their business, to use Calla's words.

It was only because of her parents—who had refused to cower under the press's long eye and had instilled that in their daughter—that Eleni had not only survived but thrived in the environment. As she'd demonstrated today, she loved messing with the press. Sending them on wild-goose chases. In her words, if they were dumb enough to chase her outlandish statements after she'd established that she liked to tell them nonsense, that was their problem.

His brother had found his match. Kostas was happy

for him, but most women hadn't grown up in the "I don't care what anyone thinks" environment that Eleni had.

"Don't you have a patient to prep for?" Calla's tone wasn't hostile, but she'd dismissed him. There was no need for him to hover. No professional need anyway.

"How have you felt this week? Any contractions, cramps? Discomfort?" Calla didn't look at him as he stepped toward the door.

"Discomfort? Have you met any almost-nine-months-pregnant women who are comfortable? I'd love to meet such a mythical creature…and destroy her!"

Calla's laugh joined Eleni's, and Kostas's heart clenched. The two women could be friends…sisters.

No. He pushed the selfish thought away. They'd had a perfect night. That had to be enough.

CHAPTER FOUR

"HAVE A GOOD NIGHT, Calla. Don't stay much longer!" Alexa called as she waved and headed for the clinic door.

Calla waved back and walked into the break room to gather her lunch bag and purse. The clinic was nearly silent—a weird sensation. The clinics and hospitals she'd worked all had quiet periods, but they were never silent.

She, Alexa and the other midwife lived close enough to the clinic that unless a mother had recently given birth, they didn't maintain a twenty-four-hour presence. Even Kostas's palace was less than fifteen minutes from the clinic. A commute that most doctors in Seattle would love.

In the unlikely event that all of them were unavailable, Dr. Stefanios had agreed to be on call for Kostas. It was a tiny clinic, despite its location in Palaío's capital city, and yet Kostas had avoided her for the last week and a half. Except for her first day when she'd treated Queen Eleni, he was always with a patient or in the office, with the door closed, when she was free.

In a larger facility with a staff twenty times larger than the ten on rotation here, it might happen. In Seattle, she'd had friends who shifted from night to day shift, and she occasionally wouldn't see them for a few weeks. But in a clinic this size, it had to be intentional, and she was tired of it. She crossed her arms and looked at the closed office door. Calla felt her brows knit together as she stared at the door.

She could barge in, but a better idea crossed her mind. Calla wasn't waiting for Prince Kostas to simply acknowledge her presence anymore. She was not leaving the island before her contract was up. Besides, she liked it here.

It felt like her place; a weird sensation for a woman who'd never left Seattle before traveling halfway around the world. Her apartment was nice and walking on the warm beach every morning had done more for her soul than she'd thought possible.

Her contract was a year, with the opportunity to extend, if there was a need. She and Kostas didn't have to be friends. Calla doubted that was truly possible after the night they'd shared, but she refused to be ignored.

Dropping her lunch bag on the receptionist's desk, Calla sauntered over to the main door, opened it and then closed it. She knew the buzzer in the office would register the movement, and Alexa's goodbye had been loud enough to hear in every corner of the facility. Kostas knew she was the last midwife in the clinic—and that it was past the end of her shift.

"Ten…nine…eight…" She leaned against the door as she started her countdown. Kostas opened the office door, and she let out a frustrated sigh. "Didn't even let me get to five."

An emotion blipped across his eyes before the mask he'd worn the first morning resettled. "Five?"

"I opened the door—" Calla pushed away from her perch, trying to keep the bubble of emotions roaming through her body in check "—then started counting backward from ten." It was childish, but at least it should silence the final tiny bead of hope that she'd misread the situation. That he'd just been really busy.

Better to accept the truth than give in to any wishful thinking. "You don't have to worry that I think there is more to our night together. Or that I will ruin your reputation, Your Highness." She offered a low bow before reaching for her lunch bag.

"It's not my reputation that's the problem, Calla."

Her name on his lips stilled her feet. But it was his words that lit a fire in her belly. Liam had said it was her upbringing, her lack of societal connections, and her below-average bank account that had riled his parents. Not that her ex had argued with them.

And he'd only been a rich jerk.

Maybe she wasn't the right girlfriend for a prince, but that didn't mean he was any better than her. "*My* reputation is just fine, Your Highness. Maybe it's not good enough for you." Angry tears coated her eyes, but she refused to let them fall. "However, I will not be told that I am less than someone else again."

"Again?" Kostas's head popped back as he took another step toward her.

Calla straightened her shoulders. "You're not the first man to tell me I'm not enough. However, we are colleagues and you should act like it. Treat me just like any of the other midwives." A single tear fell and she wiped at it, furious that she'd lost control. She needed to get out of there; confronting him was a bad idea.

"I can't do that, Calla."

His hand gripped her wrist and she hated the heat climbing up her body, hated that she wanted him to hold her even as he dropped his grip. Why couldn't her body accept what her brain had? Prince Kostas didn't want her.

Men hadn't wanted her before. It had stung then, but it ached with Kostas.

"I'm not saying you aren't enough." He dragged a hand through his hair then shook his head. "You aren't like the other midwives. I've never…" He stepped even closer to her, the distance between them shrinking to millimeters.

When he didn't finish his sentence, she raised an eyebrow and finished it for him. "You never slept with them? Never told them goodbye at an airport, expecting you'd never have to see them again? Never pretended not to know them when fate threw you back together?" The words flew from her lips as she glared at him. Finally, giving in to the hurt and fury his inattention caused.

She'd put herself through nursing school. Come around the world to work on an island where she knew no one. Calla Lewis was perfect the way she was.

"I see I'm interrupting." Eleni's voice carried over the room.

Calla blinked as she stepped back from Kostas. The queen looked from Calla to Kostas, her dark eyes holding her brother-in-law's for far longer than was comfortable. "I apologize. Evan, my bodyguard," she added looking at Calla, "recommended using the rear entrance. I was on my way back from an engagement and wanted to see if you were coming to dinner tonight, Kostas. I didn't want the press to worry about the baby, but…" She shrugged. "I'll see myself out."

Calla raised her chin, knowing she looked tiny compared to Kostas and Eleni. She mustered the last of her reserves as she met the queen's gaze. "I'm sorry that you had to hear that. I'd appreciate your discretion, Eleni."

"You call her by her first name, but me you refuse to use mine?"

It was a ridiculous complaint, and she chuckled as she grabbed her things. A sad laugh that was the only thing keeping the sobs echoing from her soul. "She acknowledges my presence. I had to trick you to even see you. So, why should I use your name, Your Highness?"

She didn't wait for a response. Just spun on her feet and walked out of the clinic.

"Don't say a word." Kostas turned on his heels without looking at his sister-in-law's face. He'd spent more than a week avoiding Calla. Days of arriving early, staying late, bouncing from one exam room to the next while making sure that she was busy with her patients. It had been torture.

But he couldn't stop his response to her. Even when she was furious with him, all he'd wanted was to beg her forgiveness then spend the rest of the time kissing her. It wouldn't take long for people to notice how he responded to her.

And by trying to protect her from the rapid rumors this island liked to start, he'd made her feel unworthy of his presence. There wasn't enough punishment in the world for that…though he suspected the universe was meting out divine justice by ensuring Eleni had heard everything.

"If you think I have any intention of keeping my mouth shut, then you don't know me at all." Eleni bounced further into the room—well, bounced as much as her heavily pregnant body would allow. "At least now I can tell Ioannis why you have been such a bear.

I stopped by unannounced today because I doubted you'd answer your phone."

He wouldn't have, but Kostas left that unsaid.

He'd attended his brother's formal Sunday dinner, which was more meeting than dinner. But he'd taken all his other meals in his private rooms…while thinking of Calla. "I have no intention of discussing this with Ioannis."

Eleni fell into the chair across from the desk and smiled. "I said I would tell Ioannis. I don't care what you do."

He clicked his tongue. "I don't believe that for one moment, Eleni. You absolutely care."

"I do." She grinned. "Your brother knows returning to the island didn't thrill you. He hasn't realized you're plotting your escape yet—"

Kostas opened his mouth but Eleni raised her hand. "Don't interrupt the queen."

"You only ever pull that card when you don't want to be interrupted."

Eleni continued as though she hadn't heard his mutterings. "Ioannis is busy, but I know what escape looks like. I wore it once myself before I found my place."

"I have a place in Seattle." He forced the words through his teeth. "This island holds nothing for me."

"Calla—"

"Would end up just like Mom or Maria. Devoured by the press and hating me." Heat filled his cheeks as the truth escaped into the room.

Eleni held his gaze for a moment before pushing her body out of the seat. "You are Prince Kostas of Palaío. You can't change that."

She headed for the door. "And Maria was a teenage girl. The rumors your father allowed to circulate were not okay. Do you really think that Ioannis would follow the same path as your father did?"

Kostas wanted to say no. Wanted to think that Ioannis would put his partner before the needs of the crown. But if the pressure was too much...too distracting... He wasn't sure the answer was yes. So he kept his thoughts to himself.

"Your mother..." Eleni paused, weighing her words. "Your father should have protected her. But this generation will not allow someone to get hurt. Especially for this outdated honor code of royals that we 'don't comment to the press.' I comment all the time—exactly as I please."

"Because no one can ever get you to follow the protocol rules."

She waved a hand at him. "I follow the rules, just in my own way. And whoever you fall for will make their own rules, too, if you give them a chance."

He opened his mouth to argue but Eleni had gone without a goodbye. His brother's wife really had a way of making an entrance and delivering her exit.

"Kostas!" Calla's voice echoed from the front of the clinic, and his heart picked up. Finally, she'd called him by his name again. Not Dr. Drakos. Not Your Highness. Kostas.

His joy was short-lived when he saw her holding up a barely lucid Narella.

"Her husband called me," Calla stated as Kostas put his arm on the other side of Narella. "Said she told him she was going to the clinic, but her voice sounded off. Then he couldn't get hold of her. He's on his way now."

Calla shifted, adjusting her position to account for Kostas's height on the other side of the woman. "I found her at the edge of the parking lot, looking confused."

"Feel funny...dizzy...mind foggy." Narella glared at Kostas. "Why are you holding me?"

"She's irritable," Calla whispered and didn't flinch when Narella glared at her. "Any chance of GDM?"

Gestational Diabetes Mellitus, frequently called gestational diabetes, was the most common metabolic disease in pregnancy. He hadn't seen Narella yet, but the symptoms she'd described, combined with the usually warm and bubbly woman's irritability, were classic symptoms.

"Can you tell me how far along you are?" Kostas kept his voice low and comforting as they eased Narella into the exam chair. The woman's pregnancy was showing, but Kostas knew she had at least one child already, and women showed quicker with subsequent pregnancies. Besides, visual pregnancy clues were notoriously unreliable!

"Twenty..." she panted as she looked at him, her eyes narrowing in focus as she bit her lip. She knew how far along she was. If she couldn't remember, that was a bad sign. "Twenty something..."

Calla moved to the computer and began pulling up records. "She's twenty-three weeks along. Scheduled for her diabetes test next week. She had GDM with her first and second pregnancies. Probably why she was already walking to the clinic when the symptoms started." Calla moved without him asking to grab the finger test kit from the cabinet.

She handed it to him, and he took it, meeting her gaze. "I suspect this is coming back with a very low blood sugar result. While I do the stick, can you please get a juice box from the fridge?"

They kept several food items for their patients for such situations in the common area and Calla left quickly. "All right, Narella, you're going to feel a prick and then I am going to get a little blood to test."

She nodded, but Kostas wasn't sure how much she'd actually understood of what he'd said. If they were right, they needed to get Narella's blood sugar up quickly.

"Ouch."

"That was the only pinch," Kostas promised as he pulled a little blood into the tester. It dinged just as Calla walked back through the door with two apple juice boxes.

"Forty-two," Kostas stated as Calla put the straw in the juice box and handed it to Narella. It was a good thing she'd thought to bring the second box. Each one only had half a cup of juice, enough to get a woman with low blood sugar—anything below seventy milligrams per deciliter—into the normal range. Below fifty-four was considered a medical emergency. Below twenty, a person could lose consciousness or have a seizure.

Narella drank the juice and, within three minutes, was already acting more like herself. "I'm so sorry. I got a little dizzy and cut up an apple while waiting for my mother-in-law to arrive to watch my two little boys. I can't remember if I ate it…" Her cheeks colored. "My youngest started crying and… I must have forgotten."

"It's easy for that to happen." Kostas kept his tone calm. "I don't know why Dr. Stefanios was waiting to test you for diabetes, but with your previous history, I would have asked you to start testing your blood at week fifteen. Unfortunately, with your history, you will probably have gestational diabetes with each pregnancy. But that doesn't mean you won't have healthy babies."

"It's just…with Marcus and Atticus at home, it's hard to remember to eat at regular intervals." Narella bit her lip as she looked at her fingers. "I'm not complaining.

I love them, but it's so easy to get distracted, and Atticus is still in diapers."

Calla slid onto the corner of the exam chair and patted Narella's knee, waiting for the woman to meet her gaze before she said, "I bet you are a super mom. Two boys under the age of five and pregnant with your first daughter…you *are* amazing. Being tired and distracted is normal, but the best thing you can do for the boys and your daughter is to take care of yourself."

"Easier said than done."

"It is," Kostas agreed. Expectant mothers had so much to deal with, and he wanted to make sure Narella knew he understood that. "But taking care of yourself is the best thing you can do for your children. A healthy mom, a happy mom, a well-rested mom—those are the best things you can give your children."

"Dr. Drakos is right." Calla grinned as she picked up the finger stick test. "It's been about fifteen minutes. Want us to stick you or want to do it yourself?"

Narella glared at the small device before she held out her hand. "I may as well get used to doing it again." She pricked her finger and sighed as the monitor registered sixty-five. "So close." She held out her other hand. "Guess it's another juice box for me."

"Two or three sips should get you to seventy, if you don't want to drink the whole thing," Calla encouraged as she stood.

"Narella! Narella!" Carlos, Narella's husband, raced into the room. "Are you all right, my love?"

His wife waved a hand and gestured to the blood testing kit in her lap. "I have gestational diabetes. Again." Her bottom lip shook as the first tear rolled down her cheek.

Carlos slid next to his wife and pulled her into his arms. "I'm sorry."

"Why don't we give you a few minutes?" Kostas nodded to Calla.

"I'll test my sugar again in fifteen minutes." Narella hiccupped as the sobs racked her body. Carlos kissed the top of his wife's head.

Kostas and Calla quietly stepped from the room.

"Will you want to keep her overnight, Dr. Drakos? I am the midwife on call tonight." The energy that allowed them to work so seamlessly together evaporated as the door to their patient's room closed.

"Calla…"

"Just answer the question, please, Doctor. I don't want to discuss anything else."

Her bottom lip shook, and Kostas wished for the thousandth time since he'd met her that he was simply Dr. Drakos.

"If this was her first experience with GDM, I would. But she and her husband know the symptoms and are skilled at managing the disease."

"Do you need anything else from me tonight?"

"Yes." The word was out before Kostas could think through the moment. But he didn't wait to consider backtracking. "I need to check back in on Narella and her husband. Let them know they can go home, assuming her blood sugar came into the normal range with that second juice box. Can you wait in the office? Or out here…just wait. Please."

Calla crossed her arms, but she didn't argue or head into the office.

That was fine. He owed her an apology. And the knowledge that it wasn't her reputation that was the problem…at least not in the way she assumed.

* * *

Calla waited until Kostas headed back to the patient's room before heading to the small break room. Maybe it was petty. She knew he wanted to discuss her outburst, and she didn't want to do that in the waiting room. But the office was his space.

The midwives used it, but rarely. That was the realm of Dr. Drakos and whomever was hired to join him. Having a personal discussion in his space wasn't what she wanted.

Calla tapped the edge of the wall with her toe and wished she had the strength to just walk away. There was part of her that wanted—needed—an explanation. But if Kostas expected her to apologize for this evening, he was going to be waiting a long time.

She heard Narella and her husband offering their thanks to Kostas and her stomach tightened. Any moment Kostas would find her and say…whatever she hadn't allowed in her pique this evening.

Calla hated to admit that she'd been proud that she'd left without listening to him. It was something she'd never gotten to do with Liam. He'd always had the last statement in any disagreement.

But it hadn't brought her as much satisfaction as she'd hoped.

Because Kostas isn't Liam!

Why couldn't her brain stop that thought? She'd known the man for less than twenty-four hours and had spent the night with him. That didn't mean she knew him.

He'd had plenty of time during their time together to mention he was a prince. And he hadn't. Hadn't said where he was going or shared anything too personal.

Their connection was physical. Primal, even...but that was all.

So why was her heart so certain that Kostas was somehow different?

Before she contemplated that meandering nonsense, Kostas walked in. His tall frame filled the doorway, and she waited for him to step closer, but he kept his distance. That should make her happy...but rational thought was not something she excelled at in his presence.

When he didn't say anything, she shrugged. "I guess you didn't need anything, Dr. Drakos."

"I owe you an apology."

"Just one?" Calla flinched at her tone and closed her eyes as she rocked back on her heels. "That was uncalled for."

"No." Kostas's voice was warm as it filled the room. "It was very called for. I owe you so many apologies. I should have told you who I was in Dayton."

He pushed a hand through his hair and a muscle in his cheek twitched.

Was the nervous tic not as satisfying with his now short hair?

"Dr. Drakos, OBGYN, is the title that I love. The one that I wish defined me. It's the one I earned. When I'm not here, I try to forget that I have a hereditary title. I'm second in line to the throne, soon to be third. I will never be king, and I am fine with that. More than fine."

He shook his head as he looked at her, his eyes studying her. "When you met me, I was Dr. Kostas Drakos. Still am. Unfortunately, Prince Kostas is the only one that matters on this island."

"That's not true." The denial shot from her lips. This was not the conversation she'd meant to have. Not the one they should have. But the words kept coming, "The people here refer to you by Dr. Drakos or Kostas more than they call you 'Prince' or 'Your Highness.' You are more than your title. If you want to be."

She hated the look in his eyes. She'd seen it reflected in her mirror so often. The look of unworthiness. She'd done her best to banish it from her own gaze, following her relationship with Liam, but she knew how insidious the element was. How it lied to you; convinced you it was true even when all the evidence everyone else saw was crystal-clear.

She didn't know why Kostas, a doctor and a prince, felt unworthy. But he did.

"Maybe."

There was the word that really meant no, but she would not press him. Only he could find his worthiness within the life he had.

"Doesn't change the fact that I reacted badly when I saw you in the clinic the first day. I'd spent my three days on the island imagining you, trying to figure out if there was a way to contact you when…" His voice faltered and he shook himself.

"Then you were here, and Alexa was watching, and the press was outside. It kept me from doing what I actually wanted, or even treating you like a colleague that I'd watched work through a medical emergency in the most amazing way I'd ever seen.

"I am truly sorry, Calla. And I am sorry that after fumbling everything so badly, I avoided you. It was unprofessional."

Those were a lot of words. A lot to work through. "What's wrong with my reputation?"

It wasn't the only question hovering in her mind, but it was the one she needed an answer to. Maybe hearing him say out loud that an American nurse, a broke American nurse, wasn't the ideal candidate for a royal girlfriend would stop the fantasy invading her nightly dreams.

"Nothing is wrong with your reputation."

"You said—"

"I know what I said and how you interpreted it, Calla."

Kostas took a step toward her and Calla desperately wanted to close the distance. But she forced her feet to remain still. She pulled her arms even tighter around herself as she waited for him to continue.

"Calla." Her name slipped from his lips and her skin ignited.

What was the hold he had over her?

"You are perfect. It's me that's the problem." He continued before she could respond. "I know what happily ever after with a secret prince looks like in the movies. I've seen the holiday specials that people binge where everything falls into place with the royal and the baker or journalist or…"

"Nurse?" Calla added as his dark eyes held hers.

"Or nurse." Kostas nodded. "Multiple photographers have captured my picture every day since I returned to this island. There are rumors about my advancing age—"

"Advancing age!" Calla let out a laugh then wished she could pull it back in when the lines on his forehead deepened. "Kostas, you're what? Thirty-seven?"

"Thirty-eight." He grinned at her and took another step forward. "Anyone attached to me, even in a rumor, will be hounded by the island press. It is brutal for those caught in the trap."

That wasn't a guess. She heard it in his voice. He'd

watched others ensnared and hurt. He'd been protecting her. It was sweet in a messed-up, internal trauma way.

"Someone you loved was caught in it?" It was a personal question, and one she wasn't sure he'd answer. But she saw the pain hovering in his eyes.

"Loved is a strong word, though I guess all first relationships feel like love, particularly as a teen. My girlfriend, Maria…the press hounded her. It was stressful but she laughed about it. Until a supposed friend of hers told the press that she'd gotten pregnant and lost the baby."

"Oh…" Calla covered her mouth at the horror of that rumor.

"She left the island not long after. She's happily married now, but on the few occasions she returned to visit her parents, she'd always been greeted by at least one or two journalists. I heard a few years ago that she pays for her parents to visit her now. She doesn't come home because of me."

"That's terrible." It was, but it also wasn't his fault. He hadn't spread the rumor…

"It is." Kostas agreed before Calla could think of anything else to say. "I still should have talked to you. Should have explained." He pulled at the back of his neck as he looked at her. "Can we start over…as professionals? Colleagues?"

"Colleagues." She nodded, hoping the hurt in her heart wasn't radiating through her voice. "We work well together. We've proved that twice now." She winked, hating the feelings crawling through her.

She wanted to scream at him. To tell him that what was between them might be special. Maybe it was really something. Couldn't they at least try?

But perhaps he was right. Maybe all the emotions,

the voice in the back of her head pleading that what they'd shared was special, was just fantasy breaking through.

He was right; life wasn't made for television movies. Even when you really wanted it to be. It was time for her to leave before all her rambling thoughts slipped past her lips. No sense embarrassing herself when they'd finally addressed the issues between them.

"Good night, Kostas." She slipped past him, so close that a bit of his heat touched her shoulder.

No, that's more fantasy, Calla.

"Good night, Calla."

CHAPTER FIVE

"You made a face!"

Laughs erupted from the break room where the midwives were all enjoying their lunch. Kostas grabbed his lunch and started for his office. This was one aspect of being back in Palaío that Kostas didn't mind.

In Seattle, he saw patients from the time the practice opened until it closed and then did hospital rounds. His meals were usually snacks from vending machines and sad little sandwiches that he'd picked up from the hospital cafeteria. This clinic took an hour and a half lunch break every day. The nurses on staff always gathered in the break room.

He hesitated at the door to his office. It was lonely, and his feet ached to turn. He looked at the break room. He'd kept to himself, but what if today he joined them?

Assuming they didn't mind.

He stepped to the door and all the heads turned toward him. But it was Calla's eyes that he sought. The hazel eyes that haunted his dreams met him with a smile as he raised his lunch bag. "Mind if I join you all?"

"We'll be angry if you don't, now that you're here." Alexa winked at Calla and Kali. "Besides, maybe you can answer the question of what is wrong with our ketchup."

"There's nothing wrong with it." Calla blew out a

heavy breath as Kali and Alexa laughed. "It's good. It's just not…"

"Not right." Kali nodded as Calla's cheeks heated. "I worked all night making this recipe. It's my great-grandmother's."

"Kali—you and I both know that your husband is the cook in your family." Alexa nudged Calla before passing the dish of ketchup and the cut-up homemade fries to Kostas.

"You've been in the States for so long. Tell us, Dr. Kostas, what is wrong?"

He dipped the fry while holding Calla's gaze. The tomato paste was delicious. He let out a small sigh as he reached for another fry.

"Well, he likes it. You can leave the island, but you can't really go."

He mentally flinched at that statement, or maybe it wasn't just a mental flinch, since Calla was looking at him with concern. Reaching for a third fry, Kostas dipped the fry and brought it to his lips. "It's delicious, but it's not sweet."

"Sweet?" The other midwives both put hands over their hearts as they looked from Calla to Kostas.

Calla nodded. "Yes. It's not sweet like the ketchup I grew up with. I mean, it's good, just not ketchup."

"It's Greek ketchup." Kali shook her head. "Better."

Calla laughed, dipped a fry in the ketchup, though Kostas noticed it wasn't the full dip he'd seen her use at the restaurant. "The fries are the best."

"Pish!" Kali waved a hand. "Tomorrow, I'm trying again. We'll find something you like."

"That's sweet, but unnecessary." Calla reached for Kali's hands and squeezed them tightly.

The jealousy and need flipping through him surprised Kostas. The midwives were close. Friends… But he didn't think he could be friends with Calla. Not really. Not when it wasn't what he craved. Tomorrow he'd eat in his office, but it was too late to retreat now.

"Guess I should have put a few bottles in my luggage." Calla giggled. "Can you imagine at the airport? 'Ma'am, is there anything fragile in your bag?' 'Yes, sixteen bottles of ketchup.'"

Her laughter filled the room. It was such a delicious sound. One he loved hearing. "You know a plastic bottle wouldn't break."

"But the ketchup in glass bottles is so much better."

Kostas chuckled and leaned forward. "So it isn't just the sugar-filled tomato paste, but also the type of container?"

"Sure." Calla grinned. "If one is going to be a connoisseur, one must have tried all brands and delivery mechanisms. The best is the pumps at fast-food chains." She brought the tips of her fingers to her lips and kissed them.

The motion was silly, fun, and just so Calla, it made Kostas's heart shudder.

"A connoisseur of ketchup." Kostas shook his head as he reached his hand out to Calla. "That is the most ridiculous thing—" He made eye contact with Alexa. Her mouth was hanging open; he cut his gaze to Kali and saw the same look of astonishment hovering in her eyes.

Kostas swallowed as he leaned back in his chair, adding inches of space between him and Calla, when all he wanted was to lean closer. He'd nearly grabbed her hand in front of the other midwives. And they'd both noticed.

How could they not?

"I know it's ridiculous." Calla's voice was less cheerful now, and that killed him, too.

"But…" She brightened as she looked at Kali and Alexa. "We all have our silly things. Mine is ketchup."

"Kali's is snow globes!" Alexa laughed. "She has dozens of them on their own bookshelves."

"I love when the glitter and pretend snow falls over the little cityscapes. But you collect haunted dolls, Alexa!"

"That was a secret! And they are not haunted—"

"Just ugly," Kali countered.

The room erupted in giggles as Alexa happily slapped the table. "It started with one sad-looking doll that my youngest just loved. When she outgrew it, I couldn't get rid of her. Now…well, now it's a bit over the top." She shrugged, "But I just see the dolls previously loved by some little girl or boy and then left."

"You are such a bleeding heart." Kali winked at the midwife and Kostas thought the women had forgotten him. Until all three eyes met his.

"What?"

"Oh, come on, Dr. Kostas." Calla's voice was light, teasing, as her eyes held his. "We all shared what our weird thing was, now you."

"I don't have a weird thing." Kostas took another bite of his lunch as he met each of the ladies' eyes equally. He hoped Alexa and Kali would ignore the attention he'd given Calla earlier if he focused on everyone now.

"You do." She grinned as the other midwives nodded.

"Calla is right." Alexa nodded. "Everyone has the thing that makes them happy, that most people look at a little awkwardly. A movie you watch on repeat that's embarrassing. A food. A love of weird snow globes—"

"Or creepy abandoned dolls." Kali countered, and the table shifted.

"Ouch!" Calla's mouth fell open as she playfully glared at Kali. "That hurt."

"Sorry—" Kali looked genuinely upset "—I meant to kick Alexa."

The women laughed again, and he thought for one second that he might have gotten off the hook, but once more all eyes turned to him. He hated to disappoint them. But he couldn't think of a single thing like what they'd discussed.

His room at the palace was luxurious, but he hadn't chosen anything. In fact, no one ever asked his opinion on the décor. Kostas forced the last bite of his lunch into his mouth, swallowed, then offered the truth. "I can't think of a single thing. Being royal means conforming."

Kali giggled. "Conforming. You used to tell the press exactly what you thought of your father. I didn't think the Prodigal Prince knew how to conform."

"It was a hard-learned lesson. But even prodigal princes can learn." He winked at Alexa then looked to Calla.

She held his gaze for a moment, a look he couldn't quite understand on her face. He forced his eyes down; it would be easy to lose himself in their depths…again.

And Alexa and Kali would notice a second misstep.

The chime echoed in the break room, and Alexa and Kali both stood. They quickly exited together, making excuses for why the patient was most likely one of theirs and not Calla's or his. His hope that they might not have noticed the tension between them evaporating on their quickly moving heels.

"You have something." Calla tapped her fingers on the table. Did she yearn to reach across the table, like he did?

"I don't. My room at the palace…"

"What was in your apartment in Seattle?" Calla arched an eyebrow. "Not the palace. But what did you always bring home?"

He wished he had an answer for her. Wished he'd branched out more while in Seattle. His apartment hadn't been a home. It was simply a place he slept. The walls were blank, the cabinets full of white dishes, even the bedspread was a light gray. It held no personality.

"I know you want to hear about the funny mug I bought that said 'A Wise Doctor Once Wrote…' and then it has a bunch of unrecognizable scribbles on it. But I don't have anything like that."

"Oddly specific mug choice." Calla boxed up the containers she'd brought her lunch in and stood. "You wanted that mug, didn't you?"

"It was funny. There was another one next to it that said something far too vulgar for the office, but it made me laugh." He'd picked both up, nearly bought them, then put them back on the shelf.

Before he could say anything, she leaned close. His heart leaped at the light floral scent. The same scent he'd lost his mind to the night he'd made love to her. The urge to kiss her, to throw all his caution away, raced through him.

"Don't worry, I won't tell anyone you like funny coffee mugs—even if royals don't buy said mugs."

Then she was gone.

Calla looked at the closed office door then back at the small box in her hands. She'd found it in a shop that catered to tourists. After looking in far too many shops for the perfect one.

She bit her lip and tried to make herself walk to the door. He wasn't avoiding her…at least not like the first week. Instead, over the last week, he'd reverted to the perfect doctor with no time for small talk or lunch breaks. He'd even scheduled clients during his lunch hour.

She was pretty sure he was surviving on granola bars and yogurt. That, she knew, was common in US practices overextended with patients, but taking a break here was a perk. One she had no intention of giving up unless a mother was in labor.

It was hard not to blame the interaction they'd had over ketchup. Alexa and Kali had each privately asked if something was going between her and Kostas. She'd answered honestly…no.

And it had broken her heart to do so.

There was no reason for her to get him a gift. Particularly one so intimate…

It's a coffee mug, Calla.

But it felt intimate. She knew something about Prince Kostas she was almost certain he'd never shared with anyone else.

Shaking herself, she stepped up to the door. Colleagues could get each other a gift.

Please, Calla.

Justifying wouldn't change the truth. She'd gone looking for a mug for Kostas. She'd examined funny mugs, sweet mugs, silly mugs, even a few not-safe-for-work mugs. Then she'd found the exact one he'd wanted. The shopkeeper had checked on her after she'd squealed in delight.

Running her fingers over her heated cheek, she shifted the box and raised her hand to knock. Before her hand connected, the door opened and Kostas looked down at her. His dark gaze seemed to trip over her, like he wanted to let it linger but didn't dare.

Man, my brain really is going overboard!

"You don't have to knock, Calla. The office is for everyone."

"Yet you're the only one hiding in it." She shrugged, hoping her voice was light. She was teasing...mostly. Calla missed seeing him.

She shouldn't. But knowing that and understanding why she felt so drawn to the man in front of her were two very different things.

"I could argue that I'm busy and not hiding." Kostas winked before stepping back to let her into the office.

"But you'd be lying." Calla winked back as he closed the door.

The air in the office thickened as his eyes held hers. The tension stringing between them felt it might materialize any minute. Though, since Alexa and Kali had asked if they were secretly dating, maybe it was visible to the naked eye.

"I got you something." Kostas's words caught her off guard as he slid around the desk, his hip brushing hers.

"I got you something too." Calla held up the box and laughed as he held out one that was wrapped in fine paper with an enormous bow. It looked like something that belonged on a movie set.

She'd seen pictures in magazines of fancy and, she assumed, empty boxes. Advertisements for gifts she couldn't afford, but no one had ever wrapped something for her in such a fine manner.

She looked from the plain box in her hand to his package and felt heat creep into her cheeks again. Calla hadn't even considered wrapping the mug. The difference between them truly on display with two gifts. "I didn't wrap yours, though. I, um…"

Kostas moved to her side as she held up the plain

brown box. His fingers slid over hers as he lifted it from her. Fire coiled in her belly as she fought the urge to lean close. To rise on her tiptoes and drop a light kiss on his lips.

"Ladies first." His deep voice swirled around her as he picked up the beautiful package.

She reached for the box, surprised by its hefty weight. "You didn't wrap a box of rocks, did you?" She carefully peeled the tape from the edge of the corner. It felt almost wrong to destroy the pretty wrapping.

When she finally got the paper off, Kostas let out a sigh. "I wasn't sure you'd ever actually unwrap it."

"It's too pretty!" Calla pushed her hip against his. She regretted the connection immediately as her body burst with need.

Turning her head, she focused on the present. Not sure what he would have thought to get her…and wrap like it was worth a small fortune. Lifting the lid off, she couldn't stop the gasp. "Kostas!" Tears and laughter warred with each other as she tugged the first jar of ketchup from the paper-lined box.

Six jars of ketchup. The real deal.

"No matter how many recipes the other midwives have you try, they won't be the same as these."

"No. Though all the recipes have been good but not the same. Thank you." She pushed the tear away from her cheek as she held the precious condiment. "Sorry, homesickness hasn't really hit me. But I just got a wave of it. Over ketchup!"

Kostas took the bottle from her hands, putting it back in the box before he pulled her into his chest.

She sighed as his heat wrapped around her. The comfort of the hug, one traveler to another. He'd left Palaío, undoubtedly dealt with homesickness even though he'd been happy to be away from the title of prince, then made a life for himself in Seattle. Did he miss the rainy mornings like she did? The gray sky and moss-covered green buildings?

His home country was beautiful, but it was so different.

She inhaled, loving the scent of sea and mint that floated through her. Kostas. She squeezed him tightly then stepped back.

"All right, enough homesickness." *And wantonness!* "It's not as good as a month's worth of ketchup—"

"A month? I assumed that would get you through at least six." He grinned as he opened the plain box she had given him, his mouth falling open as he lifted the mug from the box.

He held it carefully as he spun it from front to back. It had the same design on both sides: "A Wise Doctor Once Wrote..." followed by a bunch of illegible writings.

The silence stretched out as he stared at it.

Had she guessed wrong? Was it a poor gift? Maybe he'd been joking about the mugs. He was a prince, after all.

"It's a pretty popular doctor mug, and you mentioned this one. I found it..." She twisted the toe of her shoe into the floor as embarrassment crawled through her. *Maybe this was dumb.* "I just saw it."

"Calla." Kostas set the mug down and reached for her. His hand ran along her chin as he pressed his lips together. "It's the best gift I've ever gotten."

"I doubt that." Calla trembled as his fingers danced along her skin, the need to kiss him screaming through her.

"I'm not lying or stretching the truth even a little. It's perfect." He looked at her.

There were so many reasons she should pull back. He'd made it painfully clear that he had no interest in seeing her, at least not on the island. He was a prince, heir to an actual crown, and she was the daughter of two hardworking restaurant owners. She had less than a thousand dollars to her name. Cinderella was a fairy tale.

But tonight she wanted a moment to believe the fantasy. A moment to give in. Lifting her head, she brushed her lips against his.

"Calla."

She shuddered as her name fell from his lips. She feared he'd pull away, but he wrapped an arm around her waist, drawing her tightly to him. It felt like coming home, like falling back into the place she was meant to be. It was temporary, but for a few minutes, she was going to cling to the fantasy.

He tasted of mint and the sea, of dreams and everything she couldn't have. It was precious, and it hurt. Calla flung her arms around his neck. Kostas…this was her Kostas.

Not the prince. Just the man she'd connected with weeks ago.

"Calla…"

This time, when her name slipped between them, it was to end the spell capturing them. She didn't cling to him, even though part of her wanted to. Instead, she stepped back, wrapping her arms around herself, hoping to keep some of his heat close to her.

"You don't have to say anything, Kostas. I know this—" she gestured between them "—isn't what you want."

He tilted his head, and she saw the flash of pain in his eyes. "The moment I saw you in this clinic, I wanted to pull you into my arms. Wanted to kiss you. Thank the fates that somehow, despite all the odds, you'd landed on my island."

"But…"

"Royal life isn't easy, Calla. Fairy tales are fantasy."

"Actually, the original fairy tales were allegorical morality lessons. The little mermaid turns to sea foam when she falls in love with the prince she can never have." Calla bit her lip as the explanation bubbled forth.

Kostas reached for her hand, his thumb rubbing along the edge of her palm. "Calla…" He closed his eyes, as if weighing something, then opened them. "If we try this, you'll be hounded. I need you to understand."

Her heart raced as the conversation's turn sprinted through her. "If we try…"

"Maria isn't the only woman I've seen destroyed by this." He sighed as she squeezed his hand, unsure of where the conversation was heading but wanting him to know that she was there.

"My mother… She left. Royal life was too much for her. She…"

He swallowed and Calla could see the pain radiating through him.

"Mom, Queen Sofia, was so beautiful. She did everything my father and the country had asked of her. But it wasn't enough. Her quiet answers, her shy smile, were manipulated into stories of her being stuck up. Of her thinking she was better than the rest of the island's inhabitants."

The words tumbled forth as she stepped closer to him and put her head on his shoulder. Just letting him know she was there while he got everything out.

"My father thought it was beneath the palace to respond. She tried to bear it. We're taught that from the cradle. Duty. Responsibility. Country first. She tried—she did. But…"

"But it was too much?" Calla offered.

"It was. One day she left for vacation and never came home. They never spent another night under the same roof."

He laid his head against hers. "Even leaving didn't bring her peace. She died when I was thirteen. She was swimming in the ocean and…" He sucked in a deep breath.

"She was a strong swimmer, but there were reporters on the beach. I swear she couldn't seem to escape them. In the end, the press trapped her. We think she tried to swim down the shoreline a little and got caught in a riptide. But, honestly, we don't know."

"Oh, Kostas." She pulled him into her arms, gripping him with all her strength. "I'm so sorry."

He took a deep breath and smiled at her. "She would have loved you." The words seemed to surprise him. His eyes widened and his mouth fell open, but nothing came out. She squeezed him and kissed his cheek.

"It would have been nice to meet her," Calla stated, fully meaning it.

Kostas kissed the top of her head and offered her a smile that didn't fully reach his eyes. "I don't usually speak of Mom, but I want you to understand—really understand— what dating a royal means."

"I see." Calla tried to find the right words. So many emotions were floating through her.

"I wish it wasn't the case. But your life will be controlled by things that rarely make sense—royal protocols, questions, cameras. Your life won't truly be your own. And it doesn't end when we break up, either. You'll always be the nurse that dated the royal."

When we break up...

Those words sent ice through her. *When* not *if.*

She'd been willing to try it. Willing to see if she could make life work within the confines he saw for himself and the person he cared for. The connection between them was something she'd never felt.

Except, Kostas saw this as temporary—which most relationships were—but she wouldn't enter one where one partner already knew there was an expiration date.

"I understand." She swallowed as she looked at the mug on the desk next to the bottles of ketchup. Such silly presents, things that shouldn't matter. But they spoke of the connection between them. The prince and the nurse… Kostas and Calla.

Her heart ached as she grabbed the box of ketchup bottles and hugged it to her tightly. This was the cross-roads, and she wanted to walk the other path, the one that ended with her in his arms again. But not if he thought their relationship was already destined for failure.

She didn't trust herself to say anything. Instead she looked at the ketchup and then at him. "Thank you for telling me all of that, Kostas. For trusting me with the memories of your mom." She swallowed the pain and added, "I'll ration these…well, I'll at least try."

"Good night, Calla." His voice was wistful, like he'd hoped she'd have agreed to a fling. Despite the knowledge that he didn't see her as a potential partner for life.

Liam hadn't seen her as a forever partner, either. At least Kostas had said the words up front.

Calla Lewis was worth more than temporary, even if her heart cried out for it.

Kostas had put distance between them and she'd pushed past it. Demanded he acknowledge her. She didn't regret that choice, but now she'd make sure to protect herself.

"Goodbye, Kostas."

"Dr. Drakos?" Alexa slid into the office, her head down.

Kostas lifted the mug Calla had gotten him to his lips as he looked at the normally relaxed and chatty midwife. His coffee had cooled in the last hour, but it was the mug he was reaching for, not the coffee.

Whatever Alexa had to say, he doubted it was good.

It was ridiculous that a mug from a woman who'd done her best to avoid him the last two days brought him comfort, but he didn't question it. Just like he didn't question Calla's putting the distance between them after he'd laid out the truth about what dating him looked like. And when she decided she'd had enough, her life wouldn't go back to normal. At least not while she was on Palaío.

He'd never tire of her. Of that he was nearly certain, though he shouldn't be. He'd known the woman for one spectacular night and worked with her for a little over two months now. It wasn't enough time. But his soul knew it.

If Calla had stepped into his arms the other night, told him she wanted to try it, he'd have kissed her deeply. Given her directions to the private entrance of the palace and spent the night worshipping her. He pushed those feelings aside as he looked at Alexa.

"What's wrong?" He waited briefly then added, "Is it a patient?" He doubted that. Alexa was boisterous and fun, but when a patient was involved, she was all business…and straight to the point.

"I was joking with my neighbor the other day and I said something I shouldn't have." She looked up at him, her eyes filled with unshed tears. "I am really sorry, Your Royal Highness."

The use of his title sent tingles racing across his skin. He kept his voice low and calm as he stood. "I'm sure whatever it was isn't that bad, Alexa."

"They asked how it was working with you, and about the new nurse." Alexa pursed her lips. "You know how tiny the island can feel. Everyone wants to know."

He nodded as tension pulled through his belly. *Calla.* She was an outsider, a beautiful outsider who'd arrived within hours of the Prodigal Prince. "What did you say?"

"That I thought you two would be a cute couple." Alexa's sigh echoed in the small office. "It was a joke. I swear. Gossip about colleagues. I didn't think…"

"Didn't think what?" There was more to the story and Alexa, normally so talkative and bubbly, was dribbling out the information. She pulled her cell from her back pocket, swiped a few times, and put the phone in front of him.

The *Weekly Times*, the main gossip source for the island and its surrounding neighbors, had a picture of Calla leaving the clinic. The photo wasn't overly flattering. There were a million ways they could have gotten a better image…if they'd wanted to.

But the headline made it obvious that the goal of the magazine was not to put Calla Lewis in a good light: Outsider Trying to Infiltrate the Royal Family?

He hated the phrase, but he wasn't sure how Alexa thought this was her fault. "Alexa, this is unfortunate, but, honestly, little has happened since I got back. So making up a story on a slow news day isn't all that surprising." He handed her the phone; he needed to find Calla. Make sure she was okay. But Alexa also needed to know he didn't blame her.

"Remember the story about Ioannis marrying into the British royal family before he wed Eleni? It was complete hogwash. My brother doesn't even know the granddaughter of the British monarch. But the head-line got clicks and sold ad space, which is all these rags care about."

"Thank you. I wish I could just accept that." She blew out another breath and scrolled down the page on her phone before putting it back in front of him. "The words from the anonymous source are my words to my neighbor."

Calla and Prince Kostas have a chemistry that is evident to anyone near them. It's like they're drawn to each other. Magnets circling each other, yearning to get close enough to cling together.

"I thought the magnet reference was clever, but now that I see it in print…" Alexa's lip wobbled. "I'll tender my resignation if you'd like."

"That is unnecessary. I wish I was a normal col-league, but I'm not."

"I'm not trying to infiltrate anything! Just deliver-ing babies. Excuse me." Calla's voice carried through from the front of the clinic, and Alexa turned before he could say anything else. He rushed around the desk and was in the waiting room a few seconds after the mid-wife. But it was already too late. Alexa was explaining and apologizing.

"It's no big deal." Calla hugged the other midwife

but kept her gaze away from Kostas, just like she'd done for the last several days.

What he wouldn't do to see those eyes locked on him again…

"Calla, are you okay?"

She laughed. "Of course, Dr. Drakos. I mean, they could have chosen the picture they snapped of me walking on the beach and not the one of me looking spent in my scrubs at the end of a long day."

"The beach? When did that happen?"

"Two days ago." She squeezed Alexa's hand. "I looked good that morning. Already done my hair and makeup. Very put together, which is surprising since I seem to still be battling a touch of jet lag after weeks." She yawned as she shrugged.

Kostas crossed his arms at his chest as the urge to pull her close echoed through him. Someone had taken her photo and she hadn't told him. *Why would she?*

They were colleagues. Not actual magnets. But it hurt that she hadn't mentioned it. Hadn't asked for his aid.

"Are you sure you're okay?" He hated repeating the question. She looked exhausted. And it couldn't be jet lag. Not after almost six weeks on the island. They'd had a night delivery last week, but otherwise, the tempo at the clinic had been fairly light.

Was something else going on? Was there more than just reporters at the beach? Surely they hadn't camped out at her place for one thread of gossip.

Finally, her gaze locked on his. "I'm sure it will all blow over soon, Dr. Drakos. No need to worry about me."

Dr. Drakos. For a few beautiful days, he'd been Kostas again. But since she'd given him the mug and walked away, she'd reverted to Dr. Drakos again. He hated it.

"If it doesn't…"

"It will." Calla nodded, dismissing any further concerns.

The door to the clinic opened before Kostas could argue. "Calla, I don't feel all that well. Can you please give me a quick exam?"

Eleni's voice pitched higher as she closed the door and then winked at Kostas.

"I do hope Ioannis understands you are just playing the press." Kostas fisted his hands at his sides as his sister-in-law darted to Calla's side.

She'd become Eleni's favorite midwife. Assuming there were no complications with her pregnancy that required him to perform a C-section, it would be Calla delivering the soon-to-be second in line to the throne. The two women got on well, but he hoped Eleni wasn't expecting more.

She knew far more than Alexa had even guessed at. Though he knew she'd tell no one besides Ioannis. The two had no secrets.

He envied them. That had surprised him.

His and Ioannis's parents had had a difficult relationship. Theirs was the last marriage of convenience for the sake of the throne. The throne had come first for his father. No matter what.

Ioannis and Eleni doted on their son. Treated him as a son rather than as an extension to the throne that bound them all to Palaío.

And they loved each other so very much.

Being near them had sent jealousy crawling through him. But, as Calla's plight currently showed, there were costs associated with falling for a royal. Or having someone assume you had.

"What is going on, Eleni? Or are you just playacting for the journalists again?" Calla smiled as the queen linked her arm through hers.

Does Calla understand how unique that is? How Eleni is protecting her, in her own way? How she'd protect her if she and Kostas were—

No. He would not travel that worn path.

"Those aren't journalists. They are people hoping to capture a picture or story they can sell. Nothing more." Eleni rubbed her back and cringed. "I went for coffee and figured I'd make an appearance. And my security team can help Kostas's run a bit of interference."

She grimaced. "Wow, my back just aches. Comes and goes in waves, but seriously!" She held up her hand before Kostas or anyone else could comment. "I know how far along I am. I know that at this stage I will be uncomfortable." She sucked in a weighty breath.

"Have you timed the back pain?" Calla asked as she looked at Kostas.

He pursed his lips and looked at the clock as Eleni took a few more deep breaths.

"You think it's labor. I didn't even consider it. It hurts, but it doesn't feel like my labor with Mateo. That one was basically textbook." She looked from Calla to Kostas.

"Back labor is more common when the baby is in an occiput posterior position," Kostas offered.

Eleni glared at him then looked at Calla. "Can you please say that in non-doctor-speak?"

"It means the baby is sunny-side up." Calla's voice was soft and calm. "So the head is pushing against your back instead of facing your stomach. It means nothing to your baby—they'll be fine. However, until they shift, or if they don't, it means labor is going to be tougher for you."

"Oh, great." Eleni scowled and grabbed her back again. "Kostas…" she panted as she forced herself to breathe.

"Get Ioannis?" he asked while she worked through the pain. He'd timed the contractions and at this point they were still about eight minutes apart. Eleni was in labor, but she likely had a way to go yet.

"Yes," she gasped, barely able to keep the bite from her tone. "He put me here."

"Yes, he did," Calla agreed. "Why don't you come with me to the delivery room? I'll rub your back after we get you set up. It will offer a little relief."

"At least the press will have something better to discuss than Calla infiltrating the royal family now!" Eleni called out as he started for his office.

Calla laughed. "How sweet of you to go into labor for my benefit, Eleni. Not sure it's the tactic I'd have taken, but it makes a statement. How will I ever repay you?"

"If you rub my back, I promise to do anything you want."

Eleni looked up and saw Kostas still standing by the office door, watching the comedy play out. "Ioannis! Now!"

CHAPTER SIX

CALLA YAWNED AND rubbed her back, trying to calm the achy soreness resting there. She knew it was nothing compared to Eleni's intense pain, but after tending to her patients and helping Eleni through her labor, which still hadn't progressed past five centimeters almost twelve hours later, she was exhausted.

The queen had apologized repeatedly for coming to the clinic so early. Eleni had labored at home for most of her first pregnancy, so she honestly hadn't thought the back pain was labor. The jovial woman really had stopped by to joke with Kostas, add a distraction for the gathered horde out front, and let her bodyguards help with crowd management.

It was sweet. But once Ioannis arrived, the small group of hopeful "journalists" that hung around the clinic almost constantly was replaced by the real deal. More crews had arrived throughout the day.

As had palace security.

The clinic was now basically on lockdown until the prince or princess made their arrival.

Any patient who didn't need to be seen today had been rescheduled. That left a handful of women with advanced pregnancies to navigate the crowd. Calla and the other midwives had escorted them through the parking lot, ignoring all the called questions. It was madness!

They'd discussed sending Eleni home a few hours ago. And they'd kept her here rather than ignite more rounds of speculation and questions. Besides, they figured she'd be back in a few hours anyway, which would only restart the whole process. No one had expected a twelve-hour labor…and counting.

"If you're tired, you can go home." Kostas's voice was soft as he stepped into the small break room. "I gave Eleni some Stadol. She's napping now. When she wakes, it will be time to start Pitocin if she hasn't progressed. But hopefully the rest will kick-start things."

Calla hoped the rest worked. She'd seen exhausted mothers who got pain meds, and could finally sleep for a few hours, progress immediately upon waking. Pitocin would ensure the delivery advanced, but it also intensified the contractions.

Eleni's water had broken an hour ago, officially starting the delivery timer. While some research indicated it was safe to labor for at least forty-eight hours following water breaking, many doctors only waited twenty-four hours if the patient was already at the hospital or clinic.

"Calla, if you need rest…"

"I'm fine. I took a nap after my last patient. The bunk beds in the back room are more comfortable than the ones at the birthing center I worked at. I swear they made them from concrete and covered them with foam so they could claim they were beds," Calla joked as she leaned against the wall.

Hopefully, the light tone and humor would cover the exhaustion still coursing through her. She also should have responded to Kostas quicker, but her brain seemed a little foggy these days. Chalk that up to another thing she couldn't quite place.

She wanted to believe she was fine, but if she was honest, it wasn't exactly true. She was tired. Still functional, but her body never seemed to reach fully rested these days. It was like her internal charge could only reach eighty percent. And she couldn't understand why.

She usually fell into her bed and slept straight through the night. If she woke during the night, she had no memory of it.

Today marked eight weeks since her arrival on the island. Long enough by weeks for jet lag to pass. She didn't have a cold or a virus. Calla checked her temperature every morning, just to be sure. She wasn't risking the health of her moms and their newest arrivals.

Maybe it was finally decompressing from years of hectic schedules? The clinic in Palaío was lovely and so much more relaxed than the environment she'd had in Seattle. She routinely saw between seven and ten patients a day here, rather than twenty to twenty-five.

Her delivery schedule was a fourth of what had been in the US. It was the type of nursing she'd longed to practice when she went into the field. She'd be living her best work life, if she wasn't constantly fighting off yawns!

"Do you need anything?"

Kostas's question was quiet, and he wasn't talking about being tired or Eleni.

The urge to lean into him, to tell him she wanted more, was nearly overwhelming. But before she could think of anything, Ioannis stepped into the room, shattering whatever moment they might have.

"Dinner!" Ioannis grinned, the smell of burgers and fries arriving with him. "If either of you tell my wife

I snuck a burger while she slept, I will exile you from the island!"

Kostas laughed as he sat in the chair across from his brother. The two looked so alike, but Kostas carried himself differently. A little apart. Like he wasn't fully comfortable.

Because he isn't.

The thought wrapped through Calla's mind as she looked at Kostas. He was the best OBGYN she'd ever worked with. Caring, but firm when necessary. He listened to the midwives, taking their concerns seriously. He was comfortable in the medical world.

It was his title that hung heavy. That, given what he'd told her about Maria and his mother, wasn't surprising. But he couldn't separate the parts of his life, not really. He was both an OBGYN and a prince. If only he could accept that...

She pushed herself off the wall. Tiredness was making her brain wander.

"Not sure your brother considers exile quite the threat." Calla gave Kostas a wink and immediately regretted the decision as his eyes held hers. She'd done so well keeping her distance lately. Not because she wanted to, but it was necessary, and the fluttering in her heart reminded her how easy it was for her to react to the man.

"True." Ioannis playfully pointed at her. "But I could threaten to exile you. That might be enough of a threat."

It took all her control not to lift her hands to her heated cheeks as she watched Kostas for his reaction. Reaching for the burgers and fries, Calla's mouth watered and her stomach rumbled with a hunger she hadn't noticed. It was a thoughtful meal. One she figured Ioannis had requested because she was helping his wife.

"She's one of the best midwives I've ever worked with. No. The best!" Kostas's eyes hovered on her for an instant before turning to his brother. "You don't want to deprive the island of her expertise." His words were the right ones. The ones to diffuse the tension flickering between them.

That didn't mean his rational explanation didn't cut it.

Swallowing, she picked up a fry, enjoying the salty smell. It was just what she wanted. In the last week, she'd craved salty things…another change from her normal sweet tooth. Maybe the island really was turning her into a different person.

"Wait. I brought ketchup!" Ioannis chuckled, clearly trying to smooth over the friction he'd created. If she'd ever doubted whether Eleni had told her husband about the conversation she'd overheard, it vanished.

Ioannis clearly meant to offer the joke, not to cause embarrassment. A brotherly gibe gone too far. He cleared his throat as he pulled the bottle from the bag on the floor. "Kostas spent a small fortune rush shipping the stuff from the States. And I snagged one bottle. I must admit, Calla, that I was pleasantly surprised by the taste. Sweet…"

She looked at the ketchup bottle and forced a smile to her face. The gift from Kostas was one of the kindest things anyone had done for her. But it didn't taste right.

It was tangy…and off. She couldn't quite explain it. She'd opened two bottles, thinking it was something with the first. But the second had tasted strange too.

"What's wrong?" Kostas handed her the ketchup. "And don't say nothing. I can tell."

"How?" Calla raised her chin, daring him to acknowledge he paid more attention to her than he did to anyone else. It was a dumb move. One that could only bring her heartache, but she couldn't retract the question once it was hovering in the air.

"You love ketchup." He waved the bottle at her, waiting for her to take it. "I don't pretend to understand it, but whenever you discuss it or see it, it brings a smile to your face. You frowned just now. So something is wrong."

She bit her lip then ate the fry she was holding, still not reaching for the ketchup. Kostas set the bottle down, his eyebrows knitting as he looked at her.

Her mouth exploded with salt and potato goodness. The fry was delicious, and she reached for another, careful to avoid Kostas's gaze as she answered. "It doesn't taste right."

Calla hated admitting that. She knew how happy he'd been with the present. It was sweet, but maybe the international transfer…or maybe her tastes on the Mediterranean island were just evolving. Though, she mused, something about her love of burgers and fries had changed.

"I remember when Eleni was pregnant with our first, she suddenly hated clams. She'd loved them before, but never got the taste for them back." Ioannis tossed a fry into his mouth. "I'll admit that I didn't mind when her clambakes went away, and I suspect now that you have found our local fare so much better, you might not want ketchup hiding the taste of such good food!"

She laughed, hoping it sounded right in the quiet room. "Your island's food certainly tastes wonderful. Shame about the clams, though. My parents served a buttery clam dish in their restaurant, but they only served it when there was access to fresh clams. Here, that's never a problem."

A longing for home, for the small kitchen where her parents tried new dishes for their restaurant, threatened to overwhelm her. It was silly. They'd been gone for years. The restaurant long closed. Emotions wrapped around her heart and she had to swallow the sudden swell.

Her feelings seemed closer to the surface. Maybe it was the tiredness or the excitement of a new life waiting to come forth. That had always filled her with wonder before. Something so right about a baby coming into the world, a new life that could travel this world in so many different directions.

"Fresh clams are all over the place on the island. I used to hunt for them for hours on the beach as a boy." Kostas grinned then turned his attention to his brother.

"Shifting topics, I may have found another OBGYN. Remember Dr. Bandi? She's in Greece right now, but looking for a change and a chance to come home."

The men started talking about recruiting another doctor. Any other time, she'd have paid attention to a discussion regarding a new doctor. Nurses and midwives performed a lot of the duties here, but the right, or wrong, physician could seriously impact the clinic. In one of her first positions, the OBGYN's toxic attitude had run off nearly all his nurses within two years.

She should focus on the brothers' conversation, but her ears pounded as she thought through Ioannis's statement about Eleni and clams. Mentally, she calculated back to her last period. Two weeks before she'd arrived in Palaío.

Dear God.

She was late. By several weeks. Calla's throat tightened as she tried to focus on chewing her food and nodding at the right moments.

Kostas chomped on a fry, completely oblivious to the turmoil racing through her.

All her symptoms suddenly made perfect sense. Fatigued, foggy brain, dislike of a once-beloved food... even her breasts were tender. She was a midwife. How had she missed the symptoms in herself that she'd talked about with so many women?

Because she hadn't even considered it a possibility. The only person she'd slept with in the last year was sitting at the table with her. They'd used protection. But how many times had she told stunned women that condoms were only ninety-eight percent effective, even when used perfectly—which she was nearly certain she and Kostas had done.

That meant that out of every one hundred people using that method of contraception, two would get pregnant. She'd seen women thrilled and devastated by such news. But most often it was shock they dealt with first.

She took a bite of her burger, not really tasting it as she tried to force her brain to consider everything. She was pregnant. With Kostas's baby...his royal baby.

"I know you're exhausted, Eleni, but you have to push." Kostas kept his voice level but firm as his sister-in-law glared at him.

"You can do it, honey." Ioannis leaned over to rub his wife's shoulder, and she held up a hand.

"If you touch me, I will hurt you." She let out a soft sob as she leaned back in the bed. "I'm sorry. I didn't actually mean that. I mean I did but..." Eleni let out a huge sigh as she closed her eyes. "I'm so tired."

"Of course you are," Calla stated. Stepping to the bed, she pulled the pillow off and adjusted the height just a little. "Giving birth is exhausting. There is a reason we call it labor."

Calla pursed her lips as she looked at Kostas. There was a hint of something in her gaze that he couldn't quite place. It was gone before he could consider it... though now wasn't the time.

"I think it's time to try the squat bar." Calla looked at Kostas. "What do you think, Dr. Drakos?"

He nodded. "I agree." She'd been pushing for nearly an hour and hadn't progressed. It was Eleni's second pregnancy; Kostas knew she wanted to avoid a C-section. He glanced at the clock. He'd let her push for another hour, provided she wasn't too exhausted. Then they'd have to do what was best for her and the baby.

The squat bar hadn't been an option at his hospital in Seattle, though he was aware that Calla had experience with them from her work in the birthing center.

"Squat...bar?" Eleni panted.

"Yep." Calla nodded as she helped Eleni to sit back in the bed and then raised the bar from under the bed. "The supine position, or laying on your back, is great for doctors and midwives to monitor your progress. However, some studies indicate it makes delivery for moms more difficult. Delivering in a squat or with a birth chair in the upright position was used for centuries, and still is in many nations. Gravity helping moms!"

She kept her voice bright as she explained the benefits of shifting positions, even for delivery. She was in complete control of the situation, mindful only of her patient's needs. No thought at all that she was directing the queen.

He knew that was one of the reasons Eleni had requested Calla as her primary midwife. When Mateo was born, Dr. Stefanios and the midwives had fluttered around her, paying deference but also not completely sure how to handle the propriety of delivering the queen…no matter how much Eleni had tried to explain that she wanted to be treated just like any other patient.

Calla gave her that. And it was a priceless gift, even if Calla didn't realize it.

"Brace your hands here and then get into a squat. Ioannis, give her a little support and rub her back." Calla guided Eleni, and Kostas let her take the lead while he monitored the baby's vitals.

Just before he'd left Seattle, he'd heard the arguments for birthing upright or even on all fours. The midwives and nurses were pushing for the inclusion of the option, at least. A few of the older OBGYNs had vehemently disagreed, though they'd provided no good reasons.

The nurses had lobbied him, and he'd agreed with them. He'd argued that if it made birthing easier, he'd try anything, as long as it was safe for mom and baby. Unfortunately, Ioannis had summoned him home shortly after. So he hadn't actually delivered a baby in any position besides laying down.

Eleni breathed through her teeth, almost hissing as the next contraction started.

"Brace and push for me." Calla coached as Eleni worked her way through the contraction. "That's it. Push!"

The contraction subsided, but Kostas could see that Eleni was a bit more relaxed, even though she was squatting and leaning against the bar.

"If this is easier, why the lying on your back?"

"A king of France preferred it." Calla laughed as Eleni's mouth fell open.

Kostas knew this story. King Louis the Fourteenth

was said to enjoy watching his wives and mistresses deliver babies. Scholars were divided on the reasons, but he noted that Eleni had lost interest as another contraction took over.

"I swear this little girl better appreciate me!" Eleni choked out as she gripped the bar and bore down.

"It's a girl?" Ioannis rubbed his wife's back as she let out a guttural noise and leaned against the bar as the contraction subsided.

"I dreamed of her last night. Or, at least, I think I did. I dreamed of Mateo just before his birth too." She sucked in a deep breath as she bore down again. "Stubborn too...takes after me."

"It's one of the things I love about you."

"Still want to murder you right now."

Kostas watched Calla bite her lips as she monitored Eleni's progress. She crossed her arms then uncrossed them. Was she worried about something?

The baby's vitals were great, and Eleni was doing fine. Still, Calla seemed off. Her eyes seemed to dart to him then away.

"That's it." Ioannis coached his wife as she bore down and then kissed her forehead when the contraction subsided.

His brother loved Eleni and his son, and soon-to-be daughter—if Eleni was right—more than anything. Kostas's eyes flickered to Calla again, and jealousy flared through him.

He wanted what his brother had. More than he'd ever admitted before meeting Calla. But Ioannis was king. Beloved son of the island.

Ioannis did little wrong, according to the island's inhabitants and the press. Everyone loved Eleni, even though she spoke her mind, because Ioannis loved her. There was grace given to him that Kostas never received.

Ioannis was perfect. Kostas was the opposite. The foil to his brother. It wasn't true, but truth rarely sold many papers or garnered enough ad clicks to make it worthwhile.

Carefully stated half-truths that skirted libel laws. Particularly when his father had refused to acknowledge any stories about his youngest son. The girl he'd cared for hadn't received the palace protections that Ioannis's few girlfriends and Eleni received.

He and Calla weren't together, yet they'd still run the article insinuating she was trying to infiltrate the royal family.

Infiltrate! Such an ugly word. One that didn't apply to Calla. Besides, who did they want him to wed? No one…and everyone.

"You're making progress, Eleni." Calla beamed as she looked toward Kostas. "I've delivered many babies this way. I suspect three, maybe four, more pushes and the little one will be here. Dr. Kostas, want to catch the baby?"

"Absolutely." Kostas stepped in front of Eleni where the edge of the bed had lowered to aid in the position and shifted so his hands were under Eleni. It was different from anything he'd done, but this was the reason he'd gone into obstetrics.

Caring for women and their children in these first few moments of life was a miracle. The love that appeared on parents' faces when their little ones made their way into this world had gotten him through so many long days. It was his calling, and he'd never considered another specialty.

Delivering his brother's child was a gift he'd never

expected, but he was suddenly grateful that Ioannis had called him home.

The contraction started and the room focused on the little one they were waiting for. It took two more pushes, but when a head covered with a mass of dark hair emerged, Kostas looked up at Eleni. "There's a ton of black hair."

His sister-in-law smiled and bore down again. The little princess slipped into Kostas's hands, and he nodded to Eleni. "Your daughter is beautiful."

The queen let out a soft sigh, and a tear slipped down her cheek as her daughter let out a squeal.

Calla helped Eleni lean back in the bed then took the baby from Kostas and laid it on the queen's chest.

"Zelia." Eleni crooned as she kissed the top of her little one's head. She closed her eyes, too focused on the baby to notice the delivery of the placenta.

After a few minutes, Calla tapped Eleni's shoulder and asked if she could clean up the baby. Eleni reluctantly handed the newborn over, and Kostas finished taking care of Eleni.

"She's beautiful." Kostas whispered as he watched Calla wrap the baby.

"Of course she is."

The child cradled in Calla's arms made Kostas's heart ache, but he pushed the desire away. If he was the bad boy of the royal family, and the women he cared for infiltrators, what would someone say of his children? Protecting them from all the camera bulbs, gossip and hurt wouldn't be possible.

"You should take her to Eleni and Ioannis, Uncle Kostas." Calla passed him baby Zelia, and he saw her swallow.

"Congratulations. She is beautiful." Kostas handed

the baby to Eleni and watched his brother lean over his wife to stroke his daughter's sweet face.

"Looks just like her momma." Ioannis's voice choked up.

Kostas turned to give the family a few moments. Calla had disappeared, and he couldn't keep the frown from his face. He moved without thinking, his soul needing to find her.

For reasons he didn't want to spend too much time considering.

"Tell Calla thank-you for us." Ioannis's tone was soft. "And tell her I hope the ketchup tastes right soon."

"Oh, my gosh…you ate without me! I knew I smelled hamburger on your breath. You better have one for me that you can warm up."

"Enjoy your little one." The banter between Ioannis and his wife floated around Kostas, and he was grateful that neither was focused on him.

He needed to find Calla.

Now.

She slipped into the quiet exam room and wrapped her arms around herself as she eyed the ultrasound machine. Calla looked at the door then back at the machine. If she was going to use it, now was the best time.

Kostas was busy with his brother, sister-in-law and new niece. She'd considered taking a pregnancy test, but she'd been so focused on the delivery that she was dehydrated. And she didn't want to wait.

The machine hummed as she flipped it on and grabbed the gel for the ultrasound wand. Pulling the top of her scrubs down, she dropped a sizable dollop of gel on her abdomen and tried to pretend her hand wasn't shaking as she lowered the wand. It took less than thirty seconds for her to confirm what she'd suspected when Ioannis had mentioned Eleni's sudden hatred of clams.

The little bean was moving and shifting on the small screen. She was measuring at nine and half weeks... which matched her time with Kostas perfectly. Tears coated her eyes and her glasses fogged as she watched the movements. "I love you." She whispered the words to her belly as she watched the little one dance on the screen.

No matter what happened next, no matter how Kostas reacted, or anything else, she was certain of one thing. She loved this little one.

Wiping away a tear, she tried to think of what to do next. How was she supposed to tell Kostas? Her bottom lip trembled. If this had happened with Liam, she knew he'd have accused her of trying to trap him.

How would Kostas feel?

Infiltrate the Royal Family... The ugly headline ran through her mind...as did her response to it. That brief statement of certainty uttered less than twenty-four hours ago. How was she supposed to deal with their questions? How was she to protect her child?

She ran her hand along the machine, touching the image and trying to calm herself. She could do this... had to do this. Her child was royal, but that didn't mean anything to Calla. This was her son or daughter. That was all that mattered.

But it would matter to the world.

"Calla..."

She jumped as Kostas's voice echoed in the small room. The ultrasound wand clattered to the ground and the image of her baby disappeared. How had she missed him opening the door?

Pushing the last tear from her cheek, she reached for

the wand and flipped the machine off. This wasn't the way she'd planned to tell him…well, she hadn't known she was pregnant long enough to think of a way, but this would not have made any list.

Putting it off also wasn't an option. Turning, she enfolded her arms at her waist. "Kostas…" Her mouth was dry and she mentally stumbled trying to find the right words to explain what he'd seen.

Kostas seemed frozen in place; the only movement, his mouth that opened and closed several times with no words escaping.

"Kostas," she started again, "it's going to be okay." They were words she wasn't one hundred percent certain of, but she relaxed a little just saying them. She'd find a way. No matter what.

"Are you… Calla…are…" His eyes shifted between the silent ultrasound machine and her.

"Pregnant?" She smiled as she finished his sentence. Then she took a deep breath. It was the moment of truth and she'd handle what came after.

"Yes."

One little word, so tiny, that changed everything.

Kostas ran a hand through his hair then shifted on his heels. "Does our baby look healthy?"

A weight lifted off her shoulders at the simple question. There were no accusations behind it. Kostas looked surprised, shocked even, but not disappointed.

"It was dancing. I know it doesn't realize it's doing it, but for a second it looked like the little bean was waving." She let out a nervous laugh as she gestured to the screen, as though the image of their spinning child was still on it.

He smiled as he took a step toward her. "Waving?"

He looked at her face then down at her belly. "What a sweet thing."

"Do you want to see?" Her hands shook. It was one thing to accept the truth, another to be excited, or happy.

"Yes." He grinned as he grabbed the wand, cleaned it and then picked up the gel. "Do you want to add it?"

The final weight of tension lifted from her as she looked at the happiness on his face.

She couldn't stop the smile spreading across her face as she raised her shirt. "Go ahead."

He dropped the gel on, then immediately moved the wand over her belly. The baby reappeared on the ultrasound screen, and she watched Kostas closely.

A range of emotions cut across his face. Shock, happiness, worry—all things she expected had crossed her features minutes ago.

"So what now?" The question tumbled into the quiet room and her heart flipped. They needed to figure things out, but it didn't have to be right at this moment. They'd had a long day, were both high on emotions from Eleni's delivery and the discovery that they'd be in the same position in eight months.

"We get married."

She laughed. The chuckle echoing in the room as he flipped the ultrasound machine off and handed her a paper towel to wipe off the gel. "You can't be serious."

There were dozens of things he might have stated that wouldn't have shocked her as much as that statement.

Kostas turned, his features anything but jovial. "Yes, Calla. We get married. You're carrying a prince or a princess of Palaío. There is so much that comes with that. So many responsibilities."

"Ones you want to run from! Our child will never sit

on the throne of Palaío. Our child will be even farther down the line of succession." The words spilled out; her fears gripping her as she tried to wrap her mind around all that had changed in the last few hours.

Kostas crossed his arms and raised his chin. In this moment, he looked just like the prince he claimed not to want to be. Determined. "You're right that they will never sit on the throne, but they will always be royal. That is something they can never get away from, as I have so clearly demonstrated."

His features softened as he sat beside her on the exam bed. Maybe it was the exhaustion, or the surprise of finding herself pregnant. Or maybe it was the weeks spent apart from the man she craved to be close to, but Calla couldn't keep her head from leaning against his shoulder.

Kostas wrapped an arm around her and, for just a second, the world felt right. Like this was where she was meant to be. Like everything, even the disastrous five years she'd spent with Liam, had led her here. To Kostas.

"Calla, the baby will be in the line to the throne. I cannot change that. Nor can I change that people will talk, that cameras will chase them. Leaving the island gave me a feeling of freedom, but I dealt with my royalty there too."

He squeezed her tightly. "Anyone they meet will discover the truth and that leads to people wanting to take advantage of them, or desperately seeking to join the fairy tale. I can protect them...and you."

She hadn't wanted the fairy tale, just Kostas. But she knew others who'd have been thrilled to play princess. Hell, the bride Liam had chosen had wanted to join his family because of the prestige of belonging to Seattle "royalty." To a man whose family owned so much property and controlled so many politicians.

Calla had never cared, but that didn't mean people wouldn't think she had. Or treat her child differently because of their status.

And I can't protect them.

It was a truth she didn't want to acknowledge, but it didn't make it less true. She was living in a furnished apartment. After setting aside a sizable portion of her paycheck to repay Liam, she had less than a thousand dollars to her name.

She shuddered and started to move away, but Kostas pulled her into his arms and kissed the top of her head. Her body floated with need for the man.

"Marriage." Calla whispered the word. Kostas could protect their child. Could give them everything Calla couldn't. Her bottom lip trembled. This wasn't how marriage was supposed to work. Wasn't how she'd pictured accepting a proposal...

Though Kostas hadn't proposed. He'd simply stated they would get married. It was too much after the day they'd had. She needed time to figure out her next steps. "I'm going to go home and get some sleep."

She expected him to argue, to demand an answer to his statement. But he let her go.

"Good night, Calla."

She heard the words as she raced from the room, her body letting her flee while her heart screamed for her to race back into his arms.

CHAPTER SEVEN

CALLA ROLLED OVER and looked at the clock. Nearly twelve. She blinked and rubbed her eyes. She hadn't set an alarm after getting home last night. She'd assumed she'd sleep until at least ten, not well past it.

Leaning back in bed, she sighed. For the first time in weeks, she felt rested. Maybe just learning about her pregnancy had been enough to calm her body.

She shook her head…it was the ten hours of sleep that had done it. She rubbed her belly, enjoying a few minutes of quiet, then heard the knocking. Swinging her legs off the bed, she waited for the initial wave of nausea to pass.

Seriously, Calla, how did you miss all the pregnancy signs?

Her nervous laugh echoed in the bedroom as she grabbed her well-worn robe and headed for the door. She was sure Kostas wanted to talk more. And she welcomed the discussion. Last night she'd been too tired and shocked to really discuss his marriage statement. But it was time now.

Flinging open the door, she cinched the top of her robe closed as the well-dressed young woman holding a to-go coffee cup and standing on her doormat smiled at her.

She should have thrown on actual clothes. "I'm sorry. I thought…" Calla cleared her throat. She didn't owe the stranger an explanation for being in a robe in her own home. "Can I help you?"

"I'm Natalia Kilon. Prince Kostas sent me. I think it's best if we talk inside." The young woman stepped through the door as Calla tried to figure out what exactly was going on.

"Excuse me?"

"I'm his assistant." Natalia held out the to-go cup as she smiled at Calla. "It's decaf, but Prince Kostas thought you might like to start the day with coffee."

"He did?" Calla took the cup from the aide and tried to keep her temper in check. It wasn't Natalia's fault that she was here instead of the man she'd expected… and wanted.

"And he figured that I'd want to sleep until after noon?"

"No." Natalia shook her head. "I've been here since just before eight. I've had the palace run me a fresh thermos of coffee every hour since. When noon hit, I waited a bit longer, then just took a chance that you might be awake." She shrugged as though those words made sense. Like requesting a new thermos of decaf coffee and having it delivered to a parking area while waiting for the prince's knocked-up midwife to show signs of life was normal.

Taking a deep breath, Calla offered Natalia a smile. "And where is Kostas?"

"At the clinic. He wanted me to come and see how you were doing."

"But didn't come himself." Fury quickly replaced hurt as she looked at the tall woman standing in her living room.

Natalia either didn't see the anger pulsing through her or didn't react to it. "While most of the press is focused on the birth of Princess Zelia, there are still those who would enjoy breaking the story that Prince Kostas got the nurse from America pregnant. The new royal baby won't stand a chance to that piece of juicy gossip. Even though it won't surprise most of the island that Kostas—" She quickly bit off the last of her sentence. "My apologies ma'am."

"For stating the obvious?" Calla let out a sigh. She knew coming home had been hard for Kostas. He'd been worried about expectations from the moment she'd sat next to him on the plane. And she hated how close her pregnancy was to the rumor that had destroyed his teenage crush. It would cause a scandal when the press learned. But that did not excuse him from sending an aide to her doorstep.

Color coated Natalia's cheeks as she pulled out a tablet and started hitting her stylus against it. "I think I should start making a list of the things you'd like moved to the palace. I know most of the furniture is rented. I'll ensure that it's sent back to where the clinic got it from. But what items are yours?"

"If you'll give me a minute to get dressed, Natalia?" Calla left before the woman could utter what she assumed would be a polite acceptance.

She pulled on a pair of jeans and glared at the top button. Her jeans still buttoned but they were starting to dig into her barely noticeable bump. Glaring at the ceiling, she shook her head that she'd failed to notice so many things until well past the middle of her first trimester. Reaching into a drawer, she grabbed a hair tie, threaded it through her buttonhole, and secured her jeans that way.

One didn't work with pregnant women for a decade without learning a few tricks!

Dropping an oversized shirt over her head, she slipped on shoes and walked out her front door, saying nothing to Natalia. She wanted to talk to Kostas, and that was what she was going to do.

This issue was between them...period.

It was nearly lunchtime, and the clinic was quiet as she stepped into the office. Kostas looked up as she closed the door.

"Calla." He nodded but didn't quite meet her gaze.

"Care to explain why there is an aide in my apartment right now?" She crossed her arms as she stood on the other side of the desk.

A knock echoed on the door and Kostas called for entry without even looking at her. Her mouth dropped open as Alexa opened the door. They needed to talk. Now!

"Calla! I didn't know you were here. It's your day off, and Eleni and the baby went home a few hours ago. You should use your free day!"

"Yes, you should," Kostas murmured, but she ignored him.

"I needed to see to a few things. Get something straightened out, then I am leaving...promise." She addressed Alexa, but she meant the words for Kostas. She was not leaving until they talked.

"Well, Kali and I are going to grab lunch at the bistro down the block. We don't have another patient until almost two. So—" she flicked her gaze to Kostas "—unless you need something, Dr. Drakos?"

"Enjoy your lunch, Alexa."

She was gone and Calla rounded on Kostas. "Explain. Now."

Kostas rolled his head and let out a yawn.

As the primary OBGYN in the capital, he didn't get many off days. No way to sleep until nearly noon after a long delivery. She wanted to grant him some slack, and probably would, if he'd just meet her gaze.

"It's safer for Natalia to be at your apartment. Once the news breaks that you are pregnant and we are getting married, your life is going to change. In ways that you cannot imagine yet. I wanted to give you a few more days of relative normalcy."

"By sending a stranger to ask me what I'd like to take with me? A stranger to ask me what to box and what to leave behind? Before we've even had a chance to talk?" Her body shook with emotion, but he still wouldn't meet her eyes. Last night he'd held her so tightly. Looked so excited, shocked but excited, to discover that she was pregnant. But now…

Had a night of rest made him rethink the statement of marriage? It hurt more than she wanted to acknowledge, but she couldn't really blame him. A night of passion had resulted in so many life-altering changes. However they felt about each other, they were tied together forever by the little one she carried.

"We don't have to marry, Kostas. Many people co-parent without walking down the aisle." The words tasted terrible as she uttered them. She didn't want him to marry her for the baby. But she was drawn to the man, felt like she was where she was meant to be when she was in his arms.

That didn't mean they'd make a good long-term match, though.

"We are getting married, Calla."

Such certainty. Like an order from the prince he

claimed to hate being. She felt her nose twitch as she watched him.

He made a few more notes on the page before him and she lost the bit of her temper she was still controlling.

"I am not marrying a man who won't even look up from his work at me. A man who is embarrassed by who he got pregnant." The angry words spilled out, yet it was the sob at the end that nearly broke her. It wasn't fair to make such an accusation, but he was a prince, and she really was just the knocked-up midwife.

The palace staff was too well trained to say it to her face, but others… The headlines, the questions about her status—they were inevitable. It had been one thing for Liam to point out, but for an entire island nation to question her, to judge her…

Calla wrapped her arms around herself and forced the fear and worry away. There wasn't time; and she was not weak. She was a strong woman, a soon-to-be mother who would do anything to protect her child. With or without Kostas, she'd ensure their child never questioned that Calla loved them for who they were as a person. Not the title their birth afforded them.

She reached for the door handle, ready to storm back to her apartment and tell Natalia to get out. That she wasn't going anywhere.

Kostas's dark eyes landed on her. His mouth fell open. "Embarrassed by who you are? I don't care who you are. It's you who didn't want to date a royal. Who's trapped by fate now?"

The desperation in his voice stilled her feet.

He stood, walked toward her, stopping just inches from her. "Despite your clear aversion to dating a royal, putting distance between us… Despite everything, I cannot stop looking out for you. Listening to the fluctuations of your voice so I know when you are happy, stressed, tired."

He pushed a hand through his hair as he looked at her. "Last night, when you leaned your head against me, I desperately wanted you. Still want you."

Kostas took a deep breath. "I wanted to be there when you woke up this morning. But I also want to protect you, and I know how hard that is going to be. It is safer for you, and for our child, if no one suspects anything at all until you are safely in my rooms at the palace. But all I can do is think of you, dream of you, look out for you."

The air in the room felt too thick to breathe.

Calla laid a hand on Kostas's heart. It was beating rapidly under her fingers. "Kostas..." There were so many things she should say. So many things they still needed to address, but her soul refused to voice those in this moment.

She rose on her toes and brushed her lips against his. His arms wrapped around hers. Tightening as he deepened the kiss. The world shifted just as it had the night they'd first met. Everything clicked into place.

Kostas broke the kiss but kept her close to his body, like he wasn't ready to let her go. Calla sighed, enjoying the heat coming off him. The subtle scent of clean laundry and Kostas that she'd craved for so long.

"I've missed you." His words were soft as his fingers stroked her back. "So much."

"Me too." Calla hugged him tightly. Then she made herself start the conversation they both seemed to be putting off.

"We have chemistry." She laid a hand over her belly.

"But marriage is a big deal, Kostas. A forever deal. At least, the version of it I want."

She stepped out of his arms. If she didn't put a bit of distance between them, she'd lose the smidgen of courage she'd worked up for this.

"You're carrying a royal baby, Calla."

"I am." That was a truth she couldn't escape. He might wish he was just Dr. Drakos, but that wasn't life. Their child was going to carry the title of prince or princess. Their childhood would look completely different from hers.

Still, she wouldn't cheat any child out of a loving family. "Chemistry doesn't mean we are meant to be together, though. A marriage of convenience—" Calla barely caught the laugh in the back of her throat. "This isn't a historical romance. This is our life. We get to decide."

"Marriage to me protects the baby. Ensures the entire weight of Ioannis's authority comes to his or her aid if needed," Kostas countered.

"And it won't, if we aren't married?" Calla shifted on her feet; her body aching to lean into Kostas but needing confirmation of this first.

Kostas blinked. "What?"

"If we aren't married and something happens with our son or daughter; if they need something, the palace will deny them because we didn't marry?"

"I…" Kostas opened his mouth and shut it. "I…"

"So?" Calla raised a brow as she kissed his cheek. She knew Ioannis and Eleni wouldn't deny their child the protections of the palace. His father may have refused to come to the aid of his second born, but his brother was in charge now. "Why don't we take a bit of time, get to know each other? Date."

"The press—"

"Will come for me when they find out about the pregnancy anyway. But until we are sure about marriage, we can keep this very discreet."

She inhaled a deep breath. She didn't want to be his secret, but she knew once the press learned of their relationship...her stomach twisted at the thought of press at her door. But she'd navigate it. Life was too short to accept a person for convenience. "My parents loved each other. It was a gift. Something that carried them through their lowest of lows and highest of highs. Maybe I didn't grow up with every luxury, but my home was happy and filled with love."

Calla paused briefly before continuing. "I won't accept less than that. My child—our child—deserves to see their parents love each other."

"Royal marriages don't have a great history with love." His tone was so bitter, her heart ached for him. That belief was rooted deep, and she knew of his mother's struggles. But what about Ioannis and Eleni?

"Says the man who watched his brother, the King of Palaío, fawn over his wife yesterday. Who cooed with his newborn daughter and rubbed his queen's back."

"They are the exception."

"Maybe. But our child deserves to see that, too, whether it's between us or..." Her brain caught the words as she imagined Kostas with another. It hurt, even in her imagination, but this was a point she needed to make.

"Between us or other future partners we have. I will not deprive them of that for some royal protocol issue." Calla bit her lip. "If you aren't interested in seeing if what we have is more than just passion—"

"Yes," he interjected. "Yes, I am interested." He

crossed his arms, uncrossed them, crossed them again and then reached for her hands. "But with some ground rules, to protect you and the baby."

She squeezed his hand. Ground rules sounded a lot like control, but she was determined not to give in to the baggage she carried from Liam. This would be different; she'd see to it, or she'd walk away.

Kostas laid his free hand on her belly and the hand in hers rubbed the base of her wrist. "We meet in secret, at least for now. That means no trips to your apartment or the palace. You keep palace security on speed dial in your phone, and if something threatens our child, we move you to the security of the palace. *Immediately.*"

Secret meetings. Why did that sound so different from her statement of discreet? Calla swallowed. It wasn't ideal, but it was better than a marriage of convenience. At least for now. "Any other requirements, Prince Kostas?"

His hand dropped hers and raised to her face. He stroked her cheek. "We find time for each other, each day. Even if it is only ten minutes. I've gone weeks with distance between us. I don't want that again."

"That's the easiest thing to say yes to." Calla tipped up on her toes and kissed him. They felt right together, and they owed each other the chance to see if this was the place they were meant to be. And they owed their child a happy home, even if it meant their parents weren't together.

Though Calla's heart refused to accept the possibility her brain offered.

Kostas paced the small balcony on The Grotto, his eyes trained on the trees and ridgeline for any indications of cameras or visitors that should not be in the area. The

Grotto was a secure location…mostly because it was a rarely used hideaway in the mountains.

Baby Zelia's birth had captured the nation's attention, but when word broke that another royal was on the way… The bad boy's baby, conceived with a foreign nurse out of wedlock.

The headlines his mother and Maria had faced would look like puff pieces compared to such a revelation. Kostas pulled his hand over his face at the questions that would be thrown at Calla.

And he wanted to protect her from every single sling. Wanted to wrap the weight of the palace around her to ensure no slights ever touched her. His mother hadn't felt protected. His teenage crush's concerns had simply been ignored, his pleas for aid falling on his father's deaf ears. Calla would never feel that way. He'd make sure of it.

She'd never deal with a lie or overstatement. He'd push back. He doubted Ioannis would mind, but if he did…well, Kostas planned to do it anyway. Calla would always feel protected…always.

Kostas breathed in the mountain air, forcing himself to focus on finally having Calla to himself again. Finally getting to spend time without worrying if anyone saw or suspected. Their first date!

Or was it their second date? Did they count the diner in Dayton with cheap burgers and salty fries?

"You have quite the pondering look on your face, Kostas."

Calla's voice caught him off guard. He'd not seen her hike in on the back trail. That meant he could have missed others. He scanned the horizon one more time then turned to her.

He dropped his lips to her cheek and his heart settled

as her scent floated over him. Calla was here. She was safe, and so was their baby. That was all that mattered.

"How did you get here? I was monitoring the main trail." He pushed a lock of dark hair behind her ear, his fingers unable to keep from reaching for her.

"Land trail." She pointed to the edge of the property, "It was one option on the very detailed sheet Natalia emailed me this afternoon. It looked like the easiest route from my apartment. And it's lit almost all the way back down the trailhead. Still…" She held up a flashlight before setting it on the small table.

Calla stepped closer and slid her fingers through his. He hoped it was because she couldn't keep her hands from him, either.

"So why were you looking so pensively into the trail? Scouting wayward cameras?" Her giggle hovered around them.

He knew she was trying to make light of the situation, but she needed to look for cameras. Or do like he did and just assume that they were always trained on him. If he never broke the princely expectations foisted on him in public, then people couldn't complain. Or at least they couldn't complain as much.

Rather than give a lecture she was likely to hear from the protocol office ad nauseam after she was publicly linked to him, he offered the other truth. "I was trying to figure out if this was our first or second date? Does the diner count?"

"Of course it counts." Calla's eyes widened as she held his gaze. "It's why we are here! Why…" Her hand dropped to her belly before she smiled. "It was definitely our first date."

"I like to think we'd have ended up here, even if we hadn't had the medical crisis on our flight." The hope floated into the early evening and he pulled her close. "Like to believe that you'd have landed in the clinic and our connection would have been too much to ignore at some point."

Even if I was royal. But would I have set aside a space in my heart if we hadn't met before? Kostas wanted to believe their initial connection was strong enough, but he wasn't sure. And he hated that.

Her lips twitched and her mouth opened, but whatever words initially hovered there, she swallowed as she looked over his shoulder at the retreat. Perhaps the same thoughts were floating through her mind.

"So, where are we?"

Rather than push, Kostas wrapped his arm around her and led her into the retreat. "This is The Grotto. It's a retreat my father created then rarely used. My brother updated a few rooms, but I think there are bathrooms that still have pink tile that was in fashion in the 1950s. My father planned to fully renovate it but..." Kostas shrugged.

This had been his father's place, his hideaway. On the few occasions he had come here with his mother, Ioannis and Kostas hadn't accompanied them.

"Your father?" Calla leaned her head against his as they moved into the retreat. "I'm not sure I've ever heard you mention him."

Kostas let out a small grunt. "That's because there is little to say. My father was 'the King.' Always. He was a husband and a father after caring for the country. Maybe that was the right choice, but it left little room for the rest of us. He ceded control of the throne to Ioannis only when the stroke he had made it impossible for him to carry on. He died a few weeks later. Without being king, I am not sure he had much to live for."

Calla squeezed the arm she had around his center. "That sounds hard."

"It was." Kostas bit the inside of his cheek as emotion wrapped through him. This was a heavy topic for a second date...but maybe it was best she knew. "My father wanted to control everything."

He let out a breath and shook his head. "Actually, my father did control everything. If it didn't benefit the crown, it didn't get mentioned or addressed. It's why Mom left."

"So he would have had thoughts about our relationship."

"Undoubtedly," Kostas confirmed. His father would have hated that both his sons had gotten women pregnant out of wedlock. Would have attempted to control that narrative as soon as he'd learned it. His mother...

Kostas's heart seized as he thought of his mom. And her reaction to being a grandmother. She'd died so young, but he knew she'd have loved that stage of her life.

His mother wouldn't have cared that they'd gotten pregnant out of wedlock. Wouldn't have cared that Calla was a foreigner; that she didn't have a title. All that would have mattered was the smile she brought to her son's face. "My mom wouldn't have cared, though. She'd have thought you were perfect."

Perfect for me.

Calla's lips twisted down and pulled back. "I'm hardly perfect. The best I can hope for is delightfully flawed." Her nose twitched as she looked around the retreat living room. "I love the windows overlooking the mountains here. I bet it's lovely first thing in the morning."

"It is. And at sunset, which we'll see in about two

hours." He pulled her to him. "What do you mean by 'delightfully flawed'? That is an…" he hesitated "…interesting combination of words. Did your parents say that?"

"Oh, no!" Calla laughed, but the sound was uncomfortable. "Liam, my ex, always called me that. We dated for five years, got engaged, but I didn't meet his family's expectations. I got so used to saying it for years that it still slips out."

A person she cared for; someone she'd considered spending her life with, had called her "delightfully flawed" so often it still slipped into conversation? That was horrible.

"Is he why you're here?"

He was so glad she was in Palaío, but had she been running from an ex? Her past didn't matter to him, but he wanted to know everything about the woman before him.

"In a roundabout way. He helped me pay for nursing school and when we broke up…well, he wanted the money back. It would cost more in lawyers to fight than repay. I've nearly paid it off and I'm here because the pay from your lovely clinic lets me clear the last bit off within a year."

"He wanted you to repay him?" Kostas knew his mouth was hanging open, but he couldn't help it. What a callous thing to do at the end of a relationship.

She squeezed his hand as she stepped to the window overlooking the hills. "Liam…" She hesitated, and Kostas didn't push. He wanted to know, to understand, but he wouldn't force it.

"He probably would've gotten along well with your father. He was quite controlling. I didn't realize it as quickly as I should have. But I did my best to fit the cast he and his family wanted. Blond...society fiancée, but it was never enough."

She shrugged. "And I'm glad. I am much happier being me than trying to fit someone else's mold. I won't do that again!"

Calla clapped. "But as soon as I pay off Liam, I can kick my final tie to him. Heavy stuff for date two!" She grinned and looked for the kitchen.

"The baby and I are hungry. What are you feeding us?"

She was ready to change the topic. He understood, but he couldn't stop the bead of anger pooling in his belly on her behalf. So her ex had helped her get her degree then demanded repayment when she didn't measure up to his parents' expectations? What had those expectations been that Calla couldn't meet them?

He'd called her perfect a few times, and he still felt the word fit her. Rationally, he knew no one was perfect, but Calla was caring, intelligent, beautiful, brave... what else could one want?

He made a note to have Natalia track down Liam and the loan. Preferably without Calla knowing. He'd have it paid off and perhaps send along a note thanking the man for his stupidity. After all, it had led Calla to him.

He'd surprise Calla with the news when it was done. His gift to her, a true gift, one he never expected repayment for.

"We're having moussaka." The palace cook had placed the spiced meat dish, layered with eggplant and tomato sauce, in the warmer this afternoon and he'd driven it up with him. "And there's *kourabiedes* for dessert."

"Ooh, butter cookies! I love those!" Her eyes sparkled as she pointed to the hallway. "Kitchen this way?"

Kostas took her hand and kissed the top of it. "Can't let you and the baby go hungry. Follow me, my lady."

"My lady!" Calla laughed, and the sound was relaxed. Not the nervous laugh he hated to hear come from her sweet lips. "I could get used to that phrase."

He squeezed her hand as he led her to the kitchen. If she enjoyed hearing "my lady," how would she feel when people referred to her as "Your Highness" or "Princess"? Hopefully, with the same bubbly enthusiasm he'd just witnessed.

"So now that you've fed me, what's next?" Calla grinned as Kostas put the rest of their dinner in the fridge. She hopped up on the counter just like she'd done at home for years.

Kostas turned and looked at her. For a moment, she almost hopped off. Liam had hated this habit, but she'd never managed to break it.

As a young girl, her father had placed her on the edge of the counter so she could watch her parents cook. She did it without thinking.

Rather than comment on her position, Kostas stood in front of her. His eyes burned with desire. He held her gaze before his attention dropped to where their child was growing.

"You are gorgeous. And now that you're sated, what would you like to do?" His voice was sultry, and her body hummed as its cord raked across her.

She wrapped her legs around him and pulled him closer as her arms circled his neck. She'd trapped him—though he looked like he had no intention of going anywhere. His breath caught as she lightly kissed his lips. It would be so easy to fall into bed with him, to whisper that she wanted him to carry her to bed. To lose herself in his arms.

Part of her wanted to. Cried out for her to beg him to touch her. But she also wanted, craved, more than just a physical connection to him. She brushed her lips against his then pulled back.

He let her pull away, but his palms rested on her knees.

"What movie options are there? If this was a second date between two regular people, we might go to the big screen. Pay too much for popcorn and sodas, and think about holding hands in the dark."

Kostas chuckled. "'Think about holding hands in the dark'? That sounds more like a teen rom-com." He kissed her cheek as he lifted her off the counter and then pulled her toward a door on the left.

He swung it open with flair and she covered her mouth as he flipped on the lights. She'd heard people discuss their home theaters. Known men to brag about putting in a large screen, but this...this was basically a small theater.

She blinked as she looked at the seats—or rather, couches. Designed for comfort and cuddles. The popcorn maker in the corner was only a little smaller than the one in the theater by her house.

"The bathrooms may still have pink tile, but Ioannis upgraded the theater, my lady." He winked as he walked over to the popcorn machine, flipped it on and dumped the kernels in, then looked at her. "We've got a huge library of movies. And I also have most of the streaming services, so rom-coms, drama, comedy? What's your favorite?"

The smell of popcorn started to fill the space as she

looked at the place. So this was what dating a prince was like!

"Most of the streaming services? Including the ones from the States?" She crossed her arms as the request built in her chest.

Kostas seemed to sense her hesitation. "Yep. So what is it you're craving? A talk show, reality television, baking show?"

He was so far off.

"You ever seen the ridiculous History channel show *Ancient Aliens*?" Calla felt heat flood her cheeks. "My dad and I watched it together and it's hilarious."

Kostas ran his hand through his short hair.

"Do you miss your longer hair?" Calla ran her hand along the shortened length. "I liked it. Not that the short hair doesn't look nice too."

He blinked, clearly confused by the turn of subject, which she couldn't blame him for. "Are you trying to change topics now because we can get any show in the world on a big screen, with a bucket of popcorn from an actual popcorn machine? And you want to watch a show about how aliens helped ancient people build things…a show that history can easily debunk but is like an accident you can't look away from?"

He kissed her cheek as she felt happiness bloom inside her. "You've seen it!"

"Only a few episodes. Well, almost every episode."

"So you did have a weird thing besides silly mugs. Oh, Alexa would love to know this."

"But you'll keep my secret, right?" He kissed her, lingering for a few seconds.

"I would have agreed without the kiss. But that was nice." Calla grinned as she leaned into him and kissed him again. "Besides, I couldn't out this secret without outing my love of it too.

He brushed his lips against hers again then handed her a bowl and scoop. "You get the popcorn ready; I'll go load up the show."

Calla watched him walk to the small room off the theater and let out a sigh. She was dating a prince, and everything was different, but in this moment, in this one perfect piece of time, it just felt like that first night. Like they were Calla and Kostas.

The lights and questions would come, but they'd find a way to navigate it together.

CHAPTER EIGHT

"Good morning, Calla." Kostas's voice was light as he slid his stuff into the small locker next to hers.

"Morning, Kostas." She couldn't keep the grin off her face. They'd spent the last few nights at The Grotto, watching old movies and silly alien documentaries. While working, they kept things professional, but if anyone walked into the employee lounge at the moment, she bet they'd suspect the truth.

She was happy. Really happy with Kostas. He made her feel seen. Whether it was when they cooked some of the dishes she'd learned at her parents' side or watching ridiculous documentaries, she never felt like she had to be more than who she was.

After years of agonizing over what she was wearing, how she spoke, how she held herself, it was a joy to just be herself. And made her realize how unhappy she'd been with Liam. Once she finished repaying the loan, she vowed to never think of the man again.

"How did you sleep?" His voice was low. It was a question meant to check in on her and the baby. One that he didn't want to risk the rest of the office hearing.

She was sleeping better than she'd been before. But last night she'd tossed and turned. Not with worry, though.

No matter what time they got done at The Grotto, he walked her to the top of the trailhead, then watched until she got into the car she'd parked with the others. It was sweet, but she craved more than the kisses he left on her lips.

She wanted him in her bed. Wanted to wake up next to him. To sip coffee with him, even if hers was decaf.

"Not as well as I would have liked."

He arched a brow. But before she added a suggestive statement, Alexa opened the locker room door.

"Dr. Drakos!" The panic in her voice was unmistakable, and Calla turned to see what was wrong, all thoughts of convincing Kostas to spend the night with her flying away.

"Adrian called. Myra is in labor. She requested a home birth, but Adrian says she's been laboring for too long. I couldn't get him to give me more information."

"This is their first." Kostas pursed his lips. "But Myra's mother was a midwife and she helped with dozens of births. She knows what to expect."

"I think her mother always expected she'd go into medicine, but its numbers that really make her happy," Alexa added, looking at Calla. "Still, Adrian isn't usually overly excitable."

"His wife is having their first baby, but maybe we should go out. If she's in labor, Calla and I will be there for the home delivery, anyway. I can come back to the clinic if we have any other expectant mothers needing delivery."

Calla opened the locker and grabbed the backpack she'd dropped into it just a minute before.

The door to Myra and Adrian's small house opened as Calla raised her hand. Myra looked exhausted and more than a little ticked as she tilted her head, shifting her gaze between Calla and Kostas. "So Adrian's worried self got you two out here before necessary." She cringed, grabbed her belly and breathed through the contraction.

Keeping her mouth closed, Calla monitored Myra's breathing and took stock of the mother's appearance. She looked tired, but that was to be expected. The contractions were clearly painful, but not debilitating. All good signs.

"You've been having contractions since one o'clock." Adrian's words carried over his wife, who grunted but either didn't or couldn't offer a rebuttal.

One a.m. put Myra at just over nine hours of labor. Not a terribly long time for a first-time mother. Though Myra might feel differently as the person currently experiencing the pains.

The contraction ended, and she threw her head up to the ceiling as she sucked in a long breath. "There was no need to send for anyone yet. As I've said repeatedly, Adrian. The contractions are still only six minutes apart. My water is intact—" The words left Myra's lips and she immediately looked down.

Water pooled under her bare feet as she let out a curse under her breath. Her cheeks flushed as she met Calla's gaze. "He will never stop talking about this. You know that, right?"

"I do." Calla nodded. "But now that your water has broken, I guess it's a good thing we are here."

Adrian's grin was brilliant behind his wife, but he wisely kept his mouth shut as she moved to the side to let them in.

"Contractions are six minutes apart?" Kostas asked as he stepped into the small living room.

"They are," Myra confirmed. "I'm going to change

into something less wet." She waddled off, still not looking at her husband.

"How long do you think she'll stay mad at me?" Adrian crossed then uncrossed his arms as he looked toward the hallway where his wife had disappeared.

Kostas stepped up beside him and dropped the midwifery bag with all their supplies. Offering Adrian a comforting smile, he shrugged. "Many women are mad at their significant others during labor. There is a reason it's a standard storyline in comedy shows."

"I guess. At least her snarls aren't as deep or cutting as her mother's." Adrian let out a laugh before sharing a knowing glance with Kostas.

Clearly, there was a story there Calla missed as an outsider. She raised a brow, and Adrian chuckled. "Leta, my mother-in-law, doesn't think I'm good enough for her daughter. She's quieted down about it now, but—"

"She wouldn't have been happy with anyone," Myra stated as she rounded the corner.

"Maybe a prince." Adrian grinned as his pregnant wife came to his side.

"Well, Ioannis is taken, and the rebel prince over here would have gotten an even rougher time than you. Titled or not." Color invaded her cheeks as she looked at Kostas. "No offense, Dr. Drakos. I…"

Calla opened her mouth, looking for the right words to defend Kostas. To playfully state that the man was as far from that reputation as possible. Hell, it was her putting the brakes on the marriage he'd suggested when she'd found out she was pregnant.

But before she could say anything, Kostas waved it off. "None taken, Myra." He offered them each a smile. It was only the twitch in his hand that let Calla know the words had landed close to his heart.

Reminded him once more that it wasn't really him people saw, but a caricature. That, despite the years away from the island, completing med school and then returning when the island needed him, the reputation earned unfairly in his youth still clung to him.

"Do you have the water bath ready?" Calla hoped the question redirected the awkwardness of the room back to the reason they were all there.

"Yes. It's out here." Adrian gestured for Kostas to follow him while Calla waited with Myra.

Another contraction started and she breathed through it then started pacing. "I know my mother wasn't thrilled that I married Adrian. Thought that he was beneath me since I got my master's degree and he's a carpenter." She rubbed her lower back as she walked from one side of the small living room to the other.

Calla didn't interrupt. She'd heard all sorts of tales since she'd started her career. Something about labor brought out the chattiness in some of her patients. Maybe it was wanting to drop old baggage as new life entered the world. Or perhaps it just passed the time while mothers worked through the long hours it typically took to bring forth new life.

"But he makes me laugh. And he makes the most beautiful furniture." She sucked in a deep breath.

A tear slipped down her cheek. "I can't explain it. Maybe on the outside we don't look like we should click. A mathematician and a carpenter, but he's my person. It's just that simple. Adrian is my person. Does that sound ridiculous?"

Kostas stuck his head back in the room. "Everything still okay in here? We're filling the water bath. In a few minutes, if you want to sit in it, it might give you a bit of relief."

His eyes flicked just briefly to Calla and her heart swelled with emotion. Her person. Maybe it really was as simple and as uncomplicated as that. Adrian was Myra's match…and Kostas was hers.

"No, that doesn't sound ridiculous," Calla murmured, but Myra was bent over in the throes of another contraction.

"Sorry, what did you say?" Myra wiped the back of her hand across her forehead as the contraction ended. That one was not six minutes apart.

"Nothing." Calla grinned.

"Are you okay?" Calla's voice startled him in the quiet dark of their walk back to the clinic. A clinic staffer had picked up all their gear and taken their dirty scrubs while they'd waited with Myra and Adrian for the local pediatrician to check in on the newborn.

It had been a long but wonderful day…mostly.

"Of course." The words carried through the night, and he wished he felt he could hold her hand. The last two weeks, they'd made time for each other like they'd promised. But it was always at The Grotto, or in the quiet times when they were the only ones at the clinic.

The times when he knew for sure they were alone. It was the right choice, but he envied others. Other couples walked home together, arms linked, head on shoulders. No worries about it making headlines. Just able to enjoy the moments together without realizing what a special gift that actually was.

As if she'd read his mind, Calla reached for him. The pressure of her touch sent calmness floating through him. Then concern as he tracked the empty pathway in front of them.

He squeezed her palm and pulled away. Until she

was ready to move into the safety of the palace, until he could fully protect her, he wouldn't risk anything.

"Adrian and Myra's baby is adorable." Her whisper carried in the evening air.

"She is. And Adrian will never let her forget we were there just as her water broke."

"And Myra will not let him forget that she didn't deliver for another six hours." Calla laughed.

The sound sent a thrill through him. He could hear the brilliant smile attached to it. A happy Calla, a safe Calla, was the most important thing to him. He'd had a realization today, though. He understood Adrian's panic.

Understood why the man had gone against his partner's wishes to ensure she and their child were safe. Despite all the evidence before him, they were fine.

For years, Kostas had watched nervous partners pace the halls, worry running through their features. Even when labor was progressing normally, the partner not delivering the child carried an anxiety through the entire process. Kostas hadn't planned on having children...but he'd always prided himself that he knew too much to worry over nothing.

Pride... He mentally scoffed at how little he'd really known. Heck, if Calla would let him ensconce her in the palace for the next several months so he could ensure nothing bad happened to her, he'd order it done tonight.

Six months ago, he'd have assured himself that he knew too much about delivery, understood the risks that needed worry and those that were just part of the process to be concerned if he ever found a life partner.

Now he'd side with Adrian. Rationally, he knew Myra was right. They hadn't needed to call for a midwife for at least another two hours. But the idea of Calla in pain, walking the halls for hours, cringing in agony, sent shudders through his soul.

The clinic came into view and he slowed his pace, not yet wanting to say goodbye.

"Why don't you come to my place? We can make dinner...a very late dinner." Calla bumped his hip with hers.

The refusal hung on his tongue. There were hundreds of reasons to say no. To protect Calla and their child. If anyone saw him at her place...

Before he could say anything, she offered, "I need dinner despite the late hour. You're hungry too. I heard your stomach growl. Besides, it's nearly midnight. No one will see you, and you can sneak out early before anyone else is awake.

"Don't say no." She grabbed his hands and pulled him to the path up to her apartment. "Come home with me, Kostas."

He wanted to hesitate—to think through everything. But his feet seemed to have a mind of their own.

"You aren't the rebel, Kostas." Calla squeezed his hand as they walked together. "I know that you worry about what happens when people learn about us. You aren't the stereotype. Myra was joking."

"She was." His voice sounded hoarse. He wanted to blame the late hour but...

"But the words still hurt." Calla pulled the key to her apartment out of her bag with her free hand.

He wished he could say they didn't. Wished that after all these years, it didn't bother him. That he'd developed an impenetrable skin. "She didn't mean anything by them."

The door to her apartment swung open and Kostas inhaled and let the worries pass him by. "And tonight, or what's left of it, I just want to enjoy my time with you."

Kostas dropped a kiss on her lips. She leaned into him, her body molding to his. This was his happy place.

"Calla…" He wanted to take her to bed. To lift her in his arms, carry her to her room, then spend the night lost in her arms. But they needed sustenance.

The clinic wasn't open on Sunday, so they had the day off. Assuming no mothers went into labor. He had all night. And he'd make sure he was gone before the rest of the world was awake.

"I have leftovers in the fridge." She kissed his cheek. "Leftovers that we can enjoy cold, so we can go to bed." The heat in her eyes burned him.

"Sorry, I forgot the other kitchen chair was broken. I meant to tell the landlord, but since it's only me…" She shrugged as she hopped off the kitchen counter and grabbed his empty plate.

"I think you like sitting on the counter." Kostas slid behind her at the sink, wrapping his arms around her waist as she ran the warm water over the dishes.

He dropped his lips to the base of her neck and barely contained a moan of need as her butt rubbed into him. The month of distance, the weeks of pent-up need barreled through him as her body moved against him. But he would not rush this.

Calla turned in his arms, wrapping her arms around his neck. "Kostas…"

He drew circles with his fingers lightly on her back as her head tilted up to his. Her lips beckoned and he skimmed his mouth along her jaw, grazing her skin before finally claiming her lips.

She sighed and opened her mouth. His hands slipped to her waist and he pulled her tightly to him as their tongues danced. His senses were nearly overwhelmed as heat consumed him.

Calla pulled back, running her hand along his jaw. "Come to bed?"

"Lead the way."

Her eyes lit up and she grabbed his hand. The apartment was small, and he was grateful that it took only seconds to work their way to her bedroom. He flicked on the bedside light. After weeks apart, he wanted to see her.

Needed to see her reactions to his touch.

She pulled his shirt over his head, dropping it to the floor. Her fingers trailed along his skin and his body ached for her.

"Calla." Her name sounded like a prayer as it escaped his lips. "Sweetheart." He cupped her cheeks with his hands, dropping a light kiss to her lips before slipping his fingers under her light shirt.

He sighed as her shirt dropped to the ground, then grinned as he saw the ponytail holder looping through her buttonhole.

"I know it looks silly—" Calla shrugged "—but it works."

Laying his hand on her lower belly, he kissed her again. "You're perfect." He captured her mouth once more before she could argue with him. She was perfect to him, and he wanted her to hear that so much that she never doubted it.

His fingers unwrapped the makeshift waist extender, and he pushed the pants down her hips. He unclipped her bra and smiled as he rubbed a thumb over one nipple then the other.

She rocked her hips toward him. "My breasts are sensitive."

"You'll tell me if it's too much, promise?" Kostas trailed kisses along the top of her breasts, his body screaming for him to claim her.

"I meant..." Her eyes dilated with pleasure as she looked at him. "I meant I want you to touch me." Her hand grabbed his, guiding him back to her breasts, showing him exactly how she wanted him to love her.

It was erotic, and he loved ceding to her wishes. However Calla wanted pleasure, he'd give it to her! He circled her nipples with his fingers, watching the need play across her face.

Lowering his head, he suckled each of her nipples then carefully guided her to the bed. Her skin felt velvety under his fingers as he lowered her to the mattress. He quickly stripped off the final pieces of his clothing and lay next to her on the bed, pulling her into his arms.

Her backside rubbed against him, and he nipped at the nape of her neck. "I want you, Calla. So badly. But I won't rush this."

Leaning her head back, she kissed him. Her hand stroked his thigh, desperately close to his manhood, and desire nearly overwhelmed him.

Feathering stokes down her body, he touched her heat, loving the moan echoing in the room as he pressed her bud. Wrapping his other arm under her, he grazed his thumb across her nipples, matching the motion of each hand. It was a delicate dance to bring Calla pleasure, and as she arched against him, he trailed his tongue down her beautiful body.

Her hips moved on their own against his fingers. "Kostas…" Her voice cracked as her body shuddered.

There was nothing he'd ever enjoyed more than hearing his name on her lips as he brought her to orgasm.

"Kostas, I need you." Her heady plea hung in the air as she brought her mouth to his. She seized him as she rolled on top of him.

"All of you." Her eyes glittered as she held him with her hands.

Kostas barely fought off the urge to drive into her as she slowly lowered her body on his. "Calla!"

"Does it feel good?" She feathered kisses across his jaw as she rose nearly off him again.

"Yes…" he breathed as she started the slow motion again, her eyes watching his every move. He hissed as she rose once more before fully taking him…again.

"Calla…now. Please."

As soon as the words left his lips, she eased the rest of the way down. He gripped her waist as she rocked them both into oblivion then collapsed against him.

"Nice to know I can make you beg too." Her words were light as she lay on him.

Kostas wrapped his arms around her. "Never doubt that I want you, sweetheart. So much."

The alarm he'd set buzzed and Kostas stretched, enjoying the warmth of Calla next to him. He tapped the icon on his phone, glad that he'd remembered to put it under his pillow so he wouldn't wake her.

He glared at the still dark window. He didn't want to head out. It was a simple realization with so much power behind it.

He'd suggested marriage when he'd learned she was

pregnant. It was the most pragmatic way to protect her. A job he swore he'd do better than his father.

They enjoyed each other's company. There was passion between them. That was more of a connection than so many royal couples experienced. Despite the modern era, arranged marriages in the aristocracy and wealthy classes were much more common than anyone wanted to admit. It wasn't confined to the waste bin of history; it just wasn't talked about.

Kostas had figured that he and Calla would make a good match. But it was more than that. He wanted her next to him every night. He ran a hand along her hip before draping it over her belly. There was a slight bump there. One no one would notice but that hinted at how their life was going to change.

A smile spread on his face as he ran a thumb along where the child rested. Or maybe danced while their parents rested. Soon, Calla would know, and in a few months, Kostas would feel it too.

Kostas couldn't wait.

He kissed her cheek and she rolled into his arms, leaning her head against his shoulder. Kostas looked at the clock: just after four in the morning. He needed to leave soon, but he could hold her for a few more minutes.

CHAPTER NINE

"Kostas?"

Calla's voice hovered above him in the dream. His body felt heavy, like he couldn't quite make his feet move. He frowned as he reached for something…or tried to. But his hands came up empty.

"Kostas?"

He turned again. Looking for Calla. His heart raced as he looked into the void but couldn't find her. He needed to reach her. Needed to protect her.

"Kostas."

This time his eyes shot open and he blinked as Calla grinned. She was wearing a well-worn blue robe that hit just above her knees. It was loosely tied, and he could tell she wore nothing under it.

It was the type of getup longtime lovers wore when they were comfortable around each other. The kind that wasn't designed to be sexy…though anything Calla wore would make his mouth water. Maybe it was just what she'd thrown on, but part of him wanted to believe it was because she was comfortable with him.

It is the best way to start a morning. The thought registered against his brain as he sat up, looking to the window where daylight peaked out from under her curtain.

"I overslept."

"You did," Calla confirmed as she handed him the mug of coffee. "I made you a pot of regular coffee. That is an act of…" Her voice paused as she looked at him.

His ears perked up as he looked at her. Part of him wanted so badly to hear her say it was an act of love. He'd never wanted that from a partner. Never expected it. Hell, he'd ensured no one got close enough to even risk falling in love with him before Calla.

But holding the warm mug between his fingers, he desperately wanted to hear her say it was love. Because it was for him. Calla was his other half…a simple truth that carried so much with it.

Maybe it was cowardly to want her to say it first. To want her to admit he was hers before he announced that truth, too, but Kostas felt like the world tilted as he waited for her to finish the sentence.

"An act of kindness." She laughed, but it was her nervous one.

He kissed her cheek, enjoying the intimate moment. He wanted to scream that he loved her, that he wanted millions more moments like this. But she'd hesitated and the last thing he wanted was to push her. "Thank you for the coffee."

She looked at the mug in his hand then at him. "I haven't had anything but decaf since I found out I was expecting. You don't know how much I wanted to pour myself a cup, too."

He took a sip of the coffee and sighed as the hot liquid hit his tongue. Rationally, he knew the caffeine took at least ten minutes to start showing effect, but the placebo effect was real.

"You can safely have one cup a day." Pregnant mothers were advised to limit their caffeine intake, but didn't have to resist it completely. It was a valid statement, but not the words he wanted to utter.

"If I have one, I will crave more." She looked at his cup once more as she sat next to him on the bed.

He slipped his arm around her waist, his heart calming as she settled in his embrace. He could stay like this forever, but unfortunately, duty called.

Lifting the mug, he took one more sip of coffee before broaching the topic. "So, how well do you know your neighbors?"

"Do you mean how well do I know their schedules, or do I know them enough that they might keep a secret if they see you?"

He hated the defensive tone in her voice. It was fair. This was not a conversation he wanted to have, either. Mentally, he kicked himself for not getting up when his alarm had gone off hours ago.

"Both, unfortunately." He rubbed her side as he kissed her cheek.

"Unfortunately, the answer is the same for both questions. I've never monitored the schedules of Patrick and his boys. They're teenagers. They go to school, and I think have jobs, but I don't know where or what time. Isabella and Pietro are usually leaving for work at the same time I do, but I don't know their weekend schedules."

Her voice trailed off for a moment then she started again. "As far as keeping secrets, we are on first-name, wave-and-say-hello-neighbor level. Not best friends and confidants. Certainly not 'don't sell the biggest story the island has seen since the birth of its princess to the press.'"

Their news was bigger than the birth of Zelia. The princess was exciting, but she'd been expected, and the second in line to the throne. A pregnant foreigner, an out-of-wedlock baby by the Prodigal Prince, was a bigger story. One he doubted anyone besides Ioannis and Eleni could be trusted with.

He tightened his arm around her and kissed her head. "I'm pretty good at sneaking out of places." He rushed on at the sight of her raised eyebrow. "I mean that I have spent most of my life leaving shops, restaurants and clubs through side and back entrances. Head down, ball cap on. You know, pro-celebrity stuff."

Calla grinned, and he enjoyed the light moment. "I can't think of you as a celebrity. I mean... I know you're a prince. But to me you're just Kostas. My Kostas."

He set his coffee cup on the nightstand then pulled her into his lap. "That is my favorite thing to be."

Maybe that was why their connection had felt so natural. When they'd met, he'd kept his royal status under wraps, and when she'd learned of it, it wasn't the thing she'd cared most about. Rather, it was how he was with her, how their interactions were.

If he didn't have a title, Calla would treat him the same way she did now. It was the best gift; one she likely didn't even register she was giving him.

"You could always spend the day with me. Hunker down here until it's late again." She winked, and he knew it was a serious offer. "I have enough leftovers to last us until tomorrow morning. I will even let you make a second pot of coffee tomorrow before work."

"That sounds like heaven." It was an offer he wished he could take. But Sunday was the day of the week that Ioannis set aside to have all the royals together. Something she'd have to join soon.

It gave them a chance to run over news, any issues that needed to be addressed for the country, and weekly appearances. Eleni was on maternity leave and Kostas's work at the clinic kept him busy, so it was really on Ioannis making appearances. But they discussed it every week. Even if there was nothing for him or Eleni to do, Ioannis expected everyone there.

No. His brother *wanted* everyone there. Wanted them to participate. His father had demanded their presence. Ioannis was different, but that didn't change the obligation that came with Kostas's birth. The obligation that their child would have one day too.

She brushed her lips against his. "I understand. But you should head out. The longer you are here, the later it gets, the more likely…" Calla swallowed.

He didn't need her to complete the sentence. "I will see you first thing tomorrow morning at the clinic. We can video chat this evening?"

She nodded and smiled, but it didn't quite reach her eyes.

"We could go public?" The phrase was out before he'd thought it through. But he wouldn't pull it back. He was ready to announce to the world that Calla was pregnant, that they were getting married. Ready for the world to see her by his side each day.

Calla patted his knee, kissed his cheek, and stood. "I'd like to make that decision based on how we feel. Not for a moment of us oversleeping and trying to game reactions."

"Fair," Kostas said, hoping the disappointment he felt wasn't apparent on his face. He wanted to decide based on feelings, too…and he was already comfortable. But he wouldn't push her.

Unless she and our child are caught in the press's crossfire.

Then he'd do anything he had to, to protect them.

She tightened the belt of her robe and left as he gathered his clothes.

Calla was standing by the door, holding a travel mug, when he exited her room. "Figured you might as well take the rest of it with you."

He took the coffee from her hand. "Thank you. I will see you tonight, on video chat. If you need anything…" He dipped his mouth to hers.

Her hand grazed his cheek as she deepened the kiss. It felt possessive, and he loved every second.

When she broke away, Calla's lips parted as she wrapped her arms around herself. "A kiss just to remind you of me through the day." Her cheeks colored as she looked at him. "It's a silly thing my parents always did…"

"I like that tradition!" Kostas dropped a light kiss to her lips; uncertain he'd ever make it out the door if he kissed her like that again. "We are definitely keeping that one!"

He opened her door, took a quick look. "The coast looks clear." Kostas turned once more and kissed her.

"'Bye, Kostas."

He grinned, loving the look of contentment on her face.

"Prince Kostas?" His name sent a chill down his spine as he turned to find a young man standing at the edge of the hallway, sliding his phone into his back pocket.

"Close the door, Calla." He didn't wait to make sure she did as he asked as he started toward the teen. He shifted his shoulders, donning the mask of Prince Kostas that he dropped so effectively around Calla.

"I'm checking on one of the midwives from the clinic. We had a long delivery yesterday." He hated the lie, but to protect Calla and the baby, he'd do anything necessary.

"By kissing her?" The boy raised an eyebrow, his face shifting as Kostas failed to react. With any luck, the teen was wondering if the story was worth pressing. "Calla is nice."

"She is," Kostas confirmed. *Please let that be enough to keep your mouth shut.* He wanted Calla to choose him, to choose the life they'd have together as Kostas and Calla. But that life would mean they'd also be prince and princess.

Making sure the young man was looking at him, Kostas kept his tone regal, hoping it might gain him something for once in his life. "It would be a shame if anything hurt her."

The teen looked over Kostas's shoulder, and Kostas looked back with him. Calla had shut her door. The boy frowned. Clearly hoping he might catch another glimpse, something to add to his tale.

"It would." He pulled keys from his pocket.

"She doesn't deserve that." Kostas pressed, hoping he was making it clear.

"Have a nice day, Prince Kostas." Then the young man unlocked his apartment and stepped inside without looking back.

Kostas's heart raced as he stared at the closed door then back at Calla's.

Is he going to say anything? Had he snapped a picture?

His phone dinged, and it didn't surprise him to see Calla's text.

Did Nico say anything? Patrick's car isn't in the parking lot, but I can talk to him later.

A few seconds later, a second came.

If you think it will help?

He stared at the messages for a minute, not knowing what to say. Nico seemed to agree that hurting Calla was wrong. That she didn't deserve it. With luck, he'd not gotten a picture and would keep the information to himself. Maybe just this once.

Leave it be for now. If the story breaks, we'll handle it.

He hit Send, then added,

Together. We'll handle it together.

Midwife Tempting Prince!

The headline didn't surprise her. Nico seemed like a good kid, but he had juicy gossip. Keeping that news secret would have been a miracle. Still, it wasn't the way she'd wanted the world to find out about their relationship.

Kostas was right. They should have gone public, beaten the story to the press. But she hadn't wanted him to feel trapped. So much of their relationship seemed to be outside their control.

She was pregnant. They enjoyed each other's company. Calla sighed as she pulled her hair into a bun. It was more than that.

She'd almost called making the coffee yesterday an act of love. Maybe a silly label for what so many would think of as a minor thing. But she hadn't regretted him oversleeping. She'd loved that he'd stayed the whole night.

Loved sleeping next to him. Loved him…

There was one positive to the article. It omitted the rebel or the Prodigal Prince narrative Kostas hated. In fact, based on the reading, it seemed like she was a siren who'd trapped a paragon of virtue. What would the island think when they learned she was pregnant?

She swallowed as she opened her makeup drawer. That was a problem for another day. Today she wanted to walk out of her apartment and confidently into the clinic. She twisted open the tube of mascara, glaring at it.

Calla rarely wore much makeup to the clinic. But the other thing the internet-hit piece had pointed out was her blue robe. They'd called it well-used and sad-looking.

Not good enough for a prince.

Those words hadn't made it into print, but everyone could read between the lines. Her eyes twitched to the robe hanging on the back of the bathroom door.

It was faded and she'd restitched the hem several times. Liam had hated the robe. In fact, he'd gifted her several over the course of their relationship. All frilly things that provided little to no coverage.

But her blue robe was comfortable. Her mother had wrapped it for the last Christmas they'd spent together. Maybe it wasn't fancy, but she'd liked it. It was more faded now, but still just as comfy as it had been on day one. And Kostas hadn't seemed to mind it yesterday.

She'd seen him eye the robe. Or, more accurately, the loose tie around her waist that showed off her cleavage. Yesterday morning had been so perfect.

And now everyone knew.

Calla squared her shoulders and looked at herself in the mirror. She let her hand rest over her belly for a moment as she raised her chin. She was about to walk the first of what she expected would be many gauntlets.

A smile twitched at the corners of her lips, and she gave in to it. Their relationship didn't embarrass her. Maybe it wasn't the perfect way for the world to find out. However, she would not hide herself away as though she'd done something wrong.

"And you'll have everything brought here while we're at the clinic? Just bring everything but the bed and kitchen table and chairs. Not sure what is hers, but we can send back anything that isn't tomorrow. I want all this done while we're at the clinic."

Natalia nodded and made notes on the tablet that seemed permanently affixed to her. "I'll see which room is free for the furniture." She made another note then turned to start her day.

"Room? Furniture?"

Kostas turned and smiled at his brother. "Yes. I'm moving Calla into the palace today. I told you I was pretty sure one of her neighbors snapped a picture of us. Well, they did and sold it…apparently."

Ioannis held up his hands. "Yes. That is unfortunate. I like Calla a lot. She was lovely when helping Eleni, and I know you are drawn to her."

Kostas crossed his arms, visions of his father blinking in the forefront of his memory. "But?" He was proud that his voice sounded calm.

"But moving her into the palace will give the impression that this is serious. Are you ready to take that step? Is Calla?" Eleni stepped to her husband's side and nodded, confirming that she'd read her husband's thoughts perfectly.

Would he and Calla be able to do that someday? Speak with nearly one mind?

"Is there anything I need to pick up for Calla or the baby?"

Natalia's question hit his back as he watched his sister-in-law's eyes widen. Without looking at his assistant, Kostas muttered, "Just make sure the kitchen has decaf coffee."

"And ensure no one interrupts us for a while," Ioannis added.

Kostas pushed a hand through his hair as he looked at his brother. He'd wanted to tell Ioannis and Eleni with Calla present. Wanted to announce the wedding and the baby with fanfare.

That moment was gone, but he still smiled as he looked from his brother to Eleni. "Yes. Calla is pregnant. Due in a little more than seven months."

"Congratulations. But you should have told us." Ioannis rubbed his face as he looked at him.

Kostas knew this was a lot, but he tried to make Ioannis understand. "We found out the night Zelia was born. We didn't want to steal the spotlight, and Calla wanted us to date. To make sure we were right for each other."

"Are you sure?" Eleni's question hung in the quiet hall.

Three simple words with the simplest answer. "Yes." He nodded. "I never expected this, but yes. I am certain. And I need her moved into the palace, Ioannis. Need her protected."

"Of course. We'll make sure it happens."

His phone buzzed and he took a deep breath as he saw the clinic number pop up and answered, "Dr. Drakos."

"Kali and I showed up early. There are a lot of cameras here. Even more than when the queen gave birth." Alexa sounded breathless as she called out, "No comment and stay out of the clinic. Only patients and staff!"

"Is Calla there yet?" Kostas's stomach flipped. He'd thought he had a little longer.

"No. But Kali is standing by the entrance, looking for her. We've called all the morning appoints for anyone low risk and less than thirty weeks and rescheduled."

"Good call. I'm on my way."

Calla didn't have a car. She walked the few blocks from her apartment to the clinic. If he hurried, he might make it to her place before she headed out. If the clinic was packed, he could only imagine what her apartment complex looked like.

He looked at Ioannis, but his brother waved him off.

"Go. I understand." He wrapped his arm around Eleni and kissed her cheek.

The trip to Calla's apartment felt like it took hours. He tapped his fingers on the steering wheel of his car, trying to avoid the urge to put the pedal to the floor. The parking lot was busting at the seams. He didn't even attempt to pull into the lot. Instead, he parked on a side street and walked with purpose past the comments and questions. His royal mask firmly in place.

"Calla!" He knocked on her door. "Calla." A few flashbulbs went off, but he didn't look at them.

"Good morning, Kostas." She beamed as she reached for his hand. "Quite a way to start a morning!"

"You seem to be handling it better than expected." Kostas whispered as he squeezed her hand, well aware of the phones and cameras snapping around them.

Calla nodded. "Getting angry or upset doesn't change

the facts. Besides, I'm not embarrassed to be with you. Though maybe I need a new robe."

Kostas dropped her hand and put his arm around her waist. It shielded her and the baby a little more. He'd hated the comment about the robe. Or rather, the knowledge that a stupid line in an online tabloid piece had caused it. "I like your robe."

"You're the only one," Calla muttered.

"Not true. You like it." Kostas squeezed her tightly. Her world had altered as of this morning. And it would continue to do so, but she needed to hold on to the little things. To know that she could like a comfy robe and anything else she had.

She was good enough for him just as she was…now he just had to protect her from as much of the royal world as he could!

CHAPTER TEN

THE INSIDE OF the clinic was nearly silent. Most of the noise came from the low hum of the multitude gathered outside. Clicks of cameras and shouted questions, like the door would magically open and she or Kostas would step outside.

Calla wished there was something to do...anything to take her mind off the bizarre situation taking place around her. Kostas was taking the unexpected break in patients to complete paperwork he'd let pile up. Alexa was spinning in the chair typically reserved for the office assistant they'd sent home over an hour ago. And Calla was doing her best not to pace the small room or peek out the window.

She'd offered to head back to her apartment, but Kostas had vetoed that idea with gusto. He'd pointed out that dividing the journalists, photographers and curiosity seekers wouldn't serve until the palace had security in place for her.

Security... She still couldn't wrap her head around that.

When Calla pointed out that Kostas went where he wanted, Alexa had unhelpfully reminded her that Kostas wasn't as interesting as the foreign midwife he'd fallen for. Before she could utter a word, Kostas had agreed. Then he'd stated that he had a security detail that just did little more than hang outside in the parking lot and accompany him to events.

The two men who looked like they stepped out of a movie script were currently guarding the door of the clinic. Georgios and Christos…even their names sounded like characters. But they'd managed to control the crowd outside. *Mostly.*

The phone rang and Alexa picked it up before the second ring. The person on the other line didn't have enough time to utter more than two words before Alexa stated, "No comment," and slammed the receiver down.

"Sorry." Calla frowned, wondering how many times the phone could withstand that level of damage. "I can answer the phone…"

"And deal with rude questions?" Alexa shook her head. "Nope. I slammed that too hard, must admit, I've always wanted to slam a phone down in disgust, but never really had a good excuse. My husband says I'm his overdramatic queen!"

"No. Overdramatic?" Calla playfully tossed her hand to the side and winked at Alexa. "How could he say that?"

Alexa grinned then the giggles escaped her lips. "I know, right! It's like he knows me far too well."

Calla enjoyed the few moments of levity until the phone rang again. She glared at it and braced herself for the slam as Alexa lifted it again.

"How far apart are the contractions?"

Calla's ears perked. A call not related to her dating life was a welcome respite.

"Three minutes. They came on fast. No, it's okay, Dimitra. That's normal, but we need to see you as soon as possible."

Calla's heart picked up at the mom's name. Dimitra was one of their oldest patients. She and her husband had tried for years to conceive and had never expected a pregnancy just before she turned forty-three.

Dimitra's pregnancy was textbook. There'd been no complications at all, but the woman was understandably anxious. She came to each appointment with a list of questions, having read every prenatal and postnatal book Calla had heard of, and several she hadn't.

In a normal situation, Dimitra would be nervous, and the situation at the clinic was anything but normal.

"And you're trying to get through the gaggle of people out front, but they won't let you in…"

Calla saw red. A patient—her patient—was in labor, and no one was letting her into the clinic. That would not do!

"Calla! No!"

She heard Alexa's plea as she raced for the clinic door. Flashbulbs and questions blended together as she stepped into the chaos.

"Princess!" A hand reached for her, and she blinked as one of Kostas's bodyguards gripped her arm.

"I'm not a princess." She called over the slew of questions being hurled at her.

Christos raised a brow as if to say, *Not yet*, but wisely held his tongue.

"Princess? Does that mean you and Kostas are getting married?"

"How long have you known each other?"

"Did you know each other in Seattle?"

The questions floated around her, but Calla pushed them away.

Where was Dimitra? She scanned the gathered crowd, blinking as flashes went off all around her.

"Ugh." Calla tried to push past the horde, but it seemed to morph together as she moved forward.

"I have a pregnant mom in labor at the back of this crowd. They won't let her through. Help me."

Georgios nodded and gestured to his partner. With no trouble, they created a small path through the mess.

Ignoring the questions, Calla called out for Dimitra as she walked with the bodyguards. Rising on her tiptoes, she wished for the millionth time in her life that she had more height.

"There's a hand raised to the left. Looks to be a heavily pregnant woman. Stay here, Princess."

"Not a princess!" Calla huffed but agreed. She'd argue with the Christos over titles another time.

Georgios stepped to her side but didn't say anything as he glared at the gathered crowd.

Christos was back in moments but without Dimitra. "She's breathing really hard and can't fully stand."

"Get me to her now!"

She delivered the order, and the two men seemed to part the people before her as if by magic.

Dimitra was leaning over her knees. Her face flushed. "I feel like I need to push." Her eyes were wide as she looked at Calla. Her bottom lip wobbled. "It's happening so fast. Leo dropped me off. He is back there. He can't miss this. He can't." Her sobs hiccupped as another contraction started.

Calla turned to look at the clinic door. It was a little over two hundred meters. A distance that shouldn't take more than a minute or so to walk…assuming you weren't in active labor. She looked over Dimitra's shoulder and saw Leo farther back in the group, desperately trying to push his way toward his wife.

"Dimitra." Calla waited for her to look up then she

kept her voice level. "We will not have a baby in the parking lot. I promise."

Turning to the bodyguard to her left, she pointed to the clinic. Kostas was by the entrance, or at least she thought he was, based on the shift in the questions around her. "I need a wheelchair, Christos." He looked at the clinic, but she grabbed his arm. "And Kostas needs to get washed up. Tell him that has to be his focus. I am fine, but Dimitra needs to push. We may deliver in the lobby. Tell him that!"

The man looked at Dimitra and then nodded. "Of course."

Turning her attention to the other bodyguard, Calla pointed to Leo. "Georgios! Get that man and bring him here."

"I'm not leaving you, Princess."

She understood his job, but now was not the time. She was not a princess…at least not yet. And even after she gained a title, her patients would still come first. The sooner everyone understood that, the better.

Calla grabbed his arm and turned him toward Leo. "I am not asking! That man *will* see the birth of his first child. Go get him. That's an order." If he was going to call her "princess," she may as well act like one at the moment!

The man waffled; she could see the look in Georgios's eyes as he weighed the situation before him. She understood what she was asking, but Leo deserved to be here with his wife.

"Please."

Dimitra's plea broke his final resolve and he darted off.

"I know this isn't the way you planned for delivery."

Calla kept her voice down, trying to pretend that there weren't dozens of ears around them listening in.

"With a soon-to-be princess?" Dimitra chuckled then bent over again.

She knew it was nerves and trying not to focus on her own predicament that made Dimitra laugh. Heaven knew Calla had laughed in more than one situation where it wasn't technically appropriate.

"That's what they say." Calla smiled, hoping it looked real as she focused on her patient.

"I need to push!"

"Not now." Calla tapped Dimitra's shoulder, firming up her voice. "I know it's hard. Look at me."

She saw a few eyes widen at her tone, but sometimes health professionals had to use strict voices to get their patient's attention. And if ever a situation called for it!

Holding up a finger, she bit her lip and wished the wheelchair was already there. "Pretend this is a candle and blow it out."

It was a trick her midwife mentor had taught her. The action helped mothers stop pushing, but it wouldn't stop it forever. The crush of people around her had stopped hurling questions, but she knew people were filming, taking pictures of what should be a private experience.

She would not let Dimitra deliver here. They might only get to the front of the clinic, but she deserved more privacy than this.

"Dimitra!" Leo's voice was tight as he came to his wife's side.

"Look at me," Calla ordered. She was glad Leo was there, but Dimitra and her baby were her top priority. "Blow."

"Princess!"

Seriously, was there nothing else Christos would call her? But he had a wheelchair, so she let it go…again.

They loaded Dimitra into the chair and raced for the clinic entrance.

"We're in room one!" Alexa called out.

"I need to push! I can't… I can't…dear God, Calla, there is so much pressure."

"Kostas!"

He exited the room, his eyes scanning her briefly as he took in the scene.

"I think the baby is crowning." She couldn't be sure, but based on the need Dimitra was feeling, it was likely.

Kostas bent, raising the hem of Dimitra's dress. "Calla's right. We aren't even going to make it to the room. Leo, put your hands under Dimitra's arms to give her a little help."

Dimitra took a deep breath and bore down as the next contraction took over. It took only two pushes before Kostas grinned and held up their very loud little man.

"Congratulations." Calla felt her lips tip up as Kostas laid the little one in Dimitra's arms without even detaching the cord. He then nodded to Alexa to slowly wheel the new family back to room one so they could fully take care of their patients.

"So what now?" Calla sat on the desk and dropped a kiss on Kostas's lips, then yawned as she looked at the clock. Kali had arrived about ten minutes ago. She'd watch over Dimitra and her little man until they were ready to be discharged. Calla wasn't looking forward to braving the group outside again, but she also did not want to sleep at the clinic.

Kostas stood and pulled her into his arms. He

dropped a kiss on the top of her head as he squeezed her tightly. "We go home."

"Home?" Calla looked at him. "You're going to spend the night at my place again? I mean, you're more than welcome, of course." She sighed. Sleeping next to Kostas, waking up next to him, had been perfect. Even if the repercussions were sitting outside.

"The palace, Calla. Home."

She blinked. The palace... She knew that they'd end up there eventually. Their child was a prince or princess; their father was third in line to the throne. But she had a hard time thinking of it as home.

Though if she was honest, the small apartment hadn't felt like home, either...until Kostas spent the night.

He was her home. And if that meant the palace, so be it.

"I need to get a few things."

"I had all of your things sent to the palace while we were here." Kostas released his hold on her as she stepped back.

The room spun as she tried to place those words. "So when I offered to go back to the apartment today?" She gripped her waist as she looked at the man in front of her. The one she loved, who'd moved her things...without asking. Without even telling her!

"They were moving your belongings. Yes." Kostas's voice was firm. The prince delivering the news.

She chuckled, but there was no mirth in the sound. The last twelve hours had been over the top, but there was no way the palace knew what to take and what to leave in her apartment. "And how did Natalia know what to move? I seem to remember refusing that overture two weeks ago!"

"They moved the entire apartment." Kostas sighed. "I know this is a lot—"

She held up her hand, cutting him off. "The entire apartment? The furniture is rented, as is the cutlery… and…" Calla blew out a breath and moved to the chair, flopping down.

This was fine. Everything was fine. It was.

Kostas went to the floor in front of her. Even sitting on his knees, his dark eyes were nearly at eye level with hers. "I know this a lot. But I will do everything to keep you and the baby safe. And you are safest with me at the palace, Calla."

Given the pressure of the press outside, she nodded. He got a pass. This time. But she wanted to be sure he understood her position…now. "Next time, you will tell me. If we are going to do this, we do it together. As a team. Understood."

"A team." He kissed her cheek. "I like the sound of that. A lot."

"Good." Calla nodded, her breaths coming a little easier.

He put his hands on her knees, his fingers running over them before he pushed a lock of hair that had slipped from her bun back behind her ear. "I have something else for you."

"A ring?" Calla groaned but cut the sound off as she saw the reflection of the truth in his eyes. "Kostas…"

"I know you wanted more time, Calla. But…" He flipped open the box. The shimmering diamond was massive and surrounded by smaller emeralds. "Over the top" was the best description. It was beautiful, but the exact opposite of what she'd have chosen for herself.

The ring was a thing made for a royal. Something her child would be. But she…

Calla's parents had loved each other, but they'd been lower middle class when the restaurant was doing well. When it wasn't…well, then they'd had to decide which bills were most important.

How many times had Liam's parents stated she wasn't good enough for their son?

And now she was sitting across from a real prince. A real Cinderella story. But Cinderella and her Prince Charming had loved each other. She loved Kostas, but this ring was not a declaration of love. It was protection.

A statement for others, not for her.

Her heart screamed for her to say yes. It yearned for Kostas, for happily ever after. Her brain urged caution.

"Calla?"

She looked up from the ring, meeting Kostas's eyes. "That is a lot for a ring."

Kostas moved the box, so it sparkled in the light. "It makes a statement."

She ran her hand along his cheek, working up the courage to ask the question she needed answered most.

"Are you sure?"

The words sounded wrong.

Because they are…

She should have asked *Do you love me?* That was the question she wanted answered. The one that was so important but sounded so needy.

Kostas wasn't Liam, yet the desire to be her own person, to show that she wasn't the needy girl, the one who'd stand in front of someone and ask if they loved them, was overwhelming.

A grin spread across his face until Kostas looked like he was beaming. "I'm certain!"

She let go of as many worries as possible as she let his certainty flow through her. Holding out her finger, she tried not to let her mouth gape as he slid the rock on her hand. She was engaged…to a prince.

No.

She was engaged to Kostas. And that was better than any fantasy.

"Are you ready? The second we step out the door with that ring on your finger, the entire island will know that we're engaged."

Clasping her hand in his, Calla took a deep breath. "Ready."

CHAPTER ELEVEN

"Good morning, Princess."

Kostas's words wrapped around her as she rolled over in the massive bed. *Their massive bed.* He'd slept better than he had in forever. Having Calla next to him was the best feeling in the world.

"I'm not a princess, at least not yet. No matter what Christos and Georgios said yesterday."

Running his hand down her side, he kissed her. It wasn't much of a kiss. Not passionate, but it felt special. The world looked for passion, for the big moments, but it was these little ones that made for a happy life.

Now that he'd found it, he'd do anything to protect it. To protect her and their child.

"It's a term associated with royal fiancées in Palaío too. You aren't Your Royal Highness until after we wed, but you became a princess when we got engaged. The best way to protect the baby and you."

"So you told the staff we were engaged before you asked me?" Calla blinked. "What if I'd said no?"

Kostas held up her hand, enjoying the sight of the large ring on her finger. No one would doubt that he cared for her if they saw this. The ring screamed *princess*.

But his stomach pinched at the tone in her voice.

"Calla, I assumed you didn't want to announce the pregnancy, at least not yet. Though we won't be able to keep it quiet much longer."

"Meaning?" She sat up, pulling the covers with her.

He moved with her, trying to find the right words. "I can't give palace protection to my girlfriend. Ioannis is not my father, but a full-time staff and security, who you'll meet shortly, is not possible unless we announced your pregnancy or our engagement."

"So this way we protect my privacy and the baby." Calla swallowed. There was an underlying thread to her statement, but he couldn't quite understand what it might be.

"I will keep you two safe. I promise."

"Safe? What—"

A knock at the door interrupted whatever she was about to say. It was lost as Natalia and Angeliki entered. "Good morning. Sorry to interrupt, but there are a few things we should get ahead of before the event tonight."

"Event?" Calla rolled off the bed and grabbed her blue robe, covering her tank top and short shorts. Putting on her glasses, she pushed her hair out of her face.

"The king and queen are holding a small reception to properly announce your engagement."

He understood why Calla was focused on the word *event*, but it was the beginning of the statement that sent chills down his spine. "What 'things'?"

He saw Natalia's gaze shift to Angeliki. The woman was Calla's assistant, and the fact that she adjusted her shoulders as she met Kostas's and Calla's looks confirmed his suspicions. "What does the news say this morning?"

"They are saying the princess was rude to a bodyguard and a pregnant woman yesterday. That she is already giving orders and acting like a diva. And that she will ruin you. The language is less flattering than that."

Kostas sucked in a deep breath. None of that was fair. Eleni was the loved one, and they'd cast Calla in the opposite role. The truth failing to matter.

Calla laughed. The sound echoing off the walls of the room. The women seemed as stunned as he was at seeing his soon-to-be bride's mirth at the situation. She clapped and walked to the closet.

"Look at that, Kostas. We've rehabilitated your image." She winked as she opened the door. "You just had to fall for a diva. I've had a few rows with patients, but even in the throes of labor pains, no one has ever called me a diva."

"This isn't funny, sweetheart. If they are making such statements, it means they are making you the villain. The roles they choose in the first few weeks will stick." Kostas kept his voice even though he wanted to dictate a forceful response and demand its immediate publication through their social media.

"If you're the villain, then so is our child." He pushed again. "We have to respond."

"No. We don't." Calla kissed his cheek as she emerged from the closet with a pair of worn blue jeans and T-shirt. "Do you see me as the villain?"

"Of course not." Kostas felt his head pop back at the ridiculous question.

"Do either of you?" Calla asked the assistants, who both shook their heads no. "Do you think Alexa or Kali will think me the villain, or Ioannis or Eleni?"

"No," Kostas muttered. "But that doesn't mean that we just let this stand. We need to make sure they see us as above this. Know that we won't stand for lies."

"Kostas, you can't fight every battle."

"For our child—" *for you* "—I certainly can."

He hated the exasperation he saw dripping from Calla, but she needed to understand. Ignoring the mistruths didn't make them go away. His mother and Maria hadn't had someone to respond for them. Calla would... always.

"Fine. If you want to issue a rebuttal, go for it. But I doubt it fixes anything." Calla held up her jeans then looked at the assistants.

"I hate to be a diva they're accusing me of being on day one, but any chance Eleni has some belly bands? You know, the stretchy bands most women wear early when their pants get a little snug? I should have thought to order some, but everything's been..." Calla blew out a breath as she forced a smile. "Would hate for the press to get a picture of my unbuttoned pants and jump to any conclusions. Even if they were right, this time."

Her tone was playful, but he could hear a hint of fear. She was putting on a brave face, but Calla was nervous. That, he understood.

"We'll find something, and we have a few dresses, too, for tonight's party for you to choose from. Nothing in your closet works for the function," Angeliki stated as she made a few notes on the tablet identical to the one Natalia carried around.

Kostas saw Calla blink and he reached for her hand. "Angeliki meant that, for a royal function, we need formal wear, and you understandably didn't bring that with you."

"Of course." Calla offered him a tight smile. "Not a lot of room in my bag for long gowns."

He squeezed her hand before turning back to the assistants. "I'll work on the reply for the media, run it through the press secretary, and I need to swing by the clinic and check on Dimitra."

"I'll come too." Calla brightened.

Before he could say anything, Angeliki rushed in. "We have some things we need to get set up here, Princess. It's your day off, correct?" She looked from the tablet to Calla to Kostas.

"It is." She hesitated and Kostas pulled her to him.

She softened in his arms and leaned her head against his chest. "I know this is a lot, sweetheart." He squeezed her tightly. "But we'll be fine. Promise."

"We're a team, remember."

"We are." Kostas nodded. But team or not, he would not allow the public to make the woman he loved a villain. She would not suffer the way his mother had. He'd protect her at all costs.

Kissing her again, he let her go. "I can't wait to see the dress you pick out for tonight. You'll be perfect. Everyone will think so."

Calla rolled her eyes. "I'm not trying to be perfect, Kostas." She kissed his cheek then let Angeliki direct her to the door.

"Champagne or hors d'oeuvres, Princess?"

Calla waved away the waiter for what felt like the hundredth time. The room was full of people snacking and drinking. She couldn't consume any alcohol and the small trays of food turned her stomach.

So far, she'd rarely had issues with morning sickness, but her stomach was tossing too much at the moment to put anything in it.

"How are you holding up?" Eleni's voice was quiet and only for her ears as Calla stood in the crowded room.

In theory, this was the party celebrating her and Kostas's impending nuptials, but she'd chosen nothing. No input on the flowers, the food, drinks, the messaging. Even her dress was the only one from Eleni's closet that had fit her petite frame. It was not how she'd imagined an engagement party. Though, she'd never anticipated marrying royalty. Perhaps this was just the way it was.

Pursing her lips, she resisted the urge to shrug, knowing tons of eyes were trained on all her movements.

"Overwhelming." Calla offered Eleni what she hoped was close to a cheerful smile to cover the unsettledness tugging at her back.

Eleni slid her hand through Calla's as they started toward another area of the party, casually making conversation with a few people as they walked past. Eleni was an expert at making others feel comfortable without actually saying anything too deep. It was a skill Calla had seen Kostas use too. But it felt wrong.

At least for her.

She understood the need to guard herself. But she wanted to be genuine. There would be days where she was happy, others where she was cross. She didn't want to wear a royal mask. She wanted the people of Palaío to see her exactly as she was.

A midwife, a soon-to-be mom, a wife who loved her husband…even if they fought occasionally. She wasn't interested in the fairy tale. She wanted the real thing.

Kostas found her across the crowd, saw she was with Eleni, and nodded. She'd had no time alone since she'd been in her apartment putting on makeup to prepare for the rabid press outside her door. How had that only been a day ago?

"He's talking to one of the television anchors…"

"No doubt reiterating the palace's line regarding me.

Trying to make me seem perfect." Calla bit the inside of her cheek as the words left her lips. "Sorry, Eleni."

"Don't be." The queen hugged her. "This is a lot, Calla." She paused, checked their location, and then motioned for Calla to follow her.

They stepped into a small room, and Eleni squeezed her hands. "Are you sure about this?"

Calla hesitated. She wanted to say yes. She was sure about Kostas. It was the prince she wavered on. He claimed they were one and the same, but they weren't. The mask he wore around others, the buttoned-up man trying so hard to prove that he wasn't the rebellious teen, was hard to watch.

He deserved to be who he was, the kindhearted, playful man who enjoyed silly coffee mugs and had come home to ensure the people of his island had access to a great OBGYN. He cared what they thought of him... and what they thought of her.

What if the press never changed its thoughts on her? Calla didn't mind, as long as Kostas didn't treat her differently. But could he separate the two? She didn't need protection from poisoned pens—at least, not all the time. She just wanted his love.

"I don't know." It was honest, but she saw Eleni's eyes dip. Calla hated disappointing her, but she would not pretend things were fine if they weren't. She'd sworn not to do that again after her last relationship. It was hard, but she'd stand in her own truth. Even if it wasn't what others wanted to hear.

"I lo—" She caught herself, though she suspected Eleni knew she'd been about to say she loved Kostas. He deserved to hear that first.

"A marriage of convenience..." she continued, "well, it's just not the way I envisioned things." Her stomach rumbled and she laughed. "Guess I should have eaten something."

"That is easily rectified." Eleni grinned, but it didn't quite meet her eyes. She reached for the door handle then paused.

"Calla…" She sighed as she seemed to weigh her words. "Life is too short not to be certain of your place. I think you are, but Kostas ran away rather than force the island to accept who he truly is. He came home because Ioannis asked him, though I suspect Kostas saw it as an order. He's seeking outside approval, and he may never get it. I don't have an answer for any of that, but wanted you to know."

"I do." Calla nodded. She knew who she was, what she would accept; now she had to hope Kostas would accept that person, as well. And maybe step into his true self full-time too.

"There you are." Kostas beamed as she and Eleni stepped from the room. "I thought maybe you were hiding. This is a lot."

"Do you want to hide?" Calla offered. "We can for a few minutes."

"It's our party, Calla."

"Is it?" She raised a brow.

"Of course." He gestured to the room as Eleni made a silent retreat. "Our names are even on the cake."

"What's the flavor of the cake, Kostas?"

He blinked at her question. "What?"

It was a small thing. But he'd told her yesterday that it mattered that she liked her blue robe. He'd meant it then too. But did he give himself the same grace? The same ability to choose his likes based on what he wanted?

"The flavor of the cake, Kostas. That big, beautiful

cake. My favorite flavor is a white cake with raspberry filling, and yours?"

"Dark chocolate with chocolate icing."

"Well, that cake certainly doesn't have chocolate icing. And I suspect there is no raspberry filling." She gestured to the decorations and food. "This is an experience for others, not our party."

Kostas brushed his lips against hers. "I told Natalia and Angeliki to make sure everything was perfect. That no one could find fault with it."

And there was the crux of the problem. He was still terrified of anyone finding fault, or people he didn't know thinking he was the prodigal or rebel prince. "Kostas, people are going to find fault. You—*we* are public figures. You can't stop the tongues wagging. All you can do is find happiness."

With me. Those words felt like too much in the crowded ballroom, but she held them tight within her.

"I am happy." He squeezed her.

She wanted to believe him. But as his eyes wandered the room, she saw the need for approval, the desire to control the story. She knew he wanted to protect her, but was it really for her?

CHAPTER TWELVE

KOSTAS ROLLED OVER and his hand struck Calla's cool pillow. He sat up, blinking at the sight of the empty place next to him. Rubbing his eyes, he slid off the bed and went looking for Calla.

His stomach twisted as he found the bathroom, dressing room and kitchen empty. The palace was enormous, but Calla had kept to his rooms since moving in a week ago. He sensed she was chafing at the royal life over the last two weeks.

Her life had shifted so quickly. She claimed she was adjusting, but the added attention must be difficult.

She was pushing back on things too. She'd challenged him on the protocols he'd set up for himself after his mother's death and his own fall from grace. The things designed to ensure her safety. He'd tried to compromise. But how could he not respond to the ridiculous story that she'd hated her engagement party and that Eleni had scolded her for being pouty.

He'd wanted to put out a release stating she'd loved it. She'd told him she wouldn't lie. That if they corrected the story, it needed to be with the truth. That she was finding royal life overwhelming and that the staff had done a lovely job on such short notice. But that she wished she'd had a bit more control over the festivities.

Control.

He understood. The party had been rushed, and the staff had largely put the event together using Eleni and Ioannis's favorite foods and decorations. The flowers were lovely, but Eleni's not Calla's style. The cake was delicious, but Ioannis's favorite lemon rather than his or Calla's.

Yet if they'd put out a statement regarding her wanting control…he could see the twists in real time. So he'd adjusted. Not the full pushback, but not full honesty, either. A carefully worded release that kept the emotion neutral but clarified the lies.

It seemed a new story popped up almost every day… and each day he'd struck back. Correcting the narratives. It was his mission to ensure she was treated as fairly as possible, even if Calla told him it didn't bother her too much.

Maybe it was fine now. But he knew how the stories ripped at you over time. One day it would hurt her, and he never wanted her to doubt that he'd protect her.

He pushed a hand through his hair as he stood in the empty library.

Where could she be?

The clinic? Kostas rushed back to his room. If he'd slept through a notification, surely Calla would have woken him. Except they'd argued about the clinic last night too.

No, "argued" was too strong a word. She'd simply ignored his suggestion about reducing her hours at the clinic. The press wasn't hanging out quite like vultures anymore, but they still cased the clinic more than he'd like. It was the place where she was easiest to find.

He'd already put out feelers for a new midwife. When the baby was born, she'd have to step back a bit. And Dr.

Bandi had agreed to Ioannis's terms. She'd just started. Soon Kostas would have a more regular schedule. Handle half the patients rather than all of them!

"The princess is on the beach." Christos yawned as he walked past Kostas. "Antonio is with her, though, keeping his distance."

The beach? So early?

Kostas nodded as he headed out to find Calla.

Her hair waved in the breeze as she looked across the water. She wasn't in the water, but close enough that when the wave came, it rushed over her toes. He paused and stared at her.

She was lovely, true perfection! Calla looked relaxed for the first time since they'd gone public. Looked like herself. He grabbed his phone out of his back pocket and snapped the photo.

Sliding his phone into his pocket, he took a step forward. She turned and he saw her smile fade. That tore at his heart.

"Don't worry, Antonio isn't far away." She took a deep breath before stepping a little closer to the escaping sea.

"Calla, I was just going to ask if I could join you."

She closed her eyes as the tide rolled over her feet again, seemingly lost in the moment. "I'd like that."

Stepping behind her, he wrapped his arms around her waist and rested his head on hers. For a few precious breaths, he let himself go. Just enjoying the moment with Calla, unworried about any of the responsibilities they had.

"This is nice," Calla murmured as she turned in his arms.

"It is." He tightened his grip then lowered his mouth to capture hers.

"I always wanted to live by the beach. To wake up and play by the ocean. It wasn't something my parents could afford, but I still dreamed about it. Now…" She pulled back, walked a little closer to the water, turned and grinned at him.

Then she bent, scooped a bit of water in her palms and tossed it his way. It was chilly but not cold as it splashed onto his shirt.

Kostas couldn't stop the laughter escaping his lips, even if he'd wanted to. "Is that how it's going to be, Princess?" He raced toward her, scooping water in both his hands before dumping it over her head.

She giggled as she kicked up water at him. He turned so the spray hit his back before he shifted quickly to the side.

"Wait!" Calla held up her hand.

"Calling a pause to the game so quick?" He chucked the water from his hands.

"I think the baby moved. I know it's early…" She sucked in a breath and grabbed his hand, laying it over her lower belly. Her stomach rumbled and she let out a laugh… "Oh, pretty sure that was just hunger pangs. Well, we can pretend for a moment, right?"

She closed her eyes, taking in slow, deep breaths.

They weren't feeling the baby, but as he laid his head against hers, he left his hand where their child lay. These few moments were precious, and he wanted to soak them in.

After a few minutes, she kissed his cheek. "I should probably get some breakfast."

"Probably." Kostas wrapped his arm around her waist as they started back toward the palace.

"This morning was delightful. We should make time for this."

"For playing in the ocean?" Kostas hugged her tightly. "I'd be okay with that."

She bumped her hip against his. "You know what I mean. Time for Calla and Kostas, not the prince and princess." She rose up on her toes and kissed his cheek.

"We are the same people, sweetheart. Kostas and Calla. Prince and Princess." The sooner she understood that the world wouldn't see a difference, the better.

"Are we?" She leaned her head against his shoulder and before he could say anything, she offered, "Want to help me get the sand off in the shower?"

Desire glittered in her eyes, and he let the fresh worry wash away. "I think this may be the best way to start a day!"

Angeliki's text message landed in Calla's phone, and she sighed as she saw the headline for the article. Someone had captured the image of Kostas with his hand over her belly this morning. They must have had a telescopic lens.

Honestly, it was a great photo. One that she'd set on the mantel if it had resulted from a photoshoot.

But it hadn't.

And the note above it was the reason Angeliki had given her the heads-up.

Prince Marrying Midwife Because of Pregnancy!

It was her worst fear outlined in blocky letters designed to capture a reader's attention. Angeliki and Natalia were already working with the public relations department for a response. She'd given Calla a ten-minute head start to let Kostas know before Natalia sent the text of the response to him. Waiting wasn't an option, even though her feet dragged as she started for the office.

Opening the door, she swallowed as he looked up from the stack of papers on his desk.

"Hi, sweetheart, are you about ready to head home? I know we have the fundraiser for Eleni's charity. I have a few more things to do, but if you'll just give me ten minutes, then I'll be ready."

The fundraiser to help ensure income didn't stop anyone from continuing their education. It was Eleni's passion, and she'd talked to Calla about joining it. But Calla didn't want to give up being a midwife. She'd have to step back some, but if she was going to have a public platform, she wanted it focused on access to prenatal care.

That was a discussion for another day.

"The pregnancy is public knowledge." The statement fell from her lips. There were hundreds of better ways to start this conversation, all of them flooding her brain after she'd spit out the worst option.

"How?" Kostas stood, and she handed him the phone.

The silence stretched for what seemed like forever as he looked at the article.

"It's an excellent picture." Kostas shrugged as he handed it back to her.

"I thought the same thing." Calla blinked, trying to justify the reaction she'd expected with the one she was getting. Was he finally not caring what they said about him? About her? Willing to let it flow…

And did it have to be this headline he was okay with?

"You're okay?" She bit her lip as he slid back into the chair. "Natalia and Angeliki already have a statement ready to go. It should be in your email shortly. They wanted me to tell you first."

Kostas typed a few more things before he powered down the computer. "I mean it's not the way I'd have announced the news, but at least this headline is mostly true."

"It is?" Calla felt her mouth open wide. Hurt bubbled through her as she tried to catch her breath. She loved him. Had upended her life, given up control of so many things, hoping he felt the same way about her.

Was she just a fool?

No. What they had was special. She didn't doubt that. But that didn't mean it was forever love.

How many times had she started to ask that and held back? So many relationship problems could be handled with a simple conversation…but what if you feared the answers?

"So the headline is true?" Her voice wobbled but she refused to break. Not now.

He looked up, and she could see the moment his words' meaning registered. "No." Kostas shook his head. "No."

He pushed a hand through his hair as he stood. "Calla, I am so sorry. I didn't mean that, not really. I… I just meant that of all the headlines, this one is the closest to the truth. Would you have accepted my proposal if you weren't pregnant?"

No. She bit her lip. It was true, but in this moment she couldn't seem to catch the words exiting her mouth. "You didn't ask me to marry you. You just held up a giant ring."

She gripped her side. "What are we doing, Kostas?" Waves sounded in her ears as she tried to regain her footing. This morning, everything seemed so easy. He'd held her and the doubts she'd had since moving into the palace seemed to evaporate.

Now, though. Everything raced toward her.

"We are protecting our baby..." He grimaced. "That wasn't right, either."

"I think it was." Calla blinked away the tears she felt forming.

"Can we go home? We can talk about this there? Away from any prying ears in the clinic."

"So you don't trust our colleagues?"

"I didn't say that."

"You did," she countered.

"Calla, I just meant that, at the palace, we can be ourselves. We can have this row there, get it out. In private."

"A controlled environment..."

"Exactly."

It wasn't the right answer...but he wasn't wrong, either. They'd seen their last patient, but this was still their workplace. She bit her lip as she tried to cool the emotions pouring through her.

"I'm not waiting for you." Calla stated. "I'll meet you at the palace." Before he could argue, she held up a hand. "I need a few minutes to collect myself. I'll be ready for the event tonight and then we will talk."

She left before he could say anything else.

"Calla?" Alexa's voice was soft. "Are you okay?"

She'd heard everything, but her eyes held kindness, not the look of someone savoring juicy gossip.

Rather than lie or put on a royal mask, Calla shook her head no.

Alexa pulled her into a hug, clasping her tightly. "Can I do anything?"

"Distract my security team." Calla let out a harsh sob. She needed a few minutes on her own. But that was too much to ask.

"I can do that."

"I was joking." Calla wiped a tear from her cheek.

"I wasn't." Alexa winked and waved as she headed for the entrance. "Wait two minutes, then use the emergency exit."

She nodded and then followed Alexa's suggestion.

The late-afternoon sun hit her cheeks as she looked at the sky. It was easier to breathe, but that didn't stop the tears from racing down her cheeks. Without thinking, she climbed the secluded walking path that, if she followed it, would lead her all the way to The Grotto. She wouldn't go that far, but it gave her at least a few minutes of solitude.

Finding a sizable rock, she sat and pulled her knees up to her chest, rocking herself as she gave in to all the hurt Kostas's words had caused.

Even if they are true?

That was the part that struck her hardest. He was right. They might have dated without her pregnancy; she wanted to hope so. But she wouldn't be living in the palace now, wouldn't have the giant ring on her left hand, without the baby.

Kostas was right. Their child needed protection, but Calla deserved a husband who wanted her for her too.

Her phone buzzed and it surprised Calla to see Angeliki's name under the time. An hour had escaped her.

"Is Kostas frantic?"

"You slipped your security detail, Princess. Of course, he is frantic. If anything happens to the baby..."

The baby...

"I don't need a lecture, Angeliki. I am perfectly fine. Not all that far from the clinic, actually."

"Once the new midwife starts, you'll be here more often, then he won't worry so much."

"What?" The birds took flight and Calla flinched as

she focused on lowering her voice. "What do you mean 'new midwife'?"

"Well…" She could hear her assistant swallow. "Maybe it's best if Kostas talks to you about the expectations once you're married."

Expectations.

There it was. The changes she'd feared from the moment he'd put the ring on her finger. The control, the desire for her to be someone other than who she was. Who she wanted to be.

But she wasn't the Perfect Princess the press refused to call her, despite Kostas's many official statements. Not that she wanted to be. And none of which had said he loved her or cared about her. Calla closed her eyes as that truth settled in. He'd corrected the facts of the story…but added no feelings.

"Please tell Kostas I need a little more time, but I'll see him after the charity event."

She muttered a goodbye and started for the palace. She hoped Eleni would forgive her, but Calla had other plans for her evening.

Kostas raced toward his room after the charity event. He'd waited for an hour before realizing that Calla would not attend. He'd watched the clock closely to make sure he'd been in attendance long enough. People wouldn't talk much about him leaving.

Swinging open the door, his chest lightened as he saw her sitting on the bed. She was here; she was safe.

"I'm issuing a statement about the headline. I—"

Calla held up a hand. "Did the clinic hire a new midwife?"

Kostas blinked. He'd anticipated the fight about his statement earlier. He'd spent most of the evening wanting to kick his own ass for it. He wasn't marrying Calla because of the baby, but because he loved her. That was what mattered.

He'd not expected this question. His mouth opened then closed as he tried to make his tongue work.

"Did the clinic hire a new midwife? My replacement."

Kostas shuddered as the word *replacement* reverberated around the room. "Replacement isn't the exact right word."

Calla shook her head as she stood.

"Calla, once our child is born, the duties of a royal..."

"Stop!" She shook as she pushed a tear from her cheek. "I'm not just a royal. I'm a daughter. A friend. A woman. And a midwife. I like my job and even if I didn't, I still owe Liam—"

"No." Kostas shook his head. "Natalia found him and let me know how much. I paid it off before we got engaged."

Calla pursed her lips. "'Paid it off before we got engaged.' Of course you did. Can't have the island think you're marrying a gold digger? That's certainly not the right image. Very far from perfection."

"Hey!" Kostas hated his raised voice. That was not how he'd meant this. He'd done it to free her. So it was one less worry.

Sucking in a deep breath, he tried to keep the emotions he rarely let loose in check. "I did it for you. A fresh start."

"And you never wondered what people might say if they found out I was here paying off a loan to my ex. My wealthy ex."

He hesitated. That hadn't crossed his mind...had it?

She walked to the closet and pulled out her beaten-up

luggage. "I wanted Kostas. The funny man who plays in the water with me. Watches bad documentaries and laughs at me sitting on a counter. Not the one so scared of making a mistake in public he tries to control everything possible."

God, she'd spent the evening packing.

She'd never planned to stay with him. To find a middle ground.

"We'll find a way to co-parent." Calla sobbed and swallowed. "But I won't live under a microscope, Kostas."

"That's royal life."

"No." Calla shook her head. "It's not the island's microscope I'm leaving. It's yours. I wanted to be on your team…"

"We are a team!" he challenged.

"Sure. You're just the star and get to make all the decisions, right? Make sure the image is correct, right? Make sure no one thinks we make mistakes! Always controlling the narrative. More worried about what *they* think than what *I* want."

The words cut deep. He'd done his best to make sure no one hurt her like his mother and Maria. He understood this world, understood the challenges. He'd been burned by the scandal, watched his mother lose herself, endured Maria's disgrace because of a teenage romance. He was protecting Calla.

She walked past him.

He wanted to say something. But in the end, he stayed, lost for words as the woman he loved walked out.

CHAPTER THIRTEEN

"THE BABY AND I are fine... Please give the rest of the apartment some space... No, it is not true that I am returning to Seattle." That insidious rumor had popped up as soon as she'd left the palace.

There was nothing in Seattle for her. Her parents were gone, and the clinic had filled her position almost as soon as she'd put in her two-week notice. She'd already let the travel nursing agency know she wouldn't be accepting any more assignments. The island of Palaío was her child's place. And she'd find her path here.

Hopefully, one that didn't involve as much of a spotlight after she had the baby. She smiled through the pain as she nodded to the crowd that had gathered after the reports she'd moved back to her apartment had emerged. She swore some of them were camping out at her home.

Home...

The apartment wasn't home. She'd didn't even have all the furniture back. Though Ioannis had ensured the dishes were returned, the living room furniture was in Dr. Bandi's temporary apartment. A delivery was scheduled at the end of the week, but until then, this was just a sparse shell.

Calla hugged her waist as she stood in the empty living room. She'd managed the last three days by keeping one foot in front of the other. And ensuring she only worked during the new doctor's shift.

Kostas hadn't sought her out.

After making sure he knew where she was and that everything was safe for weeks, he'd simply dropped it. She bit the inside of her cheek, but it didn't stop the tears from falling.

She'd meant what she'd said. She didn't want to live under his microscope. Didn't want to be perfect for the cameras. Calla wanted to be herself, wanted that to be enough. But she wished he'd stopped her. Wished he'd said something...

But what was there to say?

Liam had wanted to mold her into the society wife. It hadn't worked. Kostas had wanted her to be the perfect princess. Above any kind of reproach. Never mind that the island wouldn't see her that way...at least not right away.

After a few years, when the baby was older, when she and Kostas were still a happy couple. Maybe then the narrative might change.

The narrative, the one she claimed not to care about, seemed to encompass her now. The questions, the shouts, the sideways glances, the rumors. They took a toll.

One that would have been worth it...if she and Kostas were a real team.

That was the hurt that cut the deepest. That he hadn't talked to her. Told her the game plan. He'd acted like the prince, taking control and shaping the world to his liking.

Today she'd taken back a piece of the narrative, though. She'd sent half of her paycheck to the palace.

At least this way no one could say she'd taken more from Kostas than she was owed.

A knock sounded on her door, followed by a raised voice claiming to be from some blog site. She closed her eyes as she slid down the wall of her apartment. She would not answer…but they'd effectively trapped her.

Her finger itched to call Kostas…but pride stilled it. She was fine; she was fine…

If you say it long enough, will it be true?

"What do you mean she sent part of her paycheck here?" Kostas pushed a hand through his hair. He'd started letting it grow back out after Calla's statements in The Grotto a few weeks ago. There'd been a few comments from people on the island and more than one cruel statement on social media calling it unprofessional. But he felt more like himself.

And Ioannis hadn't cared. He'd changed himself because of his own perception of expectations rather than what they actually were.

Natalia looked at the tablet in her hands and stated the sum before adding, "Based on my calculations, she'll have paid you back in full in the next six months."

"I don't need to be paid back."

Don't want it.

"Perhaps not, but if anyone asks, it will be good to show the record of her repaying it now that you two aren't together."

Natalia's crisp words struck Kostas. "What?"

She opened her mouth but Kostas stopped her. "No need to repeat, that was rhetorical."

Natalia nodded as she looked at her tablet again and started listing the day's events. He was scheduled at the clinic until four, which meant that Calla wouldn't be there.

He closed his eyes as that pain washed over him. In the three days since she'd walked out, she'd successfully avoided him in the one place they hadn't been able to escape each other for months. He'd pushed through his regular schedule, his body aching with hurt and need that he made sure not to show.

"There is a concert this weekend, benefiting…" Natalia frowned as she tapped a few things onto the tablet. "I just had it here."

Kostas waved a hand. "I'm not interested in attending a concert right now." He was stunned she'd even suggest it. He was barely managing to do the things he had to do. If he could've gotten away with calling off at the clinic for a week, he would. But duty and responsibility…

Duty and responsibility. The words tasted bitter, even though they remained unspoken.

"Oh." Natalia pursed her lips and dragged her finger up on the electronic planner. "Eleni mentioned you might not be interested in things for a while, but you seem so fine."

Fine? He looked at his assistant. She was serious. How could she be serious? Surely, he wasn't that good of an actor…his mask wasn't that secure. Was it?

"Where is Eleni this morning?"

"It's breakfast time, so probably with the children in their rooms. They like to do a relaxed—"

"Thanks, Natalia," Kostas called as he hustled to his brother and sister-in-law's suite. A hard bubble of truth was settling under his skin, and he wanted to confirm it with someone he could trust.

"Good morning, Kostas." Eleni's voice was warm as she looked up from nursing Zelia.

"Do people not realize I'm heartbroken?" The question was awkward, but he couldn't pull it back or ask it better.

His world had fallen apart when Calla walked out. She'd let the press see her tears. He'd run his hand over the images, hating the pain, but uncertain what he should do.

He'd kept up the regal face. The images captured showed a doctor in control, a man exiting the clinic on time. Going about his day, as always. But he was still devastated.

"No. You hide behind your mask well, Kostas. I wasn't sure until now."

If the mask could fool his sister-in-law, what about Calla?

She softened her tone as she looked at him. "You control so much that the world doesn't see you. They see Prince Kostas."

Control.

He'd tried to control everything since returning to the island. He'd promised himself that no one would find fault with him. And that if they made something up, he'd rebut it.

But it wasn't real. Who he was with Calla was the real Kostas. And he'd let that go for—what?—an image he didn't even want.

His father had failed to listen to his mother. To hear what she wanted. And he'd done the same. Unintentionally and with much better motives. But that didn't change the fact that he'd hurt the woman he loved.

"I need to see Calla." He turned without waiting for a response.

Just before he heard the door close, Kostas caught Eleni's whispered, "About time."

"Prince Kostas, what are you doing here?"

"Seeing the woman I love and begging forgiveness." He saw a few heads pop up at that statement and hated that it was surprise coating them. It was oddly freeing to say exactly what he wanted rather than couch it.

They shouted a few more questions at him as he hit the top of the stairs. He knocked on Calla's door and his heart broke as she called through, "No comment."

A few cameras followed, and he knew they were capturing this moment. But for the first time in his life, he didn't care. He loved Calla. He wanted everyone to know it, full stop.

"It's me, Calla."

He waited, the silence stretching as he leaned his head against her door, aware of the additional eyes watching him.

"No comment," Calla called again, but there was a hiccup of a sob behind it.

"Fine. I'll sit outside this apartment until we talk. We can even talk through the door, sweetheart. But I'm not giving up." He slid down the door.

He waved to the camera as he leaned back. He was a man in love, and he was determined that no one was going to doubt that. Most especially the woman on the other side of the door.

"That will make quite the story." Her voice was soft, but he could still hear her. She must be sitting right by the door.

"Maybe." He responded. "But I don't care what the story is. I love you, and that is the only story that matters. And if the only people that ever know it are the two of us, then that is enough. I'm done caring what the headline or narrative is." He didn't shout the words, but he didn't whisper them, either.

Let the world know the truth. All he cared was that Calla heard him. That she knew he loved her.

The lock clicked and he couldn't stop the grin from spreading across his face. Standing, he opened the door, sliding inside. His breath caught as he saw her sitting on the floor next to the door, tears streaming down her face.

"Calla." He bent next to her.

"I'm fine, Kostas. Or I will be. Don't worry, I won't let them see me break. At least not like this, promise."

He brushed away a tear, his heart shattering at the sight of the woman he loved hurting. Worried about how it looked to someone else. He'd done this. His quest for perfection, even though he'd said he didn't care about the narrative anymore…part of her still wasn't sure.

"Calla, I am so sorry. I don't need perfection, honey. I just need you." He reached for her hands, grateful when she let him hold them. It was more than he deserved.

"I love you. I should have said that when we fought. Hell, I should have said it the moment I realized it. Should have told you then shouted it to the world. I don't have a good excuse for why I didn't. Fear. The need to protect myself. A lifetime of keeping things inside."

Calla's bright eyes lit up as she looked at him. "You love me, not who I could be or because I'm carrying your child?" She hiccuped as she looked at him.

"Just you." He placed a hand over where their child slept. "I love this little guy or gal too. But it's their mother that I'm here for. I want to be a team, Calla. A real one."

Calla threw her hands around Kostas's shoulders. "I love you too." She kissed him before pulling back.

Pursing her lips, she stood, looking at the door and then back at him. "But I also owe you an apology. That is a lot!" She gestured to the door. "I've done my best to handle it, but…"

"Your best was pretty great." He dropped a kiss to her nose.

"Maybe for a day or so. Over the long term…" Calla glared at the door. "I am not saying we have to refute everything, but I also understand your desire to.

"I let the trauma of my past cloud my present. I was so worried that you'd find fault with me eventually. That the narrative was meant for me, not them. That I wasn't enough. I'm sorry."

"Oh, Calla. You will always be enough." He brushed his lips against hers.

"I have something for you." Kostas grinned as he slid to one knee. "Calla Lewis, will you marry me?" He flipped open a ring box, watching carefully how Calla's eyes brightened.

"It's a different ring." She beamed as her eyes looked at the ring. "Oh, it's beautiful. Yes, Kostas. Yes, I will marry you."

He took the ring from the box and slid it on her finger. The diamond was smaller, and it had two sapphires on either side. It was gorgeous, reminding him so much of Calla the moment he'd seen it.

Maybe it wasn't large, and it wouldn't be easily identifiable in pictures like the other, but it was meant for her. And that was all that mattered.

Dropping his lips to hers, he relaxed as she slid into him. The world was simply right when she was in his arms.

EPILOGUE

THE PHONE IN the clinic rang for the hundredth time in the last hour, and Dr. Bandi sighed. They had to keep the phone on in case a patient needed them, but the calls were only the press. The front desk assistant had been instructed to give no updates on the royal baby.

"I swear they are calling more now than they did for Eleni's delivery," Calla muttered as Kostas wiped her brow.

"Well, they love you, sweetheart," Kostas whispered in her ear. "Love" was too strong of a word, but Kostas's declaration of love outside her door had changed the tone of most of the reporting. They might never be granted the grace that Ioannis and Eleni had, but no one doubted that Kostas and Calla loved each other.

Another contraction started and Calla squeezed Kostas's hand, aware she was probably being too forceful but...

"Push, Princess."

"Alexa, if you call me that one more time, I will—" Calla groaned as she bore down. The contraction subsided as she laid her head back against Kostas, releasing her death grip on his fingers—which he flexed without complaining.

He'd climbed into bed with her when she'd started

pushing. It was sweet and comforting, but she was so ready to be done. To hold her child and rest.

"Sorry, Pr—" Alexa caught herself as Calla shot her a glare.

Dr. Bandi looked up. "You're almost there. A few more pushes."

"A few more pushes." Calla moaned. "You keep saying that!" She took a deep breath as the next contraction started.

"You've got this, honey." Kostas kissed her cheek as she squeezed his hands and pushed. His fingers must be screaming, but he hadn't complained at all.

The pressure released and Calla sighed as the doctor looked up.

"They've got a full head of hair! One more push, Calla."

Bearing down, she followed the instructions and let out a sob as the doctor placed her squealing daughter against her chest.

"She's nearly perfect." Kostas whispered as he kissed the top of Calla's head.

"Nearly perfect?" Calla opened her mouth and made a face at her husband before kissing the top of her daughter's head. "Nearly perfect" had become their running joke in the last few months. Calla might not like the term "perfect" but "nearly perfect" she'd accepted. And Kostas used it as often as possible.

"Would you prefer perfect? Seems like a lot to lay on a newborn still covered in vernix, but…"

"Nearly perfect, she is." Calla closed her eyes as she soaked in the first few minutes of their daughter's life. They were a family of three now.

Her nearly perfect little family.

* * * * *

COMING SOON!

We really hope you enjoyed reading this book.
If you're looking for more romance, be sure to
head to the shops when new books are
available on

Thursday 24th November

To see which titles are coming soon, please visit
millsandboon.co.uk/nextmonth

MILLS & BOON®

Coming next month

RESISTING THE SINGLE DAD NEXT DOOR
Louisa George

'Carly.'

She turned to face him, her belly dancing with lightness. 'Yes?'

'Thanks again.' He leaned in and pressed a friendly kiss to her cheek.

She closed her eyes as the touch of his skin sent thrills of desire rippling through her. She pulled back, looked at him and caught the heat in his gaze, the need.

She should have turned then and climbed into her truck. She should have driven away into the darkness. But she was transfixed by the way he was looking at her, as if she was…everything.

His previous words about not being distracted seemed to melt from her brain and all she could focus on was his face, his heated eyes, his delicious mouth. So tantalisingly close.

Later, when she thought back to this moment—and she thought back to this moment a lot—she wasn't sure how it had happened. One minute they were looking at each other, the next moment they were kissing. Hot, hard and greedy. Desperate. Frantic. Out of control.

The heat of his mouth made her moan and stoked the burning in her belly. She spiked her fingers into his hair and pressed her lips against his, her body hard against his. The outline of his muscled chest pressed against her and, lower, she could feel just how much he was enjoying this. How much he wanted her.

'God, Carly…' His hands cupped her face and held her in place as he captured her bottom lip in his teeth, then took her mouth fully again and kissed her, kissed her and kissed her.

He tasted of hot chocolate and a warm, delicious spice that she couldn't get enough of. He smelt of the smoky fire. He tasted of coming home and of somewhere new, exotic and enticing. Exciting.

It was too much and not enough all at the same time. She didn't want it to end, this night, this kiss lasting for…

Someone committed to staying around.

His words came back to her in a hard jolt of reality. She had an interested buyer visiting tomorrow. A plan to be gone as soon as feasibly possible. So kissing Owen was an impossible and ridiculous idea and a sure-fire way of ruining the fledgling friendship they'd grown.

What on earth was she doing?

'Sorry. I've got to…' She took two shaky steps away from him, jumped into her car and got the hell away.

Continue reading
RESISTING THE SINGLE DAD NEXT DOOR
Louisa George

Available next month
www.millsandboon.co.uk

MILLS & BOON

THE HEART OF ROMANCE

A ROMANCE FOR EVERY READER

MODERN

Prepare to be swept off your feet by sophisticated, sexy and seductive heroes, in some of the world's most glamourous and romantic locations, where power and passion collide.

HISTORICAL

Escape with historical heroes from time gone by. Whether your passion is for wicked Regency Rakes, muscled Vikings or rugged Highlanders, awake the romance of the past.

MEDICAL

Set your pulse racing with dedicated, delectable doctors in the high-pressure world of medicine, where emotions run high and passion, comfort and love are the best medicine.

True Love

Celebrate true love with tender stories of heartfelt romance, from the rush of falling in love to the joy a new baby can bring, and a focus on the emotional heart of a relationship.

Desire

Indulge in secrets and scandal, intense drama and plenty of sizzling hot action with powerful and passionate heroes who have it all: wealth, status, good looks…everything but the right woman.

HEROES

Experience all the excitement of a gripping thriller, with an intense romance at its heart. Resourceful, true-to-life women and strong, fearless me face danger and desire - a killer combination!

To see which titles are coming soon, please visit

millsandboon.co.uk/nextmonth